THE SEVENTH PLAGUE

THE SEVENTH PLAGUE

A Σ SIGMA FORCE NOVEL

JAMES ROLLINS

WILLIAM MORROW
An Imprint of HarperCollins*Publishers*

THE SEVENTH PLAGUE. Copyright © 2016 by James Czajkowski. All rights reserved. Printed in the United States of America. No part of this book may be used or reproduced in any manner whatsoever without written permission except in the case of brief quotations embodied in critical articles and reviews. For information, address HarperCollins Publishers, 195 Broadway, New York, NY 10007.

HarperCollins books may be purchased for educational, business, or sales promotional use. For information, please email the Special Markets Department at SPsales@harpercollins.com.

FIRST EDITION

Library of Congress Cataloging-in-Publication Data has been applied for.

ISBN 978-0-06-238168-2
ISBN 978-0-06-256585-3 (international edition)
ISBN 978-0-06-256620-1 (international edition)
ISBN 978-0-06-267356-5 (Barnes & Noble signed edition)
ISBN 978-0-06-267357-2 (Books-A-Million signed edition)

16 17 18 19 20   DIX/RRD   10 9 8 7 6 5 4 3 2 1

ACKNOWLEDGMENTS

A long litany of people helped make this book better—through their help, guidance, criticisms, encouragement, and, most important, their enduring friendship. I must thank my critique group, that close-knit bevy of readers who serve both as my initial editors and who are not above holding my feet to the fire to make me push farther and dig deeper: Sally Ann Barnes, Chris Crowe, Lee Garrett, Jane O'Riva, Denny Grayson, Leonard Little, Judy Prey, Caroline Williams, Christian Riley, Tod Todd, Chris Smith, and Amy Rogers. And, as always, a special thanks to Steve Prey for the great maps . . . and to David Sylvian for making sure I put my best foot forward at all times . . . and to Cherei McCarter for the many great historical and scientific tidbits found within these pages! And of course, to everyone at HarperCollins for always having my back, especially Michael Morrison, Liate Stehlik, Danielle Bartlett, Kaitlin Harri, Josh Marwell, Lynn Grady, Jeanne Reina, Richard Aquan, Tom Egner, Shawn Nicholls, and Ana Maria Allessi. Last, of course, a special acknowledgment to the people instrumental to all levels of production: my editor, Lyssa Keusch, and her colleague Priyanka Krishnan; and my agents, Russ Galen and Danny Baror (along with his daughter Heather Baror). And, as always, I must stress that any and all errors of fact or detail in this book, of which hopefully there are not too many, fall squarely on my own shoulders.

NILE RIVER BASIN

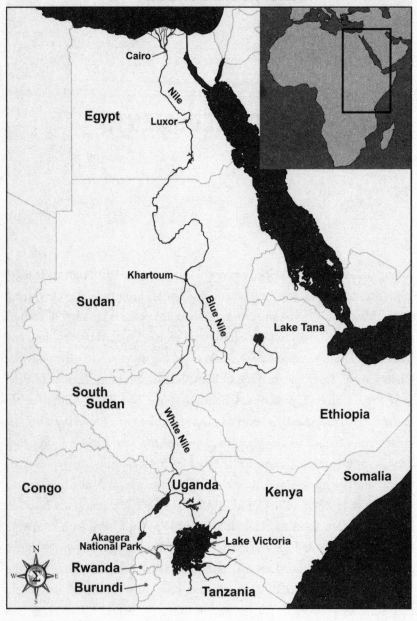

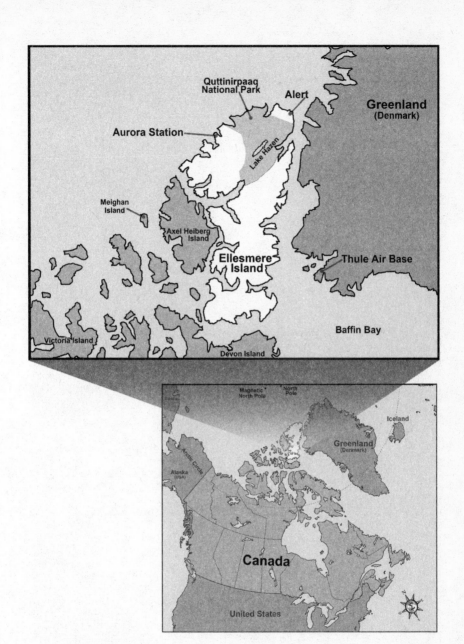

NOTES FROM THE HISTORICAL RECORD

And Moses said unto his people, "Remember this day, in which you came out from Egypt, from the house of slavery; for the LORD brought you out of here by the strength of His hand. . . ."

—Exodus 13:3

Few stories in the Bible are as harrowing or as often retold—both in print and on screen—as the story of Moses. Starting with his fateful salvation as a baby, when he was floated in a reed basket into the arms of Pharaoh's daughter, to his later confrontation with that same Pharaoh's son, Moses became a figure of legend. To free the Jewish tribes from slavery, he afflicted Egypt with ten plagues and eventually parted the seas and led his people through the desert for forty years, delivering the Ten Commandments as a template for a new system of laws.

But did any of this truly happen? Most historians, even many religious leaders, have discounted the story of Exodus as a myth, a moral lesson rather than a historical reality. As support for this stance, skeptical archaeologists point to the lack of Egyptian sources in documenting any series of plagues or a mass exodus of slaves, especially within the time frame indicated in the Bible.

Yet now, recent discoveries along the Nile suggest that such naysayers may be wrong. Could there truly be evidence supporting the story of Moses, of a great exodus from Egypt, of miracles and curses? Could the ten plagues of Egypt have truly occurred? The startling answers found within these pages are based on facts as solid as the name *Israel* found carved into the stela of Ramesses the Great's son.

And if the plagues of Egypt could have truly happened—could they happen again, only on a global scale?

The answer to that is a frightening . . . *yes*.

NOTES FROM THE SCIENTIFIC RECORD

Climate is what we expect, weather is what we get.
—attributed to Mark Twain

Things are heating up of late—not just in regard to global temperatures but also in regard to the debate about climate change. In the last few years, the question has evolved from *Is climate change real?* to *What is causing it and can anything be done about it?* Even many former skeptics now recognize that something *is* happening to our planet, what with glaciers melting worldwide, Greenland's ice pack vanishing at a breakneck pace, and oceans steadily warming. Even the weather is growing more extreme, from persistent droughts to massive flooding. As reported in February 2016, Alaska experienced its second-warmest winter on record, with temperatures more than 10 degrees Fahrenheit above average, and in May of that same year, satellite measurements of the arctic ice cap revealed that it had dwindled to the lowest level ever recorded.

But the more frightening question—and one explored in this novel—is *Where are we headed next?* The answer is a surprising one, little talked about, but based on concrete evidence and science—and most shocking of all, it's happened before. So whether skeptic or believer, to be forewarned is to be forearmed. It's time to learn the staggering truth about the future of our planet.

And the LORD spake unto Moses, "Say unto Aaron, 'Take thy rod, and stretch out thine hand upon the waters of Egypt, upon their streams, upon their rivers, and upon their ponds, and upon all their pools of water, that they may become blood; and that there may be blood throughout all the land of Egypt, both in vessels of wood, and in vessels of stone.'"

—EXODUS 7:19

Denial ain't just a river in Egypt.

—MARK TWAIN

THE SEVENTH PLAGUE

Spring, 1324 B.C.
Nubian Desert, South of Egypt

The high priestess knelt naked in the sand and knew it was time. The omens had been building, growing more dire, becoming certainty. To the west, a sandstorm climbed toward the sun, turning the day's blue sky into a dusty darkness, crackling with lightning.

The enemy was almost upon them.

In preparation, Sabah had shaved all the hair from her body, even the brows above her painted eyes. She had bathed in the waters to either side, two tributaries that flowed north out of the deeper desert and joined at this sacred confluence to form the mighty river that the ancient kings of *heqa khaseshet* called the *Nahal*. She pictured its snaking course as it flowed past Luxor, Thebes, and Memphis on its way to the great blue sea that stretched past the river's fertile delta.

Though she had never set eyes upon that region, she had heard tales.

Of our old home, a place of green fields, palms, and a life ruled by the rhythmic flooding of the Nahal . . .

It was from those lands that Sabah's people had fled over a century ago, escaping the time of plagues, starvation, and death, chased by a pharaoh now long dead. Most of the other tribes in the delta had sought refuge in the deserts to the east, conquering the lands out there and creating a kingdom of their own—but her tribe had lived in an area farther south along the river, near the village of Djeba, in the Upper Egyptian district of *Wetjes-Hor*, known as the Throne of Horus.

During the time of darkness and death, her tribe had uprooted itself and fled up the river, beyond the reach of the Egyptian kingdom and into the Nubian Desert. Her tribe had been scholars and scribes, priests and priestesses, keepers of great knowledge. They had retreated into the empty ranges of Nubia to protect such knowledge during the turbulent times that followed the plagues, when Egypt was beset and overrun by foreigners from the east, a fierce people with faster chariots and stronger bronze weapons who conquered the weakened Egyptian towns with barely an arrow fired.

But that dark time was coming to an end.

Egypt was rising yet again, chasing out the invaders and building monuments to their many victories and spreading ever in this direction.

"*Hemet netjer...*" her Nubian assistant—a young man named Tabor—whispered behind her, perhaps sensing her distress or merely trying to remind her of her role as *hemet netjer...* the maid of God. "We must go now."

She understood and rose to her feet.

Tabor's eyes were upon the storm to the west, clearly the source of his worry, but Sabah noted a wisp of smoke due north, marking the destruction of a town alongside the fifth cataract of the Nahal, the latest conquest by the Egyptian armies. It would not be long before those same forces reached this mighty confluence.

Before that happened, Sabah and the others of her order must hide what they had protected for over a century, a wonder unlike any other: a blessing by God, a cure hidden at the heart of a curse.

Watching the Egyptians creep and spread up along the river, consuming town after town, preparations had been under way for the past thousand days, mostly acts of purification, all to ready her and her order to become immortal vessels for God's blessing.

Sabah was the last to be allowed this transformation, having already overseen and guided many of her brothers and sisters on this path. Like the others, she had forsaken all millet and grain for the past year, subsisting on nuts, berries, tree bark, and a tea made from a resin carried here from foreign lands. Over the turning of seasons, her flesh had dried to her bones, her breasts and buttocks gone sallow and sunken. Though only into her third decade, she now needed Tabor's strong back and arms to help her move, even to slip her linen robe back over her head.

As they set off away from the confluence, Sabah watched the sand-storm roll inexorably toward them, laced with lightning born from the roiling clouds of dust. She could sense that energy flowing across the desert. She smelled it in the air, felt it stir the small hairs along her arms. With God's will, those same blowing sands should help cover their handiwork, to bury it under windswept dunes.

But first they had to reach the distant hills.

She concentrated on putting one foot before the other. Still, she feared she had waited too long at the river. By the time she and Tabor reached the deep cleft between two hills, the storm had caught them, howling over-head and scouring any exposed skin with burning sand.

"Hurry, mistress," Tabor urged, all but picking her up. Carried now, she felt her toes brushing the ground, scribing the sand underfoot with indecipherable glyphs of beseechment.

I must not fail . . .

Then they were through the dark doorway and hurrying down a long, steep passageway to the greater wonder sculpted out of the sandstone below. Torches lit the way, flickering shadows all around them, slowly re-vealing what was hidden, what had been created by artisans and scholars working in tandem for over seven decades.

Tabor helped her over the arcade of large stone teeth and across the sprawl of a sculpted tongue, carved in exquisite detail. Ahead, the chamber bifurcated into two tunnels: one that dove through the rock toward the stone stomach below, the other ringed by small ridges and leading to the cavernous chest cavity.

It was the latter route they took now in great haste.

As Tabor helped her, she pictured the subterranean complex beneath these hills. It had been dug out and fashioned to model the interior work-ings of a featureless figure in repose, one whose body lay buried under these hills. While this sculpture had no exterior—for the world was its skin—all of the internal details of the human body had been meticu-lously carved out of the sandstone, from liver and kidney to bladder and brain.

Beneath the hills, her order had created their own stone God, one

large enough to make their home within, to use its body as a vessel to preserve what must be kept safe.

*Like I must do now . . . to make of my own body a temple for God's great
blessing.*

Tabor led her to where the ridge-lined passageway split yet again into
two smaller tunnels, marking the same division of airways found in her
own chest. He took her to the left, requiring that they duck slightly from
the curved roof of the smaller passage. But they did not have far to go.

Torchlight grew brighter ahead as the tunnel ended and opened into
a massive space, seemingly supported by stone ribs that arched up to the
carving of a mighty spine overhead. In the room's center sat a stone heart,
rising four times her height, again rendered in perfect symmetry, with
great curving blood vessels that fanned outward.

She glanced to the handful of other Nubian servants, all on their
knees, who awaited her in the chamber.

She stared over to the colonnades of curved stone ribs. Between those
ribs, fresh bricks had been used to seal the many alcoves hidden there.
They marked the tombs of her brothers and sisters of the order, those who
had preceded her into the future. She pictured them seated or slumped on
their chairs, their bodies slowly finishing their transformations, becoming
vessels for the blessing.

I am the last . . . the chosen maid of God.

She turned from the walls to face the stone heart. A small doorway
opened into one of the chambers, a place of great honor.

She shook free of Tabor's arm and took the last steps on her own.
She crossed to the doorway, bowed her head low, and climbed inside. Her
palm felt the cold stone as she straightened. A silver throne awaited her
inside, equally cold as she sat upon it. To one side rested a bowl of carved
lapis lazuli. Water filled it to just shy of its silver-embossed brim. She lifted
the bowl and let it rest on her thin thighs.

Tabor leaned toward the opening, too pained to speak, but his face
was easy to read, full of grief, hope, and fear. Matching emotions swelled
within her own breast—along with a fair amount of doubt. But she nodded to Tabor.

"Let it be done."

Grief won the battle in his face, but he matched her nod and bowed out.

The other servants came forward and began sealing the entrance with dry bricks of mud and straw. Darkness fell over her, but in the last flicker of torchlight from outside, she stared down at the bowl in her lap, recognizing the dark sheen to the water. It was colored a deep crimson. She knew what she held. It was water from the Nahal, from when the river had been cursed and turned to blood. The water had been collected ages ago and preserved by their order—along with the blessing held at its cursed heart.

As the last brick was set, she swallowed hard, finding her throat suddenly dry. She listened as a fresh coat of mud was smeared over the bricks outside. She also heard the telltale scrape of wood being stacked under the base of the heart, encircling it completely.

She closed her eyes, knowing what was to come.

She pictured torches igniting that bonfire of wood.

Slowly came confirmation as the stone grew warm underfoot. The air inside the heart—already stifling—did not take long to become heated. Any moisture dried away, escaping up the flue of the sculpted vessels. In moments, it felt as if she were breathing hot sand. She gasped as the bottoms of her feet began to burn. Even the silver throne became as hot as the scorched lip of a dune under a summer sun.

Still, she kept quiet. By now, those outside should have exited this underworld, sealing the way behind them. They would leave these lands under the cover of the storm, vanishing away forever, letting the desert erase all evidence of this place.

As she awaited her end, tears flowed from her eyes, only to be dried from her cheeks before they could roll away. Through cracked lips, she sobbed from the pain, from the certainty of what was to come. Then in the darkness came a soft glow. It rose from the basin on her lap, swirling the crimson water with the faintest of shimmers.

She did not know if it was a mirage born of pain, but she found solace in that glow. It granted her the strength to complete her last act. She lifted the bowl to her lips and drank deeply and fully. The life-giving water flowed down her parched throat and filled her knotted stomach.

By the time she lowered the empty bowl, the heat inside the stone heart had intensified to a blistering agony. Still, she smiled through the pain, knowing what she held within her.

I am your vessel, my Lord . . . now and forever.

Now this is more like it . . .

With his goal in sight, Samuel Clemens—better known by his pen name Mark Twain—led his reluctant companion through Gramercy Park. Directly ahead, gaslights beckoned on the far side of the street, illuminating the columns, portico, and ironwork of the Players Club. Both men were members of this exclusive establishment.

Drawn by the promise of laughter, spirits, and good company, Twain increased his pace, moving in great, purposeful strides, trailing a cloud of cigar smoke through the crisp night air. "What do you say, Nikola?" he called back to his chum. "According to my pocket watch and my stomach, Players must still be serving dinner. And barring that, I could use some brandy to go with this cigar."

Younger by almost two decades, Nikola Tesla was dressed in a stiff suit, worn at the elbows to a dull sheen. He kept swiping at his dark hair and darting glances around. When he was nervous, like now, the man's Serbian accent grew as thick as his mustache.

"Samuel, my friend, the night is late, and I still have work to finish at my lab. I appreciate the tickets to the theater, but I should be off."

"Nonsense. Too much work makes for a dull man."

"Then you must be exceptionally exciting . . . what with your life of such extreme leisure."

Twain glanced back with an exaggerated huff. "I'll have you know I'm working on another book."

"Let me guess," Nikola offered with a wry smile. "Huck Finn and Tom Sawyer get into more trouble."

"If only those two bastards would!" Twain chuckled, drawing the eye of a passerby. "Then I might be able to pay off my creditors."

Though Twain kept it quiet, he had declared bankruptcy last year, turning over all of his copyrights to his wife, Olivia. To help pay off his debts, he was due to head out on an around-the-world lecture tour over the next twelve months.

Still, the mention of money had soured the moment. Twain kicked himself for mentioning it, knowing Nikola was struggling as much as he was with financial hardships, despite his friend being a veritable genius, a polymath who was equal parts inventor, electrical engineer, and physicist. Twain had spent many afternoons at the man's South Fifth Avenue laboratory, the two becoming great friends.

"Maybe one drink," Nikola conceded with a sigh.

They headed across the street toward the portico under the hissing gas lamps. But before they could reach the entrance, a figure stepped from the shadows to accost them both.

"Thank God," the man said as he ambushed them. "I heard from your doorman that you might end up here tonight."

Momentarily taken aback, Twain finally recognized the fellow. Surprised and delighted, he clapped his old friend on the shoulder. "Well met, Stanley! What are you doing here? I thought you were still in England."

"I only arrived back yesterday."

"Wonderful! Then let's celebrate your return to our shores by raising a glass or two. Maybe even three."

Twain moved to draw the other two men inside with him, only to be stopped by Stanley at the threshold.

"As I understand it," Stanley said, "you have the ear of Thomas Edison."

"I . . . I suppose I do," Twain answered hesitantly, knowing all too well of the deep-seated friction between Edison and his companion this night, Nikola Tesla.

"I have a matter of urgency to discuss with the inventor, something to show him, a task given to me by the Crown."

"Truly? What a tantalizing bit of intrigue."

"Perhaps I could help," Nikola offered.

As the two men were unacquainted, Twain made proper introductions, acting as a potential matchmaker for this strange affair. "Nikola, this is Henry Morton Stanley—soon to be *Sir* Stanley if the rumors hold true—famed not only as an explorer in his own right but also regaled for his discovery of David Livingstone, a fellow explorer lost in the darkest heart of Africa."

"Ah," Nikola said, "I remember now, especially how you greeted him. '*Dr. Livingstone, I presume?*'"

Stanley groaned. "I never said those exact words."

Twain smiled and turned to his other friend. "And this is Nikola Tesla, as much a genius in his own right as Edison, perhaps more so."

Stanley's eyes grew wider upon this introduction. "Of course. I should have recognized you."

This drew some color to Nikola's pale cheeks.

"So," Twain began, "upon what dire mission has the British Crown assigned you?"

Stanley wiped a damp palm across his thinning gray hair. "As you know, Livingstone was lost in Africa while seeking the true source of the Nile. Something I've sought myself in the past."

"Yes, you and many other Brits. Apparently it's a quest on par with finding the Holy Grail for you all."

Stanley scowled but did not discount his words.

Twain suspected that the drive behind such a concerted search by the British had less to do with geographical curiosity than it did with the country's colonial ambitions in Africa, but for once he held his tongue, fearing he might scare his friend off before the night's mystery revealed itself.

"So how does the source of the Nile concern the British Crown?" Twain pressed.

Stanley drew him closer and pulled a small object from his pocket. It was a glass vial full of a dark liquid. "This was only recently discovered among the relics of David Livingstone's estate. A Nubian warrior—someone whom Livingstone had helped by saving the man's sick son—had given

David an ancient talisman, a small vessel sealed with wax and carved with hieroglyphics. This vial holds a small sample of the water found inside that talisman, water which the tribesman claimed came from the Nile itself."

Twain shrugged. "Why's that significant?"

Stanley stepped away and raised the vial toward one of the gas lamps. Under the flickering flame, the liquid inside glowed a rich crimson.

"According to Livingstone's papers, the water was said to be thousands of years old, drawn from the ancient Nile when the river had turned to blood."

"Turned to blood?" Nikola asked. "Like in the Old Testament?"

Twain smiled, suspecting Stanley was trying to set him up. The explorer knew of his personal disdain for organized religion. They'd had many heated discourses on that very subject. "So you're claiming this came from Moses's biblical plague, the *first* of the ten he cast upon the Egyptians?"

Stanley's expression never wavered. "I know how this sounds."

"It can't possibly—"

"Twenty-two men are dead at the Royal Society. Slain when the Nubian talisman was first opened and its contents tested in a laboratory."

A moment of stunned silence followed.

"How did they die?" Nikola finally asked. "Was it a poison?"

Stanley had paled. Here was a man who had faced all manner of dread beast, debilitating fever, and cannibal savages with nary a sign of fear. He now looked terrified.

"Not a poison."

"Then what?" Twain asked.

With deadpan seriousness, Stanley answered, "A curse. A plague out of the distant past." He closed his fist around the vial. "For this is indeed a remnant of God's ancient wrath upon the Egyptians—but it's only the beginning if we don't stop what is to come."

"What can be done?" Twain asked.

Stanley turned to Nikola. "You must come to England."

"To do what?" Twain asked.

"To stop the next plague."

FIRST

MUMMIFICATION

1

From the coroner's nervous manner, Derek Rankin knew something was wrong. "Show us the body."

Dr. Badawi gave a small bow of his head and lifted an arm toward the morgue's elevator. "If you'll follow me, please."

As the coroner led them away, Derek glanced to his two companions, uncertain how they would handle these last steps of this grim journey. The older of the two women, Safia al-Maaz, stood a head taller than her younger companion, Jane McCabe. The group had arrived by private jet from London this morning, landing at the Cairo airport before being whisked to the city's morgue, a nondescript set of blue buildings within a stone's throw of the Nile.

As they followed the coroner, Safia kept a protective, motherly arm around the younger woman, who was only twenty-one.

Derek caught Safia's eyes, silently asking her, *Can Jane handle this?*

Safia took a deep breath and nodded to him. She was his boss, a senior curator at the British Museum. He had joined the museum four years ago, hired as an assistant keeper, a low-level curatorship. His specialty was bio-archaeology, with a focus on investigating past human health. By studying the condition of dental, skeletal, and tissue remains, he tried to piece together a more complete assessment of the physical conditions of ancient peoples, sometimes even calculating a cause of death for certain individuals. During his prior fellowship with the University College London, he had investigated various epidemics, including the Black Death in Europe and the Great Famine in Ireland.

His current project with the British Museum involved analyzing mummies recovered from a region surrounding the Nile's Sixth Cataract, where a new dam was being built in the Sudan. That arid zone had been rarely studied, but with the new construction under way, the Sudan Archaeological Research Society had sought the assistance of the British Museum to help salvage the region of its archaeological treasures before it was all lost. Just in the last few months, the project had managed to preserve significant swaths of rock art, including digging up and transporting the 390 blocks of a small Nubian pyramid.

It was this very project that led them all here, a project many considered cursed when the lead researcher vanished two years ago, along with an entire survey team. After months of searching for the group, the loss was eventually attributed to foul play, likely due to the region's instability following the Arab Spring uprisings and subsequent political unrest. Though half the survey team was Sudanese, it was still unwise for foreigners to be traipsing in such remote areas where bandits and rebels held sway. Even an act of terrorism was considered, but no group ever claimed responsibility, nor were there any ransom demands.

The entire museum had been shaken by this loss. The team leader, Professor Harold McCabe—while not beloved due to his intractable nature—was well respected in his field. In fact, it had been Professor McCabe's involvement with the project that had convinced Derek to join this salvage effort. McCabe had been Derek's teacher and mentor during his early years at the University College London, even helping him attain his fellowship.

So the man's death had hit Derek deeply—but not as deeply as the youngest member of their group today.

He studied Jane McCabe as she entered the elevator. The young woman stood with her arms crossed, her gaze a thousand miles away. She was Harold's daughter. Derek noted the slight pebbling of sweat on her forehead and upper lip. The day was sweltering, and the morgue's air-conditioning did little to hold back the heat. But he suspected the perspiration had less to do with the temperature than with the trepidation at what she must confront.

Safia touched her elbow before the elevator doors closed. "Jane, you can still wait up here. I knew your father well enough to handle the identification."

Derek nodded his support, reaching out to stop the doors from gliding shut.

Jane's stare steadied and hardened. "I must do this," she said. "After waiting two years for any answers—about my father, about my brother—I'm not about to . . ."

Her voice cracked, which only seemed to irritate the young woman. Her older brother, Rory, had accompanied her father on the expedition, vanishing along with all the others, leaving Jane alone in the world. Her mother had died six years ago following a protracted battle with ovarian cancer.

Jane reached forward and knocked Derek's arm down, allowing the elevator doors to close.

Safia let out a small sigh, plainly resigned to the young woman's decision.

Derek had expected no other response from Jane. She was too much like her father: stubborn, willful, and brilliant in her own right. Derek had known Jane for as long as he had known her father. Back then she had been sixteen and already in an accelerated undergraduate program at the same university. By the age of nineteen, she had a PhD in anthropology and was now in a postdoctoral program, clearly determined to follow in her father's footsteps.

Which unfortunately, in the end, only led her here.

As the elevator descended, Derek studied the two women. Though they both shared a passion for antiquities, they couldn't be more different. Safia's Middle Eastern heritage was evident in the light mocha of her skin and the long fall of dark hair, half-hidden under a loose headscarf. She was dressed modestly in dark slacks and a long-sleeved light blue blouse. Even her manner was soft-spoken, yet she could easily command attention. There was something about those emerald green eyes that could stop a man cold if necessary.

Jane, on the other hand, was much like her father, who was Scottish. Her hair was a fiery red, cut in a masculine bob. Unfortunately, her personality was just as fiery. Derek had heard stories of her browbeating fellow students, sometimes even her professors, if they disagreed with her. She was plainly her father's daughter, but in one way the two were very different. Harold's skin had been tanned to a wrinkled leather from decades under the desert sun, while Jane's skin was pale and smooth from her years spent in university libraries. The only blemish was a slight freckling over her nose and cheeks, giving her a girlish appearance that many mistook for naïveté.

Derek knew better than that.

The elevator bumped to a stop. As the doors opened, the biting smell of bleach wafted into the cage, along with an underlying whiff of decay. Dr. Badawi led them all into a basement passageway of whitewashed concrete walls and worn linoleum floors. The coroner moved quickly, his small frame wrapped in a knee-length white lab coat. He clearly wanted to dispose of this matter as quickly as possible—but something also had him on edge.

Badawi reached the end of the hallway and brushed through a thick drape of plastic that closed off a small room. Derek followed with the two women. In the room's center rested a single stainless steel table. Atop it, a body lay under a crisp sheet.

Despite her firm insistence on being here, Jane faltered at the threshold. Safia stayed at her side, while Derek followed the coroner to the table. Behind him, he heard Jane mumble that she was okay.

Badawi glanced to the women, nervously bumping into a steel scale hanging beside the table. He whispered to Derek. "Perhaps you should view first. Maybe it is improper for women to be here at this time."

Jane heard him and responded to the veiled misogyny. "No." She stalked forward with Safia. "I need to know if this is my father."

Derek read more in her expression. She wanted answers, some way to explain the years of uncertainty and false hopes. But most of all, she needed to let the ghost of her father go.

"Let's get this over with," Safia urged.

Badawi bowed his head slightly. He stepped to the table and folded back the top half of the sheet, exposing the naked upper torso of the body.

Derek gasped and took a full step back. His first reaction was negation. This could not be Harold McCabe. The corpse on the table looked like something dug out of the sands after being buried for centuries. The skin had sunk to the sharp contours of the facial bones and ribs. Even stranger, the surface was a dark walnut color with a shiny complexion, almost as if the body had been varnished. But after the momentary shock wore off, Derek noted the grayish red hair sprouting from the body's scalp, cheeks, and chin and knew his initial assessment was wrong.

Jane recognized this, too. "Dad . . ."

Derek glanced back. Despair and anguish racked Jane's features. She turned away and buried her face in Safia's chest. Safia's expression was only slightly less despairing than the girl's. Safia had known Harold for far longer than Derek. But he also read the crinkle of confusion on her brow.

Derek could guess the cause of her consternation and voiced it to the coroner. "I thought Professor McCabe was still alive when he was discovered ten days ago."

Badawi nodded. "A family of nomads found him stumbling through the desert, about a kilometer outside the town of Rufaa." The coroner cast a sympathetic glance toward Jane. "They brought him by cart to the village, but he died before reaching help."

"That timeline makes no sense," Safia said. "The body here looks so much older."

Derek agreed, having had the same visceral reaction. Still, he returned his attention to the table, perplexed by another mystery. "You say Professor McCabe's remains arrived two days ago by truck and that no one had embalmed his body, only wrapped him in plastic. Was the vehicle refrigerated?"

"No. But the body was put into a cooler once it arrived at the morgue."

Derek glanced to Safia. "It's been ten days, with the body kept at stifling temperatures. Yet I'm seeing very little evidence of postmortem decay. No significant bloating, no cracking of skin. He looks almost preserved."

The only damage was a Y-incision across the torso from the autopsy. Derek had read the coroner's report while en route from London. No cause of death was confirmed, but heat exposure and dehydration were the most likely culprits. Still, that diagnosis did little to tell Professor McCabe's true story.

Where had he been all of this time?

Safia pursued this very question. "Were you able to get any more information from this family of nomads? Did Professor McCabe offer any explanation for his whereabouts prior to being found in the desert? Any word about his son or the others?"

Badawi gazed at his toes as he answered Safia. "Nothing that makes sense. He was weak, delirious, and the group who came upon him only spoke a dialect of Sudanese Arabic."

"My father was fluent in many variants of Arabic," Jane pressed.

"That's true," Safia said. "If there's anything he was able to communicate before dying . . ."

Badawi sighed. "I didn't write this in the report, but one of the nomads said Professor McCabe claimed to have been swallowed by a giant."

Safia frowned. "Swallowed by a giant?"

Badawi shrugged. "Like I said, he was severely dehydrated, likely delirious."

"And nothing else?" Safia asked.

"Only one word, mumbled over and over again as he was being driven to the village of Rufaa."

"What was that?"

Badawi looked toward the young woman next to Safia. "Jane."

Harold's daughter had stiffened at this revelation, looking both wounded and lost.

As Safia kept hold of her, Derek used the moment to gently examine the body. He pinched and tested the elasticity of the skin. It appeared oddly thickened, almost hard. He then slipped free a bony hand and checked the fingernails, which were a peculiar shade of yellow.

He spoke to Badawi. "Your report said you found a collection of small rocks in the man's stomach, all the same size and shape."

"Yes. About as big as quail eggs."

"You also found pieces of what you believed to be tree bark."

"That's correct. I suspect hunger drove him to eat whatever he could find in the desert, to perhaps dull the pangs from starvation."

"Or maybe their presence was due to another reason."

"What reason?" Safia asked as she held Jane.

Derek stepped back. "I'll need more tests to confirm my suspicion. Skin biopsies, definitely a toxicological study of those gastric contents." In his head, he ran through everything he wanted done. "But most importantly, I'll want a scan of his brain."

"What are you thinking?" Safia pressed him.

"From the state of the body—its ancient appearance, the peculiarly preserved nature of the remains—I think Professor McCabe has been mummified."

Badawi flinched, looked both aggrieved and affronted. "I can assure you that no one has molested this man's body after his death. No one would dare."

"You misunderstand me, Dr. Badawi. I don't think he was mummified *after* his death." He looked to Safia. "But *before*."

4:32 P.M.

Five hours later, Derek crouched over a battery of computer screens. Above his head, a bay of windows overlooked an MRI suite, with its long table and giant white magnetic tube.

Due to bureaucratic delays, they could not transport Professor Mc-Cabe's body back to England until tomorrow, so Derek had sought to gain what details he could from the body before any further decomposition occurred. He had already collected skin biopsies and hair samples and had the coroner seal and box up the strange gastric contents: the odd quail-egg-sized stones and pieces of what appeared to be undigested bark. Badawi had also arranged for Derek to use a neighboring hospital's MRI facility.

He studied the results of the second scan. On the screen was a para-sagittal image of Professor McCabe's head, showing a lateral cross section of the man's skull. The arch of the cranium, the bony nasal bridge, and the eye sockets were all crisply defined by the device's strong magnetic forces and radio waves. But within the skull, the brain itself was a featureless gray wash—not what he'd normally expect.

"These results look even less clear than the first pass through the machine," Safia said at his shoulder.

He nodded. The first scan had at least shown some details of the brain's surface, such as the wrinkling of the cerebrum's outer gyri and sulci. Still, dissatisfied with the lack of further detail, Derek had asked for a second imaging scan before the body was returned to the morgue. But these results showed even fewer internal features.

Derek straightened. "I don't know if it's a calibration issue with this particular machine or if postmortem decay has already degraded the architecture of Professor McCabe's brain."

"What about another scan?"

He shook his head, staring at the empty MRI scanner. The professor's body had already been returned to the morgue. "From here, our best hope is to conserve what we can before there's further decomposition. I've asked the coroner to collect cerebrospinal fluid and to remove the brain so it can be preserved and set in formalin for proper examination once we return to London."

Safia's brows pinched worriedly. "Does Jane know about all of this?"

"I got her permission before she retired to the hotel."

After identifying her father's remains and filling out the proper paperwork, Jane had become more drawn and pale. Still, Derek had told her all he wanted to have done before the body was returned to England for burial. She had agreed, wanting answers as much as he, probably more so. Still, she had no desire to observe such matters firsthand. There were plainly limits to even her stoic resolve.

Safia sighed. "Then that sounds like all we can do for now."

He stretched a crick from his back and nodded. "I'm going to head back to the morgue and make sure everything's in order. Perhaps you can pop in on Jane and see how—"

A phone rang, cutting him off. The lone technician in the room picked up the receiver, spoke briefly, then turned to Derek. "It is the coroner. He asks to speak to you."

Frowning, Derek took the receiver. "This is Dr. Rankin."

"You must come immediately," Badawi said in a rush, his voice sounding desperate. "You must see this yourself."

Derek tried asking a few questions, but Badawi refused to give any further details, only stressing the urgency of his return to the morgue. Derek finally hung up the phone and explained the situation to Safia.

"I'm coming with you," she said.

The two of them exited the hospital and headed down the two blocks toward the morgue. The sun was blinding after the hours spent indoors, the heat nearly unbearable. Each breath threatened to scald his lungs.

As they traversed the crowded streets, Safia seemed little bothered by the scorching temperature, striding easily beside him. "Derek, you mentioned that you believed something was done to Harold, some process that could explain the strange state of his body. What did you mean about him being mummified before he died?"

Derek had wanted to avoid this conversation, silently admonishing himself for speaking out of turn earlier. His words had clearly only added to Jane's anxiety, and until proven to be true, he should not have raised the matter.

He felt his face grow hotter now, and not from the heat. "It's only a conjecture—and a wild one at that. It was imprudent of me to voice such a suspicion prematurely."

"Still, tell me what you were talking about."

He sighed. "It's called self-mummification, where someone deliberately prepares his or her body in such a way as to preserve their flesh after death. It's a practice most commonly seen among monks in the Far East. Specifically Japan and China. But the ritual has also been noted in certain cults in India and among ascetic sects in the Middle East."

"But why undergo that? It sounds like a form of suicide."

"On the contrary. For most participants, it's a spiritual act, a path to immortality. The preserved remains of those who have undergone such a transition are revered by their sects. The mummified bodies are believed to be miraculous vessels capable of bestowing special powers upon their worshippers."

Safia made a scoffing, dismissive noise.

Derek shrugged. "It's not just remote cults. Even Catholics believe the incorruptibility of a corpse's body to be one of the proofs of sainthood."

Safia glanced at him. "If that's all true, how does someone go about mummifying themselves?"

"It varies between cultures, but there are some common elements. First, it's a long process, taking years. It starts by shifting one's diet, avoiding all grains, and eating a specific regimen of nuts, pine needles, berries, and a resin-rich tree bark. In fact, ancient practitioners of this art in Japan, known as *sokushinbutsu*—or Buddhas in the flesh—call their diet *mokuji-kyo,* or 'tree-eating.'"

"So was it the coroner's mention of finding bark in Harold's stomach that started you on this train of thought?"

"That, and the fact that small stones were also found in his belly. X-rays of *sokushinbutsu* mummies also reveal small river stones in their guts."

"But how does any of this process preserve a body after death?"

"It's believed certain herbs, toxins, and resins, once infused into bodily tissues by chronic consumption, have an antimicrobial effect, inhibiting bacterial growth after death and basically acting like a natural embalming fluid."

Safia looked sickened by this thought.

"The final step in this process is usually to enshrine yourself into a burial chamber with a small opening to allow in air. In Japan, the monks undergoing this process would chant and ring a bell until they died. Then those outside would seal the tomb, wait three years, then open it to see if the monk was successful."

"To check if the body was uncorrupted?"

He nodded. "If it was, they would smoke the body with incense to further ensure its preservation."

"And you think Harold did this to himself?"

"Or he was forced to undergo this process by his captors. Either way, the ritual was not complete. I'd estimate Harold's procedure was started only two or three months ago."

"If you're right, then proving this was done to him might give us some clue to who kidnapped that survey team."

"And it might offer hope that others are still alive. Perhaps they're being held captive and undergoing this same slow process. Including Jane's brother, Rory. If we can find them quickly enough, they could be treated in time to make a full recovery."

Safia's lips tensed for a few breaths, then she asked, "Do you think you could identify the type of bark—or the tree it came from? It could help pinpoint where the others are being held."

"I hadn't even thought of that. But, yes, it's possible."

By now they had reached the morgue and climbed the steps to the main doors. Once inside, the air felt a hundred degrees cooler. A small woman, dressed in green scrubs, hurried across the lobby toward them, plainly recognizing them.

She nodded to Derek, then Safia. "Dr. Badawi asked me to take you directly to him."

Before the woman could turn away, Derek noted the fear shining in the woman's eyes. Maybe she was intimidated by her boss, but Derek suspected it was something else. He found himself hurrying after her, wondering what had gone wrong.

She led them down a set of stairs to another section of the morgue and took them to a bench-lined observation room that looked out upon a pathology lab. Beyond the window, a stainless steel table occupied the room's center with a halogen lamp hanging above it. Both the morgue and the neighboring hospital were affiliated with Cairo University's school of medicine. Clearly this was a teaching suite meant for students to observe actual autopsies.

But at the moment, the only audience in attendance was Derek and Safia, along with their escort. Out in the lab, a small group milled around the table, all in scrubs with their faces obscured behind paper masks. Badawi noted their arrival. He raised an arm and shifted a wireless microphone to his hidden lips. His words reached them through a small speaker above the observation window.

"I do not know the meaning of this, but before I continue with removing and preserving the subject's brain, I wanted you to witness what we've found. I've also taken the liberty of filming the same."

"What did you find?" Derek asked, shouting a bit. The escort pointed to an intercom next to the window. He stepped there and repeated the question.

Badawi waved his team away from the table. The body of the sixty-year-old archaeologist lay naked under the glare of the halogens, with only a small cloth over his privates for modesty. A second damp surgical towel covered the top of his skull. The table was angled such that the corpse's head pointed toward the window.

"We already collected the samples of cerebrospinal fluid as you requested," Badawi explained, "and had just started the process to gain access to the brain for removal."

The coroner removed the cloth to reveal his team had already peeled back the scalp and circumferentially sawed open the cranium. Badawi lifted off the back of the skull, where he must have gingerly returned it in place after first accessing the brain.

Derek glanced sidelong at Safia to make sure she was okay with observing this process. She stood a bit too stiffly with her hands clutched at her waist, but she remained in place.

Badawi placed the section of skull to the side and stepped away. Now exposed, the two gray-pink lobes of the brain glistened under the lamps, draped by folds of meningeal tissue.

Derek found it incomprehensible that here, exposed for all to see, was the source of his mentor's genius. He remembered the long conversations with his friend deep into the night, covering everything from the latest scientific articles to which soccer teams had the best chances at the World Cup. The man had a laugh like a wounded bear and a temper to match. He could also be one of the kindest men, and the love for his wife and two children was both bottomless and unshakable.

Now that's all gone . . .

Badawi's voice through the tinny speaker drew him back to the moment. Derek missed the first few words. "—see this. It was only chance that we happened to note this phenomenon."

Note what?

Badawi motioned to one of his team. The man doused the surgical lamp, then darkened the room's overhead lights. It took several blinks before Derek could believe what he was seeing.

Safia let out a gasp, confirming she was seeing it, too.

From the ruins of his mentor's skull, the brain and meningeal tissues softly glowed in the darkness, a pinkish hue, like the first blush of dawn.

"It was brighter earlier," Badawi explained. "The effect is already fading."

"What's causing it?" Safia asked, voicing the very question echoing in Derek's own skull.

Derek struggled to understand. He remembered his conversation earlier with Safia, how one of the goals of self-mummification was to create an incorruptible vessel, an immortal chalice capable of preserving the miraculous.

Is that what I'm witnessing?

Safia turned to him. "No more testing. We need that body bagged up and sealed. I want everything ready for transport back to London immediately."

Derek blinked a few times at her abrupt manner, noting the new urgency in her voice. "But we can't ship Professor McCabe's remains until tomorrow."

"I'll pull a few strings," she said confidently.

"Still," Derek warned, "whatever is happening here is beyond any-thing I've seen. I'll need more help."

She swung toward the door. "I know someone."

"Who?"

"An old friend who owes me a favor."

2

Painter Crowe sat behind his desk, staring at a mirage out of his past.

Safia al-Maaz's image filled his monitor's screen. The last time he had seen her was a decade ago, in the sun-blasted deserts of the Rub 'al Khali, the vast Empty Quarter of Arabia. Stirrings of old feelings washed through him, especially when she smiled. Her eyes sparked with amusement; she was plainly happy to see him, too.

The two had first met when Painter was still a field agent for Sigma Force, back when the newly minted agency was still under the directorship of Painter's former mentor, Sean McKnight. The covert group—operating under the auspices of DARPA, the Defense Department's research-and-development agency—was composed of former Special Forces soldiers who had been retrained in various scientific disciplines to act as field agents for DARPA.

A decade later, Painter now filled Sigma's directorship—but that wasn't all that had changed.

Safia reached to an ear and brushed back a lock of her dark hair. "That's new," she said, letting her fingers linger by her ear.

He touched the same patch of his own hair, which had gone a snowy white from a traumatic event a while back. It remained in sharp contrast with his black hair, like a snowy feather tucked behind his ear. If nothing else, it served to accent his Pequot Indian heritage.

He lifted one eyebrow. "I imagine I have a few wrinkles to go along with this, too."

Before he could drop his hand, she noted another change. "Is that a ring I see?"

He grinned, turning the gold band around his finger. "What can I say? Someone finally agreed to marry me."

"She's lucky to have you."

"No, *I'm* the lucky one." He lowered his hand and turned the focus on her. "So how's Omaha doing?"

She sighed and gave an exasperated roll of her eyes at the mention of her husband, Dr. Omaha Dunn, an American archaeologist who had somehow won the affections of this brilliant woman.

"He's off with his brother, Danny, on a dig in India. He's been out there a bloody month. I've been trying to reach him, but as usual he's holed up somewhere where communication is spotty at best."

"So that's why you called me," he said, feigning a wounded air. "Always your second choice."

"Not in this case." Her attitude turned more serious, worry shadowing her features. With pleasantries finished, Safia addressed the reason behind her urgent call. "I need your help."

"Of course, anything." He straightened in his chair. "What's wrong?"

She glanced down, possibly searching for a place to start. "I don't know if you're aware that the British Museum has been overseeing a salvage project in northern Sudan."

He rubbed his chin. *That sounds familiar, but why?* Then it struck him. "Wasn't there some sort of mishap early on?"

She nodded. "One of our initial survey groups disappeared out in the desert."

Reminded now, he remembered receiving an intelligence report about the matter. "As I recall, the general consensus was that the team had crossed paths with rebels in the area and had met a foul end."

She frowned. "Or so we all thought. Then ten days ago, the leader of the group—Professor Harold McCabe—reappeared, stumbling out of the deep desert. He died before he could reach a hospital. It took almost a week before the locals were able to identify him by his fingerprints. In fact, I just returned two days ago from Egypt. He was a dear friend, and I wanted to accompany his body back to London."

"I'm so sorry for your loss."

She looked down. "I also went there hoping there might be some clue to the fate of the others, including Harold's son who was part of the expedition."

"Was there?"

She sighed. "No, in fact, I only uncovered more mysteries. Harold's body was found to be in an inexplicable state. One of the museum's experts who came with me believes Harold might have been subjected to some sort of self-mummification process intended to preserve his flesh after death."

Painter frowned at such a gruesome thought. A thousand questions filled his head, but he let Safia continue uninterrupted.

"We collected tissue samples and are finalizing some tests to confirm what happened. We're hoping if we can identify some of the plants and herbs used in this process that it might help pinpoint where Harold had come from, where he had been all of this time."

Smart, Painter thought.

"But one postmortem detail has raised a concern, a strange alteration to the tissues of Harold's brain and central nervous system."

"Strange how?"

"You should see this for yourself." She tapped at her computer's keyboard. "I'm sending you a file, a video taken roughly forty-eight hours ago by a morgue attendant in Cairo."

Painter opened the file as soon as it downloaded. On the video, he watched a commotion around a stainless steel table. There was no audio, but from the silent tableau, something had stirred the group in attendance. A figure, likely the coroner, waved everyone back and motioned the camera operator closer. The image jittered, then settled upon a body draped atop the table. The skull had been sawn open, exposing the brain. The room suddenly darkened, and the cause behind the agitation became immediately clear.

Painter squinted at the video. "Am I seeing this right? It looks like the insides of his skull are glowing."

"They were," she confirmed. "I witnessed the effect myself, though it was already fading by the time I arrived at the morgue's lab."

As the video ended, Painter returned his attention to Safia. "Do you know what caused that effect?"

"Not yet. Tissues and fluids are currently being tested. But we believe it's some biological or chemical agent, something Harold was exposed to, either accidentally or intentionally. Whatever it was, discovering the source has now become critical."

"Why's that?"

"Two reasons. First, I called Dr. Badawi this morning, to light a fire under him regarding some reports he had failed to transmit to our labs. I discovered he and his entire team are sick. High fevers, vomiting, muscular tremors."

Painter recalled the time frame Safia had described. "They're *that* sick in only forty-eight hours."

"The first symptom—a raging fever—occurred eight hours after they opened Harold's skull. Now family members of those exposed are showing the same initial signs. Quarantine is already being established, but at the moment we don't know how many people have been exposed."

Painter had been to Cairo. He knew how hard it would be to lock down that crowded, chaotic city, especially if panic spread.

A more immediate concern struck him. "Safia, how are you feeling?"

"I'm fine. I was outside the morgue's lab when the autopsy was performed. But when I saw the strange state of Harold's body, I had his remains and all of his tissue samples sealed up tight."

"And once the body reached London?"

Her face turned grim. "We took precautions, but I'm afraid there were some lapses before we realized the extent of the danger. Customs at Heathrow reported the seal on Harold's transport casket had been damaged during transit, either back in Cairo or while en route."

Painter's stomach tightened uneasily. Both Heathrow and the Cairo airport were major international hubs. If contamination occurred at those locations, they could have a worldwide pandemic on their hands.

From the fear shining in Safia's eyes, she recognized this risk. "Two technicians who secured Harold's body in our labs are already showing early symptoms. They've been placed in quarantine, along with anyone they came in contact with. In addition, public health agencies both here and in Cairo are questioning baggage handlers and airport personnel for any signs of illness. I'm still awaiting word, but with the levels of bureaucracy involved, I might be the last to hear anything."

"I'll see what I can do at my end to get an update."

Painter had already begun running a checklist through his head. He had recently read a risk-assessment report from MIT about the role airports played in spreading disease. The same report highlighted this danger by reminding how the H1N1 flu pandemic managed to kill 300,000 people worldwide back in 2009.

She frowned. "I . . . I should've been more diligent."

Painter read the guilt in her eyes and tried to assuage it. "You did all you could considering the circumstances. In fact, if you hadn't the foresight to seal up everything so quickly, many more could've been exposed."

She gave a small shake of her head, as if trying to dismiss his support. "I only acted on a gut feeling, a hunch . . . but when I saw what was happening, I suddenly had a suspicion *why* Harold might've been put through that mummification procedure."

From past experience, Painter knew to trust Safia's suspicions. Her intuitive leaps had proven to be uncannily accurate. "Why?"

"I think it was to protect whatever was in his head. I believe this mummification process had been employed to turn his body into some sort of vessel for this unknown agent, to preserve his flesh, especially after death, so that it could act as an incorruptible container for what was hidden inside."

A container that had been inadvertently opened.

Painter suddenly remembered something Safia had said earlier. "You mentioned there were *two* reasons this matter concerned you. What's the other?"

She stared out of the screen at him. "Because I think this has happened before."

5:02 P.M. BST
London, England

Safia waited for Painter to absorb this news before continuing. "After I learned of Harold's reappearance, I pulled all of his records and studies, even some of his handwritten journals, stored here at the museum. I hoped there might be some insight in them, something we missed in the past to explain his disappearance and sudden return."

"Did you learn anything?"

"Maybe . . . something that only struck me as significant in hindsight."

"What?"

"First, you have to understand that Harold was a bigger-than-life character, both here at the museum and to the academic world at large. As an archaeologist, he loved to challenge accepted dogma, especially in regards to Egyptology. He was equally loathed and admired, both for his wild conjectures and for his fierce advocacy of his positions. He was always willing to listen to opposing positions, but he could cut a colleague's legs out from under them if he felt they were too closed-minded."

A smile formed on her lips as she remembered some of those heated debates. There were few men like Harold—with maybe the exception of his son, Rory, who could go toe-to-toe with the old man. Still, the two were often at odds, arguing deep into the night on some historical or scientific point. Even when red-faced from such a debate, Harold could not hide the pride he held for his son. It shone from his eyes.

Safia's smile faded as grief overwhelmed her again.

To lose both of them . . .

She fought back her sorrow, replacing it with a steely determination. If there was any chance Rory was still alive, she owed it to Harold to find his boy. She also owed it to Jane, who over the last two years had steadfastly refused to accept that her father and brother were dead. Safia suspected that what drove Jane to study so diligently, almost relentlessly, was to prepare herself to hunt for them, to learn the truth.

Painter drew Safia back to the matter at hand. "What does Professor McCabe's past eccentricity have to do with any of this?"

She returned to the matter at hand. "There was one aspect of Egyptology of special interest to Harold. It was where he butted heads with many of his colleagues. It concerned the biblical story of Exodus."

"Exodus? As in Moses and the flight of the Jews from Egypt?"

She nodded. "Most archaeologists consider the story to be no more than a myth, an allegory, versus a historical event."

"But not Professor McCabe?"

"No, he believed the story could be a true account, one that was possibly exaggerated and mythologized over the passing millennia, but nonetheless real." Safia had many of Harold's field journals piled on her desk, full of her colleague's speculations, theories, and fragments of support, some quite cryptic. "I believe one of the reasons he led the expedition into the Sudan was to find proof for his theories."

"Why search out there?"

"That was Harold. While most biblical archaeologists sought proof by scouring the lands to the *east* of Egypt, looking to the Sinai Peninsula, Harold believed there could be evidence to the *south*. He thought it was possible that a smaller group of Jewish slaves might have fled in that direction, escaping along the Nile."

"What was he looking for in particular?"

"For any signs of a plague, especially in the mummies recovered from that remote region of the Nile. In fact, Harold specifically hired Dr. Derek Rankin for this task, a bio-archaeologist who specializes in the study of ancient diseases."

Painter sat back in his seat. "And now Professor McCabe comes stumbling out of the desert two years later, harboring some sort of disease, while also having been the victim of a bizarre self-mummification ritual. What do you make of it?"

"I don't know."

"But you mentioned that the sickness seen in Cairo had happened *before,* sometime in the past. Were you referring to the plagues of ancient Egypt?"

"No." She grabbed one of Harold's journals and flipped to a section she had marked with a Post-it tab. "Before setting off on his expedition, Harold had sought any references from the area that might hint at the presence of a disease or contagion. He discovered something in the museum archives here, going back to the famous explorers Stanley and Livingstone. The two men had both independently sought the source of the Nile, traveling deep into the Sudan and beyond, searching for those headwaters."

"If I remember my history lessons well enough, Livingstone vanished into the jungle and was believed dead."

"Until six years later, when Stanley found him sick and impoverished in a small African village on the shores of Lake Tanganyika."

"But what does any of this have to do with Professor McCabe's expedition?"

"Harold had become fixated on this pair of men, less for their famous encounter in Africa than what became of the two explorers later in life."

"Why? What did they do?"

"Livingstone remained in Africa until his death in 1873. Harold was especially interested in the fact that natives close to Livingstone mummified the explorer's body before returning him to the British authorities."

"He was mummified?"

She nodded, recognizing the strange coincidental nature of this detail. "His body is now buried in Westminster Abbey."

"And what about Stanley?"

"He eventually returned to Britain, married a Welsh woman, and served in Parliament. It was that part of the man's life that most interested Harold."

"Why?"

"You have to understand that Stanley's fame was forever tied to Livingstone's. Because of that, he was often consulted in regards to Living-stone's legacy. After the man died in Africa, most of the artifacts gathered during his journeys ended up here at the British Museum. But there were some objects of personal significance that remained with the Livingstone estate. It was only after the dissolution of that estate in the late nineteenth century that those last objects came into the museum's possession. It was the record of *one* of those artifacts that drew Harold's attention."

"What was it?"

"It was a talisman given to the explorer by a native as a gift for saving the man's child. The object was inscribed with Egyptian hieroglyphics, and according to the native's story, the sealed artifact held water from the Nile, collected when the river had been turned to blood."

"Turned to blood?" Painter's voice rang with skepticism. "Are you talking about the time of Moses?"

Safia could understand his doubt. She'd had a similar reaction herself. "It could all be a tall tale. Livingstone was a well-known Christian mis-sionary, preaching where and when he could in Africa. So it's possible the native concocted that biblical connection about the talisman to please his Christian friend. But either way, due to the authenticity of the hieroglyph-ics, Harold was convinced that the object had a true Egyptian connec-tion."

"But what about all of this struck *you* as significant? How does this talisman tie into what's happening now?"

"Beyond a drawing of it found in Livingstone's personal papers, there is only one other mention of the talisman. At least that Harold could un-earth. It's a reference to some curse associated with it."

"A curse?"

"After its acquisition, the artifact was opened and studied here at the museum. Within days of that event, all those associated with the project became ill and died of—" She read from where Harold had copied the lone record of this tragic event. "*—of a great feverish affliction accompanied by violent fits.*"

She lowered the book and saw the understanding in Painter's face.

"Sounds like the same symptoms reported in the patients in Cairo," he said. "So what happened back then?"

"That's just it. Harold attempted to discover more. And even though twenty-two people died during this outbreak, he could find no corroborating evidence."

"Even for records from the nineteenth century, that's suspicious. Almost sounds like someone was trying to expunge all accounts of this tragedy."

"Harold thought so, too. Yet, he eventually did learn that Stanley was consulted about the matter. He was brought before the Royal Society and questioned."

"Why?"

"It seems he and Livingstone continued to have communication up until the man's death in Africa."

Painter's brow furrowed. "Where Livingstone was also mummified."

She lifted an eyebrow. "Unless the order of events surrounding his death was wrong."

"What do you mean?"

"What if Livingstone had undergone the mummification process *before* his death, like with Harold?" She shrugged. "Records only show that Livingstone's body arrived back in England already in a mummified state. Back then, everyone would have simply assumed he'd been mummified after his death."

"It's an intriguing thought. But even if you're right, where does this line of inquiry get us?"

"I'm hoping it'll lead us to where Harold and the others vanished. It's possible Harold discovered something—either here at the museum or out in the field—that led him to the source of this disease. What happened after that, I have no idea, but maybe discovering the source could lead us to the others."

"Not to mention, if matters get worse with this outbreak, finding the source could be vital." Painter stared hard at her. "What can I do to help?"

"I'll take anything." She gave him an earnest look, trying to put into words the fear in her gut. "Call it one of those hunches again, but I think we're looking at the tip of a bloody iceberg."

"I think you may be right."

"I also fear we're running out of time. It's been almost two weeks since Harold came stumbling out of the desert."

He nodded his understanding. "Which means his trail out in that desert is growing colder by the day."

"I've got Jane—Harold's daughter—searching the boxes of her father's personal papers for any further clues. Meanwhile, medical personnel from Public Health are trying to isolate the cause of the illness."

Painter nodded. "I can send a team to assist you there in London. We'll also need boots on the ground in the Sudan, to try to find where Harold came from."

Safia saw the gears turning in the man's head. Before they could work out further plans, her office door opened.

I thought I had locked it . . .

She turned her chair toward the door—then relaxed when she saw it was a junior curator, a postdoctoral student named Carol Wentzel. "What can I—?"

A stranger shoved past the young woman and into the office. He lifted a gun and pointed it at Safia.

She raised an arm, but it was too late.

The muzzle flashed twice. Pain flared in her chest. Gasping, she twisted toward the computer, toward the panicked look on Painter's face. She reached a hand up to him, as if he could somehow help.

A louder retort exploded behind her. The round buzzed her ear and shattered the screen under her palm. The image went immediately dark—and a moment later, so did the rest of the world.

3

Jane McCabe fought through the ghosts haunting her attic. She felt like a trespasser in her own family cottage. Everywhere she turned in the cramped, cobweb-strewn space were reminders of those who were gone. The old worm-eaten wardrobe in the corner still held some of her mother's clothes. Discarded in the corner was her brother, Rory's, old sports equipment: a dusty cricket bat, a half-deflated football, even a tattered rugby jersey from his schoolboy days.

Still, one specter loomed above all else, a shadow from which none of them could escape in life, and now even in death: Her father dominated this space. Squirreled up here were mountains of old file boxes, some going back to her father's university days, along with stacks of books and field journals.

At the request of Dr. al-Maaz, Jane had already sifted through the least grimy of the boxes, those from the last two or three years before her father vanished into the desert. She had lowered the crates down to Derek Rankin, who was in the kitchen going through their contents, searching for some clue to the fate of her father and brother.

The task seemed futile, but it was better than sitting alone, struggling to come to terms with the finality of her father's death and the mysteries of his body's condition.

Better to keep moving.

She stretched a kink from her back and stared out the small attic window that overlooked the village of Ashwell. The town was an idyllic mix of medieval cottages and homes with thatched roofs and plaster-and-timber walls. From her high vantage, she could spy upon the square tower of the parish church, which dated back to the fourteenth century. Rising from that direction, the faint chords of music reached her. The annual Ashwell Music Festival had been under way for the past ten days. Though it ended tonight, when Saint Mary's held a great pageant, called the Choral Evensong.

She stared toward the ancient bell tower, rising in crenellated sections and topped by a leaden spike that pointed toward the heavens. She remembered her father taking her inside the church when she was nine years old, showing her the medieval graffiti carved along the walls. Scribblings in Latin and early English described the calamity of the Black Plague as it struck the village in the 1300s. As a child, she had done charcoal rubbings of several inscriptions. While doing so, she had felt a strange kinship with those long-dead scribes. In many ways, those moments may have planted the seeds that inspired her to follow in her father's footsteps, to pursue a career in archaeology.

She turned from the window, from the sounds of merriment wafting from the festival, and stared across the attic filled with the shadows of her father. She remembered one inscription from the church, copied from the side of a pillar. This bit of graffiti had nothing to do with the Black Plague, but it felt particularly apt at this moment.

"*Superbia precidit fallum,*" she recited, picturing the Latin scratched into the wall.

Pride goes before a fall.

Though Jane loved her father, she was not blind to his faults. He could be stubborn, obstinate in his beliefs, and was certainly not free from the sin of pride. She knew arrogance had driven her father into the desert as much as the quest for knowledge. His contrarian position regarding the truth behind the biblical Exodus had left him open to ridicule and rebuke by his colleagues. And while he presented a self-assured and confident face to the world, she knew how the scorn ate at him. He was determined to prove his theory was right—for the sake of history as much as his own pride.

And look where it led you—and Rory, too.

She clenched a fist as anger momentarily overwhelmed her grief. But underlying all of that was something deeper, something that had been eating at her for the past two years. Guilt. It was one of the reasons she seldom returned to the family cottage, leaving it empty, the furniture covered in drop cloths. Though the commute from Ashwell to London was less than an hour by train, she had taken a studio apartment in the city center. She told herself it was because of the flat's convenient proximity to the university, but she knew better. It was too painful to come back here. Only necessity ever drove her back to Ashwell, like this request from Dr. al-Maaz.

A shout rose from the kitchen below. "I think I found something!"

Relieved to escape the ghosts up here, Jane crossed back through the shadows to the glow of the open trapdoor that led down into the cottage. She descended the ladder to the second-floor hallway and hurried past the closed bedroom doors to reach the stairs down to the main floor.

As she passed through the parlor to the small kitchen, she discovered Derek had opened all the curtains. The sunlight made her squint after so long in the attic. She paused to blink away the glare. The brightness seemed too cheerful considering the circumstances.

Ahead of her, Derek sat at the kitchen table, surrounded by boxes from the attic. At his elbows were stacks of books and journals, along with a scatter of loose papers. He had shed his jacket and rolled up his sleeves.

The man was six years older than her. Her father had taken Derek under his wing, mentoring him through his years at the university and eventually luring him out into the deserts. Like so many others, Derek had been unable to escape the gravitational pull of her father. He ended up spending many days in the family study, often camping overnight on the sofa.

Back then, Jane hadn't minded the intrusion, especially when her mother had become sick. Derek had always been easy to talk to, an ear to listen to her when there was no one else. Unfortunately, Rory did not share this sentiment. Her brother had always bristled at the young protégé in their midst, plainly feeling Derek was a competitor for their father's attention and, more important, for his accolades.

At present Derek was bent over what appeared to be a leather-bound archive. From the cracks in the leather, it looked to be far older than anything written by her father. As she stepped over, she noted the day's worth of dark stubble across Derek's chin and cheeks. Neither of them had managed to get much sleep since returning from Egypt.

"What did you find?" she asked.

He turned and grinned, which served to light up his tanned face and accentuate his sun wrinkles and smile lines. He hefted up the large volume. "I think your dad pilfered this from a library in Glasgow."

"Glasgow?" She frowned, remembering her father had made several journeys to Scotland before turning his attention to the Sudan.

"Come see," he urged.

She peered over his shoulder as he opened the book to a place marked with a slip of paper. As she leaned over, she caught a whiff of his cologne, or maybe it was his shampoo. Either way, the scent helped clear her nose of the moldering odor of the attic.

"According to a catalog tag," Derek said, "the book came from the Livingstone Archives at the University of Glasgow, where a majority of the explorer's documents are kept. This particular volume contains copies of his correspondences, starting from his early years exploring the Zambezi River in southern Africa through his later years as he searched for the source of the Nile. The section bookmarked by your father covers letters written by Livingstone to Henry Morton Stanley, the man who so famously found him in the darkest depths of Africa."

Curious, Jane pulled a chair over and joined Derek. "What do the letters say? Why was my father so interested in them?"

Derek shrugged. "Most of the content appears to be innocuous, just two old chums commiserating, but if you look through these marked pages, they also contain pages of biological and anatomical sketches drawn by Livingstone. Your father marked this page in particular. It caught my attention because of the taxonomy of this little bugger. Come look."

Jane leaned shoulder to shoulder with Derek to view the hand-drawn sketches of what appeared to be a beetle.

Ateuchus sacer

The detail captured by Livingstone was indeed impressive. The sketch showed the insect both with its wings unfurled and not. She read its scientific name aloud, scrunching her nose. "*Ateuchus sacer.* I don't get it. Why's this beetle important?"

"Because it was given its name by none other than Charles Darwin." Derek cocked an eyebrow at her. "He also called it 'the sacred beetle of the Egyptians.'"

Jane suddenly understood. "It's a scarab beetle."

"Classified nowadays as *Scarabaeus sacer,*" Derek explained.

She began to get an inkling of her father's interest. The ancient Egyptians worshipped this little coprophagous beetle because of its habit of rolling dung into small balls. They believed the practice to be analogous to the actions of the god Khepri—the morning version of Ra—whose task it was each day to roll the sun across the heavens. Scarab symbols could be found throughout Egyptian art and writing.

She leaned closer to the old book. "If my dad was researching the history behind the talisman given to Livingstone, it makes sense he would've been interested in anything related to Egypt in Livingstone's notes or diaries." She sat back in her chair. "But why would he steal this book from Glasgow? That's so unlike him to violate such a trust."

"I don't know. There are other pages marked here, too. He seemed particularly interested in the letters with those sketches on them." Derek closed the book and pulled over a field journal. "What's odd is that months before he left for the Sudan, he clearly became fixated on that talisman. Yet, he never mentioned a breath of it to me. He simply tasked me to look for some pattern of illness in the mummies collected from the salvage operation in the Sudan."

"Did you find any such sign?"

"No." Derek sighed. "I feel like I let your father down."

She touched his elbow. "It's not your fault. Dad always wanted . . . no, *needed* some proof to support his Exodus theory. He wouldn't let anything stand in his way."

Derek still looked dissatisfied and opened the journal. "Your father took extensive notes about the talisman. The museum destroyed it after so many inexplicable deaths, incinerating it completely. But he uncovered a charcoal rendering of the object, along with a copy of the hieroglyphics found inscribed on its underside. He recorded it in his journal."

Derek showed her the page. She recognized her father's meticulous handwriting. On the top of the page, he had taped a small photocopy of the original charcoal rendering.

"It looks to be an *aryballos,* or oil vessel," Jane noted. "One with double heads. Looks to be a lion on one side and an Egyptian woman's face on the other. Strange."

"According to the written description, the artifact was composed of Egyptian faience with a turquoise-blue glaze."

"Hmm . . . that makes sense. Especially if the vessel was made to hold water." Egyptian faience was an early type of pottery made from a slurry of quartz, silica, and clay. Once kilned, it was actually closer to glass than true pottery. "How large was it?"

"According to the account, the object stood about six inches tall and could hold about a pint of liquid. To access the inner chamber, the museum had to chip out the vessel's stone plug, which had been glued in place with a wad of hard resinous wax."

"Making the *aryballos* watertight."

He nodded. "And look here on the bottom of the page. Your father copied down the hieroglyphics inscribed on the artifact's underside."

She recognized the set of figures without needing to consult a book and translated it aloud. "*Iteru.*"

"The Egyptian word for *river.*"

"Which was also their name for the Nile." She rubbed her forehead. "I guess that supports the story told by the native who gave Livingstone the *aryballos.*"

"That the water came from the Nile."

"When it had turned bloody," Jane reminded him. "The first of Moses's ten plagues to strike Egypt."

"Speaking of that, look at this." Derek turned to the next page, to where her father had listed those ten disasters.

1) Water into blood
2) A rain of frogs
3) An affliction of lice
4) A plague of flies
5) Diseased livestock
6) A rage of boils
7) A thunderstorm of hail and fire
8) An invasion of locusts
9) Three days of darkness
10) The death of the firstborn

The record was written in chronological order, but for some reason, her father had circled the seventh on the list: *A thunderstorm of hail and fire.*

Derek noted her deep frown. "What do you make of that?"

"I have no idea."

The cottage's phone rang, startling them both.

Jane stood with a scowl, irritated, believing it was Dr. al-Maaz calling to pressure them for answers. But so far all they had uncovered were more mysteries. She stepped to the old phone on the kitchen counter and picked up the receiver.

Before she could even say hello, an urgent voice cut her off. "Jane Mc-Cabe?"

"Yes? Who is this?"

"My name is Painter Crowe." The caller spoke in a rush, his voice distinctly American. "I'm a friend of Safia al-Maaz. Someone attacked her at the museum a little over an hour ago."

"What? How?" Jane struggled to absorb this news.

"Others are dead. If this is about your father, they might be coming after you next. You must get somewhere safe."

"But what about—?"

"Just go. Find a police station."

"Our village doesn't have one."

The closest constabulary was in neighboring Letchworth or Royston—and she didn't have a car. She and Derek had traveled here by train.

"Then get somewhere public," the caller warned. "Put people around you, where you're less likely to be assaulted. I have help on the way."

Derek spoke from where he stood at the table. "What's wrong?"

She stared wide-eyed at him, her mind whirling, and spoke to the caller. "I . . . there's a pub and diner around the corner. The Bushel and Strike."

She looked at her watch. It was after seven, so the place should be busy.

"Get there!" he urged her. "Now!"

The line cut off.

Jane took a deep breath, trying to stave off panic.

If the caller is right about my dad . . .

She pointed to the table. "Derek, grab my father's journal, and that archive from Glasgow, anything you think might be important."

"What's happening?"

Jane hurried over to help him gather the research into his leather messenger bag. "We're in big trouble."

7:17 P.M.

Derek held the cottage door open for Jane, struggling to understand what was happening. All of this seemed impossible.

He waited as Jane paused on the porch. Her eyes searched the overgrown front garden and the narrow street beyond the low brick fence. Though the sun had yet to set, it sat low on the horizon, casting the roadway in deep shadows.

"What is going on?" he pressed. "Who could be coming after you?"

With no apparent sign of a threat, Jane headed to the small iron gate that opened onto Gardiners Lane. "I don't know. Maybe no one. Maybe the same ones who attacked Dr. al-Maaz and the others at the museum."

Derek pulled the strap of his bag higher on his shoulder as he followed Jane through the gate and onto the street. Worry for his friends and colleagues at the museum helped harden his resolve to keep Jane safe.

"Can you trust this caller's word?" he asked.

Jane glanced to him, plainly considering this for a breath. "I . . . I think so. The man suggested surrounding ourselves with people. That doesn't sound like someone leading us into a trap."

That's certainly true.

"If nothing else," she said, "I could use a tall pint. Maybe two. To help settle the nerves."

She offered him a small smile, which he matched.

"Since it's for medicinal purposes," he said, "the first round's on me. I am a doctor after all."

She looked askance at him. "Of archaeology."

"Of *bio*-archaeology," he reminded her. "That's almost as good as a medical doctor."

She rolled her eyes and waved ahead. "Then prescribe away, my good doctor."

After a short walk, they reached an alley that led to the back patio of the local pub. The Bushel and Strike stood across Mill Street from the massive bulk of Saint Mary's Church and its surrounding parklands. Beyond the pub, the top half of the church tower stretched into the sky, its prominent lead spike aglow in the last rays of the day.

Closer at hand, it looked as if twilight had already fallen over the pub's rear patio. Shadowy patrons occupied most of the tables. Through the open rear doors came the murmur of others in the pub.

The familiar cadence, punctuated by bouts of laughter, helped dampen Derek's fear of some faceless menace. He had spent many nights in the Bushel and Strike with Jane's father, sometimes closing the place down before stumbling back to the cottage.

Coming here felt like coming home.

He also heard a woman singing, her voice echoing from the churchyard across the street, reminding him it was the final night of the Ashwell Music Festival.

No wonder the pub sounded so packed.

Still, considering the circumstances, maybe that is just as well.

Drawn by the cheerfulness, he and Jane hurried down the alley and through a gate in the picket fence that bordered the back patio. They reached the rear doors without being molested by any unknown assailants and soon found themselves parked before the bar with two pints of Guinness before them. A few local patrons recognized Jane and offered their condolences. The story of her father's inexplicable reappearance and death had hit all the major newspapers and was surely the topic of much of the local gossip.

Jane sipped at her beer, her shoulders hunched, plainly uncomfortable with the attention, by the repeated reminders of her loss. While not impolite, she fixed a false smile on her face or would nod woodenly at some anecdote about her father. Derek eventually shifted to shield her from the others, to give her some measure of privacy.

He also kept a watch on the front door to the establishment. He judged each person who entered with a wary eye, noting the volume of strangers due to the festival. Still, after a full forty-five minutes, he began to suspect the caller must have been mistaken or overly cautious. There appeared to be no threat or any sign of an enemy.

Then someone burst through the front door, looking frantic.

"Fire!" he hollered into the pub while pointing outside.

A beat later, patrons from the back patio piled inside, sounding the same alarm. En masse the packed pub emptied out onto Mill Street. Jane and Derek followed. In the press of the crowd, Derek got separated as they were pushed and pulled by the excited tide of people.

"Jane!" he called out.

By now, night had fallen, and the temperature had dropped precipitously. He stumbled into the middle of the dark street and searched around. Down the block, flames licked into the sky, illuminating a thick curl of black smoke.

It can't be . . .

He finally spotted Jane a few yards ahead of him. She stood with her back to him. He shoved and elbowed his way to her side, hooking an arm around her. Her face was frighteningly blank. She also recognized the likely source of the blaze.

"It's our house," she mumbled.

He gripped her tighter.

"They set it on fire."

Derek searched the surroundings, suspicious of everyone. The glow of the rising flames cast the street and the milling throng in a hellish light. The alarm of fire engines echoed through the village, adding to the sense of dread and urgency.

"We have to get out of here," he warned Jane, pulling her back, getting her moving.

If someone had set fire to the cottage, the intent must have been to destroy her father's research. The weight of the satchel over his shoulder suddenly grew heavier. Its contents were now even more important, but it remained the least of his concerns. If the enemy wanted to eliminate all ties to Professor McCabe's life and work, there was one final target surely high on their list.

His daughter.

Derek turned Jane around, putting her back to the flames. "We have to—"

Someone grabbed his shoulder and shoved him aside. Caught by surprise, Derek stumbled a few steps. A hulking figure loomed over Jane. The man looked like something out of a nightmare with a brutish face and a massive physique.

Still, Derek refused to back off. He lunged for the attacker, ready to defend Jane—only to be met by the man's fist. Derek's head snapped back, pain flared with a crunch of bone, lights burst and dazzled his eyes.

He fell hard to the street.

Through a haze, he watched Jane be dragged away.

No . . .

4

Kathryn Bryant had never seen her boss so distressed. Her office overlooked the communication hub in Sigma's subterranean headquarters. Through a window, she watched Director Crowe stalk across the breadth of the neighboring room. A U-shaped bank of telecommunication stations and computer monitors glared back at the man, as if taunting him with his impotence.

"He looks ready to wear a hole down to the next subbasement," Kat's husband noted. "Maybe you'd better slip some Valium into his next cup of coffee."

"I know you're joking, Monk, but it may come to that."

Kat rubbed the line of a small scar across her chin. It was a nervous tic, a measure of her own desire to do more than shuffle calls and monitor chatter from various global intelligence agencies. But as the director's second in command, she knew her place. She had been recruited into Sigma out of a position in naval intelligence, and there were few people in the world who matched her expertise.

"Any further word out of Cairo?" Monk asked.

"Only news that's grim."

She glanced over to her husband. Monk Kokkalis stood a few inches shorter than her, but he had a true bulldog of a physique. Furthering the image, he kept his head shaved and had never bothered to fix the kink to his nose from an old break. Four hours ago, when all of this blew up,

Monk had been at the facility's gym, so he still wore sneakers, sweatpants, and a camouflage T-shirt with the Green Beret emblem—a pair of crossed arrows and a saber—stretched across his chest. From looking at him, few would doubt his years in Special Forces, but many underestimated the brilliance hidden behind his pugilistic exterior.

Sigma had come to value Monk's expertise in medicine and biotechnology—as did DARPA. But for them, Monk was more of a resident guinea pig. He had lost a hand during a prior mission and had gone through a series of prostheses, each more advanced as the technologies improved. His current hand was tied to a neural implant that allowed him even finer control of his fingers.

He fiddled with the wrist connection, still plainly getting accustomed to the upgrade. "Kat, what do you mean by *grim*?"

"It's total chaos out in Cairo at the moment."

"What about the quarantine?"

She snorted a breath. "Even before this outbreak, Cairo's medical infrastructure was frayed at best. Emergency services are little better. If this gets any worse, it'll be like trying to halt a brushfire with a squirt gun."

"How about the cases in the U.K.?"

"So far—"

A red-bannered interdepartmental brief popped up on her monitor, coming from the CDC. She scanned it quickly.

Monk noted her posture stiffening. "Not good news?"

"No. Several airport personnel in both Cairo and London are reporting cases of high fevers." She glanced over to Monk. "Including a British Airways flight attendant."

"Sounds like the cat's clawing out of the bag."

"The report is preliminary. It's still too early to say if this is the same disease that afflicted the morgue staff in Egypt, but we can't keep sitting on our hands. I'll need to coordinate and mobilize multiple health agencies, both here and abroad."

She shook her head. When it came to organizing such efforts, international red tape and bureaucracies bogged everything down. She found her finger again rubbing at the scar on her chin. She forced her errant hand back to the computer keyboard.

Beyond the window, Painter made another pass across the neighboring room. Kat knew Painter wanted to be in London rather than holed up here at Sigma command. Their headquarters had been built in a warren of old World War II–era bomb shelters beneath the Smithsonian Castle. The location allowed Sigma easy access to both the halls of power and to the country's preeminent scientific institutions and laboratories. But clearly for Painter, none of that mattered at the moment. He wanted to be topside, out in the field leading the hunt for those who had attacked the British Museum.

From reading an old mission dossier, Kat knew of the director's history with Safia al-Maaz. The woman was important to him. As if sensing this line of thought, Painter stepped to one of the computer stations and played back the footage captured on the conference call with Dr. al-Maaz.

Kat had already viewed the video four times. It showed Safia assaulted by a masked assailant who barged into her office. The man shot her with what had been identified as a Palmer Cap-Chur tranquilizer gun. A pair of feathered darts struck her in the chest. He had then shot out the screen with a regular pistol, the same weapon he had used to kill two museum personnel, including a young woman, a junior curator, who was seen briefly in the footage.

By the time help arrived, Safia was gone.

Out in the communication hub, Painter had stopped the video, freezing it on the last image of the woman, her palm lifted toward the screen.

"If they'd wanted her dead, she would be," Monk murmured. "They clearly need something from her."

"But what about after that?" Kat asked.

Monk grimaced. "Let's hope we reach her before that bridge is crossed."

Kat checked the clock on her monitor. "Shouldn't Gray already be here? Your jet to London is scheduled to be wheels up in thirty-five minutes."

Monk shrugged. "He's at the hospital with his dad and brother. Said he'd meet me at the airfield."

"How's his father doing?"

"Not great." Monk ran the palm of his prosthesis over his shaved scalp. "But it's his brother that's the real issue."

4:14 P.M.

If it's not one thing, it's another . . .

Commander Grayson Pierce sat at his father's bedside. They had just returned from a series of medical tests at Holy Cross Hospital and were getting him settled at a skilled nursing center for further care. Even the ride here by ambulance had taken its toll on the old man.

As Gray watched the nurse tuck his father's sheets around him, he searched for the hard Texas oilman who had run roughshod over their family. His father had been a rugged figure, fiercely independent, even after an accident had sheared one of his legs off at the knee. For most of his life, Gray and his father had butted heads, both too stubborn to bend, too full of pride. The fighting eventually drove Gray away from home, first into the army, then into the Rangers, and eventually into Sigma.

Sitting here now, he studied the map of lines across the old man's face, noting the sallow complexion and sunken eyes. His father heaved a hard breath as the nurse fluffed his pillow. Normally such a lungful would have unleashed a litany of curses, lambasting such doting attention. Jackson Pierce was not one to be coddled. Instead, his father's chest sank with a defeated sigh; he was too exhausted to object.

Gray spoke up for him and waved the nurse away. "That's enough," he said. "My dad doesn't like to be fussed over."

The young woman stepped back and turned to Gray. "I'll still need to flush his central line."

"Can you give us a minute or two?" He checked his watch.

That's about all the time I have left.

Pressure to get moving wore at him. He needed to be at the airfield. He glanced over to the door.

Where's Kenny?

Gray imagined his brother must have stopped off somewhere on his way over from Holy Cross. Likely trying to eke out his last moments of freedom. With Gray leaving, Kenny had to assume "dad duty"—as they had come to call it—a responsibility that only seemed to weigh heavier upon them both as time passed.

Impatient, Gray took in the new room. Though private, it could only be generously described as Spartan. It held a wardrobe closet, a privacy curtain on rails, and a small rolling bedside table. This would be his father's home for the next six weeks.

After slipping and falling last month, his father had gouged a deep tear in the stump of his leg. After an emergency room visit and minor surgery, everything seemed to be fine, but a low-grade fever developed and persisted. The diagnosis was a secondary bone infection and mild septicemia, not an uncommon complication in senior patients. Another surgery and hospital stay later and his father had been assigned here, where he was scheduled for six weeks of intravenous antibiotic therapy.

And maybe that's for the best, Gray thought guiltily. *At least here, he'll have around-the-clock attention while I'm gone.*

Even at the best of times, Kenny was not the more responsible caregiver.

A rasp rose from the bed. "I'm ready to go."

Gray turned back to his father. "You have to stay here, Dad. Doctor's orders."

Of late, his father had only a tentative grasp on the present. What had first started as bouts of forgetfulness—losing his keys, repeating the same question, mixing up directions—eventually led to a diagnosis of Alzheimer's, one more blow to a man grasping to hold on to his independence. Last year, Gray had risked an experimental treatment, a drug he had stolen from a lab that showed promise for degenerative neuropathies—and amazingly it worked. A series of PET scans had showed no new amyloidal deposits in the brain, and clinically his father's decline seemed to have stopped.

Unfortunately the therapy had failed to reverse the damage done—

which was a double-edged sword. His father remained somewhat coherent and engaged, but he would never return to the man he was before the disease ravaged him. He was trapped somewhere in between, lost in a fog that never lifted.

His father spoke again, more adamant now. "I want to see your mother."

Gray took in a deep breath. His mother had died a while back. Gray had explained this tragedy to him many times, and clearly his father had absorbed it at some level, often expressing his sorrow or sharing some funny story about her. Gray cherished those moments. But when his father was exhausted or stressed—like now—he lost his tether on the passage of time.

Gray reached to his father's shoulder, unsure whether to allow him this delusion or to explain the harsh truth once again. Instead, he looked into his father's ice-blue eyes, a match to his own. Deep in there, he recognized the lucidity shining back.

"Dad . . . ?"

"I'm ready to go, son." His father repeated these words plainly. "I . . . I miss Harriet so much. I want to see her again."

Gray froze in place, momentarily struck dumb. His father had always raged against the world, against any assumed slight, even against his own bullheaded son. Gray could not balance this complete resignation with the hard man who had raised him.

Before he could respond, Kenny arrived, barging into the room like a whirlwind. There was no mistaking the family resemblance. The two brothers stood the same height, with dark, thick hair and ruddy Welsh complexions. Only, while Gray kept fit, Kenny nursed a prominent beer belly, a feature earned from his deskbound job at a software company and too many nights of partying.

Kenny lifted a plastic bag with a 7-Eleven logo on it. "Got Dad some magazines. A *Sports Illustrated. Golf Digest*. Also bought him some snacks. Chips and candy bars."

Kenny hauled another chair to the bedside and fell heavily onto it as if he had just run a marathon. Gray caught a strong whiff of whiskey on his breath. Apparently his younger brother had bought more than just staples at the convenience store.

Kenny pointed toward the door. "Gray, you can leave. I got it from here. I'll make sure Dad is taken care of." A lilt of accusation slipped into his voice. "I mean somebody has to, right?"

Gray gritted his teeth. Kenny knew Gray worked for the government, but he didn't have the clearance to know about Sigma Force or the importance of Gray's covert work. In fact, Kenny was never all that curious about his older brother in the first place.

As Gray stood to leave, his father gave him a stern stare, accompanied by a small shake of his head. The message was clear. Dad didn't want Gray mentioning what was said a moment ago. Apparently that poignant admission was only meant for Gray's ears.

Fine . . . what's one more secret?

Gray stepped to the bedside and gave the old man a final hug. It was awkward, both from the bed's half-reclined position and because such public displays of affection were rare between them.

Still, his father freed an arm and patted Gray on the back. "Give 'em hell."

"Always." From trouble in the past, his dad had learned about the true nature of Gray's work. "I'll see you when I get back."

Gray straightened and turned. Inside, he felt the tidal shift as he readied himself for the coming mission. Years in the Army Rangers had taught him to go from idle to full throttle in seconds, whether it was rolling from his bunk at the whistle of an incoming mortar or diving for cover at the crack of a sniper's shot.

As a soldier, when it was time to get moving, you moved.

Now was one of those times.

He headed toward the door, but his father stopped him, his voice ringing out with surprising strength, sounding more like his old self. "Promise me."

Gray looked back, wrinkling his brow. "Promise what?"

His father blinked, his stare wavering. He had propped himself up on an elbow, but even this small effort had taxed him to the point of trembling. He fell back to the bed, a familiar confusion settling over his features.

"Dad?" Gray asked.

A hand weakly waved, dismissing him.

Kenny reinforced it with a frown. "Christ, man, if you're going, *go*. Let Dad get some rest. Quit dragging this out."

Gray balled a fist, looking for something to strike out at. Instead, he turned on a heel and strode out the door. As he exited the nursing facility, he sucked in deep breaths and crossed to his parked motorcycle, a Yamaha V-Max. He hauled his six-foot frame onto the bike, tugged on his helmet, and ignited the engine into a throaty growl.

He let it roar, giving voice to his own frustration. With the rumble coursing through his bones, he set off. He took a sharp turn from the parking lot onto the street, leaning his bike hard, and sped away.

Still, his father's final words chased him.

Promise me.

He didn't know what that meant. Guilt gnawed at him, both because he was leaving and because down deep he was relieved to be going. After so many months of dealing with the ebbs and flows of his father's health, of wrestling demons that seemed to have no substance, Gray needed something he could truly battle, something he could grab with his hands.

Focusing on that, he called up Sigma command and reached Kat. "I'm on my way to the airfield. ETA is fifteen minutes."

Her voice answered inside his helmet. "Monk'll meet you there. He has a full mission report waiting for you on the plane."

Gray had already received the bullet points from the director. Painter had a personal stake in all of this and had requested Gray take point in London.

"What's the status out there?" he asked.

"The museum is in lockdown. Unfortunately the security cameras in the employee wing failed to capture the intruders. At the moment, police are canvassing the area for witnesses."

"What about the other potential target?"

"Jane McCabe? Still no word from the field."

Gray sped faster, sensing matters were growing more dire by the hour. Unfortunately, their flight wouldn't land until dawn, touching down at Northolt, a Royal Air Force station in a western borough of London.

Because of the delay, Painter Crowe had already activated two Sigma operatives who were closer at hand: one who had been attending a conference in Leipzig, Germany; the other who had been in Marrakesh, investigating the black-market sale of stolen antiquities from the Middle East.

The two made for an odd couple, but necessity often created strange bedfellows.

The turnoff to the private airfield appeared ahead. Gray throttled up and raced for the entrance, picturing that pair of operatives in the field.

God help anyone who got in their way.

Of course, that's if the two didn't kill each other first.

5

Surely he can't be this stupid . . .

Seichan grabbed Joe Kowalski's wrist and jammed her finger into a cluster of nerves at the base of his thumb. The big man yelped, but he finally let go of Jane McCabe's arm.

The young woman stumbled back a step. Before she could bolt, Seichan blocked her escape. She held up both palms. "Ms. McCabe, I'm sorry. We didn't mean to frighten you."

Jane gaped at her pair of assailants. The crowd milled around them, seemingly oblivious to the brief assault. Then again, most of their attention was fixed on the flames licking into the dark sky.

As sirens echoed through the dark village, Seichan explained. "We were sent by Painter Crowe. To get you somewhere safe."

Jane rubbed her bruised forearm. From her appalled expression, she didn't look swayed by Seichan's assurance. Her eyes took in Kowalski. The man looked like a steroid-addicted linebacker. Even the black knee-length leather duster failed to hide his overly muscled frame, well over six feet tall. To make matters worse, his face was a brutal terrain of scars, craggy brows, and thick lips, all of which was centered around a squashed nose and supported by a squared-off chin.

Kowalski's expression at the moment had turned sheepish. "Sorry about that." He waved a mitt-sized hand. "I saw you standing in the street. Thought some guy was trying to attack you."

Jane glanced over her shoulder. "Derek . . ."

As if summoned, a gangly tall figure broke through the crowd. Twin trails of blood dripped from a broken nose. His eyes were already starting to swell. He lunged toward Jane, clearly ready to defend her.

Seichan allowed him to join the young woman. She recognized Dr. Derek Rankin from his photograph included in her mission brief, an identification that had clearly escaped Kowalski before he threw himself headlong into the mix.

Derek glared at Kowalski, looking ready to take the man on yet again, but he glanced sidelong at Jane. "Are you okay?" he asked, his voice nasally from the injury.

She nodded.

Seichan stepped forward. "There's been a misunderstanding."

Only then did the archaeologist notice her. He did a bit of a double take. She was not unaccustomed to this response. She knew her Eurasian features—her long black hair, almond complexion, high cheekbones, and emerald-green eyes—were striking, exotic enough to seduce targets in the past, back when she worked as an assassin for the Guild, a terrorist organization destroyed by Sigma. She was lean and muscular, dressed modestly in black jeans, leather boots, and a loose denim jacket over a dark red blouse.

Derek looked between her and Kowalski. "Wh . . . Who are you two?"

Jane answered, still keeping back. "They were sent by the caller on the phone."

"Despite appearances," Seichan assured them, "we are here to help."

As proof, she slipped a picture that Painter Crowe had sent her. She held it out to Jane. The young woman took it and shifted closer to a streetlamp. Derek looked over her shoulder. It showed Crowe in a photograph with Safia al-Maaz. Both were younger, smiling at the camera, the Omani desert in the background with a large lake shining under moonlight.

"That's our boss," Seichan explained. "He helped Dr. al-Maaz a few years back."

Derek looked up. "I've seen this bloke's picture in Safia's office. She once told me the story of how they met . . . though I suspect she had highly edited that account."

The suspicion slowly dimmed from his eyes.

"So should we trust them?" Jane asked him.

Derek half-turned toward the flames and churning smoke. "Don't think we have much choice." He gingerly touched his nose and scowled at Kowalski. "But just so you know, next time a simple hello would suffice."

Jane crossed her arms, anger hardening her features. She looked less willing to forgive and forget. "I'm not about to—"

Seichan lunged forward and tackled Jane to the side. The gunshot cracked loudly, cutting through the cacophony of sirens. On constant alert to her surroundings—a survival instinct born from her feral years on the streets of Bangkok and Phnom Penh—she had spotted a shadowy figure lift an arm toward their group. She responded reflexively to the threatening gesture, even before a weapon glinted.

Jane tripped, but Seichan scooped an arm around the woman's waist and kept her upright. "Stay low," she warned, while still spinning and freeing a SIG Sauer pistol from the shoulder holster under her jacket.

She pointed it toward the shooter, but the crowd had reacted to the gunshot and surged in confusion, allowing the assassin to fade into the crowd.

Off to the side, Kowalski had pushed Derek down, sheltering him under his bulk. He had freed his own sidearm from under his duster. It looked like a snub-nosed shotgun, but it was a Piezer, a new weapon developed by Homeland Security's Advanced Research Project. Rather than firing standard 12-gauge shells filled with buckshot, the gun's rounds were packed with piezoelectric crystals, which the battery-powered weapon kept charged. Upon firing, the shells would burst open, releasing a shower of electrified crystals, each carrying a voltage equivalent to a Taser. The nonlethal weapon had a range up to fifty yards, perfect for crowd-control situations.

But in a rare instance of restraint, Kowalski held off firing.

Good . . . we don't need more panic on the street—at least not yet.

She got Jane moving away from the shooter's last position and gathered Kowalski and Derek with her. She kept alert for other gunmen hidden among the crowd. Unfortunately their flight was taking them farther away from their vehicle. Minutes ago, she and Kowalski had reached the hamlet in time to see flames spiraling into the sky. She was forced to park and work upstream through the crowd of onlookers to reach the Bushel and Strike.

"Where are we going?" Derek asked.

"To get somewhere safe." She searched around. "We're too exposed out here."

Jane pointed past a stone fence to where a group in white robes was gathered before the open doors of an old stone church. "The Choral Evensong is tonight."

Seichan frowned, not understanding.

"Means the place is usually packed," Derek explained.

Good enough.

Seichan guided them in that direction, hiding her weapon under her jacket. "Is there a way out the back?" she asked, hoping for a chance to break free from whoever was hunting them.

"We can exit out the north side," Jane said breathlessly. "It leads to a cemetery behind the church."

"A cemetery at night." Kowalski grunted next to her. "Well, at least the bastards will have an easier time burying our bodies."

Ignoring him, Seichan hurried them through the fence gate and across the churchyard. "What's beyond the cemetery?" she asked Jane.

"Parklands mostly. Centered around a set of springs that feed the River Cam." Jane waved ahead. "But past those marshy grounds, about a quarter mile, is Station Road. We could hail down a car there. It's only a couple minutes' ride to the train station."

Seichan nodded.

Not a bad plan.

Derek checked his watch. "The next train to Kings Cross London leaves in under an hour."

Even better.

Seichan set a harder pace. "Let's not miss that train."

Ahead of them, the robed choir group chattered loudly, their expressions a mix of worry and excitement. They were bathed in lamplight spilling from the open doors and across the south porch. The robust notes of a pipe organ flowed forth from inside as musicians prepped for the night's celebration. All of them must be wondering if the event would be held or not. It would undoubtedly be hard for any choir to compete with the wailing sirens of the fire trucks.

As their party reached the porch, Seichan urged the others through the crowd and past a set of iron-strapped doors to enter the church. Moving cautiously, Seichan studied the interior layout. To the left was the arched entrance to the tower. To the right, the church's nave extended toward a wide altar, overhung with a candlelit figure of Christ framed in an iron cross. More people mingled in that direction, mostly around the choir stalls and at the base of a massive pipe organ.

Identifying no immediate threat, Seichan focused on their goal. On the far side of the church, an identical set of medieval-looking doors stood open to the night.

Must be the north exit.

Jane confirmed this, pointing ahead. "That way."

Seichan set off, but a commotion drew her attention around. The crowd outside shouted angrily, drowned out a moment later by the coarser growling of an engine. The group hurriedly parted, diving to either side of the doorway. A dark shape blasted toward them with a roar. It was a motorcycle, carrying two helmeted riders. The passenger in back had a pistol leveled over the driver's hunched shoulder.

As the bike skittered across the long porch toward the doors, Seichan turned and pointed toward the tower, to the entrance of a spiral staircase.

"Kowalski, get the others in there and moving up."

He nodded and took off, only glancing back to ask, "What're you—?"

She turned in the other direction and leaped headlong toward the nearest pew. She twisted to land on her shoulder and rolled cleanly to her feet. Sheltered by the thick wooden bench, she aimed her SIG Sauer toward the door as the cycle shot under the archway and into the church. The engine's snarl echoed throughout the nave, a devil's chorus of exhaust and torque. The driver braked hard, tires smoking across the stone floor.

The passenger pointed toward the tower entrance.

Kowalski must've been spotted.

The gunman hopped off the back of the bike, plainly intending to chase down his prey on foot. Seichan aimed her pistol at the base of the helmet and fired. The gun's sharp retort cut through the cycle's growl. The shooter's back arched, blood spraying from his throat. He fell hard, his helmet bouncing off the stone tiles as he hit.

Before she could get a bead on the driver, the man spun around in his seat. He tugged out an assault rifle from a holster at his knee and sprayed wildly in Seichan's direction. She barely had time to duck for cover. Rounds pelted the old wood, chipping at the edges of the pew. From under the bench, she spotted the driver hopping off his bike and using its bulk as a shield to retreat through the tower archway.

She fired from under the pew, aiming for the man's legs, but he made it to safety. She cursed under her breath but respected the man's skill.

Guy's good under pressure . . . too good for an amateur.

Fearing the worst, she darted out of cover and kept her weapon aimed toward the tower entrance. She skirted across the floor, alert for any shift of shadows beyond the archway. Before she could reach there, a new chorus arose.

A wailing cacophony of engines, growing ever louder.

She twisted toward the source. Beyond the porch, a cadre of dark shapes charged across the churchyard, aiming her way.

Cavalry's coming . . . but for the wrong side.

With her plate about to be full, she glanced back toward the tower. She pictured the assassin vanishing away, likely pursuing his target, determined to complete his objective. There was nothing she could do about him for the moment. She had to hold the ground here if they had any hope of escaping.

She cast up a silent plea as she readied for the coming assault.

Kowalski, don't do anything stupid.

9:44 P.M.

To hold back panic at the noise of gunfire below, Jane ran her hand along the walls as she scaled the tower's spiral stairs. Its solidity helped steady her nerves. The bell tower had been built of locally quarried chalkstone. Centuries of rain had worn its façade, but it still endured. She took strength from that.

Under her fingertips, she also felt the medieval inscriptions carved into the soft chalk. It was a reminder of the steadfast people who once lived here, villagers resolute in the face of plagues, wars, and famines.

I must be as firm.

Her fingers dragged over another inscription, reminding her of her father, of the trips here with her as a child. She refused to let the night's attackers erase him from the world, not by fire, not by murder. She would fight with her last breath.

Not only for her father's sake, but also for Rory.

If there's any chance he's still alive, I will not stop until I find him.

She increased her pace.

Derek climbed ahead of her, while the bulk of the American, the fellow named Kowalski, followed behind her.

"Where does this damned place go?" the big man asked.

"The belfry," Jane answered. "Where the tower's bells are housed."

She looked upward. The ringing of the bells had been a constant of village life, chiming every fifteen minutes for over a century. Though of late, because of noise complaints, the bells' peals had been muffled at night, which she found particularly sad, as if history itself were being stifled.

A new noise—much more modern—suddenly intruded, rising up from below. The roaring of multiple engines echoed to them. It sounded like demons chasing them up the stairs. The American cocked his head and hesitated on the stairs, his face a mask of concern for his partner.

"What do we do?" Derek asked.

Kowalski growled and waved his weapon. "Keep going. All the way to the top. We'll hole up there. Should be safe until—"

A gunshot cut through the rumble of distant engines.

Kowalski winced and ducked. The round had sparked off the stone wall near his head, pelting him with stinging shards. "Run!" he hollered and barreled toward them.

Jane turned and ran ahead with Derek.

A loud blast made her jump. Kowalski had fired his shotgun blindly behind him. The buckshot—or whatever was loaded in the stubby weapon—scattered and ricocheted off the walls in a cascade of brilliant blue sparks.

Shock made her lose her footing on the steps.

Derek caught her arm. "I got you, Jane."

"What was—?"

"I don't know. I don't care. Keep going."

He kept a grip on her arm as they rushed up the stairs. From his worried expression, there was only one thing he cared about. It shone from his face. He didn't fear for his own life—only hers.

Not wanting to let him down, she ran faster.

Far below, the echoing screams of the engines abruptly faded. Only the group's anxious panting filled the passageway. The continuing quiet unnerved her.

She glanced below, wondering what was happening.

Was the sudden silence good news or bad?

9:50 P.M.

Seichan crouched low over the stolen motorcycle's handlebars as she sped across a dark grassy lawn. She kept the headlamp doused, mirroring those that followed behind her.

Moments ago, as the pack of enemy bikes had headed toward the south porch of the church, she snatched the helmet from the rider she had shot and tugged it over her features. She then hopped atop the abandoned bike. With the engine hot, she throttled it to a scream and shot the cycle to the north exit. As she reached the open doors, she skidded the bike and slid into the shadows beyond the threshold. She twisted in time to see the first of three motorcycles barrel into the church.

From her position, half-hidden in the dark doorway, she waved and hollered gruffly. She hoped the helmet muffled her voice enough to be indistinct and that the enemy spoke English. At least, the dead man on the floor had been Caucasian.

"This way!" she yelled. "They went this way!"

She then shot off into the night, luring the others with her.

As she rumbled across the dark yard behind the church, she checked her mirror to make sure the other bikes pursued her. She let out a breath of relief.

Three bikes, all running dark, spread out across the grass.

Behind them, beyond the tile roof of the church, the ruddy glow of the fire lit the skies. So far, the flames had kept all attention from the commotion and gunfire inside the church.

All the better . . .

She didn't need civilians in her way. Focusing on the task at hand, she searched ahead as she crested a low grassy hill. Past the summit, the lawn dropped toward a glade of trees that spread in a black line two hundred yards away. Unfortunately the landscape immediately in front of her was littered with upright stones and small crypts.

It was the cemetery Jane had described.

Without slowing, she aimed for the old graveyard. It would be tricky to traverse in the dark, but she had no other choice. As she swept into the cemetery, she did her best to avoid any obstacles, but the grave markers and tombs grew more congested as she continued. Still, she forged ahead, even throttling up.

She risked quick peeks at her mirror. The others, still believing she was chasing their prey, swept down the slope behind her. She waited until they had entered the graveyard—then jammed on her brake, twisted the handlebars, and spun her bike fully around to face the enemy.

Her thumb clicked the bike's headlight. A spear of blinding light burst forth into the night. She made it worse by toggling on the high beams. The pursuing riders—now blinded and caught off guard—could not avoid the marble obstacles.

One bike struck a crypt head-on, catapulting the rider into a wall. His body crumpled to the ground, his neck bent at an angle.

Another sideswiped a gravestone. The driver lost control, laid his bike on its side, and rolled across the grass. Seichan followed his course with her SIG Sauer and fired as he came to a dazed stop. His helmet's faceplate shattered, and his body fell slack to the ground.

The third rider proved more adept. He angled away from the blinding spear of light, carving a wide path and expertly slaloming through a grove of gravestones.

Seichan shot in his direction, but his jagged course defied her aim. The rider fled away. With a curse, Seichan spun her bike around and gave chase. She feared the enemy would turn back once the glare faded from his eyes. She needed to take advantage while she had the opportunity.

The rider cleared the cemetery ahead of her. With the remaining open stretch of parkland free of obstacles, the enemy had enough confidence to twist sideways in his seat. It was Seichan's only warning. The rider raised a pistol and fired at her, emptying the clip toward her bike.

Seichan dropped low behind her windshield. Rounds pelted the ground to either side; one pinged off her front fender. She flogged her engine, weaving back and forth to present a harder target, but a lucky shot doused her headlamp. Shadows fell back over her path, momentarily making it harder to see.

Cursing, she reluctantly slowed—but not fast enough.

Ahead of her, a supernova exploded. The world vanished, washed away in a blaze of light. She knew exactly what had happened. The enemy had pulled the same trick on her, spinning his bike around and flashing his high beams at her.

Fearing he would use this moment to reload, Seichan sped faster into the brilliance. She freed her pistol and fired toward the source. Her shot struck true, and darkness again collapsed around her. Unfortunately, the enemy's motorcycle sat riderless and upright, leaning against a tree, only yards from her.

With a collision imminent, Seichan dropped her bike and skid-ded tires-first toward the crash. She tumbled away at the last moment as the two bikes struck each other. Without waiting for a breath, she used the momentum of her last roll to leap to her feet and dive into the cover of the neighboring forest.

Seichan put her back against the bole of a heavily bowered ash tree. The chase had ended at the small glade she had spotted from the hill above the cemetery.

But where was the enemy?

Her ears strained for any telltale sign: a rustle of leaves, the crack of a branch. Somewhere deeper in the woods, water tinkled and burbled. She remembered Jane mentioning that these parklands surrounded a set of natural springs that fed the River Cam.

From that same direction, a louder splash sounded, then another.

The enemy must be attempting to flee.

Seichan headed toward the splashing. She could not let the survivor call for reinforcements or circle back and set up another ambush. Still, she proceeded cautiously, suspicious that the noise might be a decoy, one intended to lure her into a trap. She moved with great stealth, breathing evenly through her nose, taking care with each step.

As her eyes adjusted to the deeper shadows under the bower, she spot-ted a gravel path that must lead to the springs. She moved parallel to it. Ahead of her, a soft sparkling shone through the trees. After a few more yards, a wide expanse of water appeared before her, its black surface re-flecting the stars and moon. It was a spring-fed pond, about half the size of a football field. A few park benches lined its wooded shores.

Movement on the far side drew her attention.

A shadowy figure ran across the water's surface, moving without rais-ing even a ripple.

How—?

Seichan looked closer and noted a row of square stepping-stones, al-most flush with the pond's surface. They ran in a line across the water. The unusual path must offer visitors a way to cross the pond.

Nearby, a helmet floated in the water. Her target must have tossed it aside while crossing, likely aggravated by its limited range of view.

Seichan raised her pistol, but by now the figure had reached the far side. Before vanishing into the dark woods, her target turned. The moon's reflection in the pond illuminated the enemy's features.

Surprise made Seichan pause.

It was a young woman, her shoulder-length hair as white as snow. Even from this distance, Seichan noted a map of tattoos darkening half her face. Then the figure spun away and vanished into the shadows.

Seichan weighed the risk of crossing the stepping-stones, of pursuing the stranger, but she would be too exposed out there, an easy target for a sniper in those woods. She considered circling around, but she knew her target would be long gone before she reached the far side.

Still, she hesitated.

Then a new noise intruded.

The peal of bells rose from the church tower behind her, echoing far and wide. The ringing sounded raucous and wild, no melody, just alarm and discord.

She stared in that direction, knowing the likely source of that cacophony.

Kowalski . . .

10:04 P.M.

"Hurry it up back there!" the hulking American demanded.

Kowalski crouched at the top of the tower staircase and fired his strange shotgun, blasting a load of sparking crystals down the steps.

As he reloaded, he cast Derek a grim look and lifted a pair of fingers.

He was down to his last two shells.

Knowing they couldn't hold out much longer, Derek dug in his toes and rolled the bronze bell across the floor. Anxiety clutched his throat, making it harder to breathe—or maybe it was the fact that he was pushing an unwieldy bell that weighed over four hundred pounds.

After winding around and around the tower stairs, their group had finally reached the belfry a few minutes ago. The room encompassed the entire top floor. A large timber bell frame filled most of the space overhead. It housed the church's six bells, the oldest of which dated back to the seventeenth century. The bells were of various sizes, each hung with ropes that fell through holes in the plank flooring.

While Kowalski had exchanged fire with the gunman hidden below, Derek and Jane had followed his instructions to free one of the bells.

His explanation was terse.

I have a plan.

So Derek grabbed a ladder, while Jane found a maintenance toolbox in a corner of the belfry. With sweat stinging his eyes and blood dripping from his broken nose, Derek had unbolted one of the smaller bells from its wooden arch. It fell heavily to the floor, clanging loudly.

He and Jane now fought to roll it toward the American.

Another rifle shot echoed up from the stairwell. Kowalski returned fire with a dazzle of scattering crystals.

One shell left.

Kowalski turned and ran over to join them. Together they all manhandled the bell to the threshold and toward the first step.

The plan was now obvious.

"Time to get out of here," Kowalski grumbled next to Derek.

As one, they shoved the bell down the stairs. It tumbled and bounced along the steps, ringing loudly off the walls, the peal of its descent nearly deafening.

Kowalski pointed after it. "Go!"

The big man set off, taking the lead. Jane followed. Derek paused only long enough to snatch his leather satchel from the floor, then he gave chase. He understood the urgency. The plummeting bell might succeed in chasing the hunter out of the tower, but the bastard could still lay in wait below.

Kowalski clearly had other plans.

They raced around and around, following the riotous clanging of the bell. Then at one turn, Derek caught sight of the bell and a glimpse of a darker shadow fleeing from its path. Kowalski fired his final round. A blast of scintillating crystals shot over the bouncing bell and sparked off the curve of the wall. But some struck their target in the back, raising a sharp scream of pain.

Another turn of the stairs revealed the gunman, stunned and compromised now, stumbling forward. The assailant managed to turn his face upward—just in time to see four hundred pounds of beaten bronze rebound off the stony wall and crush him flat against the steps.

Undeterred, the bell tumbled ever onward.

"Don't look," Derek warned, scooping an arm around Jane.

He led her past the broken body, skirting the smear of blood.

Kowalski collected the gunman's rifle and waved the weapon forward. "Keep going!"

Derek read the concern in the man's face. He was worried about what could be waiting for them below. They followed the bell the last of the way. At the bottom, the bell shot free of the tower and barreled out into the church's nave. It crashed into the pews, breaking through the first row until it finally came to a rest against the next.

Their group remained sheltered in the tower. Kowalski held back Derek and Jane, his gaze sweeping the church for any sign of a threat. On the far end of the nave, several terrified members of the choir huddled behind the pipe organ.

Sirens echoed from outside, while smoke wafted in from the south porch through the open doors. Derek turned in that direction. The fire must be spreading. In a village of thatched roofs and timber-framed homes, the windswept spread of fiery embers threatened all.

A piercing whistle drew all their attentions in the other direction. A figure stepped from the shadows of the north porch.

It was Kowalski's partner.

"If you're done making a bloody racket," she called out, "let's haul ass out of this damned town."

Jane pushed forward and stalked into the open. "Smartest thing I've heard all night."

6

Someone sure as hell's cleaning house.

From beyond a police cordon, Gray scowled at the fiery ruins of the medical lab. The Francis Crick Institute—a part of the British National Institute of Medical Research—was located in Mill Hill, on the outskirts of London. From the center of the sprawling complex rose a towering brick building with four large wings. Smoke poured from the guttered windows on its northwest side, where a bevy of fire engines cast flumes of water at the smoldering structure.

Painter had alerted Gray and Monk of the lab's firebombing as their jet landed at a British air base. They had been instructed to come straight to Mill Hill, to meet someone who the director believed could provide useful intel.

They had been waiting for over thirty minutes, which only exacerbated Gray's frustration. He wanted to keep moving, to pursue those involved not only in this attack—but also the assault up in Ashwell. Painter had informed him of the attempted abduction of Jane McCabe. Seichan and Kowalski had managed to secure the professor's daughter, along with a colleague. Their group was currently holed up in a nondescript hotel in central London. Gray was anxious to join them.

Monk lowered his prosthetic hand from his radio earpiece.

"What's the latest from Sigma command?" Gray asked.

"Not good. Kat confirms what everyone feared." Monk nodded to-

ward the smoking ruins. "The body, the samples . . . they were all incinerated."

Gray shook his head. Professor McCabe's body had been quarantined
at one of this institute's biohazard labs. Staff had been tasked with isolating and identifying the contagion found within the man's mummified
remains.

Monk frowned. "But why go to all this effort to burn the guy's body?
Others are already sick with whatever disease he was carrying."

And according to Kat, many of them had died.

Gray squinted at the smoke choking into the morning skies. "I don't
think the arsonists were worried about the pathogen. I wager their real
intent here was to burn bridges."

"What do you mean?"

"Besides getting a handle on the disease, the game plan had been to
analyze the dead man's stomach contents—like the strange tree bark—and
use those clues to identify the possible location where he was held all of
this time . . . and maybe where the rest of his survey team could still be."

Including the professor's son.

Monk sighed. "So we're back to square one."

"And not only here. We're still no closer to discovering who abducted
Safia al-Maaz."

According to initial reports, whoever had raided the British Museum
had left behind no clues. Similarly the bodies of the assault team in Ashwell had been searched by local authorities. No IDs were found. Fingerprints and photos were already being circulated, and a manhunt was under
way for the one assailant who escaped on foot.

Still, Gray did not hold out much hope. Whoever was behind all of
this had ample resources and considerable knowledge of their targets. The
strikes had been performed with a surgical precision, all intended to erase
any clues to the mysteries surrounding Professor McCabe.

*But why? And why kidnap Dr. al-Maaz? Was it just to interrogate her?
To discover what she knew about all of this?*

Gray sensed he was missing something important. It buzzed at the edge of his senses, struggling to come into focus. One of the reasons he had been recruited into Sigma was his ability to piece puzzles together, to discover patterns where no one else could, but even his considerable skill had its limits.

Like now.

He shook his head, knowing he needed more pieces before he had any hope of solving this particular puzzle.

The potential source for those pieces came striding across the street from the institute. Kat had forwarded a picture of the woman: Dr. Ileara Kano. As Sigma's intelligence expert, Kat had developed a network of contacts across the globe. Gray had tried to find out how Kat knew the British woman, but Kat had answered cryptically: *I'll let her explain.*

Dr. Kano was in her midthirties, the same age as Gray. She wore jeans and a half-zippered white jacket, revealing a prominent necklace of coral beads. Her dark hair was cut in a close crop, and her features were fine, almost stately. According to her bio, she had emigrated from Nigeria with her parents when she was twelve and eventually went on to earn a PhD in epidemiology, a discipline that focused on the pattern of disease outbreaks. She currently worked for a British unit called the Identification and Advisory Service.

Though the woman surely had been up most of the night, she showed no exhaustion. Her dark eyes shone brightly, though her lids narrowed slightly as she took in the two Americans.

"You must be Commander Pierce," she said, her accent distinctly British, then she turned with a slight smile to Monk. "And the infamous Dr. Kokkalis. Kat has told me much about you."

"Is that so?" Monk held out a hand. "Sounds like I'll have to explain the word *confidentiality* to my wife when I get back home."

Her smile broadened as she shook his hand. "Don't worry. It was all good." She gave half a shrug. "Well, mostly."

"It's the *mostly* part that worries me."

Gray directed the conversation to the matter at hand. "Kat said that you might have some insight about all of this."

Ileara sighed, casting a worried glance at the blasted lab. "Insight might be too strong a word. I have some answers, but unfortunately most of those only raise more questions."

"At this point, I'll take any answers."

Monk grunted his agreement.

Ileara waved for them to follow her. "My car is parked in a lot around the corner."

Gray kept to her side, matching her long-legged stride. "Where are we going?"

"Didn't Kat tell you?" She frowned over at him. "It's urgent I speak with Jane McCabe."

"Why?"

"Kat informed me that Ms. McCabe managed to secure some of her father's old papers, particularly pages that suggest this is not the first time that this disease has reached British soil."

Gray had been similarly briefed about the outbreak at the British Museum over a century ago, and while he was anxious to join the others, years of fieldwork had taught him to be guarded. While Kat trusted this woman, she was a stranger to Gray. He pressed her for clarification as they reached her car. Gray placed a palm on the door, barring her from opening it.

"Why is the history of the disease so important?"

Ileara gave him an exasperated look, as if he should already know the answer. "I don't know if you've heard. I only got word myself within the past hour. Scores of new cases are being reported throughout Cairo and neighboring Egyptian cities. Here in London, we're scrambling to avoid a similar pattern, but we may already be too late. And now we're hearing anecdotal reports of new cases, people who traveled through Heathrow or Cairo's airport. They're showing the same spiked fevers, the same disturbing hallucinations."

Monk interrupted. "Hallucinations?"

Ileara nodded to him. "It's a new clinical sign, seen in patients close to death. We believe it's secondary to advancing meningitis."

Monk stepped closer. With his background in medicine, he was clearly intrigued by this news and wanted more details.

Gray interrupted this line of inquiry. "That's all good to know, but again *how* does this old outbreak from the eighteen hundreds bear on today's events?"

Ileara began ticking off items on her fingertips. "We've got cases now in Berlin, in Dubai, in Krakow. Even three cases in New York City and one in Washington, D.C."

Gray cast a worried look at Monk.

"But the worst conditions are still in Cairo, where panic is beginning to spread, which is further exasperating efforts to control the situation." Ileara pulled Gray's hand from the car door and faced him. "Why my interest in the past outbreak? Because my nineteenth-century colleagues somehow stopped this plague from spreading. If there's any clue in Professor McCabe's papers about *how* they accomplished this, we need to discover it straightaway before matters get worse."

"She's right," Monk said.

Gray stood pat. "But why you?" he pressed. "Why are you looking into this by yourself?"

Ileara sagged a bit, but she waved toward the column of smoke in the sky. "Because the people on the Medical Research Council who are overseeing the analysis of the pathogen have their heads up their asses. They've put their full faith in modern science, in electron microscopy, in DNA analysis, in genome mapping. They've no trust in the work of scientists from a century ago, which is daft."

Monk nodded. "I've met plenty of those types myself. And not just in the scientific field. That old adage—*those who fail to learn from history are doomed to repeat it*—falls too often on deaf ears."

"Precisely. It's one of the reasons I joined the Identification and Advisory Service," Ileara explained.

"Which does what?" Gray asked.

"It's a unit connected with the British Natural History Museum. We're tasked with investigating unexplained phenomena, specifically scientific mysteries that baffle conventional study. Our unit searches museum records and files, while employing modern methodologies to look into enigmatic cases."

Monk lifted a brow. "Let me guess. You have someone named Mulder or Scully working for you."

Ileara smiled and pulled the car door open. "Trust me. The truth is out there—if you're not too afraid to look."

Gray rolled his eyes as she hopped behind the wheel.

Monk grinned. "No wonder Kat likes her."

Gray glanced to him. "Why?"

"She's as much a crackpot as any of us."

8:39 A.M.

Derek rubbed his eyes with one hand, while suppressing a yawn with his other fist. Spread before him across the kitchenette's table were all of the books, journals, and papers he had managed to shove into his leather satchel before fleeing the McCabes' cottage with Jane.

There's gotta be something important here.

It was his mantra that kept him up all night, not that he could have slept anyway. After last night's escape from Ashwell, he had arrived in London still on edge, his nerves frazzled with adrenaline. Of course, his nose, which had been crudely set and taped, throbbed and ached, defying the handful of pain relievers he had downed.

He glanced to the side. Somehow Jane had managed to fall asleep on the hotel's sofa. Seichan napped on a nearby chair, her chin resting on her chest, a pistol on her lap. Derek suspected that woman would be on her feet at the first sign of danger. The last member of the group, the giant named Kowalski, took his turn standing guard by the window. After arriving by train in the middle of the night, they had secured the hotel room under false names, but no one was taking any chances.

Derek returned to his research. He had the leather-bound collection of Livingstone's old correspondences open before him. He found himself staring at another of the pages tabbed by Professor McCabe. The marked letter was addressed to Stanley and contained a meandering account of the flora and fauna found in the swamps surrounding Lake Bangweulu, where Livingstone had been continuing his quest for the source of the Nile. The page also held another of Livingstone's naturalist drawings, this time of a species of caterpillar and butterfly.

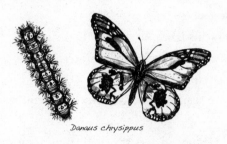

Danaus chrysippus

Though not an entomologist, Derek recognized the name of this particular insect: *Danaus chrysippus*. It was the common tiger or African monarch, indigenous to the Nile basin. With his background in archaeology, he knew about this rather large specimen because it was one of the first butterflies to be illustrated in ancient art. It was discovered painted on an Egyptian fresco in Luxor, some 3,500 years ago.

Derek rubbed his tired eyes again.

What did any of this mean?

He flipped one last time through the book, unable to discern what had interested Professor McCabe in this volume of old letters. He returned again to the first image he had shown Jane, a picture of a beetle, an Egyptian scarab.

Ateuchus sacer

He tried to focus, but exhaustion blurred his vision.

He sighed loudly, ready to give up.

This is all a wild goose—

Then he saw it. What had escaped his determined attention all night revealed itself because of his fatigue. Shocked, he scooted his chair back rather loudly.

The sudden noise disturbed Jane on the sofa. She lifted her head from the crook of her arm. "What is it?"

Derek wasn't ready to tell her.

Not until I'm sure.

He reached for his iPad, needing to make certain. He took a picture of the page and used the hotel's wireless Internet to do a Google search.

Please let me be right.

Jane must have suspected he was on to something. "Derek, what are you doing?"

"I think . . ." He looked over at her. "I think I know where your father went."

A gruff voice spoke behind him. "We got company," Kowalski said, swinging away from the window. "Time to go."

8:51 A.M.

Her heart pounding, Seichan was on her feet immediately. She cursed herself for being so lax. Her mind ran through the possible ways they might have been followed, but nothing made sense. She pictured the assassin from last night, her pale face shining in the moonlight reflecting off the spring-fed pond in Ashwell. Seichan should have known better than to underestimate this particular adversary.

Kowalski frowned at the SIG Sauer clamped in her fist. "Calm down. It's just Gray and Monk." He glanced back to the window. "They've brought someone with them."

Seichan kept her weapon up, weighing whether or not to shoot the man for needlessly panicking her. She took a deep steadying breath. She noted the frightened looks on the other two and holstered her pistol.

"You're safe," she assured them. "It's the colleagues I mentioned would be meeting us here."

Derek licked his lips and nodded. Jane had moved closer to the man, partly sheltering behind him.

Seichan waved to the table. "Gather everything up. Kowalski is right. We should be ready to go."

Derek remained where he was. "But I think—"

"Think while you're moving," she ordered. "The longer we're in one place, the more likely we'll be tracked down."

The short-term plan was to secure Derek and Jane at a safe house near the coast, a place arranged by Director Crowe. Everything was on schedule, which only made Seichan's heart pound harder. Again the assassin's tattooed face flashed before her eyes. She was glad Gray had arrived. She wanted to talk to him, to help her gain perspective.

It can't be . . .

Ever since she had stood frozen alongside the bank of that dark pond, trepidation wore at her. She had run the scene through her head countless times. At that moment, her instinct had been to continue the chase, but she knew she would have been too exposed out on the pond, needlessly putting herself at risk. Still, she had considered it—until the church bells had rung, calling her back to her duty, reminding her that she was no longer an assassin for the shadowy Guild. She had other responsibilities now, other lives to protect. But deep down she had wanted to continue the hunt, regardless of the risk to her own life.

She studied Derek and Jane, all but smelling their fear as they hurriedly collected the research material from the table. Disdain iced through her. It was a reflex, like a phonograph needle grinding deeper into a well-worn track. The reaction only made her angrier, at herself, at them.

She turned away.

What am I doing here?

A knock sounded at the room door. Kowalski had already moved to the threshold, anticipating the arrival. He pulled open the door, and the newcomers piled into the room.

Seichan caught Gray's attention as he entered first. He smiled at her, which helped calm the tempest inside her, but only barely. Past the doorway, Gray quickly swept the room, taking everything in. Monk and a tall black woman followed behind him, the two in a deep discussion, their heads bowed together.

Seichan motioned Gray aside, needing to confess what she had witnessed, especially before they continued to the safe house.

Monk's voice interrupted, shock sharpening his voice. His eyes were still on the stranger at his side. "And you think that's what killed Professor McCabe?"

The woman answered, "Either that or the process that led to his mummification. We didn't have time to complete the analysis before his body was burned."

Jane pushed past Derek, facing the two, her face pale with shock. "What are you talking about?"

Monk finally seemed to realize he had an audience. He stammered, plainly chagrined to be caught speaking so brusquely about the death of the young woman's father. "I'm . . . I'm sorry, Ms. McCabe."

Gray intervened and explained. "Someone firebombed the quarantine lab where you father's body was being held."

Jane stepped back, but Derek slipped an arm around her shoulders to steady her. "But why?" she asked.

Derek answered, "Probably the same reason they destroyed your family cottage. Someone is trying to cover everything up."

Gray nodded and tried to explain more, but Jane cut him off, her gaze turning to Monk and the stranger.

"You also said something about what killed my father."

Monk exchanged a look with the tall woman, then pointed to Jane. "She has a right to know."

"Then best I show her." She slipped a messenger bag from her shoulder and stepped toward the table. She removed a laptop from inside and set it down. "Though you must understand these results are still preliminary."

As everyone circled the table, Seichan pulled Gray aside. "I need to tell you something about last night, something I held off telling Director Crowe."

His brows knit together with concern. "What is it?"

She had trouble meeting his eye, not only afraid of what he might think about her withholding this information, but also anxious that he might see the desire buried deep in her heart. She pictured the woman blithely escaping across the pond, pausing only long enough to look back, as if challenging Seichan to follow. In that fleeting glimpse, there had been no fear in the other's face, not even anger. Instead, freedom had shone forth, along with a wild abandon that had called out to Seichan, stirring what she was fighting so hard to keep buried.

All too well she remembered what it had felt like to be that woman, of surviving at the edge, beyond right and wrong, of living only for one's self.

"What's the matter?" Gray pressed.

Seichan kept her face turned, resisting when Gray gently brushed her cheek with his knuckles. They had been apart for over a month, and she missed his touch, his smell, his breath on her neck. She knew he loved her, and his love had been the anchor to which she had moored herself during the tumult of these past few years. Still, was that fair to Gray? In an attempt to answer that, she had taken that assignment in Marrakesh on purpose, to give herself some breathing space.

Instead, she had found something else as a piece of her past was dangled before her.

"The woman who escaped last night," she said. "The one with the tattoos."

"What about her?"

"I recognized her." Seichan faced Gray with the undeniable truth. "Or at least I should say I knew *of* her. By her reputation."

"What are you saying?"

She refused to look away. "She's an assassin for the Guild."

7

That's impossible . . .

Gray fought through the shock of Seichan's revelation, ready to dismiss her words, but he noted the stony certainty in those green eyes.

"But that makes no sense," he said. "We destroyed the Guild."

Seichan turned toward the hotel window, her voice going bitter. *"I'm still here. I was part of that same murderous group."*

Gray reached to her shoulder. "That was the past."

"Sometimes you can't escape your past." She turned, folding herself into his embrace. Her body trembled. "We may have chopped off the head of the snake, but who's to say another hasn't grown in its place."

"We were thorough."

"Then maybe something *new* grew in its place, filling that power vacuum." She looked up at him, her expression guarded, as if she were hiding something from him. "Either way, the Guild certainly employed others like me, others who had been brutalized and trained to work for them, and who likely vanished into the shadows afterward."

"Where they could have found new masters to serve," Gray acknowledged.

"Like I did." She broke from his side.

"Seichan . . ."

"Once you're in the shadows, you can't ever come out. Not fully." She stared up at him. "You very well know I'm still on multiple terrorist lists. Even the Mossad maintains a shoot-to-kill order on me."

"But Sigma will protect you. You know that."

She snorted under her breath. "As long as I'm useful."

"That's not true."

She kept her gaze fixed on him. "Do you truly believe that?"

Gray considered her question. He knew Sigma's inner circle, which included the director, would never betray her, but he could not deny that her past had been kept secret from everyone else, including those in DARPA who oversaw Sigma. What would happen if she were ever dragged out of the shadows into the light?

Before he could answer, Dr. Kano straightened from where she had been hunched over her laptop. "This is what we're battling," Ileara announced. "And why it's so important that we stop it."

Gray touched Seichan's elbow, silently promising that they'd continue this discussion. Though still unsettled, she waved to the table and crossed with him to join the others.

"What are we looking at?" Derek asked, leaning on the back of a chair to get a closer peek at the window she had opened on the screen.

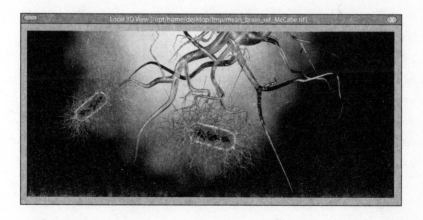

Ileara explained, "It's a three-dimensional volumetric rendering of an electron microscopic image of a nerve cell. Those fluorescent roots are the ends of a neuron collected from Professor McCabe's brain. The neighboring rods, covered in hairlike projections, are the unclassified pathogen discovered throughout the deceased's inflamed neural tissues."

"So the contagion is not viral," Monk said, sounding surprised. "It's bacterial."

Ileara shook her head. "I'm afraid you're wrong on both counts."

Monk frowned. "How's that possible?"

"That single-celled microbe is not a bacterium. It has no nucleus and no other organelles inside. It's also biochemically very different from ordinary bacteria, even from most forms of life."

"What is it?" Jane asked, looking slightly sickened about this discussion of her father's fate.

"It's an unclassified member of the Archaea domain."

"Ah . . ." Monk nodded, plainly understanding. From the confused looks on everyone else's faces, he was the only one.

Ileara thankfully elaborated, "Life has three primary branches or *domains*. There are bacteria, which we're all familiar with. Then there are eukaryotes, which encompass most everything else. Algae, fungi, plants, and even us. But it wasn't until 1977 that Archaea were identified as unique unto themselves, having an entirely different evolutionary pathway from the primordial slime that gave rise to all life. They are one of the most ancient forms of life and quite strange."

"How so?" Gray asked.

"They reproduce asexually, by binary fission, but they are really efficient at incorporating other life into their biochemistry and genetic makeup, including viruses. Some evolutionary biologists believe the two developed alongside each other, a codependent relationship going back two billion years. In fact, the specimen on the screen is chock full of viral particles, most of which we've yet to identify."

Gray pictured that hairy cell churning with a slew of viruses.

What the hell are we facing?

Ileara continued, "This strange genetic makeup has allowed Archaea microbes to survive in the most extreme environments. Like the blistering heat found in geysers. Or across frozen tundras. They also thrive in highly acidic or alkaline environments."

Gray sensed the woman was getting somewhere and pointed to the screen. "What about this species?"

She put her fists on her hips, frowning at the screen, as if facing a tough opponent. "To be such hardy survivors, Archaea employ a variety of energy sources. Sugars, ammonia, metal ions, even hydrogen sulfide. Some can fix carbon, others use the sun's energy."

"Like plants do?" Derek asked. "Using photosynthesis?"

"Actually, no. They employ a different chemical pathway, unique to their species. But like I said, they're innovative. Especially this bloody bugger."

"What does it survive on?" Gray asked.

Her gaze swept the room. "Are any of you familiar with *Geobacter* or *Shewanella*?"

Monk stirred, his eyes widening as he leaped ahead of everyone else. "You're not suggesting—?"

"I am."

Kowalski, who maintained a post by the window, interjected. "Just spill the beans already."

Gray appreciated this sentiment and looked to Monk for answers.

He obliged. "The bacteria she mentioned are both electricity eaters."

Ileara nodded. "And it's not just those two. There are *ten* other bacterial species, all different, found across the globe, and probably countless more still undiscovered. But this is the first Archaea species to do the same."

Seichan scowled. "You're saying these bugs actually *eat* electricity."

"It's not all that different from what our own cells do," Monk explained. "We basically strip electrons off of sugar molecules and store them as ATP, which powers our life functions. In the case of these electrical bacteria, they simply cut out the middleman and harvest electrons directly from the environment."

"But from where?" Derek asked.

Ileara shrugged. "Off the surface of minerals, from the electrochemical voltage streaming across seabeds. Scientists are discovering new species by simply shoving electrodes in the mud and seeing what comes up to feed."

Gray studied the laptop's screen. "And this specimen does the same?"

"Admittedly I don't know how it harvests its electricity," Ileara said. "But if we knew where it came from, maybe I could answer that."

Gray noted Jane and Derek sharing a look.

What's that about?

"But what I do know," Ileara said, drawing back his attention, "is that this bug didn't choose Professor McCabe's brain by accident. I believe the microbe, once it infects an individual and gets into the bloodstream, settles in the one part of our anatomy that's rife with energy."

Gray understood, picturing neurons firing in a cascade of energy.

Ileara continued, "Those hairlike projections latch on to nerve cells, acting like energy vampires. In turn, the body reacts like it would against any foreign invader, resulting in inflammation."

"Triggering meningitis," Monk said. "And the hallucinations you reported."

Ileara nodded grimly. "Yes, but instead of *bacterial* meningitis—which is hard enough to treat—we're dealing with an *Archaeal* meningitis. This is a disease we have never seen before. And that may not even be the worst of it."

"What do you mean?" Gray asked.

"As this microbe finds a place to grow, they multiply rapidly. It's why we believe the clinical signs advance so quickly. But with each multiplication, the dividing cells cast out the loads of the viruses harboring inside, a slew of different species. We still barely have a grasp on what that spread might be doing."

"So for any hope of a cure," Monk said, "we'll need to fight a battle on multiple fronts. Not only do we need to find an antibiotic that can kill that hairy bugger, but also an arsenal of antiviral medications."

"Exactly. As of now, we still have not assessed the mortality rate, nor do we understand how it spreads, though we're pretty sure it can pass directly through the air. Models also project that it will likely infect non-human species."

"That makes sense," Monk agreed. "Anything with an electrical nervous system could be at risk. Dogs, cats, mice. Hell, maybe even insects. This is going to go bad and fast."

"But how bad?" Gray asked.

Ileara tried to answer. "The CDC has developed a Pandemic Severity Index, used to rank the levels of risk from various pathogens, ranging from Category 1 to 5."

"Same as with hurricanes."

"That's correct. And in this case, it's estimated we could be facing a Category 5 superstorm." She turned and focused her attention onto Jane. "This is why it's vital that we discover what your father might have learned about the outbreak in the past—when that artifact of Dr. Livingstone was opened at the British Museum."

Jane glanced to Derek, as if urging him to answer.

Gray pressed the man. "Do you know something?"

"Not about any potential cure," he said hesitantly. "But I think I know where Professor McCabe might have gone when he disappeared."

Gray could not keep the shock from his voice. "What? How?"

Derek turned to the scatter of papers sharing the tabletop. "I'll show you."

9:55 A.M.

I hope I'm right . . . for Jane's sake.

As Derek pulled out the book that Professor McCabe had stolen from the Glasgow library, he saw the hope shining in her eyes. He knew her thoughts were on her brother, Rory, and on the possibility that he was still alive. Derek didn't know if the theories he had discussed with her a moment ago were valid or only a path to more disappointment. Still, he knew he couldn't keep silent any longer, not if what Dr. Kano had revealed about this pathogen was true.

He placed the book on the table and rested his palm atop it. "You have to understand that Professor McCabe was determined to ferret out any evidence that could verify the story in the Book of Exodus. It's likely how he stumbled across Livingstone's account of an artifact given to the explorer by a local native."

Derek opened McCabe's field journal to the page depicting a sketch of the *aryballos*, the oil vessel bearing the face of a lion on one side and the profile of a woman on the other. He also showed them where the Egyptian name for the Nile had been inscribed in hieroglyphics on the jar.

Ileara leaned closer. "So this is the artifact that was unsealed and led to the death of those in attendance at the museum?"

"It is," Derek said. "Or so the story goes. Though keep in mind the same tale also states that the contents preserved in the *aryballos* were collected from the Nile, back when it had turned bloody."

"But whether that's true or not," Jane added, "such a story would have intrigued my father."

"Enough so that it led him to an exchange of letters between Livingstone and the man who rescued him, Henry Morton Stanley." Derek opened the compilation of old correspondences. "Professor McCabe seemed particularly interested in a handful of those letters, specifically those that contained some of Livingstone's biological drawings."

He opened to the page containing the sketch of the scarab beetle. "At first I thought the professor had tabbed this letter because it was another connection to ancient Egypt. But then I noted something off about the drawing, so I took a picture of it that I could manipulate."

He pulled out his iPad and opened it to the photo he had taken of the old sketch. "I had just begun to work on it when you all arrived."

The others gathered at his shoulder as he used a stylus to rotate the image of the beetle until it was positioned vertically, balanced on its wingtip.

"What about it?" Monk asked, scrunching up his nose.

"The veining of the wings suddenly struck me as wrong, not that I'm an expert on insect morphology. But watch when I do this."

Derek used the pad's art program to erase most of the wings away, until only the strange veining was left.

Gray stood straighter. "My god . . ."

Derek glanced to the American, surprised that the man seemed to already glom on to what he was trying to show.

Jane encouraged Derek to continue with a measure of pride in her voice, which stoked a fire inside him. "Go on," she urged him. "Show them the rest."

He rubbed away the remainder of the scarab's body, then drew the two halves of the veining together, connecting one to the other.

"It looks like a river," Ileara said, squinting at the image.

"Not just any river," Derek said. "Note what looks like a delta at the top and a set of lakes—one small, one large—at the ends of two tributaries."

"It's a map of the Nile," Gray said, his eyes glancing to Derek with a measure of admiration.

To further support this assertion, Derek brought up a satellite scan of the region, where he had highlighted the river's watershed. He positioned one next to the other.

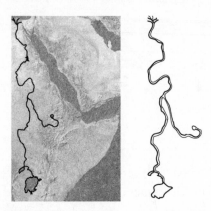

"As you can see, they're almost a perfect match," he said.

Still, Gray raised a valid concern. "But could Livingstone have produced such an accurate map of the Nile back then on his own?"

It was Jane who answered. "Certainly. Livingstone had already successfully mapped large swaths of Africa, including much of the Zambezi River. He even earned a gold medal from the Royal Geographical Society for his work."

"So it's indeed possible," Derek said. "In fact, much of the Nile's route had been charted before his death."

"But why hide it?" Monk asked. "Why sketch the river into the wings of a beetle?"

Ileara offered an answer. "Such subterfuge had been done in the past, by British spies around the same time. Take for example, Robert Baden-Powell. He was an officer in military intelligence who posed as an entomologist and used hand-drawn illustrations of bugs, leaves, and other natural elements, wherein he hid details of military installations and army forces. He did all of this under the very noses of the enemy."

Gray frowned. "Why does his name sound familiar?"

Ileara smiled. "Maybe because the man went on to found the Boy Scouts."

Monk snorted. "Talk about being prepared." He pointed to the iPad. "Still, it doesn't tell us why Livingstone hid a map of the Nile in a beetle's wing."

Derek sighed. "I believe he was trying to secretly share something of great importance with his friend Stanley, showing him where to find it."

"How?" Seichan asked.

Derek returned to the first image of the scarab. "Look how Livingstone split the river's course into *two* halves, with the body of the beetle positioned between them. The beetle itself would have been highly significant to Stanley."

"Because it was an Egyptian scarab," Gray said.

"That's right. Both men had an interest in ancient Egypt. I believe Livingstone was using the scarab's body like a big X, marking on the course of the Nile's flow where something of importance lay waiting to be found, something with a tie to the ancient Egyptians."

"If my father came to the same conclusion," Jane said, "he could have been tempted to lead a search party to find it."

Derek drew an X on the drawing, at the place where Livingstone had divided the river. The mark rested near where the Nile split into its two main tributaries: the Blue Nile and the White Nile.

Derek pointed to the X. "This site is not far from where the new hydroelectric dam is being built in the Sudan. I can easily see Professor McCabe using the engineering survey as a cover story to go search this region."

"And from the state of his body," Gray said, "he clearly must have found something."

"Or something found him," his partner Monk added.

Ileara had stepped over to stare down at the professor's journal, at the sketch of the double-headed *aryballos*. "Either way, he returned infected with the same contagion preserved in Livingstone's artifact." She turned to face the others. "We don't know if any of the other members of the survey party are still alive, but if these clues could lead us to the source of the disease, it could shed more light on its nature . . . and a possible cure."

"Then we go look," Gray decided firmly.

Everyone murmured an agreement, except for one holdout.

"This is all fine," Seichan said, "but there's still one mystery that we're no closer to solving."

Gray's expression sobered as he voiced aloud that mystery. "What became of Safia al-Maaz?"

Derek felt a stab of guilt at having forgotten about his friend's abduction in all the excitement.

Jane crossed her arms in concern. "What can we do?"

"For now, nothing," Gray admitted. "The investigation at the museum hasn't turned up any new leads. Until that changes, we go where we can."

Derek stared toward the window, fearful of abandoning Safia like this, but Gray was right. Resigned to this decision, he did the only thing he could and cast out a silent prayer.

Please be all right.

8

Safia placed her palm against the window, feeling the bitter cold through the triple-paned glass. While there were no bars, her accommodations were no doubt a prison cell. Beyond the window, a frozen landscape spread to the horizon, the skies socked in with low clouds. Near at hand, a stretch of glacier-scarred black granite was painted in swaths of white snow, while in the distance, cliffs dropped toward a sea caked in broken ice.

Where am I?

The question had plagued her since waking aboard a helicopter. She had been strapped to a stretcher and had only a hazy recollection of events, fleeting images as she slipped into and out of consciousness. Someone had attacked her in her office at the museum, drugging and kidnapping her. While out, they had stripped her and changed her into a set of gray coveralls. She crossed her arms, hugging herself, feeling violated. She turned back to the cement-block room, which was barely large enough to hold a bed, a toilet, and a washbasin.

Thankfully, her captors had left her with her wristwatch, a gift from her husband on their third anniversary. She found her hand clutching it, holding on to this piece of herself. From the time, she knew that less than twenty-four hours had passed since her abduction.

Over the past four hours, she had slowly regained her faculties, though her head still throbbed and her mouth was cotton-dry. From the camera bolted to the ceiling, they surely knew she was no longer sedated. Yet, no one had come for her; no one had even spoken to her.

What do they want with me?

The cell door was bolted steel with a small vent at the bottom where she imagined a food tray would be shoved to her—though that had not happened. There was also a tiny hatch at eye level, presently sealed closed.

She returned her attention to the frost-etched window. The view afforded her the only clues to where she might be. She studied the frozen tundra, the ice-strewn sea.

Somewhere in the Arctic, she imagined.

She had no idea of her time zone, but she had followed the sun's path over the past four hours. It had barely moved above the horizon, like it had been sitting there all day, which she suspected it had. If she was right, that would mean she was somewhere north of the Arctic Circle, in the land of the midnight sun.

She clenched a fist at her throat and studied one other feature of the landscape. It looked like a steel forest sprawling across the tundra for hundreds of acres. Each tree was a ten-story antenna, its branches X-shaped crossbeams near the top. Cabling ran across the granite linking everything into a massive networked web.

She squinted at the complex, guessing it must be some type of antenna array.

But for what purpose?

In the center of the complex, a massive man-made crater had been excavated into the rock, its mouth a good quarter-mile across. The dig appeared to be far older than the antenna installation. The hole had a hoary-edged appearance of an obsolete mining pit.

Safia knew the Arctic region was an important geological resource for oil, rare minerals, and precious metals. And with more of the northern hinterlands becoming accessible due to warmer winters and thawing permafrost, mining activities had been increasing throughout the region. It was becoming a veritable gold rush in the Arctic, straining international tensions.

Yet, despite the evidence here of prior mining, she knew this site had become something much different.

But what? And why was I brought here?

She heard a soft whirring behind her and turned.

Overhead, the camera swung its glass eye toward her.

Safia stared belligerently back, bottling up her fear.

Looks like I'm about to get those answers.

10:22 A.M.

"It will be difficult to get her to cooperate," Simon Hartnell decided.

He stood with his hands folded behind his back, fingering the cuffs of his Armani suit, rubbing the worsted silk fabric. It was a contemplative habit whenever he faced a challenge. He had lorded over many boardrooms in this same pose. But now he studied the video feed displayed on the wall monitor, noting the stubborn set to the prisoner's face, and sizing up his adversary.

A voice, frosted with a Russian accent, spoke behind him. "Perhaps we employ the same leverage used against Professor McCabe."

Simon turned and faced his head of base security. Anton Mikhailov had a whip-slim, muscular build, accentuated by a snug set of black track pants and matching jacket. His white-blond hair was trimmed and gelled flat, his hairline coming to a sharp V between his brows. After months up in the Arctic, his skin was pale, bordering on translucent, not that days under an equatorial sun would have improved his complexion. Anton, like his older sister, Valya, suffered from albinism. Yet both siblings defied the stereotypical assumption that all albinos had red eyes; instead, their irises were a pristine blue.

The only blemish to Anton's features was a black tattoo on the left side of his face. It depicted a half sun, with kinked rays extending across his cheek and shooting above his eye. His sister, Valya, carried the other half on her right cheek.

Simon had tried to discover the meaning behind the pair of symbols, but he never got a satisfactory answer from either of them, only some veiled reference to their former occupation. Simon had recruited the two mercenaries after they'd been orphaned, at no fault of their own, following the breakup of their prior employer's organization.

The pair had proven to be ruthless, cunning, and, most important of all, loyal. He expected nothing less, especially considering what he was paying them. Then again, such expenses were negligible, considering his net worth fluctuated between four and five billion dollars, depending on the daily stock valuations of Clyffe Energy. He had founded the company after dropping out of Wharton, anxious to pursue his true passion—the end goal of which was now just beyond his grasp.

I'm so close . . .

His fiftieth birthday was next month, and he was determined to make a milestone of it, even if it meant shaking the foundations of the world. He intended to prove his naysayers wrong, those who dismissed his ambitions as those of an eccentric billionaire, someone indulging in a personal vanity project.

A familiar anger stoked inside him at this thought.

Those were the same idiots who had ridiculed Richard Branson for his exploration into private spaceflight or who cast a derisive eye toward Yuri Milner, the Russian billionaire who sought to answer the fundamental question: *Is there other life in the universe?*

In the past, such visionaries had changed the course of humankind. At the beginning of the twentieth century, when the American government was gridlocked and unable to deal with rising global threats, it was wealthy entrepreneurs—great barons of industry like Howard Hughes, Henry Ford, and John Rockefeller—who wrested control from complacent politicians and faced those challenges head-on, ushering in the technological age.

Yet the world had turned round once more, with governments again stultifying. Politicians had become deadlocked, mired in one-upmanship, incapable of attending to a plethora of new dangers. It was high time for a new set of forward-thinkers to step in, to advance new technologies.

The Norwegians coined a phrase for such projects, calling them *stormannsgalskap,* or "the madness of great men." While the term was meant to be disparaging, Simon took it as a badge of honor. As history showed, *stormannsgalskap* often proved to be the true engine for change. And now more than ever, the world needed such pioneering innovation. It needed great men who were willing to defy governments and do what was necessary, to make the hard, bold choices.

I intend to be one of those men.

But there remained an obstacle.

He stared at the video feed on the monitor, at the determined glint in the British woman's eye, and came to a decision.

"While your sister failed to secure Jane McCabe in the U.K.," Simon said, "she did send us this gift. We cannot let it go to waste."

"I understand."

Simon faced Anton. "Now make *her* understand. Let Dr. al-Maaz know what is at stake—and the cost if she refuses."

10:38 A.M.

Safia heard the scrape of the door's bolt being pulled and braced herself for the worst. Still, she was unprepared as a slim figure was shoved into the room. The young man stumbled across the threshold, dressed like her in nondescript gray coveralls.

The shock of recognition drew her a step forward. "Rory?"

It was Harold McCabe's son. He was paler than the last time she had seen him, his cheekbones more pronounced, his eyes sunken. His auburn hair, normally neatly kept, had grown shaggy to his collar, curling in a way that made him appear boyish.

She also read the fear in his green eyes.

"Dr. al-Maaz, I'm so sorry." He glanced to the man who had pushed him into her cell.

The stranger remained in the doorway, blocking any means of escape. He also rested a hand on a holstered pistol at his waist, but it was his steely-eyed stare that frightened her more. The dark tattoo shadowing his face only compounded her fear.

This was a man who had killed before.

Still, Safia ignored him and stepped to Rory's side, grasping his shoulder. "Are you okay? What is going on?"

He trembled under her grip. "I don't know where to start. There's so much to tell you."

"That can wait," the man barked from the doorway. He stepped aside and waved. "Out. Both of you. Now."

Rory immediately obeyed, ducking his head like a beaten dog. Safia hurried to follow. The tattooed man trailed them, his hand never leaving the butt of his sidearm. She had noted his Russian accent and pictured the frozen landscape beyond her window.

Did that mean we're somewhere in Russia, maybe a gulag in Siberia?

She kept close to Rory, seeking that answer. "Do you know where we are?"

"Canada," he answered, surprising her. "Up north in the Arctic archipelago. A place called Ellesmere Island."

Safia frowned, struggling to reorient herself to this revelation.

Why Canada?

"It's my fault you were brought here," Rory mumbled. "All my fault."

"What do you mean?"

Rory looked over his shoulder, his voice going even softer. "They were keeping me here to force my father to cooperate. If he didn't help them with their efforts in the Sudan . . ."

Rory lifted his left hand. His pinkie finger was gone.

Dear God . . .

"My father had no choice," he said, his face pained. "Neither did I. I had to cooperate with the project here, or they'd do the same to my dad. They even threatened Jane."

"It's all right," she said, trying to soothe his guilt.

"Then my father escaped." Rory rubbed his forehead with a palm. "I don't know why he took that risk after so long."

She had wondered the same and came to one possible conclusion. "Maybe he learned something he didn't want your captors to know."

Rory's eyes pinched. "That's what they believed, too. Or at least considered it a possibility. After hearing of his death, they pressed me hard. They needed someone to fill my father's shoes. They made me name names, to list people with the knowledge to continue his work."

She understood. "And you named me."

"You were at the top of my list. You knew more about my father's work than anyone else." He gave her an apologetic look. "The only other one who understood my father better was Jane, but I insisted she was too inexperienced. I . . . I tried to protect her."

Like any good brother would.

Unfortunately, it had put Safia in harm's way.

"After kidnapping you," he continued, "their plan was to destroy any evidence of what my father was working on—both past and present—and to transfer the subject of his study here to keep it safe."

"And that came from the Sudan?" She pictured Harold weaving drunkenly out of the deep desert. "Was that where they were holding him?"

"I think so." Rory hid a scowl. "Along with another research team."

"What were they working—"

"That's enough chatter," the guard warned, his tone brooking no argument.

By now, they had reached the end of a windowless white corridor. The passage ended at a set of double doors.

The tattooed man swiped a card to unlock the way and motioned for Rory to take the lead. Cowed by his captor, Rory pulled the door open. It was accompanied by the soft hiss of a pressure seal breaking.

Rory led the way across the threshold into a small anteroom that held benches and lockers. Beyond a wall of glass, the next room contained a sprawling state-of-the-art lab. To enter required passing through a series of airlocks where yellow biosafety suits hung like limp balloons. Inside the lab, stainless steel equipment, along with refrigeration units and freezers, lined the walls. Most of the instruments were beyond Safia's comprehension.

Still, she knew why she had been brought here.

In the center of the lab stood a tall, glass-fronted sealed case. It held what appeared to be a tarnished black throne. The design motif was distinctly Egyptian. The crest rail across the back supported two sculpted finials: One was the profile of a lion, the other that of a woman, maybe an Egyptian queen.

But it was the figure seated *atop* the throne that drew Safia's full attention. It held the desiccated remains of a woman. Her mummified body appeared to be welded to the chair; the skin along the edges looked charred. Still, as the woman rested there, with her chin bowed to her sunken chest, her withered features looked oddly serene.

"Who is she?" Safia asked.

Rory's voice went bitter. "Someone we need answers from."

She frowned. "What's this all about? What's going on?"

The explanation came from a stranger who had appeared out of nowhere behind them. He stepped next to the tattooed man. The newcomer was older, with salt-and-pepper hair, and dressed in a flawless suit. He looked vaguely familiar, but she was too shaken to put a name to that face.

The man lifted a hand toward the sealed case. "We need your help in solving this mystery, Dr. al-Maaz."

"And if I refuse?"

He smiled, showing perfect teeth. "I promise no harm will come to *you*."

His gaze flicked toward Rory, who took a step back.

Anger burned through her at this threat, but she kept her face stoic. "Then tell me what you're doing here."

"Fear not." His smile widened. "We're merely trying to save the world."

SECOND

EGG OF COLUMBUS

9

"I come bearing good news and bad," Monk said.

Gray looked up from his inventory of the team's gear. Packs, along with weapons and ammunitions, were spread across a long table under an open tent. Beyond the shelter, an expanse of tarmac stretched toward a waiting C-130 U.S. military transport plane.

His team was scheduled to hitch a ride aboard the turboprop aircraft for the two-hour hop from Cairo to Khartoum. The capital city of Sudan lay a thousand miles to the south, nestled at the confluence of the Blue and White Nile, where those two main tributaries merged to form the mighty Nile River.

From there, the group would head out and search the surrounding region for a trail of bread crumbs that might lead them to where Harold McCabe had been held. He pictured the professor stumbling forth across the desert, near death, half-mummified, and carrying a plague inside his feverish skull.

What had happened to the old guy?

To help answer that, Jane and Derek were holed up in a hotel neighboring the airfield, poring through field journals and searching historical references. Gray had left them to their work, guarded over by Seichan and Kowalski.

Gray shaded his eyes against the glare of the Egyptian sun. Heat mirages shimmered over the tarmac as midday temperatures crested the century mark. He watched Monk duck under the tent, followed by Dr. Ileara Kano.

"So good news or bad?" Gray pondered. "I'm not sure which I want first."

Monk swiped a damp brow with an equally wet palm and gave a tired shake of his head, clearly not sure himself of where to start.

Ileara let out a gasp of relief once inside the shade. "No wonder my parents emigrated from Nigeria. Remind me never to complain about London's rain and fog again."

The pair had spent most of last night and this morning at NAMRU-3, the U.S. Naval Medical Research Unit located in Cairo. The base had been established back in 1942 to combat a typhus outbreak during World War II. Since then, the unit had grown into one of the largest U.S. biomedical research laboratories outside of the States, the goal of which was to study and combat emerging diseases.

So NAMRU-3 had become ground zero for monitoring and investigating this new pandemic in its own backyard. The unit's military doctors and scientists were working with the Egyptian Ministry of Health, the World Health Organization, and the U.S. Centers for Disease Control and Prevention to coordinate a worldwide effort to stop its spread and find a cure.

Monk and Ileara had been attending scientific briefings and talking to the frontline researchers investigating the new pathogen, a strange organism that subsisted on electricity. From their puffy red eyes, the pair looked like they'd gotten little sleep.

"Let's start with the good news," Gray decided.

He'd had his fill of the bad. And it might get worse, even on the personal front. His brother had left him a voicemail, asking Gray to call him first thing in the morning, which with the six-hour time difference between D.C. and Cairo would not be for another hour or so. He knew the sudden call must concern his father's health, and that worry sat like a stone between his shoulders.

But one disaster at a time . . .

"The good news," Monk started, "is that some patients are showing signs of recovery. Which means the disease is not one hundred percent fatal."

"Yet, at the moment, we don't know *why* some rebound and others succumb," Ileara cautioned.

"Still, that is good news," Gray admitted.

"I'd call it *somewhat* good." Monk shared a worried look with Ileara. "While there are survivors, current estimates still put the mortality rate between forty-five and fifty percent. We're lucky the rate isn't higher, but it's rare for an infectious disease to kill every person it afflicts. Even the Ebola virus isn't one hundred percent fatal. In fact, it shares the same mortality rate as this microbe, around fifty percent."

Gray grimaced.

"But it's still early for such firm conclusions," Ileara said. "It's only been five days since the first reported case. Much is still up in the air."

"Okay, then if that's the somewhat good news, what's the bad?"

Monk turned to Ileara, who answered, "We've determined the disease can spread via the air. One sniff of the microbe and it latches on to the nerves inside the nose and travels straight to the brain, triggering encephalitis. But even more frightening, it can take as little as *two* hours from exposure until the pathogen is settled in the brain, where treatment becomes problematic."

Monk rubbed his palms. "And like a cold bug, this bastard spreads easily. It's why we're anticipating this pandemic will quickly grow into a firestorm."

Gray was not surprised. He remembered the trip from the airport to their hotel yesterday. Cairo was normally a bustling city, but the streets had been nearly deserted. The handful of pedestrians in sight had worn paper masks or scarves over their mouths and noses. They had hurried along with their shoulders hunched, sidestepping one another. According to news reports, people were already hoarding essentials. Fights had broken out. Many had been killed—either out of fear of the sick or from altercations during looting.

It seemed *panic* was proving to be as deadly and contagious as this disease.

Even now, Gray heard a scatter of gunfire echo in the distance.

"But all of this raises one other mystery," Ileara said.

"What's that?"

"It's strange that the *first* people to become sick were those who attended the autopsy of Professor McCabe."

Gray recalled the shocking footage of that event. "But why do you find that surprising? Clearly the morgue team would have been directly exposed when the professor's skull was opened."

"True," Ileara said. "In fact, I suspect the electromagnetic stimulation from the prior MRI may have exasperated the situation by exciting the microbes in the brain. Which probably also contributed to the glowing effect caught on video. We know these electricity-eating organisms not only consume electrons as a food source, but in the right circumstances, they can shed them if overfed, too. For that reason, it might be better to consider these specimens to be electricity *breathing* rather than *eating*."

"She's right," Monk said. "I did some reading. Researchers right now are looking into practical uses for such microbes. A lab in Denmark cultured vats of these electrical bacteria, showing how they could form daisy chains and carry electrons over some distance, like living wires."

Ileara nodded. "And Archaean biology is extraordinary. They're true shapeshifters. Some are capable of fusing together to form supercells. Others link up into hairlike filaments."

Gray pictured the frilly cells that Ileara had shown them on her laptop and imagined them tying together, one after the other.

"I think," Ileara continued, "that this microbe might be capable of doing the same. It could explain why there are persistent reports of vivid hallucinations. Maybe these living filaments are rewiring the brain and directly stimulating those hallucinations. Maybe even on purpose."

"What do you mean?" Gray asked.

"Perhaps these hallucinations are intended to inflict *fear*, which would further fire up the victim's brain, creating a richer energy source for the microbes to feed upon."

"Like stuffing a goose to make foie gras," Monk added.

Gray's stomach churned at the thought.

"Still," Ileara conceded, "this is all preliminary."

"And perhaps off track for the moment." Gray returned the conversation to the original train of thought. "Dr. Kano, you never explained *why* it's a mystery that the morgue team was the first to be infected."

Ileara cringed. "Sorry. You're right. It's strange because they shouldn't have been the *first*. Remember the group of nomads who found Professor McCabe in the desert? They transported him in their cart for hours, caring for him until he died. Yet, they still remain perfectly healthy. They never got sick."

"Which makes no sense," Monk said, "especially considering how contagious we now know this pathogen to be."

"Could they be immune?"

"We can only hope so," Ileara said. "The family has been quarantined for testing. But so far, the doctors have no explanation."

Gray read something shining in the woman's eyes. "But you have an idea."

She nodded.

Gray's mind raced to catch up with her.

What possibly could be the reason for—

Then it struck him.

His back straightened. "You're thinking it's connected to the strange state of Professor McCabe's body."

From Ileara's shocked look, he had hit the nail on the head.

Monk chuckled. "It's okay, Ileara. After a while, you get used to Gray making these damned intuitive leaps. Sure, it pisses you off at first, but then you learn to roll with it. But never play poker with him. Trust me. That's a real bad idea."

Gray appreciated his partner's support, but he stayed focused. The one detail of this story that made no sense was the mummified state of the professor's body. The supposition was that the man had been tortured by his captives into undergoing this painful process and had escaped before it was finished.

But maybe we got this all wrong?

Gray stared at Ileara. "You're thinking the mummification could have been *self*-inflicted. That it was done on purpose by the professor."

"Possibly. Especially after talking to his daughter over the past two days. While Professor McCabe was certainly stubborn in his theories, he sounded like a kind man. So it got me thinking *why* he would come out of the desert carrying a disease that could trigger a pandemic. I think he would've sacrificed himself before allowing that to happen."

"Unless he believed he could do so safely."

Ileara nodded. "Maybe this process of preservation poisoned the body enough to kill the organism throughout his peripheral tissues, driving it into the only place it could survive."

"His brain."

"Where it became bottled up."

Gray imagined this threat like a snake coiled inside the professor's skull.

Ileara squinted toward the burning tarmac. "Perhaps the professor set off across the desert, hoping he could live long enough to tell his story, to warn us of some threat, something his captors were planning."

Gray considered this, his heart pounding harder. He knew this entire region was a hotbed of terrorist activity. He also recalled Seichan's story of the assassin who attacked her group at the church in Ashwell. The tattooed woman had a connection to the Guild, a group notorious for twisting scientific discoveries to their own ends. If someone were planning an act of bioterrorism, this Archaea organism would be the perfect ready-made weapon.

He considered how it had taken only *one* patient zero—Professor McCabe—to inflict this much death and panic.

What if the enemy unleashed a whole infected army?

Monk drew him back to the moment. "Okay, Gray, we've given you the good news and the bad. Now how about the truly terrifying?"

Gray braced himself. "There's worse?"

Monk glanced to Ileara, then back to Gray. "Oh, yeah. We've only been talking about the *first* plague. There's more to come."

Ileara turned away. "But this is something Jane McCabe needs to hear."

1:48 P.M.

This is all going to get much worse . . .

Jane huddled at the end of the hotel room sofa, hugging her knees as she watched the newscast on the television. Her lunch sat forgotten on the end table next to her. She cradled a cup of coffee between her palms, needing its heat to ward against the cold certainty of what was to come.

For the past hour, she had been flipping between the BBC and local stations. She was fluent enough in Egyptian Arabic to follow the various talking heads on the Cairo broadcasts. There were persistent reports of growing chaos, of lawlessness in the streets. But she didn't need the news to tell her that. Sirens echoed continually from outside. A glance out the suite's fourth-story window showed an achingly blue sky marred by multiple columns of black smoke.

The city was coming apart at the seams.

And all because of my father.

Guilt weighed on her. She had to make this right somehow. Her father had always sought to leave his mark on the world, to forge a legacy, one that could be carried on by his children. It was what drove him so adamantly to pursue his belief that events recounted in the Book of Exodus were more than allegory. He wanted his name known to the world at large.

Well, Dad, you've accomplished that in spades.

Her father was mentioned on many of the broadcasted updates, often showing his smiling face, his features tanned and sun-wrinkled. Snatches of old video were sometimes played, the footage shot around the time the survey team had vanished. Seeing those images, hearing his voice again, pained her, but she could not look away. One photo showed the entire vanished party, including a stern, determined-looking Rory.

The picture reminded her that more was at stake than just her father's legacy.

For the thousandth time, she prayed her brother was still alive.

A harsh laugh drew her attention to the window. Kowalski leaned there, watching the street below. His neck was crooked as he cradled a cell phone to his ear.

"Maria," he said, "I might be on the same continent, but I don't have time to check on Baako. I'm sure the big kid is fine. He's probably making all sorts of new jungle friends."

Jane eavesdropped on the conversation, glad for the distraction. From prior talks over the past days, she'd gotten to know the big guy better. He had a girlfriend who was in Germany, working with her sister at some lab. He had been visiting them when he had been called to London.

His partner, Seichan, was out in the hotel hallway, keeping guard.

A weight fell heavily onto the sofa. She turned to find Derek rubbing his eyes. He propped his shoeless feet onto the coffee table. She noted a hole in the toe of his left sock. For some reason, she found it inordinately charming, a testament to Derek's absentmindedness concerning the everyday details of life, like buying new socks.

He caught her staring and curled his toes to better hide the hole, then grinned at her. "As you recall, we didn't have much time for packing."

A small laugh escaped her, catching her by surprise.

Derek's smile broadened. "At least I'm *wearing* socks."

She drew her bare feet closer, tucking them under her.

He gave a scolding shake of his head. "Simply shameless, Ms. Mc-Cabe."

A sharp voice drew both their attentions to the television. A robed man was yelling in Arabic, jabbing a finger at the newscaster. He was a local imam, clearly fired up.

"What's he saying?" Kowalski asked.

Jane translated. "He's insisting that everyone should ignore the health ministry's warning to avoid public places. Instead, he wants them to gather for services at the city's mosques. He's even telling them to bring the sick to be prayed over rather than seeking medical help. It's insane. Thousands more would be infected."

Derek sat straighter. "He believes this is a punishment from God. Only by beseeching forgiveness can people be saved."

Jane listened closer. "He's now claiming he's prayed with one of the sick and heard the man speaking in tongues and experiencing visions of locusts darkening the skies, of people dying beside blood-red rivers, and of lightning ripping apart the heavens."

Derek shook his head. "I didn't think it would be long before someone tried to tie this epidemic to the biblical plagues."

Jane heard her father's name mentioned. "Quiet."

As she listened, her blood grew colder.

Derek slid across the couch and put an arm around her. "Just turn it off. The guy's clearly a nutcase."

"What did he say?" Kowalski pressed.

Derek took the television remote and muted the sound.

Jane fell deeper into the sofa's cushions. "He said that my father was the vessel for God's wrath. He went out into the desert, looking for proof of Exodus, and returned carrying the very plagues of that time to punish this world for its infamy."

Derek faced her. "Jane, that blathering idiot is a fearmonger, a bloody opportunist. He's only glomming on to this angle because of your father's well-publicized positions. You know his theories were mentioned in the news when his team vanished. Back then, these same religious nuts claimed they went missing because Harold dared to seek the truth of Exodus through science instead of faith. Now they're spinning it the other way to suit their own ends."

The hotel door burst open, making them all jump.

Seichan stalked in, cupping a hand over her radio earpiece. "Gray's on his way up."

Kowalski frowned. "Are we leaving already?"

"Not yet. Monk and Dr. Kano are with him. They want to go over something first."

Derek stood up. "What?"

Seichan's eyes settled on Jane. "Something about a new set of plagues."

Jane's gaze shifted to the silent television screen. The imam was up on his feet now, red-faced and shouting at the newscaster. Her father's photo hovered to the side. She wanted to believe Derek's dismissal of the imam's words, but one worry fought against it.

She stared at the blustering figure on the screen.

What if he's right?

10

Gray noted the tension as soon as he entered the hotel room. Jane McCabe stood with her arms hugging her chest. Derek hovered near her with concern. Kowalski and Seichan were whispering together, both staring toward a muted television.

As Monk and Ileara crowded into the room behind him, Jane unfolded her arms and took a step forward. "What's this about a new plague?"

Gray turned to his two companions. "Catch them up first and let me know when you're done."

He strode toward the neighboring bedroom, needing a moment of privacy. He checked his watch and slipped out his satellite phone. It should be a little after eight in the morning in D.C. He owed his brother a return call.

Once in the bedroom, he partially closed the door, then dialed his brother's cell. It rang several times before a bleary voice answered.

"Wh . . . who is this?"

"Kenny, it's Gray."

"Oh, hey." His brother coughed to clear his throat. "What time is it?"

Gray felt a familiar twinge of irritation. "Never mind the time. You asked me to call you. What's wrong? Is Dad okay?"

"Yeah . . . no. Hell, I don't know."

His grip tightened on the phone. "Kenny, just tell me what's going on."

"I was at the nursing home yesterday. Dad's under an isolation order.

You have to wear gloves, a mask, and gown before entering. Real pain in the ass."

Gray rolled his eyes. *Cry me a river already.*

"Dad's got some kind of new infection. Resistant staph or something."

Concerned, Gray sat down on the bed. "Staph? Are you talking about MRSA?"

"Huh?"

"Methicillin-resistant *Staphylococcus aureus.*"

"Yeah, that's it. Doctors are afraid it might go septic. So they put him on a bunch of new antibiotics. May mean Dad has to stay even longer."

Great . . . just great.

"How's he holding up?"

"He's in and out when I visit. Something to do with his blood pressure. They're also watching a spot that might blow up into a bedsore."

Gray fought a pang of guilt for not being there. He pictured the frail figure of his father in the bed, hooked up to machines and IV lines. He could only imagine the anxiety the old man must be experiencing, lost in that fog, unable to understand what was happening to him.

His father's last words still haunted him.

Promise me.

Gray suspected his dad wasn't talking about a pledge to return and see him before he passed. Instead, the old man's earlier words had stayed with Gray.

I'm ready to go.

The statement had been accompanied by a silent plea shining in his father's eyes, asking for help, for Gray to make the hard decision when the time came.

But can I do it?

"That's all I got," Kenny said, winding up the call. "I'll let you know if anything changes."

"Thanks . . . thanks for being there, Kenny."

There was a long pause. When his brother finally responded, his voice was softer, drained of its usual bitterness. "You got it. I'll hold down the fort until you get back."

Kenny hung up, and Gray lowered the phone. He sat for a few breaths, hearing the murmur of the others in the next room. With a sigh, he hauled to his feet. He turned to find a figure shadowing the room's doorway, hovering at the threshold as if reluctant to intrude.

"Everything all right?" Seichan asked.

He pocketed his phone. "Not really, but there's not much I can do about it."

At least, not yet.

Promise me.

She came forward, slipped her arms around his waist, and pressed her cheek against his chest in sympathy. He pulled her closer and tightened his embrace, knowing she was struggling with her own ghosts out of the past. Still, they took advantage of this brief respite to share this moment together.

Finally, a shout rose from the next room.

"Gray!" Monk called. "You're going to want to hear this next part."

Seichan leaned back, her eyes glinting with amusement. "Or we can simply leave. Right now. When I canvassed the hotel, I spotted a fire escape."

Despite her attempt at levity, he read something deeper in her eyes, a seriousness that underlay her words. He found himself considering it. What would it be like to turn his back on everything and be truly free, to take that fire escape and never look back?

But before he could contemplate this further, Seichan broke their embrace. She turned away quickly, as if perhaps fearing he would see the depth of her own desire.

"Duty calls," she said and headed toward the door.

Gray followed, drawn by his responsibilities, both here and back home.

Promise me.

2:22 P.M.

Derek kept close to Jane, sensing the cloud of despair building around her.

For the past several minutes, they had listened as Monk and Ileara updated them on the status of the growing pandemic, but in all that gloom there had been one bright spot, concerning Jane's father.

"So you think it's possible he was attempting to protect us by undergoing the mummification process?" Jane asked, hope and relief in her voice.

"I do." Ileara touched Jane's shoulder. "Unfortunately with his body gone, we can't confirm it."

"Still, it could be one of the reasons why the medical lab in London was firebombed," Monk said. "To cover this detail up."

Jane swallowed. "But you mentioned something about *other* plagues on the horizon."

"Yes, the other shoe that's yet to drop." Monk waved to Gray and Seichan as they joined them from the neighboring room. "You're just in time."

Gray nodded to Ileara. "Tell us what you meant."

The woman scrunched up her face, clearly struggling with how to explain. "Are any of you familiar with the term *gene drive*?" After getting blank stares, she continued. "How about Zika then?"

Gray frowned. "You mean the virus that swept through South America and now threatens the U.S.?"

"Exactly."

Even Derek knew about this disease. It caused tragic birth defects, including microcephaly in newborns. He remembered seeing photos of those poor children.

"Some countries, including the U.S., are considering combating the spread of this disease by employing gene drive technology, specifically targeting the mosquitoes that carry the virus."

"How?" Jane asked. "What is gene drive technology?"

"It's when scientists add or modify genes in such a manner that the change is inheritable across an entire population. In Florida, scientists are proposing releasing genetically altered swarms of *Aedes aegypti*—the mosquitoes that carry Zika—into the wild. When these altered pests breed with ordinary mosquitoes, the next generation of females are born sterile, while fertile males continue to carry this damaging gene forward into the succeeding generations. From estimates, *Aedes aegypti* could be extinct in Florida within a year, eradicating the threat of Zika at the same time."

"But I don't understand," Derek said. "Are you proposing this gene drive technology as a way to fight this new pandemic?"

"No." Ileara looked around the room. "On the contrary. I think what we may be facing here is a *natural* version of this gene drive technology, but in this case, *we* are the target of extinction rather than the mosquito."

Ileara twisted around and pulled out her laptop. "Let me show you." As she powered up her computer, she continued. "I told you before how Archaea microbes evolved alongside viruses, and that this particular specimen is crammed full of a slew of different viral particles, which it releases when it infects a patient."

"Think of it as a Trojan horse," Monk said. "Once it enters the castle, it unleashes what is hidden inside."

"Luckily most of the viruses are proving to be harmless, except for one, which happens to be in the same flavivirus family as Zika. It's proven to be a particularly nasty fellow."

"What does it do?" Gray asked.

"It attacks cells undergoing *meiosis*," she explained. "Most of our body heals and grows through *mitosis*, where a cell divides to produce two identical daughter cells. But meiosis occurs in ovaries and testicles to produce gametes. Sperm cells and eggs. Which carry only half of the mother cell's genetic code."

Derek didn't like the sound of this. "What damage does this virus do?"

"It's very specific, targeting a single chromosome." Ileara stepped back from her computer. "Humans—and most mammals for that matter—have gene pairs that determine our sex. XX for females, and XY for males."

She pointed to her laptop. "Here is a volumetric rendering of those two genes in a healthy individual. As you can see, the X chromosome is significantly larger and more robust than its diminutive Y companion."

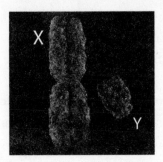

Ileara tapped the smaller image on the screen. "The virus in question targets only the Y chromosome. We don't know why. It might be a weaker target. It might be pure chance. Either way, on this next rendering, you can see how much damage it does."

On the screen, a large section of the chromosome was now missing.

"It looks like an oven glove," Kowalski noted.

"I suppose it does," Ileara said.

The large man grunted, apparently satisfied with his contribution to the discussion.

Ileara continued, "The damaged section has been analyzed by geneticists. They believe that males who survive this disease will have sperm cells that carry this defective Y chromosome, which would have an impact on any children he sires. Baby girls should be fine, as they would be carrying the normal XX complement, but any boys, if not stillborn, would be born with the damaged Y chromosomes and likely die within months."

Derek began to understand the threat. "That means, even if we survive this Archaean pandemic, we could still be doomed as a species because of this virus."

Jane took a step back from the desk, her face gone notably paler.

"What is it?" Derek asked.

"It's the tenth plague," she mumbled.

He frowned. "What do you—?"

She crossed to a table strewn with books, picked up her father's Bible, and flipped to a tabbed page. She read a passage from the Book of Exodus. "*And all the firstborn in the land of Egypt shall die, from the firstborn of Pharaoh that sitteth upon his throne, even unto the firstborn of the maidservant that is behind the mill; and all the firstborn of beasts.*"

She lowered the book. "Even *the firstborn of beasts*," she repeated. "Dr. Kano, you mentioned that this microbe was likely to infect not just humans but also most *animals*."

"Correct. Anything with an electrical nervous system."

"So this virus could be the scientific explanation for the tenth plague," Jane said. "One that strikes both people and beasts. Back in ancient Egypt, the change in the Nile would have taken months to wash out of the watershed, while this secondary genetic damage could have lasted even longer. I can easily see how all these deaths of male offspring—both human and animal—could have been transformed and folded into the story of the plagues, its final curse."

Ileara nodded, looking as if she had expected Jane to come to this conclusion.

"And Professor McCabe had his own theory about the rest of the plagues," Derek added, drawing everyone's attention. "I spent many long nights challenging Harold about the truth behind the Bible's ten plagues. He proposed a theory for explaining them that's not dissimilar to what we're talking about."

"What was his theory?" Gray asked.

Jane answered before he could. "He believed it all started when some environmental change turned the Nile red. There are certainly plenty of reports of bodies of water spontaneously changing color. Due to algal blooms, bacterial overgrowth, even heavy metal contaminations."

Ileara agreed. "And one of the most dramatic of those changes occurs seasonally right here in the Middle East. Lake Urmia in Iran turns to a bright crimson every summer due to an overgrowth of *Halobacteriaceae*." She turned to Gray, lifting one brow for emphasis. "Which happens to be an Archaea microbe."

"Like the pathogen we're facing." Gray's eyes pinched. "So there's precedent for this happening in the region."

"And not just *here*," Ileara said pointedly. "There's another Archaea microbe that turns your Great Salt Lake in Utah a blushing pink at times."

"Okay," Gray conceded, "but how does this lead to the other nine plagues?"

Derek answered, "If the Nile—the lifeblood of the region—turned toxic, the subsequent plagues could be explained without needing the hand of God."

He crossed and opened the professor's journal to where Harold had jotted down the ten plagues. He ran his finger down the list, while sharing the professor's thoughts on the subject.

> 1) Water into blood
> 2) A rain of frogs
> 3) An affliction of lice
> 4) A plague of flies
> 5) Diseased livestock
> 6) A rage of boils
> 7) A thunderstorm of hail and fire
> 8) An invasion of locusts
> 9) Three days of darkness
> 10) The death of the firstborn

"The next three plagues—frogs, lice, and flies—could have been triggered after the waters turned red. Frogs would have flooded out of the poisoned waters of the Nile, where they subsequently died. Their sudden drop in population would have led the frogs' prey—mosquitoes, flies, and lice—to explode in numbers."

"And remember," Jane said, "bloodsucking insects are major vectors for disease, which would have wreaked havoc on the area's livestock. In addition, boils would have spread from all those bites."

"So plagues five and six," Gray said, looking over Derek's shoulder at the list.

Derek tapped the next three items. "Hail, locusts, and darkness have a different explanation, one unconnected to the poisoning of the Nile."

Gray looked at him. "What's the cause?"

"A volcano named Thera up in the Greek Isles. It erupted about thirty-five hundred years ago, with an explosive force never seen before, casting out billions of tons of ash, which would've swept over Egypt. In fact, archaeologists have discovered pumice—rocks formed from cooling lava—throughout Egyptian ruins."

"And Egypt has no volcanoes," Jane reminded them.

Derek continued, "The plume from that eruption would've produced dramatic atmospheric effects, especially if it coincided with the rainy season. Meteorologists have shown that seeding hot ash into thunderclouds can result in dramatic hailstorms and violent lightning."

"And I suppose those same ash clouds would have darkened the skies," Gray said. "But what about the plague of locusts?"

"Locusts prefer damp conditions to bury their eggs," Jane explained. "With all that hail melting and changes in atmospheric conditions following Thera's eruption, it could have led to a proliferation of locusts."

"Which brings us to the tenth plague," Derek said. "Harold attributed it to the fact that the firstborn sons were revered by their families. They got the most food. So if the locusts ate most of the grain and what was left had turned moldy, those sons would've become sick first, dying of fungal poisoning."

Jane turned to Ileara. "But even my father wasn't entirely convinced about that last explanation. Many others would have eaten the same contaminated grain and died, too. And it certainly didn't justify why the firstborn of *livestock* were also succumbing."

Derek stared at the laptop's screen. "Maybe now we have a better explanation, a clearer path to connecting the first plague to the last."

Seichan spoke for the first time. "But why is number seven circled on the page?" She pointed to where Harold had highlighted that plague, a storm of hail and fire.

Derek shrugged and looked to Jane, who could only shake her head. "We have no idea," he admitted.

Gray raised another question. "If we're right about this microbe being the trigger for most of the plagues, including the last one, how did the Egyptians stop it?"

Jane struggled to answer. "It was a different world back then. More isolated. The disease could have burned through the region locally, then died away again."

Ileara scowled, clearly dissatisfied with this explanation. "Unless there's another reason. Something hidden out in the desert that your father stumbled across."

Gray cast a skeptical eye at her. "Do you truly think these ancient people could have found a cure for a disease that challenges the best medical researchers today?"

Ileara shrugged. "It's happened before. Take MRSA, for example."

Gray stiffened, looking more sharply at her. "What about MRSA?"

"While that superbug has been the scourge of hospitals, a researcher at the University of Nottingham tested a recipe for an eye salve found in a ninth-century medical text called *Bald's Leechbook*. It's basically a preparation using garlic, onions, and leeks, along with wine and cow bile."

"Cow bile?" Kowalski muttered. "If that's the cure, I'd rather be sick."

Gray ignored him and waved for Ileara to continue. "And what happened?"

"Microbiologists tested the concoction against cultures of MRSA and discovered it was capable of killing up to ninety percent of the bacteria."

"So it worked," Gray said.

Ileara nodded. "And who's to say the Egyptians hadn't stumbled upon a similar cure? Even if it's a slim possibility, we must search for it."

Gray checked his watch. "Then we'd better get moving. Our transport plane is scheduled to be wheels-up in fifteen minutes. We don't want to miss it."

Everyone scattered to get ready.

As Derek gathered his pack together, Monk pulled his partner aside. "I spoke to Painter earlier, before meeting you at the airfield. He wants

Ileara and me to remain here in Cairo, to coordinate with everyone at NAMRU-3."

"Let me guess. He wants you to be Sigma's eyes and ears on ground zero of the plague."

"He's also concerned about the political unrest. Religious groups are freaking out. Some are claiming it's the apocalypse. In a region that's already a powder keg, all this fiery rhetoric isn't helping matters."

"Then it sounds like you'd better grab a helmet and a fire hose."

Monk clapped him on the shoulder. "Still, I'm better off than you."

"How's that?"

"At least I'll have air-conditioning."

Seichan joined them, interrupting. "Monk, when you spoke with Painter, did he mention anything about identifying that assassin who attacked us at the church in Ashwell?"

Derek's ears piqued sharper at this question. He was equally concerned about some killer still hiding out there.

Monk shook his head. "He's still working that angle with Kat. But trust me, Painter is motivated. That tattooed woman may be the only lead to the whereabouts of Safia al-Maaz."

Seichan glowered. "Then he'd better find her before I do."

11

Valya Mikhailov lowered the binoculars to the windowsill of her rented room. She continued to watch the C-130 Hercules bank across the blue sky. It turned like a heavy bird toward the south. Earlier, she had used the binoculars to spy upon her targets as they scurried into the rear hatch of the plane. She had to make sure Jane McCabe remained with the group.

Satisfied now, she pulled her Bluetooth receiver closer to her lips. "They are en route to Khartoum," she reported to her younger brother.

Anton's voice whispered in her ear. "Then all is going as planned. Our best chance to secure the professor's daughter without raising an alarm will be out in the desert. I'll have an extraction team waiting for you at the rendezvous site."

"Understood."

She ended the connection.

For the past two days, Valya had trailed her quarry. Few could match her skill at tracking, a talent honed from decades of training with the Guild. She bore the crisscrossing of scars on her back as proof, punishment from whenever she was spotted by her prior masters. To avoid such punishment, she had learned to become the true ghost that her pale skin and countenance portended.

Pairing that skill with the resources of her new employers, she had easily followed her targets from the train station in Ashwell to their hotel in Cairo. At every step, she had sought a way of separating the young woman from her guardians. But Valya had learned patience during her training. To move with haste only earned one another scar.

But there was a better reason for such caution now.

Moya sestra . . .

Valya had studied the woman who caught her off guard in Ashwell and who so efficiently dispatched her men. Valya had spotted her briefly across the pond behind the church, but it wasn't until she was tailing her targets that she came to truly recognize her adversary. Less from her features than from her manners and skills. Three times the woman had come within a breath of spotting Valya.

No one did that—not unless they shared her past.

So the truth slowly grew to a cold clarity inside her.

She knew whom she faced: a dark sister, a shadow of herself.

Valya had heard stories of a woman who had betrayed the Guild, someone of Eurasian descent, one of the Guild's most skilled assassins. The consequence of that traitorous act had left her and her brother destitute, near ruin, scrabbling to hide from those who sought to cleanse the world of the Guild.

But luckily I know how to hide.

So she and her brother had escaped that purge. Eventually, they had found a new employer, but it would never be the same. She owed that traitor for her suffering, for her loss. Fury stoked inside her—along with a measure of excitement.

Valya longed for a true challenge.

Now she'd found it.

She stepped over to her room's table, where her knives lay bared, freshly honed to a razor's edge. She picked up the oldest dagger. It had belonged to her grandmother, who had lived in a rural village in Siberia before being recruited to fight the Germans during World War II. She had been part of an all-women unit, the 588th Night Bombers Regiment. They had flown old biplanes—Polikarpov Po-2 Kukuruzniks—which puttered too slowly for daytime runs. Instead, the women pilots took to the air after sunset, gliding quietly across Nazi antiaircraft batteries to drop bombs on the unsuspecting enemy encampments. Their deadly efficiency earned them the nickname *Nochnye Vedmy,* or the Night Witches.

Valya smiled, knowing why her grandmother had been so attracted to that particular unit. She turned the old blade in her hands and ran a finger over the black handle. Her grandmother had carved it from a living Siberian spruce under a full moon. It was an *athamé,* a dagger used in magical ceremonies. Her grandmother had been a well-respected *babka,* a village healer. She had eventually passed this skill and its tools to her daughter, Valya and Anton's mother.

Which proved to be unfortunate.

Rural areas were notoriously superstitious and insular. A few bad seasons in such a harsh climate and people looked for someone to blame. A widow with two strange, pale children quickly became a target. They had been forced to flee their home, making their way to Moscow. Penniless, their mother had turned to prostitution. Mercifully, she died within the year, murdered by one of her patrons. Valya had come upon this crime and in a fit of rage stabbed the man with her grandmother's dagger, turning a tool of healing into one of death.

Afterward, she and Anton—only eleven and twelve at the time—fended for themselves on the streets, becoming savage and wild, until the Guild found them and turned that anger into skill.

Valya stared at the mirror above the desk. She had powdered over her tattoo to hide this distinguishing mark, but the dark sun still shone through. She and her brother had disfigured their faces in this manner, as a promise to forever be there for each other.

But nothing lasts forever, she thought bitterly.

Anton had found someone else.

She lowered her eyes from her reflection, still holding the *athamé* blade. The tip of the knife was normally used to carve powerful symbols into candles and magical totems. She had turned it to darker purposes, marking her victims' foreheads with an evil eye, one derived from these very lands, a stylized version of the Eye of Horus.

She pictured the woman who had destroyed the Guild, who cast her and her brother out onto the streets, and dug the tip of the dagger into the desktop. She slowly carved a new promise into the wood, determined to anoint the traitor with this same mark.

Once done, she stared down at her handiwork.
Unlike my brother's oath to me, I will keep this promise.

12

"Gray and company landed safely in Khartoum," Kat announced as she entered the director's office, noting the scatter of Starbucks cups across his desk.

Too many for just the morning.

Painter lifted up a hand, silently asking for a moment. He sat with his sleeves rolled up, hunched over a thick file, while the three wall-mounted screens behind him displayed various feeds. One was a muted BBC broadcast, another displayed a live map scrolling with data from the CDC, and the last puzzled her. It appeared to be a webcam feed from a bare office. The oddity drew her attention. There was a chair pushed back from a desk. She noted a bookshelf to one side, with the texts bearing titles in both English and Arabic.

Then a familiar figure dropped into the chair. Her breath caught in her throat at the unexpected surprise. It was her husband.

Monk leaned closer to the webcam, spotting her and grinning. "Hey, honey, I'm home."

Kat stepped around the corner of Painter's desk, drawing nearer to the screen and microphone. "Where are you?"

He glanced around the room. "The folks at NAMRU-3 were kind enough to lend us an office. It's in the basement, but it's not far from the facility's medical library, which comes in handy."

Monk tilted back his chair and whistled off to the side.

Kat frowned. "What are you—?"

Another face leaned into view. "Hi, Kat."

It was Dr. Ileara Kano. She was dressed in a waist-length lab coat, with her dark hair modestly secured under a scarf. She carried a pile of journals under one arm.

Kat grinned at her friend. "Ileara, it's good to see you. I trust my husband hasn't been too much trouble."

"Not at all." Then she added, "Well, he could stop hogging all the jelly babies. With the shortages out here, they've become a premium."

Monk showed no sign of remorse. "What can I say, I'm a growing boy."

Kat felt a surge of affection. "He does have an insatiable sweet tooth."

"That's why I married you, the sweetest woman I know."

Oh, brother . . .

"Feel free to punch him," Kat said.

"Maybe later," Ileara answered. "Especially if that candy jar is empty when I get back from the library."

She waved and departed.

Kat had so much she wanted to say to Monk, to share with him, about their two daughters, about how much she missed him. He had been gone only a few days, but she could not discount what a huge presence he was in her life, how much she needed him, if only to sit quietly with her at night after the girls were put to bed.

"I miss you, too," Monk said, his grin softening with sincerity.

She wanted to hug him and inadvertently took a step forward, but she wasn't alone.

Painter shifted his chair away from his desk and stood up, stretching his back with a pained grimace. She knew he had been in his office all night. With his wife, Lisa, off visiting her brother in California, he had claimed he had no reason to abandon his station during this crisis.

But Kat suspected the real reason had nothing to do with his empty house, but something closer to his heart.

Safia al-Maaz still remained a ghost, and he would not rest until she was safe.

Painter stepped next to her, stifling a yawn with a fist. "Monk was catching me up on events in Cairo. Then he had to—"

"—talk to a man about a horse," Monk finished. "Even at the epicenter of a pandemic, when nature calls, a guy has to answer."

"And it proved to be a timely call," Painter said. "While he stepped away, I received a report from an Interpol office in Moscow. I'm not sure it's relevant. But it's something I'd like you to follow up on."

"Of course," Kat said.

"Sounds like you two kids are busy," Monk said. "And I have a medical briefing in ten minutes with the Research Science Directorate here. I'll report back if there's any significant news."

Monk gave her a wink and ended the feed, but not before grabbing a fistful of jelly babies.

Kat shook her head and faced Painter. "What did you hear from Moscow?"

She suspected it involved Seichan's tattooed assassin, a woman who might share her past ties to the Guild, but Kat refused to get her hopes up. For the past forty-eight hours, she had been hitting one dead end after the other in her attempt to identify her. Seichan had only known the woman by her reputation. Like Seichan, the assassin had been a notorious hunter-killer for the Guild. Kat remembered Seichan's description of the woman's skill.

Once she has your scent, you're already dead.

Seichan surmised the only reason her group survived back in Ashwell was because the assassin had been caught off guard by Sigma's involvement.

But it's not a mistake she'll make again, Seichan had promised.

Painter pulled a sheet of paper from the file he had been reading and slid it toward her. "Kat, you may've been right about the significance of this symbol."

Kat recognized what was illustrated on the page. After the attack, Seichan had transmitted a sketch of the woman's tattoo. It looked like half of a sun. The dark mark was the only concrete clue to identifying the pale woman. Kat had run that information through various criminal and police databases, but nothing had turned up.

After twenty-four hours, with no new leads, Kat had played with the symbol, wondering if it could be half of a whole. So she had mirrored those two halves together to form a full sun, which was printed on the page before her.

The sun's rays were kinked at the ends, forming a wheel-like shape. It hadn't taken long for Kat to identify the symbol. It was a *Kolovrat*, a pagan solar symbol from Slavic countries. It had once been tied to witchcraft but was later co-opted by nationalistic parties, including Neo-Nazis.

Using this information to narrow her search parameters, Kat had concentrated her investigation on Slavic countries. Through her network of contacts in the intelligence communities, she had reached out to Interpol offices in those thirteen nations and asked them to canvass local police records in smaller towns, records that might not have reached the Interpol's main database in Lyon. To be thorough, she had also requested the same of Moscow's office, as many Slavic countries had once been part of the former Soviet Bloc.

That had been twenty-four hours ago.

"You got a hit on this?" Kat asked. "Has someone found a record of a woman with half this symbol on her face?"

"No," Painter admitted, squashing her flicker of hope.

"Then what—?"

"Moscow found a single record of a young *man,* a boy really, sixteen years old, with half of this symbol tattooed on his face. He had been convicted of petty theft and immoral acts about a decade ago in a small town of Dubrovitsy, not far from Moscow. He ended up escaping before going to prison."

Kat sighed, sensing another dead end. "Director, it's not much to go on. I anticipated we might get several false hits, especially with the Kolovrat symbol becoming popular with Neo-Nazi groups. An Internet search will show hundreds of white supremacists, mostly men, bearing this tattoo."

"But what about someone with only *half* the symbol?" Painter pressed.

She had to admit that was odd.

"And what about this?" Painter opened the file and slid out a printout of the kid's mug shot. Angry lines of Cyrillic lined the bottom of the page, likely listing the boy's crimes. He tapped the photo. "Look familiar?"

Kat stared down at the young, unlined face. His skin was notably pale, his hair snowy white. He was actually quite handsome, with thin lips and a sharp nose. Unfortunately, the prominent tattoo across his left side marred those features, turning them beastly.

Painter placed a finger on a boxed-off word in Cyrillic.

$$\boxed{\textbf{альбинос}}$$

"It states here, he's an albino."

Kat's eyes widened, remembering Seichan's description of the woman's ghostly countenance. "Okay, maybe this *is* worth pursuing further. What's his name?"

"Anton Mikhailov."

She held out a hand for the file. "I'll see what I can find out about him."

As she took the bundle, she read the worry shining in Painter's eyes.

She didn't need him to spell it out for her.

Time was running short for Safia al-Maaz.

12:10 P.M. EDT
Ellesmere Island

It's all my fault . . .

With guilt eating at her, Safia had a hard time facing Rory McCabe. A step away from her, Harold's son had stripped to a pair of boxers and now struggled to climb into the yellow biosafety suit. She kept her gaze diverted, not out of modesty of his half-naked form, but from her own shame. Rory's right eye was purplish and almost swollen shut.

Yesterday, she had tried to drag her feet. With a rigorous schedule set for her, she had attempted a passive protest, feigning exhaustion, moving slowly, only pretending to read through Professor McCabe's volumes of old notes. Instead, she had used the time to study her surroundings, contemplating how she might escape. The conclusion she came to was grim.

There's no way out of here.

The base on Ellesmere Island was surrounded by thousands of acres of open tundra, bordered to the northwest by a sea of shattered ice. At night, unable to sleep, she could hear those jagged floes moaning and cracking as they ground together in a continuous chorus. She imagined they went silent only in the dark of winter, when the Arctic Ocean froze solid again and the sun vanished for months on end.

Even if she attempted to escape across that frozen landscape, there were other dangers. From her window, she had spotted gray-white humps slowly shifting across the black granite. Polar bears haunted the island's shores, hunting for seals, for anything to eat. This morning, before being summoned to work, she had noted a handful of workers out at the antenna array, checking cables and jotting notes on clipboards. All of them had protective rifles slung over their shoulders.

She still had no idea as to the purpose of that hundred-acre steel forest, or the huge excavated pit at its middle. From the vantage of a window in the station's library, she had spotted something poking up from the center of the hole. She could only glimpse the very top, which appeared to be a massive silver sphere, easily twenty yards across.

She had tried to ask Rory about the installation, but he had ducked his head lower and glanced to their pale guard, Anton. Apparently this information was beyond her pay grade. Still, she was not surprised by Rory's reticence. She had already assessed that the workload here was highly compartmentalized. Everything was on a need-to-know basis. The handful of other technicians she passed in the hallways had all stayed together in their own cliques, each wearing the same-colored uniform, which she guessed corresponded to their duties.

She stared at the folded set of gray coveralls on the bench before her. They matched Rory's. From the way the other personnel shied away from them, refusing even to make eye contact, she could guess the implication of this particular color.

Prisoner.

Or perhaps the better term was *forced labor,* with the emphasis on *forced.*

Rory winced as he pulled the hood of his suit over his head, brushing the plastic against his swollen eye. Anton had sucker-punched Rory last night, catching the young man off guard. Rory had ended up on his backside, too stunned to even gasp. Anton's gaze never left her. His words were curt, stilted by his accent.

Tomorrow you work better.

Apparently Safia's work ethic had been found wanting.

This morning she had done everything asked of her, which mostly involved reading through the guidelines for working in a biosafety lab. She was asked to memorize them and was tested by Anton afterward. This time, the Russian nodded, satisfied.

Safia ran through the main instructions as she suited up.

> —*All personnel must wear a positive pressure air suit.*
> —*Biological samples must be double-sealed and passed through a disinfectant dunk tank or fumigation chamber.*
> —*Decontaminate all work surfaces.*
> —*Before exiting, the outer suits must be cleansed in a chemical shower.*

There were scores of other details and procedures, and she knew the punishment for any violation would fall upon Rory's shoulders.

If that mistake doesn't kill me first . . .

She could not dismiss the tremor of fear as she pulled on her hood and sealed the suit, feeling a moment of claustrophobic panic. Working quickly, she snapped and twisted the air hose in place. The hiss of cold air swelled through her suit, which helped stave off full panic. She took several gulps of the metallic-tasting air.

Rory stalked in front of her, like some tethered astronaut. "Are you okay?" he asked, using the voice-activated radio system.

She nodded, maybe a bit too vigorously.

"Are you sure?"

"Yes," she managed to squeak out, then answered again with more as-surance. "I'm fine, Rory. Let's get this over with."

She didn't want to make it look like she was balking from her respon-sibilities. Anton stood in the outer antechamber, his hands behind his back. He wore an earpiece to monitor their radio chatter.

"Let's go," she urged Rory.

He led the way through the next set of doors. They passed through the chemical shower station to reach the main facility. From the condition of various stations along the walls, others had been here this morning. They must have been ordered to leave so she and Rory could have this private audience with their subject.

The tall sealed crate awaited them, as did its contents.

Despite her terror, Safia found herself fascinated by the figure of the mummified woman seated atop the tarnished silver throne. The serenity in her bowed head helped calm Safia. She took it all in, noting the finer details now that she was this close. The woman's scalp was smooth and bald, but Safia suspected it wasn't decomposition that had stripped this Egyptian princess of her dark locks.

She had been shaved.

There was not a hair on her body; even her eyebrows were missing.

Curiosity drew her closer.

"This must have been a ritualized death," she whispered to herself, but the radio picked up her words and transmitted them.

"My father thought the same," Rory said. "He believed she was sealed up in her tomb while still alive. Worst of all, there was a rim of old ash around its base, suggesting she had been baked inside after being imprisoned."

"I don't think she was imprisoned. I think she went in there voluntarily. Look how she sits so peacefully on that throne. She's not shackled or tied down. The pain must have been excruciating." Safia tilted her hooded head, studying the charred edges where the woman's skin came in contact with the silver chair. "Yet, she never left that burning seat."

Safia reached for the latches to unseal the transport crate.

"Let me," Rory said.

Safia nodded, stepping back to allow him to work, experiencing a flicker of impatience. Yesterday, Safia had been assigned to review Professor McCabe's work—or at least, the little that was left of it. Though the exact details were kept from her, she had learned that Harold had tried to destroy his research prior to his escape. He had been only partly successful. Snatches of his work survived, bits and pieces of a more comprehensive study. It was Safia's role—with Rory's help—to put that patchwork together again.

Yet, it was plain they were keeping secrets from her.

She still had no clue *where* this woman had come from or *why* she was so important.

Rory finally freed the last latch and swung the door wide.

Anxious for answers, Safia moved forward until she stood toe-to-toe with the princess. Her gaze swept the figure, noting the details she had missed from a distance. The carved finials on the back crest rail were masterworks of Egyptian art, from the curled lip of the lion—frozen in midgrowl—to the bashful sweep of the queen's cheek on the other side.

But her eyes settled on the true wonder before her. This dramatic work had faded with age, but there was no mistaking its beauty.

No wonder her body had been shaved.

Across the surface of the woman's skin, hieroglyphics had been tattooed. They ran down her body, row upon row, from the arch of her skull to the tops of bare feet.

My god . . .

Desperate to read what was written, Safia found it hard to breathe. She knew the woman had died to preserve this story for eternity.

She stared again at her serene countenance and whispered softly.

"Tell me everything."

2:13 P.M. EDT
Washington, D.C.

"I got another hit!" Jason called from the next room.

Kat turned from her desk. Her office window looked out onto Sigma command's communication nest. A single monitor glowed in the darkened room, illuminating the face of her chief analyst, Jason Carter. He was former navy, like herself, only he was a decade younger. Kat had recruited him into Sigma after the kid broke into DoD servers with nothing more than a BlackBerry and a jury-rigged iPad. Despite his towheaded and boyish appearance, Jason was a savant, especially when it came to analysis.

She stood up and crossed into the next room. "Show me."

Over the past two hours, they'd had three other hits on their quarry—Anton Mikhailov—but each of them had failed to pan out.

Jason hunched over this terminal, tapping away. "This one's promising."

"I'll be the judge of that." Her voice came out more scolding than she intended. She put a hand on his shoulder. "Sorry."

"Not a problem." He glanced back. "I understand the pressure you're under. I ran into the director in the hall. He's . . . well, intense."

"He's worried. We all are."

He nodded. "Maybe this'll help."

He brought up a passport photo on the screen and placed it beside the composite they had created of an *older* Anton Mikhailov. The latter had been constructed by running his young mug shot through age-progression software. She had then forwarded the altered photo to a global facial-recognition database, hoping for a match. As a precaution, she also sent two versions: one with the prominent tattoo and another without it. She could not discount the possibility that the man had covered or removed this distinguishing mark to better hide himself.

She was glad she had chosen to send both versions, because the man in the passport photo had no tattoo.

Still, Kat compared the two faces. They appeared to be a close match. She read the name on the passport. "Anthony Vasiliev."

Jason cocked an eyebrow. "Anthony . . . Anton. Surely that can't be a coincidence. So I went ahead and ran a background check under that new name. Found this." He brought up a new photo.

It was an employee ID.

Kat leaned closer and read the company's name. "Clyffe Energy."

"According to his file, Anthony is head of security at a research base—called Aurora Station—up in the Arctic."

In the Arctic . . .

Kat began to wonder if she could be wrong. Maybe the similarities in features and name were merely coincidental. Clyffe Energy was a multinational conglomerate with hundreds of patents on sustainable energy platforms. It had its fingers in multiple pies. Its CEO—Simon Hartnell—was a wunderkind, a tech billionaire who was pushing the boundaries of solar, wind, and geothermal energy. In addition, while other such industry giants bought basketball teams or lived glamorous lifestyles, Simon Hartnell was a philanthropist, donating millions to charities, especially throughout Africa.

"If this is truly Anton Mikhailov," Kat said, "his new identity must have been bulletproof to pass that corporation's background check. Clyffe Energy oversees multiple government contracts, including working with DARPA. Maybe this isn't our guy."

Instead of answering, Jason typed and brought up what appeared to be a medical file for the man.

"How did you access—?" Kat shook her head. "Never mind. I don't want to know. Why are you showing me this?"

He pointed to one line. "He's on a regular prescription of nitisinone."

"Which does what?"

Jason brought up a Web page for the National Institutes of Health and read from it. "It treats *oculocutaneous albinism, type one-B, a genetic defect in the production of tyrosine, an amino acid needed for pigment production in skin and eyes.*" He glanced back to her. "In other words, Anthony Vasiliev is an albino."

Kat stood straighter.

"He's gotta be our guy," Jason said. "But that's not all."

"You have more proof?"

"Better than that." Jason typed again, then leaned back and stretched his arms, cracking his knuckles. "He has a sister."

On the screen glowed another Clyffe Energy employee badge. The photo showed a stern woman with the same pale complexion and white hair. Again there was no tattoo visible, but that dark sun could have been eclipsed under a thick coat of makeup.

"Her name's Velma Vasiliev," Jason said, "but I doubt her name is any more real than her brother's."

A thrill passed through Kat as she stared at the woman's face.

"Send this picture to Seichan's phone," she ordered. "See if she can make a positive ID. Then pass an alert to passport security both in the EU and northern Africa. I want to know if Velma Vasiliev made a recent visit to the U.K., and if so, where she might be now."

Jason nodded and returned to his terminal.

Even if Seichan could not confirm this was the same woman, Gray's team should be on the alert for her.

She turned, ready to share this breakthrough with Painter, but she gave one last order to Jason. "While I'm gone, pull everything you can about that Arctic station where her brother works."

"You got it."

Riding on adrenaline, Kat headed out and crossed in firm strides over to the director's office. His door was ajar, but she heard him speaking inside, so knocked on the jamb. "Sir?"

Painter sat on the edge of his desk, facing one of his wall monitors. He waved to her. "C'mon in, Kat."

Another voice also encouraged her. "Great. Now it's a real party."

She entered to find her husband's mug up on the screen again. Monk's meeting with the Research Science Directorate at NAMRU-3 must have finished, and he had been briefing the director.

Monk grinned at her, which went a long way to tempering her anxiety. "Hey, gorgeous."

"Hey, yourself."

Monk's left eye narrowed. "Babe, what's wrong?"

As usual, he easily read her tension. "I believe we've identified the woman who attacked Seichan and the others in Ashwell. And maybe even played a role in the abduction of Dr. al-Maaz."

Painter swung toward her. "Tell me."

Kat ran through the chain of analysis, interrupted by a sporadic question or two from Painter or Monk. As she finished, the doubt in Painter's eyes hardened to certainty.

"Well done," Painter said.

Kat couldn't take full credit. "Most of the heavy lifting was done by Jason Carter."

Painter nodded, rubbing at his lower lip in thought.

"Still, no matter the assist," Monk said, "it's a slam dunk."

Painter stepped back around his desk. "I know about that Arctic installation. Aurora Station. Or at least I'm familiar with it."

"How?" Kat asked.

"The place is partly financed by DARPA."

Monk snorted from the screen. "Really? Why?"

"Bad press," he answered cryptically and dropped back into his seat. He began typing at his desktop computer.

"Back in 2014," he explained, "the U.S. Air Force closed down its HAARP facility up in Alaska. Which stands for *High Frequency Active*

Auroral Research Program. Funded by DARPA, the program's purpose was to study the earth's ionosphere, that shell of plasma enclosing the planet hundreds of miles overhead, a layer that's vital to satellite and radio communication. Experiments involved sending high-frequency signals from ground-based radio antennas up into the sky. Doing so allowed HAARP scientists to study how to improve communications to our submarines, along with performing countless other tests. One project—the Lunar Echo Experiment—once bounced a beam off the moon."

"Why?" Monk asked. "Were they trying to blow it up?"

Kat smiled, but Painter took him seriously.

"No. In fact, that's the least crazy charge against the facility. Once the public learned of a remote subarctic base that was shooting invisible rays into the sky, all sorts of accusations arose. It was a space weapon, a mind-control device, a weather-control machine. Even the 2011 Japanese earthquake was blamed on HAARP."

"So lots of bad press," Kat said.

"That HAARP could never fully shake."

"But what does any of this have to do with Aurora Station?" Monk asked.

"Aurora Station is basically HAARP reborn, only on a much bigger scale. Its antenna array is tenfold larger, its technology beyond cutting edge. And being privately owned versus run by the military, the place has garnered less attention, especially due to its remoteness. Because of this, DARPA has been quietly funding part of the project, in order for HAARP's experiments to continue away from the public eye."

Kat understood Painter's interest in this project. Before becoming director, Painter's area of expertise with Sigma had been in high tech, basically anything with an on/off button. Not only had he earned a PhD in electrical engineering, but he also held several patents.

Painter transferred an image onto the wall monitor behind him. It was the familiar logo for the corporation running Aurora Station. It depicted an egg inscribed with scientific nomenclature that was about to tip over.

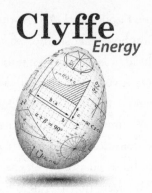

Clyffe *Energy*

"This pretty much tells you everything you need to know about the company and its CEO, Simon Hartnell," Painter said. "In fact, it's his involvement that likely further insulated the facility from public scrutiny."

"Why?" Monk asked.

"With all of his charity work, he's developed a sterling public persona. Plus everyone uses his tech. From his fast wireless chargers to his powerful batteries. With all of that goodwill, no one's accusing him of building a mind-control device."

Monk scrunched up his brow. "But what did you mean about that egg telling us everything we needed to know about the man?"

Painter glanced over his shoulder at the Clyffe Energy logo. "It's supposed to represent the Egg of Columbus."

"Which is what?" Monk asked.

"According to a story, Columbus once claimed he could balance an egg on its tip and challenged his critics to do the same. When they tried and failed, he took the egg and cracked its end atop a table, thus flattening its bottom. This, of course, allowed the egg to sit upright."

"In other words, he cheated," Monk said.

Kat scowled at him. "The story is intended to be a lesson on *creativity*, about thinking outside the box to find a solution to a seemingly impossible problem."

"Which pretty much encapsulates Simon Hartnell's philosophy," Painter said. "But the logo also has an additional layer of significance.

Hartnell considers himself to be the intellectual heir to the inventor Nikola Tesla, practically worships the guy."

Monk waved to the logo. "But what does this obsession have to do with that egg?"

"At a world exposition in 1893, Tesla set out to repeat Columbus's accomplishment, only this time scientifically. He set a copper egg to whirling within a rotating magnetic field. The gyroscopic forces along its major axis turned the egg up on its end, spinning on its tip. Thus winning Columbus's centuries-old bet."

"And without cheating," Monk added, sounding impressed.

"Columbus didn't—" Kat gave up and waved to Painter. "What exactly is Clyffe Energy doing with that expanded facility in the Arctic?"

"A slew of new projects. Like mapping the shift of the magnetic north pole. Or testing plasma clouds in the upper atmosphere. But the main emphasis is on studying climate change. The facility is using ELF and VLF signals—transmissions normally used to communicate with submarines—to monitor the thickness of the Arctic ice pack."

Kat felt a twinge of concern. "That's becoming a huge industry up north."

"And a political firestorm to boot," Painter said. "With the Arctic melting, the wealth of resources under all of that ice has become a territorial free-for-all. Canada, Russia, Denmark are all fighting to stake out claims. It won't be long before someone pushes someone else too far."

A scuffle of feet sounded behind them, followed by an urgent knock on the office door. Jason Carter pushed into the room. "You all gotta see this."

2:39 P.M.

Painter shifted to the side, allowing the young man access to his computer. He could tell the kid was worked up about something.

Jason spoke as he worked. "Kat asked me to look into that base up in the Arctic. Everything in that region is under surveillance. Military satellites, NOAA weather stations. Canada's Northern Watch program has drones in the air, on the ice, and under the water, monitoring traffic throughout the region to protect their interests. It's getting to be that a polar bear can't fart up there without triggering a seismic sensor."

"Jason . . ." Kat warned.

"I know, I know. Give me a second."

Painter shared a look with Kat, silently acknowledging how Jason's observations dovetailed into their prior discussion.

"I thought," Jason continued, "why not take advantage of all that surveillance? So I set up a search protocol around Aurora Station, specifically for the twenty-four-hour period following the abduction of Dr. al-Maaz."

Painter clenched a fist.

"And I found this on a Norwegian Polar Institute satellite."

Jason transferred a video clip to the room's third monitor. The footage showed a grainy overhead view of a helicopter sitting on a stretch of snow and black rock. The rotors spun, and small figures labored around the aircraft. Then a closed stretcher was hauled out of the cargo hold and carried toward a cluster of boxy buildings.

Jason glanced to Painter. "I couldn't get a look at whoever was being transported. But it seems odd that someone is being medevacked *to* that remote base."

Painter pictured the tranquilizer darts striking Safia, the shock on her face, her hand lifting toward him in a silent plea for help.

"What do you think?" Jason asked.

The fury smoldering for days inside Painter erupted. His vision narrowed, his throat tightened. He couldn't speak. He simply stared as the footage looped again. He watched the stretcher being whisked away, vanishing into the building.

"Sir?" Kat pressed.

"I'm going out there," he said tersely, barely able to unclench his jaw.

"Someone should," Kat agreed. "But we have others who—"

"I'm going." Painter turned his back on the screen and faced the others. He took a deep breath, but his features remained stony. "DARPA has a vested interest in Aurora Station. It's high time that place had an inspection."

Kat studied him, clearly running the merits of his plan through her head. "I suppose we could get General Metcalf at DARPA to orchestrate such a cover story."

"Still, to pull it off, it would take someone with a solid tech background."

"Like you." Kat glanced to Monk. Both of them were clearly concerned about his personal stake in all of this. Finally, Monk gave Kat a small nod, and she faced Painter again. "Then I'm going with you."

"It's better if I—"

This time Kat cut him off. "You go, I go." She waved to Jason. "Carter can hold the fort. And if need be, Monk can help him from the field."

"Not a problem, sir," Monk said.

Painter recognized he needed Kat's cooperation for any chance of rescuing Safia. He might be Sigma's director, but in many ways, Kat was the true puppet master here.

Accepting this reality, he nodded. "Then grab your parka."

13

As the sun sank away, Gray stood at the headwaters of civilization.

The spit of parkland lay between two rivers. To his left, the White Nile rolled sullenly past his position, churning with chalky clay, which gave the waterway its name. To Gray's right, the Blue Nile streamed past in a thinner black course.

But it was what lay *before* him that held him transfixed.

The two tributaries wove together, mixing their waters, merging to form the lifeblood of this region: the Nile River.

He gazed down its length as it snaked north toward Egypt. He could feel the agelessness of this place, accentuated by the haunting call to evening prayers echoing across Khartoum. Overhead, a sickle moon hung in the twilight skies, reflecting in the dark waters like a set of silvery bull's horns.

Seichan joined him and slid an arm around his waist. He recalled her suggestion in Cairo, that they simply cast everything aside and take off. He felt that pull even stronger in this timeless moment.

She sighed next to him, as if sharing this reverie, but knowing it could not be—at least not yet. "Kowalski called in," she said, drawing his attention to the present. "He's on his way back with our transportation. Should arrive in another ten minutes."

Painter and Kat had arranged a vehicle sturdy enough to take them into the deep desert. Kowalski had gone to collect it, along with food, water, and extra diesel. Where they were headed next, they'd be on their own.

Hopefully.

Seichan had shown him the photo Kat had sent, of a glowering woman with white hair and dead eyes. Back in Ashwell, Seichan had only managed to get a glimpse of the assassin's face, so she couldn't be sure it was the same woman.

Still, following that encounter, Seichan remained more wary, her gaze always moving. To spook someone like Seichan, this woman must be big trouble.

A bright laugh rang out behind him—coming from above.

He looked back. A small Ferris wheel turned a few yards away, part of a tiny amusement park, which took its name—*al-Mogran*—from its location, meaning "confluence."

He stared up at Derek and Jane as they rode round and round, their heads bowed together, smiles on their faces. While it wasn't the wisest way to occupy their time, maybe it was for the best, especially considering what lay ahead.

The team had landed two hours ago in Khartoum. The late afternoon had been unbearably hot. The plan had been to set out after sunset, when the desert temperatures plummeted. The first leg of their journey was a seventy-mile trip to the south, to the small village of Rufaa, where the family who had found Professor McCabe lived. They were currently under quarantine because of their exposure to the sick man, but a local villager—one of that family's cousins—had agreed to serve as a guide and take them into the desert.

The Ferris wheel slowed to a stop and began to unload its riders. Seichan stood to the side, studying the darkening park for any threats.

Gray met Derek and Jane as they climbed off. They both looked more relaxed, years younger in fact. Derek helped Jane out of her seat, holding her hand. His grip lingered a little longer than necessary.

"That was fun," Jane said. "You could see for miles all around."

Derek nodded. "I had hoped to spot the site of the new dam construction, where all of this trouble started. But it's too far away, about a hundred miles to the northeast."

Gray knew the project—located at the Nile's Sixth Cataract—was where Professor McCabe's survey team had started its fateful journey two years ago. The group had vanished into a harsh terrain of broken rock, blowing sand, and towering dunes, a desolate landscape that covered thousands of square miles.

And we're about to head out there ourselves.

Gray got them all moving. "Kowalski should be here soon. Let's get back to the street."

As they crossed the amusement park, Jane glanced back toward the silvery confluence of the two rivers. "I've read so much about this region, but to see it for yourself . . ."

Her eyes were wide with wonder.

Gray was reminded of how truly young she was, only twenty-one. While clearly smart, most of her education must have come from classrooms and libraries, seldom from fieldwork. Still, after everything that had transpired, she was holding up remarkably well.

He stepped alongside her.

"Jane, as we're about to follow your father's footsteps out into the desert, maybe we should know more about the theory he was trying to prove. You mentioned before that most archaeologists found his theories about the Book of Exodus to be controversial."

"Not just archaeologists, but also Jewish rabbis." Jane looked down as she walked, clearly uncomfortable discussing this, but she went on. "Many people believe the story of Moses to be allegorical, rather than historical. They base this decision on the fact that the real-life Ramesses the Great is mentioned in the Book of Exodus, but because there's *no* archaeological evidence of a plague or slave revolt during his reign, they dismiss the story of Moses as a fairy tale."

"Sounds cut and dry, so what's your father's take on this?"

"He—and several colleagues—questioned some inconsistencies found in the Book of Exodus concerning the name *Ramesses*, calling into question if Ramesses the Great was truly the pharaoh who Moses cursed with his ten plagues. It's all rather complicated."

"But why does that matter?"

"It matters because it allows archaeologists the freedom to look *elsewhere* for evidence of Exodus and not be pinned down to the reign of Ramesses the Great."

"And with this newfound freedom, did your father and his colleagues find anything?"

"They found *everything*." She stared toward the distant desert hills. "If you look to an era four centuries before Pharaoh Ramesses, you discover all the missing archaeological evidence for Exodus." She ticked items off on her fingers. "A town of Semite slaves. Signs of a massive plague. The frantic emptying of the city. There's even a crypt discovered that bears a striking resemblance to the tomb of Joseph that's described in the Bible. It all lines up."

"And this is what your father was trying to verify?"

"It's called the New Chronology. He believed if he could find proof of a series of great plagues from around that time, then he could authenticate this theory."

No wonder the man was so obsessed with the biblical plagues.

Jane sighed, clearly no longer wanting to talk about it, which was just as well.

By now, they had reached the street bordering the park.

It appeared Kowalski had beaten them here. At the curb, a large truck idled heavily, as if out of breath. It was a reconditioned dark green Mercedes Unimog, a true beast of a four-wheeler. It had a wide-framed double cab with a small open bed in the back, all sitting atop hip-high tires with aggressive treads. It was a vehicle built to eat through the toughest terrain. And if it ever bogged down, the truck came equipped with a large winch on its front bumper to help haul itself out of trouble.

Kowalski sat behind the wheel, his elbow resting on the sill of the open window, cigar smoke wafting out. "Now *this* is a truck," he grunted, slapping the outer door with his palm.

Gray understood Kowalski's affection. The pair made the perfect match. Both were slow, loud, and somewhat crude.

Seichan waved everyone aboard, but she kept watching the streets.

"We good?" Gray asked her.

"For now."

Then that'll have to do.

8:08 P.M.

In the truck's backseat, Derek worked on his iPad.

After forty-five minutes riding south along a two-lane road that hugged the curves of the Blue Nile, Derek had lost interest in the passing landscape. They had left the bright lights of Khartoum far behind and were now traveling back in time. Most of the surrounding terrain was the same as it had been for centuries: dark tilled fields cut through by silvery irrigation channels, stands of palm trees, the hulking forms of idle water buffalo, the occasional mud-brick hovel.

But the Blue Nile was only a trickling shadow of the mighty flow that coursed north through Egypt, the source of that kingdom's fertile bounty. The river here was less generous. The farmlands and plantings did not stretch as far, needing to huddle closer to the restrained river.

Derek could easily see low hills in the distance, limned in silvery moonlight, barren and empty. They looked like bent-backed old beggars, dying of thirst. Beyond those hills, a sun-blasted desert awaited them, spreading for thousands of miles.

To traverse it, they needed a plan.

This was what he focused on now—fine-tuning what had been discussed earlier. Once they reached the village of Rufaa, the team was scheduled to travel overland through the desert to where the professor was found. From there, the plan grew sketchy. But Derek had an idea.

Jane stirred beside him. The engine's grumble, the rocking of the suspension, and the strain of the past few days had lulled her into a light slumber. "What are you doing?" she asked, stifling a yawn.

The iPad's screen illuminated her face in a soft glow. He found himself transfixed by the fine curl of her eyelashes as she looked down at his work.

He cleared his throat. "I was trying to map a possible route for us. Or maybe I'm deluding myself."

She leaned against his shoulder. "Show me."

He was surprised at how much he wanted to share this with her. Plus it helped to talk it out.

"We know your father left from Nile's Sixth Cataract with his survey team, only to reappear two years later hundreds of miles to the south, not too far from the village of Rufaa. Unfortunately no one knew *where* he was during that time or what route he and the survey team took through that trackless desert. But now, from the clue hidden in Livingstone's old sketch of an Egyptian scarab, we might know where your father was drawn."

He shifted his iPad so she could see. "I took a satellite map of the region and drew a line across the two tributaries of the Nile that corresponds to where Livingstone had split the river between the two scarab's wings."

He showed the result.

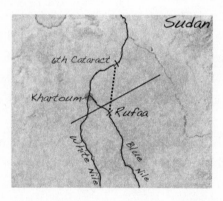

"I then connected a dashed line from the Sixth Cataract—where your father left from—to the village of Rufaa, where he ended up." He tapped the X formed on the map where those two lines crossed. "I think this is where we should start looking."

"That's brilliant," Jane said, placing a hand on his knee.

A second person concurred. "She's right," Gray said from the far side of the backseat.

Derek's cheeks heated up. He hadn't known Gray was eavesdropping. "Thanks."

Gray held out his hand. "Can I see that?"

Derek passed him the iPad, and Gray leaned forward to show Seichan and Kowalski, who were seated up front.

Seichan's praise was less enthusiastic. "Guess it's better than just driving aimlessly through the desert."

From behind the wheel, Kowalski pointed forward. "Got lights up ahead."

Gray checked the map on his satellite phone. "That should be Rufaa."

Jane removed her hand from Derek's knee, suddenly looking nervous. He could guess the cause of her anxiety. Her father had died trying to reach here.

"It'll be okay," he said softly.

He hoped that was the truth.

8:28 P.M.

The village was larger than Jane had expected. She had pictured a cluster of huts surrounded by walls made of millet stalks, but Rufaa was actually a good-sized town clustered against the curve of the Nile.

"It looks like it'd be easy to get lost in there," Derek commented.

She agreed.

Dirt roads divided the sprawling place up into a veritable maze of square, flat-roofed buildings, set off by narrow alleyways or sectioned into small walled courtyards. Everything appeared constructed of the same mud bricks, giving it a uniformity that confounded the eye. The only landmark that stood out was the local mosque. Its white minaret shone like a beacon.

Jane knew that the Rufaa people, who gave this town its name, were of Arabic descent, practicing a Sunni form of Islam. Many of the families had roots here but still maintained a nomadic lifestyle. This was certainly true for the group who found her father. They were part of the Jaaliyin tribe, who still roamed the desert as they had for thousands of years, claiming to be descendants of Abbas, an uncle to the prophet Muhammad.

As their truck slowed to a crawl through the outskirts of the village, children peered at them from the roadside, while goats fled from their grumbling path, bleating in irritation. Finally, a thin figure waved them down and stepped into the road.

"Is that the guy we were supposed to meet?" Kowalski asked.

"Seems so," Gray answered. "They were told to watch for us."

As the truck drew to a stop, their escort hurried to the open window on Kowalski's side. He appeared to be a boy of sixteen or seventeen with skin the color of dark mocha. He was dressed in a purple-checkered football jersey, beige shorts, and sandals.

"I am Ahmad. Be welcome."

Kowalski glanced back to Gray, who nodded, seeming to recognize the name.

"I take you to my family. We eat." He pantomimed putting food in his mouth. "Then go. Yes?"

Kowalski shrugged. "I could eat."

Ahmad pointed to a stretch of open dirt. "Put truck there. Not far to go." From their worried looks, he added, "It safe. No worry."

Seichan frowned at this suggestion. "I should stay with the truck."

Gray nodded and ordered Kowalski to park their vehicle. Once the engine cut with a final cough, he climbed out and fitted an earpiece in place.

"Seichan, radio us if there are any problems."

Concerned, Jane followed Derek out the other side. Her eyes were on the boy. "Do you think we can trust him?"

"Considering he's about to lead us into the wilds of the Sudanese desert, we might as well start now."

With everyone ready, Ahmad led them into the main village, but not before letting out a sharp whistle. In response, a thin, rib-chested dog raced from the shadows to his side. Its tail wagged vigorously. It looked young, with bristly black-and-gold fur, dark eyes, and stiff, wide-splayed ears.

"She good girl," Ahmad said proudly.

Jane held out a hand for the dog to sniff. "What's her name?"

His grin widened at her interest. "Anjing."

Jane frowned in confusion.

"What's that mean?" Kowalski asked.

She knew enough Sudanese to answer. "It means *dog.*"

Kowalski shrugged. "Well, I guess that works."

Derek leaned closer to Jane as they walked. "I think his *pet* is an African wild dog. Or at least a mix."

Jane eyed the beast with more respect. She had heard tales of the infamous pack hunters. She remembered offering her hand to it a moment ago.

Luckily, I still have it.

Ahead of them, Ahmad looked like he wanted to run, barely keeping his excitement in check. He talked and talked, playing proud tour guide.

"Over there." He pointed to a low green domed structure. "Tomb of Sheik Tana. Very important. And on that corner. A man once ate a whole goat by himself." He glanced at them. "It true."

Kowalski was the only one who looked impressed with this claim.

They finally reached an arched gateway into a courtyard. As they all ducked through, the smell of baking bread stirred a hunger in Jane she hadn't been aware of. The sizzle of a grill also drew her forward. A clutch of robed figures, men and women, came out to greet them, as if they were all old friends. A few barefooted children hung at the fringes or stayed shyly in the doorway.

Ahmad stepped over to a tethered donkey, gave the beast a quick hug around its thick neck, and introduced his new friend, "Kalde."

Kowalski glanced to Jane again.

She translated. "Means *donkey.*"

The big man shook his head. "I don't get it. Does the kid have no imagination or is he trying to teach us his language?"

More introductions were made. When Jane's name was mentioned, the group became more somber, clearly realizing whose daughter she was. They came forward, one by one, heads bowed, and offered their condolences. Their sincerity touched her. She felt tears welling and had to turn away for a moment.

Derek stayed beside her.

She leaned into him. "Sorry. I don't know why I'm suddenly so upset."

He slipped an arm around her shoulders. "Grief does that. It can catch you off guard when you least expect it."

She took a few breaths to settle herself. "I'm okay. We shouldn't be rude."

Off to the side, an open-air table quickly filled with food, a veritable feast of Sudanese cuisine: pungent stews redolent with spices and meats, a thick sorghum porridge, platters of dates, a mound of yogurt-and-carrot salad, and piles of flatbread to scoop everything up.

They all tucked into the spread, while Gray spoke to an elder who spoke fluent English, gaining as much insight as possible into where they were headed.

Jane refrained from eavesdropping. She preferred to appreciate the meal, thanking the women, sharing a piece of grilled sheep's liver with Anjing, who seemed as welcome at the table as any of the guests. With her stomach quickly full, she leaned back. Small twinkling lights lined the castellated walls of the courtyards, but they paled in comparison to the sweep of stars overhead.

For this brief moment, she felt content and at peace.

Still, deep down, she knew it couldn't last.

9:22 P.M.

It's about time . . .

Seichan lay flat on the roof of an abandoned home, about a block from where the Unimog sat parked in an empty lot. Ten minutes after the others had left, she had stepped out of the truck and cupped her ear, feigning a radio call. After a moment, she had responded, continuing the charade: *Understood. Everything's quiet here. I'll be right there.*

She had then grabbed her pack and followed in the others' footsteps. She hiked for several blocks, as if heading over to them. Once she was certain she wasn't tailed, she circled back and climbed atop a home that offered a view of the abandoned truck.

She then waited to see if anyone took her bait.

The truck might tempt a would-be crook in the village, but such a thief was not her target. Ahmad had seemed confident that the Unimog would be unmolested by those in the village. She had learned over the years that such towns often had a strict code. It was okay to steal from strangers, but if a guest was under the protection of a family from that village, they were not to be touched.

So, for the past forty minutes, no one approached the vehicle.

Until now.

A figure appeared to Seichan's right. The stranger was wearing a jalabiya, a collarless, ankle-length white robe with long sleeves and a matching woven turban. Many men in the village wore the same attire, as the light color and loose fit helped keep them cool. So his presence wasn't unexpected. He moved with no sense of threat, casually walking toward the parked Unimog, as if curious about the hulking desert truck.

Still, something about him set off warning bells in Seichan. He glanced once to the right, then the left, then focused fully on the truck. He also carried something in his hand, but the drape of his sleeve hid it.

Seichan waited until he was fully out in the open, unable to easily fade back into the tight maze of the village. Satisfied, she rolled silently off the flat roof and dropped to the packed dirt on the far side of the building, out of view of the empty lot. Staying low, she circled the home and approached the man from behind.

She had her SIG Sauer in hand, ready to act if need be. Closer now, she could see the man wasn't carrying a weapon, but she could not make out what he held. Her nerves danced. For a brief moment, she considered shooting him in the back.

But what if I'm wrong?

Murdering an innocent man in cold blood would not win over the cooperation of these desert nomads. So she took another step toward him. Then another. Though she moved without disturbing a grain of sand and held her breath, something alerted her target.

The man swung around, his eyes flashing, his dark face hard and cold.

She knew immediately this was no common thief. She fired, but her target dove to the side, rolled over a shoulder, and gained his feet. He took off without a moment's hesitation.

She ran after the man, tracking him with her gun. She refrained from firing when he dashed across the face of a home, the windows aglow with life. She feared striking someone inside if she missed.

The man took advantage of her restraint and vanished up a narrow alleyway leading into the village. By the time she reached the alley, he was gone. She was not dumb enough to risk following him into that twisting dark labyrinth, where he could easily ambush her.

Instead, she touched the mike taped to her throat and radioed Gray. When he answered, she knew they had only one course open to them.

"Time to go," she said.

He didn't ask for an explanation. Her tone told him enough.

Three minutes later, Gray arrived with the others in tow. He gripped a SIG Sauer, guarding Derek and Jane. Kowalski brought up the rear, shouldering a shotgun.

Gray caught her eye. She nodded the all-clear and waved them to the truck.

Only then did Gray question her. "What happened?"

She told him.

"So it could have been a simple thief," he said.

She remembered those eyes, how he had moved. "No, it wasn't."

He took her at her word.

A figure suddenly came running out of the village. Seichan whipped her weapon up, but it was only Ahmad.

"Wait! I go with!" he shouted to them.

Gray looked like he was about to refuse, plainly concerned about endangering the young man.

Seichan reminded him of their original plan. "We still need someone who knows the deserts around here."

Ahmad nodded his head. "I know very well."

Gray sighed, his back stiffening, as if already taking the weight of this kid's life on his shoulders. "Okay. Everyone aboard. We're leaving right now."

Ahmad smiled, then turned and whistled.

His dog came rushing to join him.

Gray accepted this last-minute addition by turning and heading to the truck.

Kowalski was not as reticent. "At least the kid's not bringing his donkey."

9:41 P.M.

The loud growl of a truck's engine reached Valya's hiding place. Her targets were leaving. Their thunderous departure echoed throughout the village, matching her mood.

Damn that woman.

Standing inside one of the local homes, Valya stripped out of the borrowed jalabiya robe and tossed aside the turban that had hidden her white hair. She stood naked, taking a deep breath. For now, she continued wearing the dark brown makeup that colored her pale skin and tattoo. She would need it again when she changed her disguise to that of an old woman. Part of her training had been to learn to vanish into the background. This she had easily mastered. She considered her white form to be a blank slate upon which she could paint any number of faces.

Two hours ago, Valya had come straight here from Khartoum, where she lay in wait for her quarry to arrive.

The team Anton had sent here were already in the deep desert, readying the true trap. She had hoped to better their odds of success. The enemy's truck was old, built before the age of GPS units. So there was no way to remotely track it, especially once the group was running overland across the desert. She had hoped to fix that problem by hiding a transceiver inside the wheel well. Such a simple solution—yet, still she had been thwarted, chased off by the other woman.

The only small advantage gained tonight was that Valya had overheard the woman's name.

Seichan.

Valya took satisfaction in this. The woman was less of a mystery now, less of a myth. She was someone who could be killed.

Still, Valya swore not to underestimate her again.

Turning, she crossed to the two dead bodies in the corner of the room. The pair lay sprawled across the bare floor with their throats slit. Pools of blood seeped into the parched dirt.

They were the elderly owners of the home. She had stalked them after arriving here, wrapped head-to-toe in a burka, following them to their doorstep like a beggar. Once inside, she shed her cloak, revealing her true pale self. She used that moment of shock to silently dispatch them, appreciating their looks of horror. In many places in Africa, albinos were thought to be magical, holding good luck in their bones. Such superstitions led to children being slaughtered across the continent, their mystical body parts sold on the black market.

She stared down at the two bodies.

Maybe we're not so lucky after all.

With time to spare, she slipped the black-handled *athamé*, her grandmother's witch-dagger, from its wrist sheath. She knelt beside the old woman and used the knife's tip to carve her mark on the corpse's forehead. Slowly the Eye of Horus opened upon that cold flesh and stared back at her, almost approvingly.

She felt calmer now, and a soft smile formed. Soon another would bear the mark, someone truly worthy of it. She whispered that name aloud.

"Seichan . . ."

14

As the Gulfstream banked over the open water of Baffin Bay, Painter studied their destination. Ellesmere Island lay directly ahead, shrouded in a haze of ice fog. The coastline was a craggy line of jagged inlets, small bays, jumbles of rock, and beaches of broken shale. Plates of ice had run aground in some sections, stacking up like a scatter of playing cards.

"Not exactly hospitable," Kat said, watching from her window across the cabin.

"But man finds a way nonetheless," Painter said, having read up on the place on the flight here. "The island's been occupied by indigenous hunters going back some four thousand years. Then the Vikings arrived later, followed by the Europeans in the seventeenth century."

"And now the pair of us," Kat said, trying to lighten the mood.

Painter simply nodded, his stomach still knotted with anxiety. Back in D.C., he had not wasted any time coordinating this mission with General Metcalf, his boss at DARPA. The man had questioned the necessity of an excursion a thousand miles above the Arctic Circle, but Painter had been adamant. He and Kat had flown due north, pushing the Gulfstream G150's engines. They had landed and refueled at Thule Air Base, the U.S. military's northernmost camp, located on the western coast of Greenland.

If Painter had any question as to the importance of the region, Thule answered it. Run by two different air force squadrons, the base was home to a ballistic missile early-warning system and a global satellite control network. It also acted as the regional hub for a dozen military and research installations peppered throughout Greenland and the surrounding islands, including Aurora Station on Ellesmere.

And that was just the United States.

Canada had additional camps, including one on Ellesmere called Alert, a seasonal military and scientific outpost about five hundred miles from the North Pole.

Painter tried to spot the place as their jet swept over the middle of the island, but the distances here were deceptively vast. The pilot navigated a course between Quttinirpaaq National Park, which took up the northern end of the island, and the spread of glaciers to the south. Below their wings, the Challenger Mountains rose up in a jumble of snowy peaks.

"We should be getting close," Kat said.

Aurora Station had been constructed on the northwest coast of the island, bordering the Arctic Ocean. According to his research, the site had been chosen for a number of different reasons, but primarily because it was closest to the magnetic north pole, which was the subject of several of the station's research projects. While the geographic north pole was relatively fixed, the magnetic pole had been drifting for centuries, slowly sweeping past the coastline of Ellesmere and up into the Arctic Ocean.

The pilot radioed back to them. "We're twenty miles out. Should be on the ground in ten. And from the look of the weather ahead, we're lucky we made such good time."

Painter turned his attention from the ground to the skies. While there were only a few clouds above, to the northwest the world ended at a wall of darkness. Painter had known a storm was coming, but forecasts had been worsening by the hour. The region was predicted to be socked in for days, maybe weeks. It was one of the reasons he had pressed General Metcalf so hard. If he missed this window, the chances of rescuing Safia would grow grimmer with each passing day.

He couldn't let that happen.

Still, there remained another problem.

Kat voiced it aloud. "Once that storm hits, we'll be trapped until it clears."

With those forecasts predicting gale-force winds, the jet would touch down at the station, drop them off, and promptly take off again for Thule, where it would weather out the storm. The commander at the air base, Colonel Wycroft, had been alerted under a confidential order to be ready for an emergency evacuation if they were successful. But even he had warned them that the storm could compromise such a mission.

Still, Painter remained undeterred.

"We have no choice but to keep going," he said.

She glanced at him, as if to argue against that statement—then thought better of it and returned her attention to the window. He knew he was driving this mission hard. She, in turn, fought to keep a steady hand on the reins, urging a more measured approach. So far they hadn't come to any true loggerheads. Down deep, he recognized she was trying to do what was best—both for their safety and Safia's.

Kat let out a small gasp.

"What?" he asked.

She kept her gaze out the window. "The photos don't do it justice."

Painter turned to look, returning his attention below as the jet swept toward the airstrip that served Aurora Station. A handful of Cessnas—the typical bush planes of the Arctic—were parked nearby. It looked like the planes were being anchored down ahead of the storm. Another jet was being rolled into a steel hangar.

But Painter knew this sight was not what had drawn a gasp from Kat.

Past a cluster of squat research buildings was the true engineering marvel of Aurora Station. The base's Ionospheric Research Instrument, or IRI, occupied more than three hundred acres of flat tundra. While its beam-generating powerhouse was buried underground, the prickly face it presented to the world were its two thousand steel antennas, all networked together. Each stood ten stories tall with crossbeams stretched out like arms.

"It almost looks like the Milky Way," Kat commented.

Painter understood. Where HAARP's 180 antennas had been set up in a rigid grid, the array here had been positioned into a fractal spiral, almost fluid looking. It was a work of engineering art, equally beautiful and practical.

At the heart of the steel constellation was a deep pit. It was a former mine, one of many such operations throughout the Arctic Archipelago. The whole region was pocked with these excavated holes, digging copper, gold, lead, zinc, even diamonds out of the frozen earth. The mineral resources of the Arctic were vast and mostly as of yet untouched. Though that was rapidly changing as the region thawed, opening more and more territory.

"What's that rising from the center of the hole?" Kat asked.

Painter squinted at the pinnacle-shaped tower of steel scaffolding. It pointed toward the sky and supported a massive sphere. The shining globe was cradled within a nest of concentric copper rings, which was wound throughout by braids of thick cables and connected to trapezoidal magnets, each the size of a Volkswagen Bug.

"Consider it a testament to Simon Hartnell's obsession," he said. "It's his attempt to replicate and improve upon the work of the man he worships, Nikola Tesla."

"But what is it?"

"It's Hartnell's version of Wardenclyffe Tower, one of Tesla's most ambitious projects."

Painter noted the similarity of design below, if only superficially. He pulled up a picture on his iPad to compare the two, then passed the tablet for Kat to see.

"Tesla purchased two hundred acres in Long Island and built a power plant that serviced an eighteen-story wooden tower topped by a giant cupola. He had dreams to build the world's first global wireless communication system, envisioning thirty or more of these towers around the world. Later he believed he could even tap into what he called the *resonance frequency of the earth* to also use this network to create a worldwide wireless *power* system."

"Sounds ambitious."

"And maybe ahead of his time. It ended in failure as funding fell through. The place was abandoned and demolished a few years later." Painter looked below. "Still, even in defeat, such lofty aspirations inspired others. In fact, Simon Hartnell picked his company's name—Clyffe Energy—as an acknowledgment of Wardenclyffe and the hopes and dreams it represented."

"And the tower down there?" Kat asked. "What's Hartnell's plan for it?"

He frowned. "That's a good question."

In his rush to get here, he had managed only a cursory review of the station's various projects. From what he read, the tower was an amplifier for the antenna array. The design and shape were merely an homage to Tesla. According to all reports, the tower was intended to magnify the same ionosphere-stimulating beam achieved by HAARP. The increased energy output, though, would expand the research capabilities of the array, along with producing more accurate results. It was basically a larger version of HAARP, one engineered for the same research goals as its smaller cousin.

But now that I'm seeing it in person . . .

Painter felt that knot in his stomach tightening. He had been so focused on Safia that he had never given this project its full due diligence, glossing past inconsistencies in specifications and protocols.

Or maybe I'm falling under the spell of the same conspiracists who looked upon HAARP and read nefarious purposes into its mysterious antenna array.

The pilot radioed again. "Buckle up, folks. We're beginning our descent."

Painter leaned back, settling on one certainty.

It's too late to turn back now.

10:22 P.M.

As Kat offloaded from the Gulfstream, she braced herself, but the bitter cold felt like plunging naked into a mountain lake. A steady wind blew off the neighboring Arctic Ocean, tasting of salt and ice. It cut through the neck of her parka.

She shivered and huddled against the gusts, clutching the collar of her hood with one hand and hauling her hard-shell carry-on with the other. The temperature hovered at record lows for early June—a few degrees above zero—and would likely break those records with the coming storm.

She stared out to sea, past the broken ice pack to the black clouds stacked to the horizon. The sun sat low on the west edge of the storm, as if cowering from the threat, but there would be no escape. At this polar latitude, the sun would not fully set until the first week in September.

To her left, something white dashed across the black tarmac of the small airstrip, then vanished over a berm of gray-white snow. It was an arctic hare, a reminder that despite the desolate appearance of this outpost, life found a way to survive, both on land and sea. This was the domain of polar bears, seals, narwhals, and beluga whales. Herds of caribou still roamed the wilds here, along with the shaggy musk ox. In fact, the old Inuit name for Ellesmere was *Umingmak Nuna,* or "Land of the Muskox."

Past the airstrip, patches of blue grass poked up from the snow, while open stretches of silt and soil were daubed with yellow arctic poppies and the white-flowering chickweed.

She took heart from these hardy pioneers, surviving against the most impossible odds.

She shifted her gaze to the neighboring cluster of concrete buildings, all painted orange to stand out from the terrain. Painter headed toward them, barely giving his surroundings a second look.

As the Gulfstream swung around behind them, readying for its flight back to Thule, Kat stared after the vanished hare.

Let's hope we prove to be as stalwart at surviving here.

She set off after Painter. Ahead, a welcoming committee awaited them at the main doors into Aurora Station. They were huddled within the steamy breath being exhaled through the open doors into the frigid cold. Painter strode purposefully toward them, as if to escape the weather, but she knew it was the fate of Safia al-Maaz that drew him forward.

She followed, noting the base was being battened down against the storm to come. A pair of Sno-Cats trundled down a ramp into an underground garage. Tarps and tie-downs anchored the handful of Cessnas parked near the airstrip. Apparently there was no room in the hangars for such minor aircraft. She saw a sleek Learjet sitting in one hangar, and as the doors to another were being trundled closed, she spotted the tail of a large-bodied Boeing cargo jet.

The place is practically a full-service airport.

But considering how isolated this station was, maybe that wasn't surprising.

They finally reached the open doors and were ushered into the warm heart of the station. Though she had been outside only for a few minutes, she sighed as the heat enveloped her.

The doors were sealed behind them, and the man in charge stepped forward, a big smile on his face. It was Simon Hartnell himself. He wore a thick wool turtleneck, jeans, and well-scuffed work boots. Kat was surprised the CEO of Clyffe Energy would serve such a lowly duty as station greeter.

"Welcome to the end of the world," he said, then waved toward the north. "Okay, maybe not the *end,* but we can certainly see it from here."

She smiled, though she suspected this was an old joke, part of a well-rehearsed greeting to put newcomers at ease. In turn, she played her role.

"Thank you." She pushed back the hood of her parka. "We weren't sure we'd make it with the storm coming."

Painter nodded, his manner reserved. "We appreciate you accommodating us on such short notice."

Hartnell waved away this concern. "Spot inspections are part and parcel of any organization. And DARPA is always welcome. Without your work over at HAARP, Aurora Station wouldn't exist." His smile widened. "Besides, it gives me a chance to show off a bit. We're all very proud of our work here and the promise it holds."

"To fight climate change?" Kat said, delicately prying.

"Exactly. Currently we have thirty-four different active projects, but the main goal of Aurora is to study, monitor, and test theoretical models for combating global warming."

"A noble effort," Painter said.

He shrugged. "And hopefully a profitable one. Despite my considerable resources, I still do have a board to appease." He turned and led them away. "But we can discuss this more in the morning. Even with the sun still shining, it's getting quite late. Come, let's get you both settled in."

He led them down a pastel blue corridor to an elevator bay.

"We built the station's lodging on its lowest sublevel," he explained as they entered the waiting cage. "It's the most naturally insulated and easier to keep warm."

He pressed the B4 button.

Kat had studied the base's schematics. The upper buildings sat atop four subterranean levels, which housed labs, offices, workrooms, storage spaces, and even an extensive recreation area that included an indoor tennis court, pool, and movie theater.

It was a veritable city.

To find Safia in this labyrinth would be difficult.

Kat had also noted the security cameras mounted in the entry hallway. She had no doubt the entire complex was watched. She remembered the pale face of the man who was head of station security: Anthony Vasiliev, aka Anton Mikhailov.

If Hartnell had employed Anton and his sister—two people with past ties to the Guild—how many others had been similarly recruited to protect this base?

She could almost feel those ice-blue eyes studying her.

She had no doubt Hartnell had thoroughly investigated his two new visitors, along with their cover story. He proved this as the elevator doors opened and led them out.

He turned to the director. "Painter Crowe. I know about you."

"You do?" Painter said, showing only mild surprise.

Under such a tight schedule, he and Kat hadn't bothered with false names. Both of them had a long record as being employed by DARPA, which was true and went to further corroborate their story. Even under the closest scrutiny, their role with Sigma—or even the existence of Sigma Force—would not be found in any records. And under a similar tight schedule, Hartnell's security team would only have had hours to prepare for this surprise inspection. Any background check could only have been cursory.

"Yes," Hartnell said. "I believe you're the same Painter Crowe who patented a temperature-controlled microrelay circuit."

Painter lifted his brows. "That's right."

Hartnell smiled. "We have over seventy thousand of your circuits installed here. Truly a brilliant bit of microengineering. How you handled heat dissipation . . . pure genius." He glanced over his shoulder. "I may have to steal you away from DARPA one of these days."

Good luck with that, Kat thought.

Hartnell guided them through a vast common room, which was mostly empty at this hour. A few faces lifted from meal trays to look their way. The neighboring kitchen still steamed on the far side, wafting with the smell of garlic. He pointed that way.

"If you're hungry, there's food offered around the clock. Unfortunately, we're on a limited menu at this late hour. But we do serve the world's best coffee."

Kat nodded, tempted by the latter.

Hartnell took them to a corridor on the left. "I apologize in advance. I'm afraid your accommodations are rather Spartan, but I did get you adjoining rooms."

"Anything will do," Painter said. "We'll be in and out before you know it."

Let's hope that proves to be true.

He passed them keycards. "The whole station is controlled electronically. Normally these cards would even learn your schedule, enough to adjust your room's thermostat accordingly. They keep track of everything."

Kat found that a little unnerving and wondered if that was his intent.

Simon lifted his empty palms. "But like I said, we'll get to know each other better tomorrow and make sure DARPA is getting its money's worth out of our efforts here."

"Thank you," Kat said, stifling a yawn that was not feigned.

"I'll leave you to make yourselves at home." With a small nod, he set off down the hall.

Painter swiped his card over his door's lock, while flicking a look at the hall's ceiling-mounted camera. "We should get some shut-eye."

"Sounds good," she said, playing along.

They both entered their respective rooms. As she crossed inside, she realized her definition of *Spartan* was distinctly different from their host's. Her accommodations could easily have been found at the Four Seasons. The room had hardwood floors, heated from the feel of them, and a king-sized bed dressed in damask and silk. One wall had drapes, which were parted to reveal a plasma screen glowing with a scene of a sunlit beach, gently massaged by waves, as if the room looked out upon the Caribbean. Soft music played throughout the room. A glimpse into a marble bath showed a jetted tub and a steam shower.

She shook her head, imagining Hartnell meant this all to be a surprise. *Well, we have our own surprises.*

She crossed to the bed and placed her bag on the duvet. Camouflaged compartments in the case hid a dissembled SIG Sauer. For the moment, she refrained from opening anything. Instead, she used the time to inspect the rest of her room.

Finally, a knock sounded on the door that led to Painter's room. She crossed over and swiped her card to allow him inside. He stepped silently into her room, while she stood with her arms crossed. He paced from one end to the other, both there and in the bathroom. He held a device in one hand, pausing every now and again to bring it closer to a wall or vent.

With a satisfied nod, he said, "Looks like both rooms are clear. Should be safe to talk."

"What now?" she asked, stepping to her bag, ready to retrieve and assemble her weapon.

"We find Safia."

She read the strained worry in his eyes, but she needed him thinking clearly, focused, for all their sakes.

"She's alive," Kat assured him. "They wouldn't have brought her all the way out here only to kill her. They need her for something."

"But for what?"

"That's a good question. If we can figure that out, we might have a better chance of finding her." She glanced toward the door. "But where to start?"

He focused on her question, his anxiety visibly waning. He finally pointed toward the hallway.

"We start with a couple of cups of the world's best coffee—then we get to know our neighbors."

11:26 P.M.

It makes no sense.

Seated in the station library, Safia rubbed her tired eyes. She and Rory had spent the better part of the day copying the hieroglyphs found tattooed on the Egyptian princess's body. The age and leathery mummification had made it a painstaking chore. It also didn't help that they had to accomplish this task while in biosafety suits.

Some sections had been easier to read, as if they'd been inked years ago instead of millennia. Others required using ultraviolet or infrared lights to draw the images from the skin. Then there was the challenge of anatomy, like trying to get to glyphs between her desiccated thighs or read tattoos on her toes that were so very small.

After nine hours, they had slowly built a copy—which they had digitized for easier manipulation, transforming each age-mauled glyph into a more readable version. She had one section of the reconstruction up on her laptop. It had a moth-eaten appearance, full of gaps and missing pieces.

Even with the most careful work, some of the tattoos ended up being irretrievable. In a final attempt to learn more, she and Rory had positioned a 3-D topographic scanner around the body seated on the throne. The device's four lasers would map every nook and cranny, delving deep into the epidermal layers. Its imaging software could even stretch and extend the skin, hopefully revealing more.

But it was a slow process, requiring hours to run.

Leaving it to work overnight, she and Rory had come to the library. They were attempting to translate the few intact sections recovered from the body, but so far they were making no headway.

"It's all gibberish," she said.

Rory worked across the table from her, laboring over the same puzzle on his laptop. "It can't be. Why would this woman go through so much effort to tattoo her entire body and have it all be nonsense?"

"They could simply be decorations. I've heard of people getting Chinese letters inked on them without realizing that what was written was pure twaddle."

"I'm not buying that."

She sighed. "I'm not, either. There must be something important she was trying to preserve."

But what?

"Then maybe we start fresh tomorrow," Rory said. "It's late and we're both tired. We can try to fill in more of the gaps in the morning."

She nodded, frustrated. "It's like trying to read a book where every other word is missing and those that are left have half their letters erased."

"And with the mummy's rear side burned beyond recognition," he reminded her, "we've also lost the back end of the book."

"True."

Rory tried to suppress a yawn but failed.

She smiled. "We'll try again when we can hold our eyes open."

"Maybe not this one." Rory pointed to his bruised and swollen eye, a painful reminder of the cost of failure.

The source of that injury sat near the door. Anton's gaze seldom shifted away from them.

"We'll figure it out," she promised Rory.

They both began to close up shop, collecting their laptops. While her computer was mostly locked down, she could still use it to communicate via e-mail or video chat with Rory, in case either of them had any insight during the night.

"One last question," Safia said. "There was that rectangular strip of missing skin. You said you believed your father cut it out for tests."

"To try to discern the exact nature of her mummification. He thought it was odd."

"Odd how?"

"He believed there was something unique about the ritual she had undergone prior to being entombed, but he never elaborated. We were only allowed to talk for one hour each week." He glanced back to Anton. "That is, if we both did what was asked of us."

She pictured the corresponding blank section of hieroglyphs on the reconstruction. "Did he ever copy down what might have been written on that excised piece?"

"I have no idea. But if he did, it was likely destroyed with everything else."

"What was your father trying to hide?" she mumbled to herself.

Rory heard her. "Apparently something worth dying for."

Safia winced and touched his arm. "I'm sorry."

He looked down at his feet, his voice edged with bitterness. "And he left me to pick up the pieces."

Rory strode toward the door. She hurried to catch up, seeking some words to console the young man. She could not imagine what it must be like. Not only must Rory be struggling with the grief of losing his father, but clearly there was some resentment toward Harold for abandoning him. His father had chosen to risk his life, while leaving his son in their captor's clutches. And now Rory was being forced to follow in his father's footsteps.

Safia wondered about that final act of Harold's.

Was it done out of selfishness or desperation?

As she reached Rory, there was a knock on the library door. Anton waved them back. He opened it, while blocking the view inside with his body. After a short exchange, a file was passed to him.

Anton closed the door and held out the folder. "Test results."

Safia was momentarily confused, but she took what was offered. She opened it and saw it was a DNA analysis on their subject. It was just one of a battery of tests, from tissue samples to carbon dating. She had not expected to get these results so fast, but she should have known better, considering who was financing this endeavor.

She stepped away from the door, drawing Rory with her. She didn't expect anything particularly surprising. She had asked for a genetic analysis of the mummy's autosomal and mitochondrial DNA in an attempt to trace the woman's ancestry. She hoped it might give them some clue as to *where* in ancient Egypt this woman might have lived.

The file held more than thirty pages of detailed results, including graphs and charts, but the summary was on the top page. She read aloud from the last line. " *'Subject carries several corroborating alleles and markers, but the most significant is the presence of Haplogroup K1a1b1a, suggestive of a Levant ancestry, while lacking any presence of the I2 subclade expected of an Egyptian origin.'* "

Rory frowned. "Archaeogenetics was never my cup of tea. What does that mean?"

Safia swallowed, picturing the ravaged body of the woman on the throne. "It says she's *not* Egyptian."

"What?"

She read the most significant line to herself again: *suggestive of a Levant ancestry.*

"I think . . ." She turned to Rory. "I think she's Jewish."

11:55 P.M.

Simon climbed naked out of the ice-cold plunge pool. With his body quaking from the frigid dip, he grabbed a towel from the heated rack and buffed his skin dry.

It was his ritual before retiring each night. His personal pool was only a yard wide and twelve feet deep, filled with water kept at a steady 55 degrees. Each night he jumped in and dropped down to grab a stainless steel ring bolted to the bottom. He held tight to that anchor for as long as his breath would last, then shot back out.

Already he felt the anxiety-ridding effect of the cold plunge, one of many benefits from this ritual. It was also said to improve lymphatic circulation, strengthening the immune system, while activating brown fat to help with weight loss. If nothing else, it obviously had a cardiovascular effect, as his heart hammered in his chest.

His whole body shook once more, then he pulled on a thick robe.

He found he slept much better after shocking his system with this bit of cryotherapy, a ritual that helped stave off his body's confusion in this land where months could be sunk in darkness or bright all day.

He could also think clearer, shedding the day's aggravations.

Like this surprise visit from a pair of DARPA inspectors.

Why now of all times?

An important experimental trial was scheduled in less than forty-eight hours. The conditions were perfect. Not only was the pending storm a warm one—a rarity up here, where conditions were considered to be desert-dry—but it coincided with a geomagnetic storm from a powerful solar flare recorded two days ago. Everything was in place, and he hated the thought of delaying.

With his mind running through the variables, he abandoned his plunge pool and headed barefoot to his library. His suite of rooms encompassed the entire breadth of a private *fifth* sublevel, where access was limited to only a handful of station personnel. He entered his library, appreciating the radiant heat rising from the hand-scraped plank flooring. The room was a mix of the old and the modern. Three walls were encased in mahogany shelves, holding books and volumes dating back centuries, along with glass-encased artifacts and treasures.

One entire wall was devoted to Nikola Tesla. It was a veritable museum to the inventor. Even the plasma screen that bloomed to life as he entered presented a view of Manhattan from the vantage of Tesla's old suite at the Hotel New Yorker—Room 3327, which still bears a memorial plaque to the man on its door.

It was in that room that his life ended and my life's passion began.

He gazed upon his most prized possession. A thick black book rested under glass, softly illuminated from above.

The morning after Tesla passed away in 1941, his nephew Sava Kosanovic rushed over to the hotel, only to find his uncle's body had already been removed and the room ransacked. Volumes of technical papers were missing, including a notebook of several hundred pages that Sava was told by Tesla to preserve upon his passing. The FBI investigated and confiscated all the remaining work and technical papers, with the government declaring it a matter of national security.

And no wonder.

Simon glanced to a framed copy of the *New York Times* on the wall, dated from July 11, 1934. The headline read: TESLA, AT 78, BARES NEW DEATH BEAM. The article described a particle-beam weapon that could bring down ten thousand planes from hundreds of miles away. But rather than a weapon of war, Tesla believed his invention could bring about world peace, stating that when all countries possessed this beam, all fighting would stop. He also envisioned using this same invention to transmit power wirelessly, even to use it to heat up the upper levels of the atmosphere, creating a man-made aurora borealis to light the night skies around the world.

Simon smiled.

The man was a visionary, ahead of his time.

But now that time had finally come.

He stared at the black notebook, each page carefully inscribed in Serbian, the language of Tesla's birthplace. Simon had discovered it while helping to fund the renovation and expansion of the Tesla Museum in Belgrade. Back in 1952, the government finally released Tesla's papers to his nephew, which were preserved at the museum. But even Sava knew a large portion was kept by the U.S. government, specifically by the National Defense Research Committee, which was run at the time by John G. Trump, the uncle of a certain New York real estate magnate.

In the end, Sava was proven right.

Simon spent millions looking for those missing documents. Then he learned that when John Trump died in 1985, he bequeathed a massive cache of scientific papers to his alma mater, the Massachusetts Institute of Technology. Simon sent a research investigator over to MIT to comb through that truckload of documents, specifically looking for anything related to Tesla.

It wasn't a haphazard request on Simon's part. Later in life, John Trump founded the High Voltage Engineering Corporation, which produced Van de Graaf generators, a current-producing device not all that dissimilar to the Tesla coil. Trump was even declared by the National Academy of Engineering to be a "pioneer in the scientific, engineering, and medical applications of high voltage machinery."

An acclaim that could easily describe Tesla.

Suspicious—especially since John Trump oversaw the shuttering of the NDRC—Simon sent that investigator poking around. Buried deep in that cache, the man found an unmarked notebook, scrawled by hand in the Serbian language.

Simon stared at that book under glass.

Tesla's lost notebook.

It was no wonder that the NDRC considered it of little value. The journal was *not* a treatise on building a particle-beam weapon—at least, not entirely—but rather told a wild tale going back to 1895. Later, Tesla would hint at the secrets found within his notebook in an interview, declaring he had discovered the true nature of power "from a new and unsuspected source."

And indeed he had.

While Trump and the NDRC might have dismissed the book as a work of fabrication and fancy, Simon took it for the truth. To verify the book's claims, he poured millions into charitable work in Africa, including funding construction and housing projects along the Nile, which in turn meant financing archeological surveys of such regions. With universities scrabbling to endow research projects, especially expensive fieldwork, it had not been hard to co-opt such efforts to serve his own ends.

Then two years ago—after a decade of searching, guided by the vaguest of clues—Simon found what Tesla had sworn never to reveal.

It was a true wonder, but one that came with great risks.

The ongoing pandemic was testament to that.

Simon frowned at the book, understanding why Tesla and his two companions had made a pact to keep silent. What they had discovered was beyond their abilities to harness, the risk of failure too great.

So they kept it buried in the desert—until the world was ready.

Simon formed a determined fist.

I will do what Tesla could not.

For the sake of the world.

No matter the cost.

A chime sounded behind him. He turned to the one wall not covered in bookshelves. It held a bank of monitors, serving as his digital eyes upon the station. He crossed over and accepted the incoming video call. He took this same call at midnight every day.

Anton's face appeared on the center screen, ready to pass on his final briefing for the day.

"Have you put your charges to bed?" Simon asked.

"Dr. al-Maaz is locked back in her room," he reported. "She made good progress today, including a discovery I believe even escaped Professor McCabe's attention."

"Concerning what?"

"The subject in the lab—the mummified woman—she's not Egyptian, but rather of Jewish descent."

"Jewish?"

Anton shrugged. "The significance is unknown, but work will continue tomorrow."

Simon sat down on the chair before the monitors, contemplating this news. After discovering Tesla's notebook and the plans found within it for the electrical microbe, Simon had sought a means of taming such a virulent organism—through both scientific means and historical.

Tesla had hinted at such a solution in his book, but the answer seemed to disturb and frighten him—enough so that he refrained from elaborating on it.

It was the *one* piece holding Simon back from the final stage of his work. From a theoretical standpoint, everything made sense. But any failure risked an ecological disaster, one that would make the *Exxon Valdez* oil spill look like an overturned cup of milk.

Still, the world faced an even greater threat.

Here on Ellesmere, warming conditions were already changing the chemical conditions of ponds and wetlands, resulting in the loss of species and habitats. And that was only the tip of the proverbial melting iceberg. Researchers estimated that, if unchecked, the global biosphere could collapse within this century.

Unless a true visionary steps in.

Simon considered the challenges before him. The test slated to commence in two days was the first phase, a localized trial. It would serve as a real-world proof of concept. But did he dare risk it, especially now with the station under watch?

"What about our guests?" Simon asked. "Our friends from DARPA?"

"Last I checked they were in the cafeteria, chatting over coffee."

"And you're confident in your background check?"

Anton nodded. "They work for DARPA, going back nearly a decade."

Good.

Simon didn't need any more problems. "We'll give them the official tourist tour tomorrow, then send them packing as soon as possible."

Still, something bothered him about them, something he couldn't put a finger on. And he trusted his intuition. As Tesla once stated, *instinct is something which transcends knowledge.*

"Anton, let's keep an extra eye on them."

"Of course."

"And what of the news from the Sudan? How is your sister faring with that other problem?"

"All is on schedule. That matter should be settled soon."

"Very good."

After a final few details were discussed, he ended the connection.

He sat for a moment, then toggled up a new feed from another secure section of the station. A view into a cave appeared, illuminated by bright halogens. It was part of the old Fitzgerald Mine, which once operated on the island, digging for nickel and lead. The cavern had flooded half a century ago and remained unfrozen at those insulated depths. He remembered seeing it for the first time when Aurora Station was being built. The waters had been a perfect blue, as if a memory of the sky.

In the end, this old bore pit had served as the perfect holding tank.

He studied the lake. Its flat surface mirrored the steel catwalk spanning its length. But the waters were no longer a crystalline azure but a dark ruby, like so much spilled blood.

He felt a shiver of apprehension, remembering another quote from Tesla, wondering if the visionary was foretelling what might happen if the secret in his journal ever came to light.

You may live to see man-made horrors beyond your comprehension.

Simon prayed for once that the man he admired was wrong.

THIRD

THE DREAMING GOD

15

Sunrise struck like a sledgehammer.

Gray swore under his breath, yanking down the visor, squinting as the leading edge of the sun crested the rocky dunes to his right. The skies had been steadily brightening for the past hour, but he hadn't been prepared for the fiery arrival of the new day.

While Gray took his stint behind the wheel, the others slept or drowsed. In the backseat, Jane nestled against Derek, whose head was lolled back, his mouth open. Kowalski sat with his chin on his chest, snoring loudly, challenging the throaty growl of the truck's engine. Seichan shared the front seat, her head resting against the window.

The only member of the party still awake raced ahead of the lumbering Unimog. The boy Ahmad rode an old Suzuki Tracker sand bike, cutting expertly back and forth, the rear wheel's thick tread chewing across the treacherous terrain. Ahmad had grabbed his bike before the group left Rufaa. Kowalski had helped him haul it into the truck's back bed, where Ahmad's dog, Anjing, now slept in a nest made of their packs.

Three hours ago, Ahmad had guided them to the spot where his cousin's family had found Professor McCabe in the desert. They had stopped and examined the site, but it had offered no clues. What hadn't been trampled over by local search crews, the strong winds and blowing sands had washed away. Those same shifting sands had also erased the professor's tracks leading there.

So they set off, aiming for the coordinates marked by an X on Derek's map. Ahmad had unloaded his bike and led the way onward, searching for any remaining footprints or signs of Professor McCabe's passage. He swept in wide arcs, far in the lead, running dark with his headlamp off. He claimed he could see best with just the light of the moon and stars.

Gray followed throughout the night, doing the same, but he didn't have the eyes of a desert nomad, so he kept his headlights blazing a path before him. Over the past hour, they had been climbing into a region of rolling hills, worn low by the sun and wind.

Seichan stirred next to him, stretching an arm, arching her back. She shaded her eyes against the brightness. "What time is it?"

"Time to look for shelter. It'll be broiling out there in a couple hours."

"How far are we from Derek's coordinates?"

Gray checked the GPS map on his satellite phone. "Another twenty miles, and all of them rough."

Looking at the broken hills ahead, split by dry riverbeds called wadis and wind-sculpted ridges, he understood the wisdom of their choice of vehicle. The Unimog might only have a top speed of sixty, but it made up for its sluggish pace with pure terrain-hugging grip. Still, before they tackled the obstacles to come, they could all use some time to stretch their legs and get food in their bellies.

Ahmad must have had the same idea. Far ahead, he whipped his bike around, casting up a rooster tail of sand. He pointed toward where a low cliff leaned away from the sun, creating a shady oasis beneath.

Gray trundled toward his position as the others woke with various sounds of complaints.

"We're going to take a short break," he announced. "And let the engines cool before the final haul."

Kowalski puffed out a long breath. "Good. Cuz I also gotta talk to a man about a camel. Drank *way* too much water."

Ahmad parked his bike and waited for them. He bounced about on his feet and waved an arm, plainly anxious for them to arrive.

How does that kid have so much energy?

Gray finally ground to a halt, pulling the Unimog into the shade. A happy bark came from the back bed, and Anjing leaped free and ran to his young master. As the dog and boy met in a timeless dance of greeting, everyone piled out.

"Come see, come see!" Ahmad urged.

Gray led the others toward him, while Kowalski headed toward a private spot to have that talk with a camel jockey.

"Look." Ahmad pointed to the sand. "Footprints."

Gray held everyone back, circling the disturbed area. "Definitely boot treads. And the sand's also scooped out, like someone sought a cooler bed for the night."

"Or for the day," Jane said. "My father knew the desert. He would've traveled only when the sun was down."

Derek agreed. "Harold was a tough bird."

"But he'd been delirious," Seichan reminded them. "Who knows who might have camped here?"

"It *was* my father. I just know it."

Jane dropped to her hands and knees in the shelter. She swept her palms over the areas, working in a spiral out from the center.

Derek touched her shoulder. "Jane, maybe it was, maybe it wasn't."

Jane shrugged off his hand. "If it was my father, he might have left—"

A brush of her fingers exposed something poking out of the sand. Startled, Jane yanked her hand back. It was the end of a glass jar, sealed with a rubber stopper.

Gray lowered to a knee beside her. "Let me."

He reached and extracted the object. It was a test tube—with something rolled and stuffed inside.

Jane sat back on her heels, her eyes wide. "My father must've wanted to keep this from his captors and hid it here in case he was caught."

"But what is it?" Seichan asked.

Gray weighed the risk of opening it, cognizant of the disease the professor had been harboring. Still, Ahmad's relatives hadn't become ill, and the professor surely hid this for a reason, hoping it would be found by the right people.

So be it.

He gripped the stopper, twisted it loose, and shook the object into his palm. It looked to be a tiny scroll of parchment. The others closed around him as he unrolled it. He did so carefully, sensing it was very old.

Once the scrap was spread out, he discovered a line of hieroglyphics written across its length.

Jane leaned avidly forward and held out her hand. "Let me see."

Derek peered over her shoulder as she took the fragment. "Look at the style of the glyphs. Like the quail chick and the reed. The writing must date back to the New Kingdom."

Jane agreed. "Definitely seventeenth or eighteenth dynasty."

"What does it say?" Gray asked.

Jane scrunched her face. "The grammar and syntax are odd. Something about taking a boat to the river's mouth. Then more about elephant bones."

She looked to Derek, who could only shrug, clearly as confused.

Gray frowned. "Why would your dad go to all this effort to hide this old scrap of parchment?"

"First of all, it's not *parchment*." Jane rubbed the material between her fingers. "It's leather. Maybe even tattooed human skin."

"And notice how clean and straight the edges are." Derek pointed. "Like it was cut free with a scalpel."

Jane squinted. "From its desiccated condition, I'd say it came from a mummy."

"But why?" Gray pressed again.

Jane turned the relic over in her hands, then stiffened. She held the piece out to Gray. "Maybe because of this."

He leaned closer. Faint numbers and letters had been hastily scrawled along the lower edge.

$$15°42'09.1"N \ 33°14'35.4"E$$

"Coordinates," Gray said.

As everyone stared at him, he pulled out his phone and plugged in the numbers as Jane read them aloud. A moment later, a glowing red dot appeared on the map.

"Where does it point to?" Seichan asked.

Gray looked up. "To a spot only two miles from where we were headed. Very close to the X marked on Derek's map."

Jane stood up. "We have to get over there."

Gray nodded. He rolled up the fragment and tucked it back into the tube, then pointed to the truck. "Let's load up."

Kowalski strode back to them, moving quickly, glancing over his shoulders and up at the sky. In his haste, he had forgotten to zip his fly.

"What's wrong?" Gray asked.

"I think we're being tracked."

"What?"

"I was taking a leak, and I saw something moving in the sky, near the horizon. It vanished into the sun's glare and was gone."

"It could've been a bird," Derek offered. "Hawks, kites, vultures hunt even this far into the desert. Especially early in the morning."

Gray looked hard at Kowalski. "What do you think?"

Kowalski rubbed a palm over the nape of his neck. "Maybe. I don't know. But, hell, even before I saw it, I felt like someone was watching me."

Jane turned to Gray. "What should we do?"

Gray weighed the odds. Kowalski might not be the brightest bulb in the box, but the guy had a keen instinct, especially when it came to surviving. Still, they couldn't go running back to the Nile, spooked by a hungry vulture. Too much was at stake.

"We go on," he decided. "But keep watching our backs."

"And the skies," Kowalski added, finally zipping up. "Don't forget the skies."

Seichan shared a look with Gray, her worry clear. Back in Rufaa, she had been adamant that the stranger sniffing around their truck had been no mere thief. Here could be further confirmation. If so, there was only one conclusion to make.

We're heading into a trap.

7:02 A.M.

Valya cursed as the drone landed in the sand near her team's encampment. The exhausted UAV—an RQ-11B Raven—had a four-foot wingspan and weighed less than five pounds. It was one of two birds that they had been using for aerial surveillance. Each had a charge that only lasted ninety minutes, so she had been alternating their flights to keep a watch on their targets, swapping batteries between runs.

After arriving from Rufaa in the middle of the night, she had followed the enemy's slow progress across the desert, monitoring from a small ground station hidden under a desert-camouflaged tent. The encampment had been set up in the hills that overlooked the flat terrain between here and the Nile. She had surmised correctly that the others would head first to the location where local tribesmen had found Professor McCabe.

Knowing there was a slim possibility she could have been wrong, she had hoped to fix a tracker to their truck. Such a device would be even handier now. With the sun up, they dared not use the drones anymore. She had already kept the last Raven aloft too long. For a brief moment, the drone's optics had caught the large man in the group squinting straight at the UAV.

Though the bird might not have been spotted, she regretted not withdrawing it sooner. She had taken that risk, hoping to discern what had stirred up the group a few moments ago. She got the briefest sidelong glimpse as they all huddled intently together, looking at something. But the overhang of the cliff thwarted her view.

What did they find?

She was especially suspicious considering the Unimog's course all night. The truck—led by a small sand bike—had been heading in a straight line toward their position, as if the others knew where they were going. She had expected the group to set a more expansive search grid, sweeping back and forth, in an attempt to pick up the professor's trail.

Instead, their aim was uncanny.

They can't possibly know what's out here.

"They're moving again," a voice sounded in her ear.

It was a scout she had sent circling wide to watch for the truck when it climbed out of the shadowy cleft again.

She swung to the right and spotted a dusty cloud rise two miles to the west, marking their trail. She had another six men spread throughout these canyons and hills. Not counting their group leader.

"What're your orders?" Kruger asked, standing stiffly at her side.

Willem Kruger—like the rest of his handpicked team—was a former reconnaissance commando with the South African Special Forces. He and his crew had been drummed out of the brigade due to accusations of offering armed support to human traffickers on the continent. She did not know if those stories were true. All she knew was their reputation: They were brutal, efficient, and uncompromising.

Kruger squinted toward the distant dust trail, tracking its progress. "Do we close in on them now?"

She considered his question, staring at the emblem fixed to the man's desert khakis. It depicted a black dagger set against a green laurel wreath. It was his old Special Forces badge—but the dark blade reminded her of another knife, her grandmother's *athamé*.

She remembered the promise made last night, an oath carved into cold flesh. Her fingers absently rubbed the black handle of the dagger sheathed under the cuff of her sleeve.

Her standing orders were to secure Jane McCabe—the others did not matter.

"No, not yet," she decided.

Kruger gave her an inquisitive look.

"I know where they're headed," she said, suddenly sure. "It's a dead end."

And even more so, if they discover what's hidden there.

8:08 A.M.

Jane gripped her door handle as the truck rode over a boulder, tilting precariously. They had been crawling through the challenging terrain for more than an hour.

"I think I can walk faster than this," Derek said as the Unimog righted itself, rocking heavily on its suspension. He held tight on the other side of the backseat.

Seichan sat between them, leaning forward to talk to Gray as Kowalski drove. "How much farther?"

That's a bloody good question.

Gray pointed ahead. "See that cleft between the next two hills? The coordinates Professor McCabe wrote down lie on the far side."

Jane spotted Ahmad, still leading the way. He and his bike vanished into the shadows between the cliffs. Anjing gave chase. The pace had been slow enough for the dog to keep up, even running off at times to check out an interesting smell or to relieve herself.

They lumbered after the boy and his dog, but their speed grew ever slower as the terrain became more difficult. By the time the truck reached the fissure a snail could have outraced them.

Still, Jane didn't complain as the Unimog forced its way into the cleft, which looked barely wide enough to accommodate the truck. She pictured them becoming stuck, pinched between the two walls of rock. With no rear hatch and no sunroof, they would be trapped, at the mercy of the sun when it climbed to noon and baked them inside.

A loud, sustained grind of rock on metal set her teeth on edge. She was sure her fear was about to become reality.

Even Gray cast his gaze back and forth, looking worried. "Kowalski . . ."

"Plenty of room," the driver insisted.

"Then why are you removing half the paint on my side?" he asked.

Kowalski shrugged. "What's a few battle scars?"

After another tense five minutes, the walls dropped away to either side. The Unimog picked up speed.

"Told you," Kowalski grumbled under his breath.

The gap opened into a bowl of sand the size of a football field. It was surrounded on all sides by rocky cliffs. A gust swirled through the valley, stirring the grains. Small dunes rimmed the edges, like waves on a wind-swept lake.

Ahmad had parked his bike in the shade covering half the floor at this early hour. He was down on one knee, letting Anjing lap water from his canteen.

"Well, I got us here," Kowalski said as he drew the Unimog into the shade and stopped. "Now what?"

Seichan frowned. "Place is empty."

Jane felt she needed to defend her father, to be his voice. "There must be something."

"Jane's right," Derek insisted. "Harold wouldn't have risked every-thing and hidden these coordinates unless they were important."

"We go look," Gray said. "We'll spread out into two teams and search the cliffs."

"Or why don't we just go see what's got that kid so excited?" Kowalski suggested.

Ahmad waved and pointed toward his dog. Anjing had finished drink-ing and must have run to one of the walls, drawn by some scent. The dog dug vigorously amid some boulders at the base of the cliff. Sand rocketed high between her hind legs.

Curious, they all offloaded. The day had already grown considerably hotter, even in the shade. The group hurried to the boy.

"Anjing find," Ahmad said. "Come see."

Jane looked past the busy dog and immediately saw what had got-ten Ahmad so worked up. Flush with the cliff face was a metal door. To further mask its presence from the casual eye, its surface had been acid washed to match the red-gray sandstone of these hills.

Derek's attention was elsewhere. He had dropped to run a hand over one of the small boulders. "These aren't rocks. They're old bricks. You can still feel the chisel marks."

Jane glanced from them to the door. "The stones must have originally sealed this place up."

She pictured her father coming here two years ago and opening whatever lay beyond, but this wasn't his meticulous handiwork. Someone had trampled over it, either ignorant or unconcerned about preserving the history found here, even if it was only an old pile of bricks.

Anjing dug at the door's base, clearing away some of the windblown sand from the bottom sill. The dog clearly caught some scent from whatever lay beyond. She remembered the disease carried forth by her father.

"Ahmad, perhaps you should pull Anjing back until we know what we're facing." She turned to Gray. "We should grab shovels. Along with the air masks and helmets."

Knowing the risk they were exploring, the team had been supplied with special face masks, similar to those worn by firefighters. Only these were equipped with filters fine enough to be antibacterial.

Or anti-Archaeal in this case.

After a short time digging and clearing the door, they all slipped on their helmets and secured their masks. They took time to check one another's seals. Only Seichan hung back. She carried her face mask by its straps. Her gaze remained on the skies, scanning the edges of the cliffs.

To guard their backs, she would remain behind with Ahmad and his dog.

Jane had almost forgotten about the threat of someone following them. On the way here, there had been no other strange sightings in the sky. Even now the desert remained quiet. The only sound was the haunting whistle of the wind through the rocks and the hissing sift of sand.

Of course, there was also the thumping of her heart.

But the hurried beat was not fueled by fear—well, not entirely at least—but rather by the thrill of discovery. She was on the verge of finding out what had happened to her father. She felt closer to him in this moment than she had in a long time. She imagined his excitement standing at this same threshold. She was sure his heart had been pounding as hard as hers was now.

Still, this moment of communion was tempered by a deep melancholy. She sensed the depth of her loss more intimately than ever before. Tears welled unexpectedly. She remembered Derek's comment earlier, how grief caught you off guard.

With her features already covered by her mask's clear face shield, she couldn't even wipe away her tears. So she turned from the others until she could collect herself. It was the sandy scrape of metal that finally drew her attention back around.

Gray and Kowalski manhandled the door open.

As they stepped aside, Jane clicked on the battery-powered lamp atop her helmet and shone the beam down the dark tunnel beyond the threshold.

"Ready?" Gray asked her.

"More than ready." She stepped forward. "I've been waiting two long years for this."

8:40 A.M.

With Gray in the lead, Derek followed behind Jane, his lamp shining on her legs. The roof of the passage was low, requiring them to keep their helmets ducked. Behind him, Kowalski was bent nearly in half, hunching along in their wake like a gorilla.

The tunnel dropped at a slight angle, delving deeper under the surrounding hills.

Jane ran her gloved fingertips along the walls. "Man-made," she called back to Derek, her voice muffled by her face mask. "Somebody excavated this out of the sandstone. I wonder how far it goes. Maybe it could even be another Derinkuyu."

Derek remembered reading about the discovery of Derinkuyu, a subterranean city in the Anatolia region of Turkey. The newly unearthed metropolis dated back five thousand years, encompassing four miles of tunnels, caves, escape hatches, and homes, all on multiple levels. It was just more proof that the ancients could produce engineering marvels with their limited tools. The Pyramids at Giza were only the tips of what truly lay hidden underground throughout this region, waiting to be discovered.

He shone his light forward.

But what's been excavated here? And why?

"It opens up ahead," Gray called out.

In another few yards, the passageway dumped into a domed cavern, sculpted out of the rock.

As Jane followed Gray into the chamber, she stepped over a lip of stone at the threshold. She straightened and gasped, all but twirling in place, casting her light all around.

Derek joined her a moment later and discovered the reason for her shock. "My god . . ."

"It's amazing," Jane murmured.

Derek looked down at his feet. The lip of stone at his toes was just that—a *lip*. It curved delicately around them, sheltering a row of stone teeth, a lower arcade of incisors and molars sculpted out of the sandy floor. A few were cracked and broken. The damage looked recent, triggering a reflexive stitch of anger at the appalling abuse to this archaeological treasure.

He cast his beam around the room, spotlighting its features. A matching lip and curve of teeth hung overhead. The domed ceiling was ridged like a hard palate. Under his feet, the floor arched up in the gentle wave of a sculpted tongue.

Kowalski stretched his back, looking around with a grimace. "Let's hope we don't get chewed up and spat back out."

Jane took slow steps, exploring everything. "The details are anatomically stunning." She pointed her light to a protruding stump of rock. "That must have been where a uvula once hung. And over there, those protrusions on the walls to either side must be tonsils."

"Looks like the left one had a tonsillectomy," Kowalski said, noting more damage there.

Derek stepped forward, illuminating the back of the chamber. Two tunnels led out from here. He knew what they must represent.

"The esophagus and trachea," he murmured.

Indeed the surfaces of one looked smooth and muscular, while the other was ribbed like the cartilage rings found along a human airway. He could even make out vague depictions of a larynx past the triangular flap of an epiglottis on the floor.

"What is all this?" Kowalski asked.

Gray stood a few feet away, shining his light along an arch of the roof, where the hard palate became the soft. "There's writing here. Hieroglyphics."

Derek joined him. Amid all the artistry displayed here, he had missed this detail. Inscribed into the stone archway were three rows of glyphs.

Jane ran her light along the first line.

Derek translated, "*Who comes to the one calling him . . .*"

"I guess that would be us." Kowalski looked around at the giant mouth. "But who is *he*? Whose mouth are we in?"

"That's answered in the next two rows," Jane said, pointing to the hieroglyphs across the arch. "They're the name of an Egyptian god written two different ways."

"What god?" Gray asked.

"He's a late pantheon deity," Jane explained. "Named Tutu. He was originally the protector of tombs."

"Great," Kowalski grumbled.

Jane ignored him. "Later he came to represent the guardian of sleep, the protector of dreams."

"Also the master of demons," Derek reminded her.

Kowalski fixed his mask more securely. "Just gets better and better."

"If this place is truly the source of the pathogen," Jane noted, "that disease could be the very *demon* this sculpted representation of Tutu is guarding."

Derek glanced over to the tunnels leading deeper, picturing an entire body sprawled under these hills, a subterranean god, sleeping for millennia, dreaming all of this time, protecting something dangerous.

But Jane's explanation bothered him. He sensed there was more going on here. Especially since one detail about this was distinctly *wrong*.

He pointed it out. "Jane, look at the last glyph, the one of the seated figure. Normally the name Tutu ends with the figure of a lion or a man."

She nodded. "Because he's always depicted as a beast with the head of a man and a body of a lion."

"Exactly." Derek pointed up. "But at the end of the second row. That's a *woman*, not a man."

Jane stepped closer. "You're right."

"What are you talking about?" Gray asked.

Derek pulled his iPad from his pack to show him. Plus he wanted to take photos to record all of this. He pulled up a catalog of hieroglyphics and showed Gray the two symbols for male and female.

Man   Woman

"See how the man sits cross-legged with an arm raised, whereas the woman kneels demurely." He pointed to the last glyph. "Clearly that's a woman."

Gray frowned behind his mask. "But why's that important?"

Derek shrugged, giving a shake of his head. "I don't know."

"Wait." Jane touched Derek's shoulder, her voice nearly breathless. "Remember that sketch in my father's journal, of the Egyptian oil vessel."

"The *aryballos*. The one with the double heads." Then he saw it, too. "My god, you're right."

"What are you talking about?" Gray asked.

Derek pulled up the picture of the vessel, glad he had taken the time to digitize Harold's old journal. "This was the talisman that was given to Livingstone as a gift for saving a tribesman's son."

"It's also the vessel that was said to hold water from the Nile—back when the river turned bloody," he explained. "After it was opened at the British Museum, the pathogen sealed up inside killed over twenty people."

Gray nodded. "But somehow the outbreak was kept from spreading across England."

"And maybe the same happened during the time of Moses," Jane said. "Maybe the ancients found a cure and somehow my nineteenth-century colleagues replicated it. The answer may lie here."

"Why do you say that?" Gray asked.

Derek answered. "Look at the two heads profiled on the vessel. One of a lion, the other of a woman." He pointed up to the last two rows of hieroglyphics. "And notice the two spellings of Tutu's name. One ends in a *lion*. The other in a kneeling *woman*."

"Same as the vessel," Jane said. "It can't be a coincidence. The *aryballos* must have come from here. It's further proof that the source of the pathogen must lie below—and maybe its cure."

Derek noticed Gray's face. Even behind the protective shield, it was plain the man was deep in thought. Then his eyes widened with some realization.

"I wonder . . ." Gray murmured to himself.

"What is it?" Derek asked.

He shook his head and swung his lamp's beam to the two passages leading deeper. "We should keep going."

They all turned toward the challenge.

"But which way?" Jane asked. "Esophagus or trachea?"

She ducked deeper into the pharynx to get a better look at their choices—then craned her neck, looking straight up.

"Jane?"

"There's an opening." As she stood, her head vanished into the roof. She shuffled her feet to turn fully around. "My god. Come see this."

She shifted to the side to allow Derek and Gray to crowd next to her.

Straightening at her shoulder, Derek poked his head up into a small cavern. The entrance into it was sealed with a clear plastic tarp that had been duct-taped in place, but their lights pierced this protective veil.

"It's a cranial cavity," Jane said.

"She's right." Derek noted how the walls inside had been carved to mimic the folds of a brain, showing even the divisions of its two hemispheres along the domed roof.

Gray shifted his light lower. "Look to the right and left."

His beam illuminated rows of small cubbies dug out of the rock. The niches held grapefruit-sized examples of Egyptian pottery. Some had been shattered in place long ago, leaving behind piles of broken shards. Other cubbies were empty. But those that remained were all a familiar shape and size: sealed jars bearing the profiles of a lion and a woman.

"They're identical to Livingstone's *aryballos*," Jane said, fixing her light on one of the empty niches. "This must be where his vessel had come from. Maybe it was stolen from here long ago."

"No wonder someone sealed this place up." Gray flashed his beam across several piles of broken pottery on the cavern floor.

A few looked freshly shattered.

Had there been an accident?

Jane turned to Derek. "For this collection to be housed here, it suggests the ancient must have known the pathogen sealed in those jars attacked the brain. Why else store it here?"

"You may be right."

Jane sank back down. "And if they knew that, maybe they knew more."

Derek followed her. "Like a possible cure."

She nodded as Gray joined them. She faced the two tunnels leading deeper. "Whatever else they were hiding must lie below." She posed her earlier question again. "But to find it, which path do we take? Esophagus or trachea?"

Derek shifted his beam to the damaged left tonsil. "It looks like there was more traffic in and out of the airway." He pointed out the evident trampling in the trachea compared to the esophagus. "So I say we ignore Robert Frost and take the road *most* traveled."

Gray nodded. "Let's move out."

Only Kowalski seemed disgruntled by this decision. "Yeah, let's go deeper into the belly of a demon-wrestling god. How could that possibly go wrong?"

16

"Ready?" Painter asked.

Kat nodded and shifted her chair back from the table, praying the director's plan would work. "Let's get the ball rolling."

After arriving at Aurora Station, she and Painter had sought to get the lay of the land. They started in the communal dining room over cups of coffee. The latter was a necessity at this late hour. Though she had slept briefly on the plane ride from D.C., her internal clock was all wonky. The caffeine had helped steady her focus.

She would have preferred more time to prepare, but the front edge of the storm would be passing over Ellesmere Island within the hour—which narrowed their window of opportunity. If they were going to attempt this rescue in time to be evacuated by the forces at Thule Air Base, they had to beat the storm.

In other words, now or never.

She eyed her target, waiting for the right moment.

After fueling up on coffee, she and Painter had moved on to the station's recreation area. They had picked a spot neighboring a trio of pool tables. A set of double doors to the right led into a dark movie theater. There was also a gym on the other side, and visible through a window on the far side, a swimming pool glowed a soft blue. A single swimmer had been doing slow laps for the past twenty minutes, reminding Kat of a restless tiger in a cage.

Having trained in intelligence operations, she knew enough psychology to recognize the signs of stress in the handful of base personnel who wandered through the center in the wee hours of the morning. The causes were easy enough to identify. The inhabitants here were isolated, cut off from family and friends. Add to that the bipolar months of endless night or eternal day, which would strain anyone's natural circadian rhythm—no matter how much of the world's best coffee was supplied to them. Also the station was clearly run around the clock, offering little relief to their daily schedule.

She gave her head a sad shake.

All the fake plasma windows looking out onto sunlit beaches and happy pastel-colored walls could not offset human nature.

As expected, the worst afflicted were those on this swing shift. She suspected the individuals assigned this duty were people who did not work well with others, the most antisocial.

And our best targets.

She had selected a broad-shouldered hulk of a brute, who from the grime permanently etched under his nails likely worked in a mechanical bay. He was shooting pool with some buddies in green coveralls, all part of the same work crew. They were blowing off steam after a shift. A row of Foster beer cans lining the edge of the table had been growing steadily longer. Her target glanced her way a few times, whispering every now and again to his mates, often with chuckles.

She imagined there were not that many women working up here.

She waited until the man headed away from the pool table, aiming for one of the bathrooms. His path would take him past their table. As he approached, she stood, telling Painter she was going to the restroom, then timed her turn to bump hard into the large gentleman. She purposefully struggled with him in confusion—then jumped back with a look of fear and affront on her face.

She swore at him and crossed an arm over her chest. She looked to Painter, who was already on his feet. "He . . . he just grabbed my breast."

Painter leaped forward, while the man lifted his palms, unsure what was happening. "What do you think you're doing?" Painter yelled at him.

The man tried to deny her accusation, but he fumbled for words, both inebriated and confused. Painter shoved him—hard. He crashed into the next table, which raised some chuckles from his bunch.

As expected, with his dignity assaulted and too addled to think clearly, the target swung at Painter. The director ducked the fist, and the fight was on. Chairs scattered, punches were thrown, and soon the pair were rolling across the floor. The giant's mates hung back, most clearly believing the wiry stranger was no match for their friend.

Kat grew concerned of the same.

Where the hell is—?

The doors behind her burst open. Three men in black uniforms and caps barreled inside. In the lead was their true target, the spider they had hoped to lure from his web. Anton Mikhailov charged forward, his pale face flushed, making his tattoo stand out angrily. Apparently he saw no reason to cover it up here.

"Stop this right now," he boomed out, his Russian accent thick with fury.

They had anticipated Simon Hartnell would have ordered his head of security to watch over the DARPA investigators, especially when they were out of their rooms. All it took was a little coaxing to get him to join them.

His two men rushed into the fray and tried to pull the fighters apart.

Painter took that moment to demonstrate how much he had been reining in his pugilistic skills. He punched his opponent twice in the face, a roundhouse followed by an uppercut square to the chin. The giant's head cracked back, and he slumped to the floor, out cold.

Painter stood, shaking a bloody fist.

Kat held back a grin.

Never should've doubted you.

"What is this all about?" Anton demanded.

Painter turned to him, his eyes flashing. "What sort of place are you running? This man assaulted my companion." He waved to the others around the pool table. "Fat lot of good they did to stop him."

His insult was sufficient to tweak the others into angry protests.

Kat backed toward Anton, eyeing them. "Can . . . can you please take me to my room?"

"Of course." He waved to his men. "Haul him out of here. We'll deal with this later."

"Thank you," Kat said, feigning great relief, shaking slightly for effect.

Anton led them out of the recreation area and across the communal dining hall to the corridor leading to their room. "I apologize for what happened," he said, stalking stiffly before them. "There will be repercussions. I promise you."

When they reached the door to her room, he used his own keycard to open her door. Clearly he had an all-access pass.

Good.

Kat positioned herself to shield what was to come from the hall camera. She did not know if anyone was still manning the security station, but she wasn't taking any chances.

As the door swung open, Painter shoved Anton into the room and followed on his heels. Kat came behind them, closing the door.

As Anton turned, Painter pointed his SIG Sauer P229 at the man's nose. "Hello, Anton Mikhailov."

The man stiffened in surprise, both at the threat and the use of his true name, but he quickly composed himself.

"What do you want?" he spat back.

Painter cocked the hammer. "You're going to take us to Safia al-Maaz."

3:04 A.M.

"What do you think?" Safia asked Rory.

His face filled her laptop's screen as he leaned closer to his webcam. "You may be on to something."

She nodded. "I'm sorry to wake you, but I couldn't sleep after learning the mummified woman might be Jewish. I tossed and turned—then it struck me that maybe we were looking at this all wrong."

She had the reconstruction of the tattooed hieroglyphics up on her screen. "The challenge of deciphering what was written on her body was difficult enough with the missing sections and glyphs. Still, some of the intact sections should've been readable, but we were assuming she was *Egyptian.*"

Rory sat straighter. "And we know that's not true now."

She pulled up onto the screen what she had been working on all night, wanting Rory as a sounding board.

"We know that Egyptians wrote hieroglyphs in *two* ways," she said. "Some images were simply representational, like a symbol for a cat means 'cat.' But sometimes scribes would phonetically spell the same out. In the ancient Egyptian language, the spoken word for cat is *miw.*"

Rory nodded. "Like the sound a cat makes."

She smiled. "Exactly. So they'd use three symbols to spell the word. Like this."

She brought up the two examples.

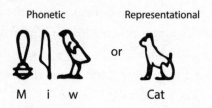

"But if this woman was Jewish and spoke an early form of Hebrew, maybe we need to rethink how we're reading her hieroglyphics. Instead of phonetically spelling out Egyptian words, maybe she was using the only script she knew to spell out her *native* tongue."

"Early Hebrew." Rory pinched his brows together. "But why wouldn't she inscribe herself with Hebrew? We know that written language goes back eight thousand years. And from the radiocarbon dating we got back, we know the mummy is from around 1300 B.C."

"Maybe she was raised in Egypt and taught to write hieroglyphics. It might be the only written language she knew. Which got me thinking."

"About what?"

"What if she's descended from those who fled the plague during the time of Moses, part of a lost Jewish tribe who escaped south rather than east with the rest of their people? That could explain why her group knew to write in hieroglyphics but spoke early Hebrew."

Rory leaned closer, clearly growing excited. "If that group was taught to write, which was rare, it would suggest they were scribes."

She nodded. "A sect that maintains records. So perhaps they sought to preserve knowledge of this plague."

"And maybe how to stop it," Rory whispered. "We could be close to the answer."

Safia knew her primary role here was to follow the thread of history to a possible cure for whatever Harold brought out of the desert. While she worked her angle, other researchers at the station tackled the same question through scientific means. But she still didn't know *what* Simon Hartnell wanted with this cure. When she first met him, he claimed her efforts could save the world.

If so, then why all the bloodshed and secrecy?

Rory drew her back to the topic at hand. "But can we be sure we're on the right track?"

As support, Safia brought more of her work up onto the screen.

S B H

"These three glyphs were marked across her forehead, about where her hairline might have been. They were encircled in a cartouche, as if important. But the three letters—S, B, and H—are gibberish in the Egyptian language, but what if instead those letters spelled out her name phonetically?" She pronounced it aloud. "*Sah-bah.*"

"Why is that significant?"

"*Sabah* is a Hebrew name derived from either Sheba or perhaps Bath-sheba."

"Like from the Bible."

She nodded. She had her own connection to that heritage, but that was a long story for another time. So she continued, "The typical meaning for that name is *daughter of the oath* . . . which can be interpreted as someone who is good at keeping secrets."

"Which she certainly is." Rory suddenly cracked a wide yawn. "But maybe we need to continue this in the morning."

She grinned. "You're right. Get some sleep, and I'll try to do the same."

They said their good nights, and Safia reluctantly closed her computer. She wasn't sure she could sleep, but she should try. She stood, stretched, and took a step toward her bed—then froze when she heard the rasp of the door bolt being pulled.

She turned, taking a step back, expecting the worst.

The door opened, and Anton entered, his face nearly purplish with fury.

Her heart pounded in her throat, panicked.

What did I do wrong?

Then suddenly he was shoved from behind. Two figures followed him into her cell. One was a stranger, but the other made her want to sob with relief.

"Painter . . ."

3:23 A.M.

Painter left Kat to guard Anton and strode forward. He embraced Safia, feeling her shake in his arms. "Are you okay?"

"Better now," she mumbled.

"Then how about we get you out of here?"

"That sounds splendid."

He let her go and guided her to the door.

"Wait." She broke away and grabbed a laptop from a small desk. "What about Rory?"

Kat glanced hard her way but kept her SIG Sauer pointed at Anton's neck. "Rory McCabe? He's here?"

Safia nodded. "A prisoner like me. It's a long story."

Painter scowled. No wonder Anton had been willing to bring them here, even at gunpoint. *The bastard had been holding an ace up his sleeve.*

"Do you know where he's being held?" Kat asked.

"I . . . I don't know. They always brought me to my room first."

Painter swung toward Anton. "Looks like we have another stop to make before we leave."

Anton glanced to a camera mounted on the room's ceiling, then smiled coldly. "No."

His expression told Painter everything. This had been his plan all along. A delaying tactic. They had marched Anton here with a pistol pressed into his lower back, avoiding cameras as much as possible.

But now?

Painter crossed to him, but Anton lifted his chin, ready to take whatever abuse was to be inflicted. But Painter had other intentions.

When you have a crap hand, your best move is to bluff.

"How much do you love your sister?" he asked. "And we know her name isn't *Velma.*"

Anton's eyes narrowed. Painter had already demonstrated knowledge of Anton's real name, so it was easy enough to get the man to believe he had the same intel on his sister.

Painter pressed his case. "You both clearly share a connection . . . or at least, the same taste in tattoos." He touched his own cheek. "Did you get them before or after the Guild hired you?"

Anton stiffened, clearly unsettled by this intimate knowledge of their past.

Now to drive it home.

"We have your sister in custody," he lied. "Interpol picked her up an hour ago. That's why we made our move just now. If you want to see her alive again, then you'll take us to Rory and escort us to the nearest exit."

Past a window in Safia's cell, storm clouds had swallowed the sun as the weather front moved over the island. Once out there, Painter planned on using his satellite phone to call in the forces waiting at Thule. If there was a problem, the backup plan was to commandeer a vehicle and take off into the neighboring icy mountains to await rescue, using the storm as cover.

But all those plans hinged on how much Anton loved his sister.

The man stared daggers at Painter, then finally heaved out a growled sigh. "He is not far."

Kat poked Anton with her pistol. "Then show us."

Painter opened the door, checked the hallway, then marched out with Safia beside him. He kept his pistol at his thigh. "Stay close."

Kat followed with Anton. She kept hold of the back of his belt with her gun against the base of his spine. They headed over two passageways and around a corner. It truly wasn't far.

Anton nodded to a door. "In there."

Painter used the all-access keycard he had pilfered from Anton and swiped open the lock. He then pulled the bolt and hauled open the door.

The room was dark. A figure jolted from a bed against the wall. "Who . . . what is going on?"

Safia stepped forward. "Rory, it's me."

"Safia?"

She quickly explained as the young man's gaze shifted all around, struggling to catch up. "Come," she said, waving to him. "We have to hurry."

Rory had already gained his feet and was tugging a pair of coveralls over his boxers. As he struggled to dress, he looked at her. "But Safia . . ."

"What?"

"The mummy. It's the only hope for a cure. If what you described about the plague spreading in Egypt and back home . . ."

Safia turned to Painter. "How bad has it gotten?"

Kat answered, "Bad."

"And likely to get worse," Painter added, remembering Dr. Kano's warning of the secondary genetic damage that could last generations.

Safia turned to Rory and lifted the laptop clutched to her chest. "I have the data we already collected."

Rory looked scared, divided between wanting to run and knowing what they might leave behind. "But you know it's incomplete."

Safia turned to Painter. "He's right. If they destroy the mummy, any hope for a cure could be lost."

Painter didn't fully understand what she was talking about, but he trusted the certainty in her eyes. "What can we do? It's not like we can haul a mummified body out with us."

She looked crestfallen. "It's also contaminated, like Professor Mc-Cabe's body. They have it locked in a biolab."

"Then we leave it," Kat said. "We can secure it once Colonel Wycroft's forces arrive."

Rory pulled on a set of boots. "I read the protocol," he said. "At the first sign of a security breach, they're going to incinerate the lab."

Painter didn't doubt such a failsafe had been established. The enemy had done the same with the professor's body back in the United Kingdom, firebombing the research lab where it had been held. Anton also offered further confirmation by sneering at Rory, furious at him for revealing this detail.

"We'll only have this one opportunity," Safia said.

Rory offered a suggestion, heaving to his feet. "The 3-D scanner."

Safia straightened. "My god, that's right. We left the mummy in a topographical scanner. To complete a detailed intradermal map of the body's entire surface." She checked her watch. "It should be done by now."

Rory nodded. "If we can pull the results and take them with us . . ."

Safia winced. "That means going back to the biolab."

Kat glanced at Painter and lifted a brow. "So one more stop?"

"We'll have to be quick."

She faced Safia. "How far away is it?"

"Not too far, but it's down three levels."

So back into the heart of the station.

Kat shared a worried look with Painter. "Maybe it's best if we don't lead a parade down there." She eyed Anton, plainly not trusting his cooperation for much longer.

"I can take Rory," Painter said. "You all hole up here."

Kat shook her head. "Two women would pose less of a threat. Especially if one is wearing a security uniform and escorting a female prisoner."

Painter wanted to argue but recognized the advantage to Kat's plan. And she certainly looked unwilling to bend on this point.

Safia stepped forward. "I can do this."

With the matter decided, Painter pointed his weapon at Anton. "Strip."

In moments, Kat had changed into his black coveralls. She tucked up her hair and pulled on his security cap. She then turned to Safia. "Ready?"

Though Safia eyes shone with fear, she nodded.

Kat led her to the door. She checked to make sure the way was clear, then ushered her outside. Before leaving, she glanced back. "I'll keep her safe."

Painter nodded and swallowed hard.

She closed the door behind her.

Painter kept his weapon leveled at Anton. In boxers and bare feet, the man looked less of a threat, but Painter refused to let down his guard. He kept Anton standing against the wall with his hands up. Those cold eyes ignored him, tracking instead Rory as he paced anxiously back and forth by the door.

Finally that gaze settled back on him. "You will never get away from here," Anton said, his accent heavy with disgust. "Both your women will suffer."

"We'll see about—"

Painter sensed the threat a moment too late. A shift of shadows, a scrape of metal on metal. He turned to see Rory swinging a desk lamp at his head. The heavy base caught him square on the temple. Pain and bright light flared across his skull. He fell down to a knee.

Anton leaped from the wall, grabbed his arm, and twisted the pistol from his grip.

Painter toppled to his side, his head still ringing.

With the stolen gun pointed at his new prisoner, Anton reached and touched Rory on the arm, almost tenderly. "Well done, my *tigryenok*."

Anton passed Rory the pistol, then efficiently patted down Painter's body, removing his satellite phone. Once satisfied there were no other weapons or means of communication, he stood and backed toward the door.

Rory's expression was apologetic. "You don't understand what's at stake," he tried to explain, as Anton drew him out of the room.

As the pair left, bolting the door behind them, Painter did understand one thing.

It seemed Anton had had more than one ace up his sleeve all along.

With a groan, he remembered Kat's last words, hoping they proved true.

I'll keep her safe.

3:40 A.M.

From the safety of the anteroom, Kat watched Safia enter the secure lab. Suited up and dragging an air hose, she looked as if she were wading into the depths of a toxic sea.

The two of them had wasted no time getting down here. Luckily they had not run into anyone in the halls at this lonely hour, and Anton's passkey had gained them easy entry into the deserted lab. The smoothness of everything set Kat's teeth on edge, even here in the locked room.

C'mon, Safia, hurry up.

Despite the urgency twanging her every nerve, Kat recognized that Safia had to follow proper safety protocols. The woman stepped over to a computer station with cables running to four laser cameras that looked like long-barreled pistols, all pointing toward a diminutive, shrunken figure seated with her head bowed on a black throne.

On the way down here, Safia had told her the body had been recovered from a dig in the Sudan, from wherever Professor McCabe had vanished. She had been assigned to learn this ancient woman's secret. The enemy believed her body held a possible clue to the cure for the pandemic spreading around the world. Safia also believed that Simon Hartnell wanted this knowledge for a very different reason—but what that might be remained a mystery.

Safia tapped at the keyboard and a tray opened to the side. She removed the silvery disk holding the data of the scan and slipped it into a plastic pouch. She had warned Kat that the pouch would also have to be bathed in a disinfectant dunk tank before being taken out. Preparing for that, Safia sought to seal the bag, but her gloved fingers hampered her efforts.

C'mon . . .

Sudden knocking on the door made Kat jump. A familiar voice called from the hallway, breathless and scared.

"Hello, hello!"

Kat stalked to the door. "Rory?"

"Thank god! Hurry!" He sounded winded, like he'd run the entire way. "Anton attacked your friend. I left them fighting. We need to go now!"

"Safia's still working. I'll let you in."

She unlocked the door with Anton's card and yanked the door hard. Caught off guard while leaning there, Rory stumbled inside. Kat helped him the rest of the way by grabbing the collar of his coverall and tossing him behind her. She then swung low across the threshold with her pistol raised. As she feared, she spotted a shadowy figure down the hall and shot wildly.

A pained gasp followed—accompanied by return fire.

Rounds shot over her head; she heard glass shatter behind her, and Rory cried out. She kept her position but dropped flat to the ground, refusing to give up the advantage of her sheltered position. The gunman, exposed out in the open hallway, was forced to retreat. He laid down a protective barrage until he reached a far corner and slipped out of view. She noted the thick blood trail leading there.

Satisfied for the moment, she rolled inside. As she slammed the door, an alarm Klaxon erupted outside, echoing through the station.

Kat shifted the smoking muzzle of her gun toward Rory. When he had arrived a moment ago, she suspected something was amiss, especially after his frantic assertion that Anton had gotten the better of Painter. That seemed unlikely, so she had acted accordingly. If she had been wrong, she would've apologized later for her rough treatment of him.

No apology was necessary now.

She stared at Rory. His act had been *too* good to be forced. He must have been playing them all along—including taking advantage of Safia's sympathy. Even a moment ago, he must have been trying to lure them out of this highly sensitive room before they barricaded themselves inside.

Rory ignored the threat of Kat's weapon. Instead, he stared in horror at the biolab. Only now did she note the two bullet holes cracked through the window.

Rory took a step back. "Oh, no . . ."

She stood, fearing the worst.

She looked into the next room. Safia was still on her feet—but one of the stray rounds had shredded through her hood, missing her head by inches. The same couldn't be said of the seated mummy. Its desiccated skull had exploded, struck by the same round or another. As Safia turned toward them, gore from the blowback coated her damaged faceplate.

Rory called to her, pointing. "Safia! Get in the chemical shower!"

Kat was surprised by the depth of the traitor's concern and reinforced it. "Do it! Hurry!"

Her sharp shout snapped Safia out of her shock and got her moving.

Rory turned to Kat and pointed above the damaged window to a timer counting down from two minutes. "With the lab's seal broken, the automatic failsafe has engaged. It allows two minutes for evacuation, then everything's incinerated in there."

Already metal gates were lowering over the window.

"Is there a way to stop it?"

"Maybe, but I don't know how."

Inside the lab, Safia had fled to the shower station. She slapped her palm on the emergency rinse. Disinfectant foam and spray swamped over her suit and the plastic pouch in her other hand. She waited until the grime was washed away, then stepped into the small changing room. She stripped off the suit in a panic, still wearing her gray coveralls beneath.

Behind her, the door into the lab was being sealed with steel shutters.

Safia glanced over her shoulder. Her eyes were wide with fear, but contamination was the least of the pressing dangers.

Rory backed away as Safia shouldered through the last door to join them. His face was a mask of guilt. "You weren't supposed to be hurt. He promised."

Safia looked between the weapon in Kat's hand and Rory. "What's happening?"

"We're getting out of here," she answered and steadied her gun on Rory. "And you're coming with us."

Kat drew them all to the door. She checked the hallway. She didn't know if Anton was still hiding around the corner or if he had sought medical attention. Either way, she knew reinforcements were likely converging here. Her only hope was to take advantage of the momentary chaos, praying a majority of Anton's crew had been off duty at this late hour, buying her an extra minute of lead time.

As an additional precaution, she grabbed a fistful of Rory's collar and positioned him between her and the far corner.

Rory noted blood trail on the floor. "Anton . . ."

Kat motioned Safia to get behind her. Using Rory as a human shield, she retreated. She had the schematic of the station fixed in her head. There was an underground garage two flights above their heads.

When she was halfway down the hall, a low roaring sounded through the wall. She pictured jets of fire sweeping the lab and shied away from that side.

Time to go.

She rushed them toward an elevator bay at the end of the hallway, punched the button, then piled into the cage as it opened. A quick ascent and the doors opened into a cavernous garage space. She hurried toward a row of parked Sno-Cats. Their square cabins sat atop treaded tracks, looked like miniature tanks.

She picked one and ordered Rory, "Get in back."

Cowed by her weapon, he obeyed.

Kat passed her gun to Safia. "Climb in front but watch him. If he even breathes suspiciously, shoot him."

Though still plainly in shock, she nodded.

Kat hurried to the other side and found keys already hanging from the ignition. She was not surprised. Who would be foolish enough to steal a vehicle up here?

That would be me.

Kat got behind the wheel, started the engine, and jerked the vehicle into gear. The treads ground along the concrete floor. She turned toward a ramp leading to a sealed garage door. A pole with a keypad stood at the foot of the ramp. Once she reached there, she willed Anton's keycard to still work and waved it over the reader.

A welcome grinding of a motor followed.

She sighed with relief—but they weren't out of danger yet.

As the door opened, winds whipped into the garage. A steady howling pierced the sealed cabin of the Sno-Cat. The storm had finally swallowed the island. Dark clouds roiled overhead, low enough that she swore the roof of the vehicle brushed through them as she trundled out into the storm.

She set a course to the northeast, aiming for the ice-capped mountains of neighboring Quttinirpaaq National Park. In less than a hundred yards, the isolated station vanished into the darkness behind her.

Still, she searched in the rearview mirror, watching for pursuers who she knew would come. But for the moment, a larger fear weighed upon her.

What would happen to Painter?

17

My god . . .

Stunned, Gray stepped into the stone thorax of the sleeping god. The others followed, casting beams of light from their helmets across the cavernous space. Surprised gasps rose behind him, but he could not rip his gaze from the sights ahead.

The chamber could easily hold a small baseball stadium. Giant stone ribs had been carved along the walls. They curved upward to connect to a row of thoracic vertebrae along the roof. The arch of the spine ran from one end of the cavity to the other and vanished into the far wall, which was bowed in the shape of a human diaphragm.

"The details are stunning," Jane murmured. "Look at the striations between the ribs."

"Intercostal muscles," Gray commented, as if giving an anatomy lesson.

Derek shone his light along a shoulder-high wall that divided the room in half. "That must represent the chest's mediastinum." He lifted his beam higher, illuminating a cloudlike formation topping one section. "They even included a thymus gland."

But none of these anatomical details were the main attraction.

As they continued deeper into the room, they were all drawn to the most singular sight in the entire chamber. In the center, a massive stone heart looked as if it hung from the roof by a tangle of muscular blood vessels, including a massive aortic arch. Each of its four chambers was meticulously carved, covered with branching carotid arteries.

Though the entire sculpture appeared weightless, the bottom of the heart rested atop a section of floor fashioned to resemble a sternum.

"There's a door into the left ventricle," Jane noted as she drew nearer.

Gray spotted ancient bricks stacked to the side. They must have been used to seal that doorway long ago. But what was hidden inside?

This question drew them all forward.

Derek shone his light through the small doorway. "It's empty."

Gray was disappointed but not surprised. Despite the wonders found here, the place had clearly been ransacked. From the condition of the debris left behind, the theft had been recent. Across the floor were tables and benches. A row of bunk beds lined the ribbed wall.

Someone had been camping inside here—and likely for a long time.

The wonder dimmed in Jane's eyes, replaced with a haunted look. "This must be where my father was held." She turned in a slow circle, as if searching for him. "But why?"

Gray studied what was left, trying to fill in the blanks. Tall pole lamps dotted the floor, while elsewhere strings of electrical lights ran up the wall. He followed the wires to where a row of generators must have once stood. One table held the smashed remains of a desktop computer. He absently wondered if its hard drive was still recoverable, but he doubted whoever had cleared out of here would have been so lax.

Nearby, a row of bookshelves had been emptied, with the last case toppled over on its back. He imagined ghostly researchers moving throughout here, working on the chamber's mysteries.

Now they were all gone after scrubbing the place.

Farther along the chamber, Kowalski crouched by the wall. "Guys, look at this."

They converged on his location.

Kowalski probed his beam into a hole at the base of two ribs. Gray had noted similar openings on both sides of the chamber. Again small stone bricks were scattered at the threshold.

As they joined him, Kowalski shifted his light to a niche above the hole. Inside stood a small wooden elephant with a curled trunk and a pair of yellowed slivers for tusks. It was beautifully wrought with some of the original bark left in place to look like the pachyderm's rough skin.

"What is it?" Gray asked.

Jane leaned closer. "It looks to be a small pot. You can see the line along the beast's back that must form the top."

"Can we take it?" Kowalski asked, looking avidly at it. Gray knew the big man had a fascination with elephants.

Jane reached for it, but Derek held her back. "It might not be safe."

She scowled at him. "My father would surely have examined it. If it was dangerous, I think he would have sealed it in plastic, like we saw with the skull." She waved to similar niches above the other low holes. "Plus this isn't the only one."

"Still, it could be contaminated."

She sighed and straightened, heeding his warning, and left it alone.

Kowalski looked no happier.

"What about the hole below it?" Gray asked, redirecting everyone's attention.

Derek crouched, shining his light inside. "I think it's an old tomb."

Gray peered inside. The chamber was narrow but deep. Definitely could hold a body. Only the walls of the tomb were blackened and covered in ash. He also spotted shards of burnt bone.

This desecration looked recent.

A red gasoline jug lay nearby, supporting this assessment.

Derek came to the same conclusion and cast his gaze to the other open tombs. "They incinerated all the bodies. Destroying everything."

Not everything.

Gray pictured the scroll of tattooed skin in the test tube. Had the professor cut it off one of the entombed mummies in order to preserve it?

Derek stood up. "But why did they cremate all of the bodies? Because of a fear of contagion? Or were they just burning bridges before they left?"

Jane glanced over to the center of the room. "I also saw some charcoal around the base of the heart, but it looked from a much older fire."

Curious, Gray headed back over.

The heart must be important.

Once there, he ducked through the low doorway and crouched inside. Its inner surfaces were pristine, decorated with a flock of butterflies etched into the stone. The work looked delicate, almost feminine.

Something strange caught his eye.

"Jane, what do you make of this?" he called out.

She crowded in with him, followed by Derek. As she looked at the walls, she accidentally stepped on a potsherd. She winced and tenderly collected it from the floor, shining her light on its dusty blue surface.

Derek looked over her shoulder. "It's a shard of lapis lazuli."

"Maybe from a bowl." She glanced around the chamber. "Lapis lazuli was a stone revered by the Egyptians for its magical properties."

Her gaze again was captured by the decoration on the walls. She swept her light all around.

"It's beautiful . . ." she murmured. "I've always loved butterflies. To the Egyptians, the image symbolized transformation. The caterpillar becoming the butterfly."

Gray studied the space, wondering about the chamber's purpose, noting the clues left here.

Magic and transformation.

He sensed he was close to something important, but maybe it wasn't for him to solve. He centered his light on the one last strange detail here. It was the reason he had called Jane inside.

She looked to where he pointed and gasped, falling back a step.

One of the butterflies had been circled—with Jane's name written there.

"My father must have done this," she murmured. Her fingers lifted to touch the mark, to make this connection to the past, but she hesitated. "Why would he do it?"

Derek tried to answer. "The nomads who found Harold mentioned he kept whispering your name over and over." He touched her shoulder. "Maybe he hoped you would find this."

Jane stepped back, looking to Derek, then Gray. "I don't understand."

"Perhaps your father thought you could solve this," Gray offered. "At least, with enough time."

He wondered if this was the same reason the enemy had been hounding Jane, trying to grab her. If the professor had left this clue behind, they might believe she knew something about it, a way to unravel this mystery.

Instead, Jane only looked more scared and confused.

"Perhaps we should keep searching," Gray said. "There may be other clues."

They all exited, but Gray did not hold out much hope. He sensed anything truly important would have been hidden here, in the literal heart of this stone god.

He was also keenly aware of the passage of time, like a pressure building around him.

We've already been down here too long.

9:38 A.M.

The only warning was a trickle of pebbles.

The thin flow dribbled down the cliff on her left side. Seichan ignored it and continued riding the Suzuki down the throat of the cleft. She was headed back to the bowl that hid the entrance to the caverns under the surrounding hills. Forty-five minutes ago, she had borrowed Ahmad's bike and began a canvass of the immediate area, sweeping back and forth along the fissure that led into the valley.

She had left the boy and his dog inside the parked Unimog with orders to hit the horn at the first sign of any trouble. She also left him with a radio and additional instructions.

She could not be certain her group had been followed, so she simply assumed it was true and planned accordingly. She had made herself the obvious target, drawing the attention of any hidden eyes. She let them see it was only the boy in the truck. She wanted them to lower their guard while they assessed the situation, to recognize the others had gone below.

Especially Jane McCabe.

Seichan imagined the young woman remained the primary target, and the enemy would waste minutes strategizing.

In turn, she used the passing time to acquaint herself with Ahmad's bike, testing the traction of the rear tire's paddled tread, discovering it was perfect for sand, less so for rock. Her only accommodation to the fall of pebbles was to shift closer to the same cliff, making an overhead shot more difficult.

She showed no other reaction. Even her heartbeat didn't change. If anything, she was relieved to see rock-hard evidence of the ghosts haunting these hills. Knowing they were truly here, she settled in, savoring the trickle of adrenaline.

Her vision sharpened.

She could guess the enemy's plan easily enough. In this situation, the only smart play would be to wait for their targets to show themselves and ambush them in the open, especially if they wanted to take Jane McCabe alive.

Seichan could not allow that.

With her face wrapped in a scarf, she whispered to activate the radio hidden at her lips. "Ahmad, be ready."

She kept the same pace as she neared the valley again.

She heard the truck engine engage, its growl echoing off the bowl's walls. Earlier, she had asked Ahmad if he knew how to drive. He had scoffed as if the question insulted his manhood. She had him prove it nonetheless, circling the bowl twice.

She trusted the enemy would believe the boy had grown bored and was preparing to take the Unimog for another joyride.

But not this time. This time it was serious.

When she entered the valley, he already had the truck trundling toward her. She lifted an arm as if greeting him—then cut her arm down.

He gunned the engine and shot toward her.

She dropped low in her seat and throttled the bike into a scream. Her rear tire spun, kicking sand, then the paddles caught traction. She leaped forward, aiming for the truck's bumper.

She spotted Ahmad's face behind the windshield. He looked scared but he didn't slow. At the last moment, she let him win this game of chicken and angled the bike sharply away. The Unimog's bulk shot past her and continued for the narrow fissure. She wanted the boy and the truck out of here—both to keep him from harm and to protect their only vehicle.

Once clear of the truck, she canted the bike sharply, shifting all of her weight to one peg. As the cycle spun around, she whipped her pistol from a holster strapped to her thigh. She aimed for the side of the cleft where the pebbles had fallen. She trusted that whoever had given themselves away had followed her the rest of the way here.

The sudden commotion on the valley floor succeeded in getting the man to show himself—if only a shift of shadows.

She fired wildly in that direction. She did not expect to hit her target, only buy an extra moment for Ahmad to reach the cover of the cliffs, which he did. The truck vanished into the shadows. She trusted the enemy wouldn't abandon the valley to go after the boy—at least not right away. The enemy would want to secure their primary target first.

Or let's hope so.

To further encourage their attention, Seichan raced into the shadows, trimming along the edge of the valley. She shot blindly at the same spot on the cliff. Finally, puffs of sand peppered the floor around her, accompanied by the faint cracks of a rifle.

Good.

She slalomed expertly across the shadows, staying on the gas, bouncing on the pegs to juke the bike into sudden turns. She returned fire as she ascertained the relative position of the sniper. As she performed her acrobatics for another minute, her heart raced in tune with the engine. A smile formed under her scarf as the ends whipped around her face.

Once satisfied she had bought Ahmad the additional time necessary to clear the cleft and reach the open terrain beyond, she swung the bike in a full one-eighty and sped for the entrance to the caverns below.

As she neared the cliff, she did not slow. She thumbed on the bike's headlamp, ducked low to the handlebars, and shot straight through the doorway.

Time to take this fight underground.

9:53 A.M.

Jane gathered with the others before the only opening that led out of the thoracic cavity and deeper into the slumbering stone god. She glanced back to the heart, now sunk into darkness behind her, still picturing the scrawled message left by her father. With no clue to its meaning, she turned toward the next step of their journey.

An archway cut through the two-foot-thick stone diaphragm at the base of chest. Their combined lights revealed masses of sandstone overhanging the far side. Ancient hands and tools had polished the surfaces almost to a glassy sheen.

"Must be the lobes of the liver," Derek said, his right hand rubbing under his own ribs as if probing for the same.

Darker shadows beckoned them deeper into what must be the abdominal cavity.

Jane felt a queasiness at venturing in there—not from any anatomical disgust about what might await her ahead, but from her fear that she might let her father down. He had left her a message, possibly dying to deliver it.

And I have no clue what it means.

Derek kept to her side, as if sensing her distress. "Maybe we should take a break and—"

Gray jerked around. "Quiet."

Then Jane heard it, too. The whine of an engine. It grew steadily louder. They all turned around. A dim light glowed from the throat of the giant, then suddenly brightened as something shot out of the airway and into the thorax. Tires skidded across the floor, slowing the object's trajectory into the chamber.

It was Ahmad's bike.

Its rider straightened from a low crouch in the seat.

"Seichan!" Gray called over to her.

But she had already spotted their illuminated group and throttled the engine back up. The roaring reverberated across the enclosed space as she raced over to them. She drew to a full stop but remained seated.

She wore no helmet, but she had strapped on her protective mask. Her gaze took in the room, but her words were for them all. "Company's coming."

"Where's Ahmad?" Gray asked.

Seichan twisted in her seat and unstrapped a pack from the back of her bike. "He's safe. For now. Sent him off with the truck." She tossed the pack toward Gray, who caught it. "Grabbed our gear. Extra magazines, flash-bangs, smoke bombs. Kowalski's Piezer is folded in there, too. It won't be long before they come down here and try to flush us out."

Her eyes settled on Jane, her emphasis easy to read.

The enemy has come for me.

Jane pictured her father's message.

Derek took her hand, plainly understanding the same. "What do we do?"

Gray turned the question back on him. "Could there be another exit?"

Derek shrugged. "I don't . . . probably, I guess."

She squeezed his hand. "He's right. These ancients often built escape galleries leading out from their sacred structures."

Derek glanced to the thoracic cavity and back to the archway leading to the abdomen. "We entered through the mouth, so if these builders continued to stick to proper anatomy . . ."

Kowalski groaned. "You've got to be shittin' me."

Gray patted him on the shoulder. "Let's hope that's the case. It may be our only way out."

He herded them toward the archway, while Seichan followed with the bike.

As they passed under the lobes of the liver, Derek shone his light on a stone sphere nestled higher up. "Gallbladder," he mumbled, a trickle of awe in his voice despite the danger.

Jane still held his hand and appreciated something solid to grip, to help anchor herself. She stayed with him as they ventured deeper into the peritoneal cavity of the abdomen. The group's helmet lamps and the headlight of the bike illuminated the wonders found here.

They rounded the bulge of a giant stomach, which rested atop a stone spleen, and discovered most of the cavity ahead was a single mass of rock sculpted into coils and tangles, representing the god's intestines. Again the details were amazing, from the hints of folded omentum wrapped around the internal organs to the tracery of blood vessels over all the surfaces.

Higher still, a row of vertebrae arched across the roof and vanished into the dark depths of the abdomen. To either side, the walls had been carved into two huge kidneys, which looked precariously hung there and about to fall down.

"Over here," Seichan said.

She guided her bike to the stomach and speared her headlight at a narrow opening in its side.

A door . . .

Gray stepped over and poked his head into the stomach. "I can see where the esophagus dumps in here." He shifted his shoulders. "And another passageway heads out."

Derek stared across the breadth of the cavern. "It must lead through the rest of the intestinal tract. Ending hopefully at another exit. It might not be the most dignified way of escaping, but we don't have much choice."

As Gray straightened, Seichan pulled him a step aside. "I left Ahmad with a radio and a GPS. Told him to get clear and that I'd radio our position if we found a way out." She glanced to Jane. "But we know *who* the enemy's true target is. Same as back at Ashwell."

Gray seemed to understand her unspoken implication. "Then you need to get Jane out of here." He glanced to the group. "But for you to truly get away, we'll have to distract the enemy, keep them focused down here. Hopefully by the time they realize you've escaped . . ."

"We'll be in the Unimog and heading for Khartoum. Once they figure that out, they'll come after us, which may allow you all the time to get free, too."

"So win-win," he said grimly, looking far from convinced of the likelihood of that outcome.

Jane resented that they were treating her like a football, giving her no say in the matter. Derek had overheard their conversation and came to a different conclusion.

"They're right," he said. "Harold left that message for you. You're too important to risk."

She saw the look in his eyes; the worry shining from his face had nothing to do with saving the world. "But I don't know what my father—"

He squeezed her hand. "You will."

She stared toward the door into the stomach. "But what if we're wrong? What if there's no exit back there?"

From a step away, Kowalski offered additional support. "I'm sure there's a way out."

"How can you be so sure?"

He urged her toward the opening. "I read it in a book."

Even Gray was puzzled by this response. "What book?"

Kowalski sighed, exasperated. "*Everybody Poops.*" He waved an arm to encompass the cavern. "That's gotta apply to this big guy, too."

Gray groaned.

Jane smiled, feeling the tension ease across her shoulders.

"Man makes sense," Derek said.

Seichan simply shook her head and pushed her bike through the door and into the stomach. They would need the cycle's speed if the two of them ever reached the desert.

With no choice but to accept this plan, Jane started to follow her, but Derek held her back.

"Be careful." He leaned forward and hugged her, appearing for a moment like he wanted to kiss her, but their masks made that impossible.

She hugged him back instead, holding tight for a long breath, then finally let go. "I'll see you soon."

"You'd better."

She turned and climbed after Seichan. Once inside, she spotted the tunnel leading out into the intestinal maze. The opening was halfway up the curved stomach wall. Her gaze swept over the rest of the gastric chamber. The surface was covered in what appeared to be shriveled ulcers—then she realized they were *faces,* with sunken eyes and blank expressions.

She balked at the sight, her skin pebbling with superstitious fear.

Jane jumped as Seichan started the engine and throttled its growl into a deafening roar.

Seichan patted the seat behind her. "Hop on."

"What are you—?"

"Get over here."

Cringing, Jane crossed to the bike, hooked a leg, and dropped onto the padded seat.

"Hold tight!"

Jane barely got her arms around the woman's waist when she gunned the engine. The bike spun in a tight circle, gaining momentum, then shot up the sloped wall and dropped through the opening.

Jane ducked from the low roof.

Ahead, the headlamp revealed the twisted roller coaster stretching before them.

"Here we go!" Seichan called back, sounding as if she were smiling.

Jane snagged her arms more tightly around Seichan.

Oh, god . . .

10:08 A.M.

Valya watched from the top of the sun-blasted cliffs.

Her vantage overlooked the shadowy bowl of the valley. She waited until the last of Kruger's men vanished through the dark doorway into the mysteries below. She could have accompanied them, but she did not trust the woman who guarded their target.

Seichan.

Earlier, Valya had watched her ride back and forth along the floor of the fissure. From her height, she had tried to read meaning in the tracks left in the sand by her bike. She had suspected the woman was doing more than just guarding the far end of that cleft, keeping them from blocking the way out.

Seichan must have suspected their presence—or at least, made plans as if they were here. She knew Valya's team would wait until the others climbed out of the hole, to trap them in the open.

So instead, you forced our hand, wanting us to play your game.

Though Valya was willing to follow along—sending Kruger and his men below—she was not foolish enough to leave the surrounding deserts unguarded and unwatched. She refused to be tricked by that traitor into loosening the cordon around these hills.

To help her in this duty, she stepped away from the cliff and picked up the second of the team's two UAV drones. She set the Raven's propellers to turning, then lifted it high. She returned to the cliff and cast the bird into the sky. It dipped for a breath, then its four-foot-long wings caught a thermal rising from the valley. It rose into the sky and started to circle out.

The bird would be her eyes, spying from on high across all these broken hills.

A handheld monitor displayed its feed, split between two screens.

The first screen showed a truck trundling across the desert.

She had already cast the first Raven aloft, sending it after the fleeing Unimog. She wanted to know if it turned back. She briefly considered sending one of Kruger's scouts to chase it down with one of their motor-cycles, but she didn't want to weaken the forces sent below.

The primary objective remained Jane McCabe.

Plus the Raven watching the truck continued to broadcast an interfer-ence net over the escaping vehicle, blocking any transmissions, isolating the driver. It would be hours before he could reach help.

She settled to a crouch, balancing on her toes at the cliff's edge.

If Kruger's men failed to handle matters below and allowed the others to pop their heads above the sand . . .

She picked up her assault rifle.

I'll be waiting for you.

18

"I hope you're comfortable," Simon Hartnell said.

Painter stared down at his wrists bound in tight handcuffs. His ankles were shackled to a steel chair. They were clearly taking no chances with him. He had been marched at gunpoint to this small library in Hartnell's private residential level. After securing him, the guards had retreated through the door. Notably absent during all of this was Anton, but what did that mean?

"Where is Kathryn Bryant?" Painter asked.

"That's a good question. The last sight we had of her was when her Sno-Cat disappeared into the storm."

Painter took grim satisfaction at the news.

So she got away.

"She's done a surprising amount of damage," Hartnell said. "More than she truly knows."

Sounds like Kat.

"But she'll be dealt with." Hartnell stalked around his desk and leaned against it, like a teacher about to scold a student. "I think we got off on the wrong foot, you and I. You're a man of science, so perhaps I should have been more up front."

Painter let him talk as he studied the room. A computer station with multiple monitors covered one wall, but the rest of the space was paneled and shelved in mahogany, with rows of dusty books and small illuminated museum cases. His gaze lingered a moment too long on a pair of tall-masted sailing ships—detailed wooden models of nineteenth-century frigates.

Hartnell noted his attention. "The HMS *Terror* and *Erebus*. They were former warships turned into vessels of exploration."

Painter knew those names and the tragic story that went with them. "As I recall, the pair vanished into the Arctic, while searching for the Northwest Passage."

"Indeed. Back in 1896, the two ships became trapped in ice off the coast of King William Island, not far from here. The crew's story became one of deprivation, madness, and death. All hands were lost, including a distant relative of mine, John Hartnell, who accompanied the voyage only to end up in a shallow grave on nearby Beechey Island." He gave a sorrowful shake of his head. "I visited the burial site myself recently, to pay my respects to such an enterprising and determined young man."

"It seems some men reach too far."

Hartnell ignored his veiled insinuation. "In John's case, his downfall wasn't his *ambition*, as it was a few bad cases of Goldner's Patent meat. Tests on the young man's cold, mummified remains showed he suffered lead poisoning from the cans, which likely drove him and the others insane." He nodded to the ships. "Still, you are right about the story being a cautionary tale—but not how you think."

"Then how?"

"Did you know that, due to the extensive melting of ice throughout the Arctic, cruise ships—full of passengers sipping cocktails and dining in fine restaurants—now sail the Northwest Passage, navigating the same waters traveled by the *Terror* and the *Erebus*?" He scowled. "Tourists come here to see the top of the world, when in fact they are witnessing its end."

"From climate change?" Painter goaded the man with the doubt in his voice, hoping to get a rise out of him, to get him to reveal more than he intended. He knew how much this topic was an obsession for the CEO of Clyffe Energy. "Don't you think you're being rather dramatic, even alarmist?"

"Everyone should be *alarmed*." Hartnell stood up. "The planet is warming at an unprecedented rate. According to NASA's analysis of ice cores, it's accelerating at a pace not seen for a thousand years. Month after month, average temperatures are hitting record highs. Kuwait broke a world record, reaching 129 degrees. Soon some places on the planet will be too hot to be habitable. We're already seeing weather events that have grown *beyond* storms of the century—they're storms of such severity that their like have not been seen in over five hundred years."

"Weather is unpredictable," Painter said with a shrug.

Hartnell looked apoplectic. "Maybe if it was only *one* such event. But in the past year alone, the U.S. has experienced *eight* five-hundred-year rainstorms. Eight!" He slammed a fist on his desk. "And don't tell me it's any natural cycle. NOAA looked at the last time the earth warmed up, rising out of the last ice age. The temperature rise recorded over this past century is *ten* times faster than that, *twenty* times faster than the average historical rate. So it's not a *cycle* we're dealing with—it's an *extinction-level event*."

Painter scoffed, "And what do you think you can do about it? From what I've read, we're already past the tipping point."

Hartnell straightened. "That's right. To stop what's to come, it's going to take someone with vision, someone willing to take big risks. It will require a Manhattan Project level of commitment. Something world governments can no longer orchestrate. For any true change, it'll be up to the private sector."

"In other words, *you*." Painter narrowed his eyes at his opponent. "What exactly are you doing here at Aurora Station?"

Pushed to the edge, Hartnell stepped over it. "I'm going to end global warming and offer the world an energy source like no other."

"How?"

Hartnell turned to a small glass case holding a black leather notebook. "With the help of a friend."

4:17 A.M.

Simon Hartnell fought the angry trembling of his hand to insert the key into the case's lock. He finally got it seated and opened the glass door. With great care, he removed the volume inside. He turned to the bound man in the seat.

He suspected Painter Crowe was purposefully trying to provoke him, but he didn't care.

"This belonged to Nikola Tesla. It was his personal journal, a notebook that the U.S. government confiscated after his death. But they failed to appreciate or comprehend what was written inside here."

"And you did?"

He smiled, calmer now as he held the book, refusing to be goaded. "Granted it took me over thirty years. And I still don't know everything. The man could be damnably cryptic when he wanted to be." He crossed over and sat at his desk. "And sadly he was more of a visionary genius than a practical one. It's why everyone knows Thomas Edison's name, but not so much Nikola Tesla. Edison was a man of his times . . . Tesla ahead of it."

"And let me guess. Those times have finally come around."

Simon looked sharper at the man, recognizing a keener mind than he first would have guessed, especially for someone working for the government.

"That's right," Simon said. "I intend to show what a genius he truly was."

Painter stared off into the distance. "Your antenna array. It's more than just a high-powered version of HAARP."

"Indeed. It's the realization of Tesla's dream. A world without war, of cheap and limitless energy, and of a healthy, thriving planet."

"And you can deliver all of that?"

"In time. We're preparing for a localized test—a proof of concept, if you will—scheduled for the day after tomorrow."

"What concept?"

"How much do you really know about Tesla's Wardenclyffe project?"

Painter frowned. "Only that it was his failed attempt at building a network of wireless power generators. His tower was to be the first."

"Wardenclyffe was going to be *his* proof of concept, to show to the world what was possible. He starting building the tower in 1901, but its engineering and design were based on theories and tests going back decades. At its simplest, he knew that to transmit energy wirelessly he would need a conductor that could carry that energy around the globe. He investigated two possible sources: the earth and the atmosphere. He believed it was possible to pump energy deep into the earth to stimulate the planet's natural resonance frequency, which would magnify that energy globally. Alternatively, the same could be achieved by projecting energy up to a charged conductive layer of the atmosphere."

"The ionosphere."

Simon nodded. "Such a layer was only speculated about at that time. It wouldn't be proven to exist until 1925."

"So again Tesla was ahead of his time."

"Unfortunately true. Because of this, Tesla looked to the only conductor he had access to: the earth. He designed Wardenclyffe to have three-hundred-foot footings, so his tower could better *grip the earth,* as he described it."

"But it was a failure."

"Only because he didn't have the technology to explore the more promising approach: the earth's ionosphere. Later, when this layer was proven to exist, he did further work, and in 1931 announced that he was on the verge of discovering a new energy source, from—and I quote— 'a new and unsuspected source.' But what that source was, he never revealed in the news article."

Painter must have noted his growing excitement. "But you know what it was."

Simon placed a palm atop Tesla's notebook. "It's all here."

Painter shifted taller. "You're talking about that electric microbe."

Simon could not hide his shock, impressed once again. "That's correct. Tesla experimented on a very dangerous organism in London."

"Was that back in 1895, at the British Museum, when a bunch of researchers opened an artifact once owned by David Livingstone?"

Simon tilted his chair back, his eyes wide.

How much did this man already know?

"What else is in that book of yours?" Painter asked.

"Tesla extrapolated a design, based on what he learned of the organism's properties and what was being discovered about the ionosphere, for a crude version of what we've built here. Again the technology and power sources necessary to pull it off weren't available to him at the time."

"So you improved and expanded this work and built Aurora Station."

"It's my Wardenclyffe. A local test station for a grander global vision."

"And what's that vision?"

"As I said before, it's the same as Tesla's. World peace, cheap and limitless energy, and a healthier planet." Simon challenged his guest. "Is that not a worthy goal?"

"Of course it is. And I'm more than happy to admit that. But it's *how* you intend to achieve such a lofty goal that concerns me."

"You're referring to the acquisition of Dr. al-Maaz."

"Kidnapping and murder would better describe that act."

Simon nodded, conceding the point.

Painter rattled his cuffs. "And then there's this."

"All unfortunate. And never intended. In fact, most of the deaths leading up to this moment you can place at the feet of Professor McCabe. If he hadn't acted so rashly, many lives would have been spared."

"It's easy to blame the dead."

"But no less true."

The phone on Simon's desk chimed. He checked the ID.

Ah . . .

He faced his guest and buzzed the guards in the hall. "I have a few matters to attend. So we'll have to end this discussion for now."

"Wait." Painter shuffled in his seat. "Tell me how you plan to bring about Tesla's vision."

Simon smiled and lifted the book. "It's best you hear this from the great man himself. Though maybe not in his native Serbian. I'll have a translated copy sent to your room. After you read it, we'll talk again. Maybe then you'll fully understand what's at stake."

The guards entered, and with a bit of clanking chains, escorted the hobbled prisoner out of the room. Once Simon was alone, he tapped the button for the incoming call and lifted the receiver.

"Anton, are you all patched up?"

"Yes, sir. I'll be joining the search crews immediately."

"Good. Find them. We need to secure the data stolen from the lab."

With the mummy incinerated, the topographic map of the body's tattoos offered the best chance for learning how to tame that deadly microbe. From the webcam discussion they had tonight, it sounded as if Rory and Dr. al-Maaz had been close to discovering something important.

Anton growled into the phone. "If they've harmed Rory . . ."

"I'm sure he's fine."

The two men had grown fond over the past two years, which Simon allowed, even encouraged. Though for Anton, *love* was a strained and strange commodity. His relationship with his sister, Valya, was unhealthy, codependent, binding the pair as surely as their shared tattoo. It wasn't sexual, thank god, but still injurious to them both. This new relationship also served Simon by weakening that sibling tie, making Valya more useful as a solo operative—and more ruthless.

Nothing like a woman scorned, even if it's by her own brother.

But now perhaps Anton's feelings for Rory were becoming a detriment.

"Anton."

"Sir?"

"Just find that disk. No matter the cost. Do you understand?"

There was a long pause, then a firmer, more determined response.

"It will be done."

4:32 A.M.

"Hello, hello . . ."

Kat knew Safia's efforts were futile. In the passenger seat of the Sno-Cat, Safia clutched Kat's satellite phone, trying to raise Thule Air Base while Kat concentrated on fighting both the treacherous terrain ahead and the storm. Icy winds buffeted the cab, howling in frustration at not being able to reach them. Dry, pebbly hail pelted the sides.

By now, they must have crossed the border into Quttinirpaaq National Park, though she couldn't be sure without GPS.

Safia lowered the phone and craned at the mountains out her window. "Maybe if we got higher."

"It wouldn't help," Kat said, squinting over the steering wheel.

The Sno-Cat's headlamps stretched only yards into the gloom and blowing snow. They were traveling alongside a frozen river, the ice melted or broken in stretches to reveal the blue waters rushing below. Black jagged peaks framed the valley, appearing and disappearing into the storm.

"Then maybe there'll be a break in the weather," Safia said.

"It's not the *weather* that's the problem." Kat looked at the roiling dark clouds overhead. "It's a different storm that's cutting us off. A geomagnetic storm from a recent solar flare. Until it calms down, we're not going to get any satellite feed."

"She's right," Rory said from the backseat. "It's forecasted to last a day or two."

Kat glanced in the rearview mirror. She had stopped long enough to tie his hands behind his back with some rope found in the rear of the Sno-Cat. She had also bound his waist to the seat's buckle braces. He wasn't going anywhere.

He caught her looking at him and lowered his chin.

She remembered his earlier concern for Safia, acting genuinely contrite and remorseful, but she also recalled the fear in his voice at seeing Anton's blood trail. She suspected the two must have developed a deeper bond.

At Sigma command, she had reviewed the record on Anton Mikhailov, back when he was sixteen years old. The crimes listed had been "petty theft" and "immoral acts."

In Russia at that time, homosexuality was still considered a crime.

Kat also recalled her review of the disappearance of Professor McCabe from two years ago. There had been reports of friction between father and son, of the two butting heads. Even Jane had mentioned the same, attributing it to her brother railing against their domineering father.

Kat didn't doubt that was part of the reason.

But maybe not the only reason.

Had Professor McCabe known about his son and never accepted it . . . or had Rory kept his orientation a secret, driving an unspoken wedge between father and son?

Rory had some explaining to do, but now was not the—

"Kat!" Safia grabbed her arm.

She pulled her attention forward. Something large loomed directly ahead, caught in her headlamp. The dark, shaggy form stood by the river, head down, drinking from the river through one of the breaks in the ice.

A muskox.

Kat swerved the Sno-Cat sharply to avoid a collision, but the only path was across a frozen stretch of the river. The treads ground across the ice. She cringed at every pop and crack, but they made it to the far bank and climbed away.

"Sorry about that," Kat said, wiping her brow.

The terrain and the storm clearly did not like being ignored.

"You need some sleep," Safia said softly.

I do. "Once we reach Alert."

That was their plan. On the far side of Quttinirpaaq National Park was the Canadian outpost of Alert, where their military maintained a garrison and a weather-monitoring station. But Quttinirpaaq was Canada's second-largest park, which meant they had to traverse one hundred and fifty miles of untamed landscape to reach safety.

The journey would take many hours, if not most of the day.

And that's if we're not hunted down first.

She posed that concern to Rory. "Back at Aurora, what type of ground pursuit vehicles do you have at the station?"

Rory shrugged. "Snowmobiles, snow bikes. But they were mostly used for recreation. Aurora's a scientific installation, not a military base."

She recognized that, knowing it was likely the only reason she had managed to escape with the others in the first place. As isolated as that facility was, the hostile terrain was probably considered security enough against most threats.

"Some guys used to hunt from the Cessnas," Rory continued with a frown. "Not exactly sporting, but it offered a way to blow off steam."

Kat studied the sky. It was the one small blessing of the storm. At least it had grounded the station's small fleet of bush planes.

But even such hunters were not Kat's biggest concern.

In the neighboring seat, Safia still clutched the satellite phone to her chest. Kat had asked her to keep trying to raise Thule Air Base. While there was only a slim possibility that a lull in the geomagnetic storm would allow them to reach Colonel Wycroft, Kat had assigned this duty to Safia to keep her distracted.

As Safia gazed out her window, one of her hands reached up and rubbed a cheek. Kat knew the fear behind that gesture, picturing the rip in the biosafety suit, the splatter of blowback. While decontamination had been prompt, had it been in time?

Kat had refrained from telling her about Dr. Kano's assessment of the disease's progression, how it took as little as two hours for infectious particles to reach the brain once inhaled.

Had our rescue attempt only ended up dooming the woman?

The Sno-Cat's heater rattled loudly, sounding asthmatic. It blew warm air throughout the sealed cabin, a noisy reminder that Safia might not be the only one at risk.

The engine suddenly coughed, jolting through the vehicle. Kat bumped into the steering wheel, but the motor steadied, rumbling smoothly again. She let out a relieved breath, but a worry remained. She imagined the station's Sno-Cats were mostly used for minor duties around the base and feared they weren't maintained well enough for a cross-country trek through the gnashing teeth of a storm.

As if everyone recognized this, they continued in silence for a long stretch—until a new noise cut through their fears.

It sounded like an avalanche, a rumbling cascade, growing louder.

Then suddenly dark shapes appeared out of the darkness behind them and swept past to either side, converging again in the headlights ahead. The thundering passage was accompanied by a panicked, mournful lowing.

It was a herd of caribou, hundreds of heads, rushing past the Sno-Cat like a river around a boulder. Then as quickly as they came, they vanished back into the storm.

Safia craned her neck to look out the back window. "What do you think spooked them?"

Kat suspected the answer and searched for lights behind them. She got the vehicle moving faster, chasing after the ghostly herd, taking heed of its warning.

Someone's found us.

4:38 A.M.

Painter rubbed his sore wrists as he paced his cell. The guards had un-shackled him, strip-searched him, and tossed him a pair of gray coveralls. They hadn't even given him any shoes.

But that was the least of his problems.

Worry ate a hole in his gut—for Kat, for Safia.

They had locked him up in Safia's old room. Her scent still lingered here, a faint hint of jasmine that conjured up their shared past, of desert sands and green oases. It also acutely reminded him of the dangers ahead.

While Kat and Safia had escaped, taking Rory with them, he didn't know how long they could keep ahead of their pursuers. Despite Simon Hartnell's cordiality, Painter knew the man would stop at nothing to re-capture them.

A scraping noise drew his attention around.

Now what?

A small grate at the bottom of the door slid open. Something was tossed through. It skittered over the floor to Painter's toes. As he bent down to examine it, the grate snapped back shut.

He picked up a thick sheaf of papers, which were punch-holed and bound together with brads. He flipped through the pages, noting large sections of the text had been redacted with thick black stripes, including what clearly hid diagrams and charts.

Intrigued, Painter crossed to the room's desk and sat down.

He knew what this must be.

A translated copy of Tesla's black notebook.

At least in this regard, Hartnell had proved himself a man of his word. Still, from the redacted sections, the man clearly refused to be forthcoming about what was truly going on here.

But I'll take what I can get.

From this gesture, Painter suspected Hartnell wanted to be understood, even respected for his brilliance and enterprise. Or maybe the guy merely needed an appreciative audience for what was to come and was willing to educate that person to fulfill that role.

Painter was happy to cooperate.

I'll even clap if it gets me what I want.

Still, Painter knew the man was no fool. He only had to look out the window to see what the man had built, under the very noses of DARPA, even funded by them. He knew better than to underestimate this guy.

Painter stared down at the bound pages.

If he's given me this, there's something more he wants from me.

So be it.

He turned to the first page and began reading.

As the story unfolded, an icy certainty grew inside him.

This is not going to end well . . . for any of us.

19

In the belly of the god, Gray listened as the muffled roaring of Seichan's bike faded behind him. He hoped there was an exit back there, and if not, he knew Seichan would hole up somewhere with Jane McCabe, trusting Gray and the others to keep them safe.

Kowalski climbed out of the archway into the stomach and gave him a thumbs-up. The big man had prepared a small surprise inside if any of the enemy opted to use the esophageal route into the abdomen. The only other entrance into this half of the slumbering god was through the opening in the diaphragm.

Gray's team kept watch on this side, guarding that pinch point. It was their best defensible position. The opening was only large enough for one person to pass through at a time. From the shelter behind a stone loop of duodenum, Gray fixed his SIG Sauer upon that archway, wishing he had more firepower.

To his right, Derek crouched behind a hill of rubble where a chunk of anatomy had fallen from on high and shattered into pieces. He kept looking worrisomely up toward the roof, as if expecting something else to fall. The man held a spare sidearm—a Beretta 96A1—and swore he was proficient with a handgun. He claimed it was a necessary skill as an archaeologist who often worked in war-torn countries or places overrun by militant rebels.

Kowalski had his own suggestion for Derek upon hearing this: *Maybe you should think about buying a whip.*

Right now, Gray would welcome any additional weapon.

Kowalski took a position behind the bulge of the stomach, staying near the opening in case there was any incursion that way. He shouldered his Piezer shotgun, the weapon loaded with shells of piezoelectric crystals, ready to deliver a shocking greeting to any uninvited guest. He also had a Desert Eagle .50-caliber pistol tucked in his belt.

No one spoke, all their ears straining for any sign of the enemy's approach.

In preparation, Gray had his team click off their lamps to make them less of a target in the dark. Their only light source came from Seichan's helmet. Gray had confiscated it before she left and positioned it on the floor with its beam pointing toward the opening.

Past the glare of the helmet, he saw no movement, but he swore he could hear faint noises: a brush of pebbles, a rasp of cloth, the creak of leather. If the noises weren't his ears playing tricks, someone was out in the next chamber, moving dark, likely wearing night-vision gear.

Then everything happened at once.

A rifle cracked, and the helmet lamp shattered, sinking the place in darkness.

At the same time, a loud blast and a brilliant flare of light burst from the archway into the stomach. Someone had hit the trip wire planted by Kowalski across the esophageal opening. It was attached to a pair of flash-bangs.

With his head turned from the brilliance, Kowalski pointed his shotgun blindly into the glare and fired. Scintillating blue piezoelectric crystals exploded inside the stomach, ricocheting all around, dazzling in their own right as the flare of flash-bang faded.

Gray used the moment to toss a smoke bomb toward the tunnel through the diaphragm. It burst at the threshold, casting a thick pall. Derek fired through it to discourage any approach.

With the view into the abdomen momentarily blocked, Gray took off his helmet, clicked on its lamp, and placed it on the floor. "Fall back to position two!"

Derek retreated with him, but Kowalski lunged headlong into the stomach with his Desert Eagle leveled. He fired a single round, likely dispatching someone stunned inside, then popped back out. He dragged something with him and rushed over.

"Thought we might need this," he said.

His prize was the black tube of a Russian RPG-7—a rocket-propelled grenade launcher—along with two rounds.

Gray turned toward the diaphragm wall with a deep sense of unease.

If the enemy had one rocket launcher, they probably have—

A thunderous boom rocked the world. The opening in the diaphragm blasted apart, herniating wider, sending huge cracks up the sandstone wall dividing the two cavities. Massive chunks rained down, forcing Gray and the others farther back. One slab struck the stomach, crushing it.

Through the stir of smoke and rock dust, dark shapes ran low across the floor, fading in and out of view.

Gunshots rang out, peppering all around.

A round hit his abandoned helmet, shattering its lamp.

Darkness fell like a black shroud.

Derek moaned beside him. "What do we do now?"

10:29 A.M.

Seichan ducked from the explosions, bobbling the bike as everything quaked around her. Jane's arms squeezed the air from her lungs as she grappled to stay seated. She braked to a stop and looked back the way they had come.

Gray . . .

Jane stared, too. "What's happening?"

"Indigestion," Seichan growled harshly, twisting back forward. "War's starting inside here. Which means it's time for us to go."

She throttled up and headed the last of the way. It appeared to be a straight shot after the looping, curving, tortuous chute that led them here.

"It can't be far," Jane said. "I think we're in the descending colon, part of the large intestine."

Earlier, the young archaeologist had described the path through the small intestine as being merely *representational*. Those twisting tunnels had been only slightly narrower than the one they were in now. The route also didn't match the detailed sculpture of the intestinal tract as seen from outside. Instead, the inner passageway was simply a looping tunnel bored through a football-field-long block of sandstone that had been carved on the outside to *appear* more convoluted than it truly was.

Seichan followed the spear of her headlight down the track, but her ears remained tuned for any clue to what was happening outside. The explosions had dulled to occasional crashes, but spats of sharper cracks warned of an ongoing firefight.

Jane pointed past her shoulder. "There. See how it narrows ahead. I think that's the sphincter. We must be near the bottom."

In this case, literally.

Seichan sped faster.

The sooner they were out of here, the sooner she could lure the enemy away from the fight here. Gray and the others had put their lives at risk to protect them.

Only fair we return the favor.

Where it narrowed, the tunnel took a final dip. As the bike reached that spot, the headlight shone down upon an impaction of rock and sand blocking the way.

"Crap," Jane swore under her breath.

Seichan braked hard to a stop. "Well, at least it's not literal."

10:32 A.M.

Derek crawled along the floor, his head ringing. Gray and Kowalski followed, popping off shots into the darkness. A single light shone out here.

It was Derek's abandoned helmet.

Gray had positioned it behind a boulder several yards back, out of the direct line of fire. While its lamp did little to reveal the enemy's approach through the rubble, the weak glow offered enough illumination to let them retreat deeper into the shadowy depths of the abdomen.

"We're running out of places to go," Kowalski said.

He was right.

To one side rose the coiled mass of the sculpted intestines; on the other, the abdominal wall swept up in a gentle curve to the arch of the spine along the roof. They were being slowly driven back to the pit of the belly, where they'd be trapped.

Kowalski fired his weapon, making Derek jump.

A pair of dark figures split up out there, looking like scraps of shadows. They vanished to either side.

"This should be far enough," Gray said.

Far enough for what?

"Everyone get behind me." Gray raised the grenade launcher to his shoulder.

"Make this count," Kowalski warned. "We only have one more round after this."

Derek jumped at the weapon's blast. A spate of flame shot out the tube's back end, while a tight spiral of smoke propelled the grenade across the cavern. But rather than firing *at* the enemy, Gray had aimed high, toward the roof.

No, not the roof.

Gray pushed them all farther back. "Go, go, go . . ."

The explosion lit up his true target, blasting it free of its attachment to the upper curve of the wall. The bus-sized kidney broke loose, taking part of the roof with it. It toppled, turning slightly in midair, then slammed across the space between their team and the enemy. More rubble followed, raining all around the dislodged kidney.

Something struck Derek's abandoned helmet and snuffed it like a candle.

Gray pulled out a spare flashlight, thumbed it on, and pointed the beam at the destruction.

Kowalski clapped his partner hard on the back. "No one's getting past there now!"

Neither are we, Derek thought. *At least not until things settle.*

But that quickly became unlikely.

Rather than slowing, the collapsing grew steadily worse, spreading wider, escalating. With a mighty tremble in the earth, a huge piece of the sandstone roof cracked away. It dropped like the palm of a god and crushed half the intestinal mass. A thick cloud of sand and dust blasted over them, threatening to smother them if not for their air masks.

Gray got them moving away. "It's all coming down."

10:35 A.M.

Jane picked herself up off the ground.

A moment ago, she had been examining the debris blocking the exit—and the next she was sprawled across the floor. Even Seichan had been knocked against the curve of the tunnel, pinned by the bike she had been sitting on. She shoved herself upright, seated again.

They both looked behind them as a ghostly cloud of dust curled down the length of the descending colon toward them.

"We need to get out of here," Seichan warned. "Right now."

More quakes and ominous crashes supported this assessment.

Jane coughed, breathing dust. Only then did she realize her air mask had been damaged from her headlong crash.

Cursing, she tore it away.

Seichan reached to her mask, clearly intending to give it to her.

"Keep it on," Jane said. "No reason for both of us to be put at risk."

She doubted there was much risk of contagion this far into the bowels of the god, but why take chances?

Instead, she faced the more immediate danger.

"This is just as fake as everything else," Jane said, patting the obstruction.

"What do you mean?"

"It's made to *look* like a natural cave-in. But watch." She slapped the boulders and scratched at the sand. "It's a sculpture like all the rest."

Seichan shrugged, looking resigned to their fate. "Fake or not, it's still a dead end."

Jane shook her head. "Derek was right before. The ancients always had hidden escape routes, often disguising them."

She examined the neighboring wall, running her palms over its surface.

Seichan hopped off her bike to check the other side.

Jane's fingertips discovered a seam in the rock. "Over here," she said and followed it around, outlining a square door. "Help me."

Together, they put their shoulders to one side of the door and pushed. The rock grated and shifted. Encouraged, they worked harder. The door pivoted around a center pole. It gave way easier than Jane had expected.

With the door opened, she wiped her hands on her pants. "My father must have discovered this in the past. He wouldn't have missed this."

A pang of sorrow immobilized her.

Seichan went back and pushed the bike to the door. "We have to go."

Jane nodded and helped her wrestle the cycle through the door and down a short tunnel. Sunlight blazed ahead, drawing them faster. The exit was sheltered by a boulder, which helped hide its position halfway up a cliff. A steep path led down between two rounded hills to either side. The shapely pair hadn't been sculpted by anything but the wind. Still, their combined silhouettes created an unmistakable piece of human anatomy—especially considering from where she and Seichan had just fled.

They headed down.

Seichan walked the bike, but her gaze remained behind them.

Jane knew her worry.

The others were still trapped below.

10:40 A.M.

Gray retreated with Kowalski and Derek, fleeing the destruction, driven farther into the depths of the dying god. Guilt ate at him, knowing the devastation his errant shot had triggered.

By now, the middle of the cavern was gone, collapsed into rubble.

More and more was coming down. Rock dust choked and clouded the air, making it hard to see.

"There's gotta be another way out," Kowalski said, looking to the two of them for support.

Gray pointed to the crumbled ruin of the intestinal tract, praying Seichan and Jane weren't still in there. "That way's blocked." He waved behind them. "And there's no going back the way we came."

"Then what about another exit?" Kowalski turned to Derek, who wore a dazed expression, nearing shock. "Didn't you say those old guys built a bunch of secret tunnels and whatnot?"

Derek shrugged. "Here it's all about anatomy. We entered the mouth. The only logical exit is the other end."

Kowalski balled a fist, thinking hard. "We got other holes," he said and waved a hand below his waist. "What about . . . you know . . ."

Gray realized the big guy could be right. "Derek, is that possible?" he glanced toward the pit of the abdomen. "Maybe through the bladder."

Derek had stopped, his brows pinched in thought. "And out the ure-thra? No." He turned and fixed Gray with a determined look. "But I think I know how to get out of here."

10:44 A.M.

At last . . .

Valya grinned at the thin dust trail rising a quarter-mile away.

Despite the past twenty minutes of quakes, buried blasts, and an up-welling of smoke through the mouth of the subterranean complex, she had maintained her cliffside vigil. With no sign of Kruger and his men, she could only imagine the pitched battle below.

Still, his team had succeeded in chasing the hare out of its burrow.

To confirm what she already suspected, she shifted over to the UAV control station and directed the Raven in the skies to sweep down upon that trail.

She wanted eyes on that target.

Crouched by the monitor, she watched a dizzying bird's-eye view of the broken hills as the drone dove toward a small motorcycle racing across the sand. It scribed a straight path away from the hills and headed toward the distant Nile. Two riders hunched atop the seat. The tail of a scarf waved from the neck of the driver, half-hiding her face.

Valya's jaw tightened, recognizing that particular flag.

Seichan.

Still, mistrust kept her fixed in place. It could be another trick. The traitor could be trying to lure her from her post, to fool her into chasing a decoy. She toggled the drone to circle closer, using the gimbaled optics to zoom in.

She needed to confirm who rode in back.

Corroboration was made difficult as the figure wore a caver's helmet and clutched tightly to Seichan's back, their face turned from the whipping sand and scorching sun.

Valya tilted the Raven, bringing it lower, trying to get the right angle to positively identify the rider. Then as if alerted—maybe by the passing shadow of the drone—the helmeted figure straightened.

Valya cursed and jerked the toggle, but she was too slow.

It *was* a trick.

The rider in back balanced on her seat, staring straight out of the monitor at her.

It was Seichan.

Using both hands, the woman leveled her pistol at the drone. On the screen those dark eyes narrowed upon Valya, as if knowing who was watching.

A flash from the gun, and the image shattered on the screen.

Valya shoved the monitor and stood. She took three sharp steps toward the cliff, staring at the dust trail still hanging over the desert. Though she didn't have confirmation, she trusted her instincts.

Jane McCabe had been the one steering the bike, her features hidden under Seichan's scarf.

Valya swung onto her motorcycle—a Ducati 1080s tuned for the desert and fitted with sand tires. It was a panther compared to her target's rabbit. And in the open desert, there would be nowhere to hide.

She paused only long enough to grab her portable UAV monitor. She recalled the other Raven, drawing it away from its patrol of the enemy's truck, and sent it winging to the coordinates of the racing bike. She kept the bird high this time, wanting it to be her eyes from above until she could close the distance.

Not that I have to get that close.

She strapped her assault rifle across her back. It was a Russian AK74M with a GP-25 grenade launcher mounted under its barrel.

She gunned the engine and began her hunt.

10:51 A.M.

Mystified, Gray followed Derek deeper into the dark abdomen. "Where are we going?"

"It shouldn't be far. If I'm right."

Kowalski trailed them, glancing frequently over his shoulder, cringing with each resounding crash. The cavern behind them grew smaller as the place imploded. They were being chased by a slow avalanche of stone and sand.

Closer at hand, the walls and roof squeezed around them, while the floor rose under their feet. They had reached the bottom of the belly.

Finally, Derek pointed ahead. "Over there. That should be the bladder."

To Gray, it looked like a flattened balloon, half-crushed under the last mass of the intestinal tract. "I thought we couldn't get out through the urinary tract."

Derek crossed toward the bladder. "Remember when we first entered, I told you something was wrong with the way Tutu's name was written."

Gray pictured the two rows of hieroglyphics. The last ended with a kneeling figure. "It depicted a woman instead of a man."

"We've been wrong all this time," Derek said. "We're not in the body of a god named Tutu—but a *goddess*."

He lifted an arm to the rounded bulk crushing the other half of the flattened bladder.

"And that's her womb."

Gray craned up at the mass of the uterus. He remembered the delicate decoration inscribed inside the stone heart, of a flock of butterflies in mid-flight. Even then it had struck him as feminine.

"How did you figure this out?" he asked.

Derek glanced back to him. "It wasn't all that hard. Remember that pile of rubble I first hid behind?"

Gray nodded. Something had fallen from the roof and shattered into ruin. Derek had kept looking for its source. Gray had thought the man was worrying about something else crushing him.

Instead, he was studying the anatomy.

"It was an ovary," Derek said. "I spotted where it broke away and rolled down to where I was standing. I could just make out the remaining fallopian tubes carved into the wall and trailing back into the darkness."

To here.

Gray turned back to the womb.

"Surely if there was another exit from here," Derek said, "it would be through there. In a symbolic act of birth."

Gray adjusted his light to sweep over the bladder and across the vastness of the stone uterus. A dark shadow marred its surface. "A door!"

A loud boom made them all jump. A huge section of the roof dislodged to their right, taking with it a large portion of the sculpted spine, breaking the goddess's lower back. It crashed on the far side of the cavity, rattling down more boulders in a deafening cascade.

"Go!" Gray ordered.

They scaled the shoulder-high edge of the bladder amid a storm of sand and pebbles. Gray's light illuminated the way to the door. Past the threshold, there was indeed a large cavity inside. They all ducked through to escape the onslaught.

Once out of the storm, the world grew quieter, the air less dust-choked. Maybe it was his imagination, but Gray was overcome by a sense of reverence, as if stepping into a cathedral.

He lifted his light high. Like with the heart and stomach, the walls here were decorated, inscribed with images. Cherub-like children danced all around them, seeming almost to fly.

Derek found a grimmer sight. "Look down."

Gray shifted his beam to his feet. Across the floor, there were more children, but from their twisted, contorted shapes, they looked dead or tortured.

Derek tried to cover his mouth, but his air mask blocked him. "It's a depiction of the tenth plague. The figures below are all boys. The ones above all girls."

Gray saw he was right.

Everything here is a lesson.

Kowalski had another one as he herded them forward, eyeing the sand sweeping across the doorway. "Keep moving or we'll be joining those boys."

They bowed as the roof lowered, the way pinching to a stone cervix. They had to drop on hands and knees to get through but could stand once past that point. Gray fixed his light down the last muscular length of the tunnel, representing the birth canal. His beam ended at a pile of rock, blocking the way.

"Great," Kowalski said. "She had to be a virgin."

Derek touched Gray's elbow. "Turn off your flashlight."

He did as the man asked. Darkness fell over them, but as his eyes adjusted, he noted faint flickers of light ahead, piercing the rockfall.

"It's a cave-in but likely fairly recent," Derek said. "With care we might be able to dig our—"

The ground jolted with a thunderous explosion. Sand and dust blasted at them from behind. Gray heard more rock cascading across the blocked opening ahead, further sealing them in.

"No time."

He crowded everyone back to the stone cervix and into the uterus. Once through, he swung the tube of the RPG launcher up to his shoulder and fitted in the last round.

"Cover your ears and open your mouth."

He dropped to his belly, pointed the launcher through the cervix, and fired.

The blast and fire overwhelmed his senses, blinding and deafening him. Rocks pelted his head and shoulders. Then something tugged on his leg.

Faint words reached him. "Run, goddamnit!"

He lifted his head as his vision cleared, only to be dazzled by a brightness that stung.

Sunlight . . .

Then dark shadows began to fall across the brilliance.

"Out!" Kowalski pushed Gray from behind. "Before it closes back up!"

Gray understood and lunged forward. Once at the threshold, he dove headlong through the cascade of rock and sand. He landed on his shoulder and rolled down a long, sandy slope.

Kowalski and Derek followed his example.

They all tumbled clear as the desert swallowed up the hole behind them.

Gray stood shakily.

Kowalski simply rolled to his rear, looking back at the ruins. "So was it good for you, sweetheart?" He gained his feet and wiped his brow. "Cuz I'm spent."

Derek stumbled a few steps away, his eyes on the ground. "There are tire tracks over here."

Gray joined him, his gaze following the trail out into the desert as relief flooded through him.

Seichan made it out.

11:02 A.M.

We're not going to make it.

Seichan hunched low over the bike's handlebars. She had switched places with Jane after shooting down the drone fifteen minutes ago and now raced across the desert. She had hoped to gain more distance before the enemy had found them.

No such luck.

Without a good lead, they would never reach Rufaa before the enemy intercepted them. Jane had tried radioing Ahmad but got no response.

Despite the treacherous terrain, Seichan had the throttle fully open, driving hard.

Jane patted her side. Still keeping one arm around Seichan's waist, she pointed to the right, to a dust trail in the distance. A small dark mote sped across the sand, the source of the smoke signal.

Seichan wanted to believe it was a mirage.

Nothing could be moving that fast.

It had to be racing well over a hundred miles an hour.

Still, she knew it was real—and knew who rode so hell-bent after them.

Seichan gritted her teeth, trying to will more speed out of their bike.

Never make it.

The mote to her right closed in, revealing itself to be a black-and-silver motorcycle. Its rider lay almost flat across the seat.

Seichan searched ahead, knowing she could never outrun that pale rider sweeping toward them. A dune rose in the distance, a crisp line stretching across their path. Their only hope was to seek cover and higher ground.

With a goal set, Seichan hunkered lower.

C'mon . . .

The dune rose higher as they approached, cresting into the sky like a frozen wave. It was steeper than it first looked. But there was no turning back.

As she reached its lower edge, she shifted her rump back, pushing Jane with her. She needed as much weight over the rear wheel as possible, adding traction to the rubber paddles of the back tire. The bike shot up the slope, kicking sand high. She didn't slow. They couldn't risk getting bogged down.

Still, the disturbed sand fought them. As she cut higher up the dune, the entire side suddenly gave way, sliding down, becoming a river. She fought against the current, shimmying the bike's rear from side to side to keep them moving, bouncing off the pegs to keep the back tire from sinking too deep.

A glance to her right revealed the hunter was upon them, only fifty yards back.

Seichan searched up, believing she might just clear the crest in time.

Then the dune exploded above her, blasting a wall of sand toward her. There was no getting out of the way. The wave flipped the bike, sending both riders flying.

Seichan hit the sand, righted herself, and used her heels to brake herself to a stop. She was perched halfway up the slope. Jane was not as fortunate. The woman continued to tumble toward the desert floor.

The enemy closed down on her, riding one-handed. Her other arm steadied an assault rifle with a grenade launcher smoking from beneath the barrel.

Seichan grabbed for her SIG Sauer, but her thigh holster was empty.

There was nothing she could do.

Her adversary wore no helmet, only a scarf over her lower face, but Seichan knew the woman was grinning savagely, savoring the kill. She knew that feeling, having been at the other end of that rifle many times before.

The bike slowed as Jane came to a dazed stop.

As the engine's roar dimmed, a new noise intruded.

Barking.

From the dune behind her.

She twisted in time to see a furry shape bound over the crest and come racing down.

Anjing.

Along the ridge, dark shapes appeared. They were figures wrapped in desert robes. They dropped flat along the sandy crest, long rifles at their shoulders. A barrage of gunfire drove her flat, but they were all aiming below, toward the woman atop the cycle.

Rounds puffed into the sand, ricocheted off rocks, and a few pinged into the flank of the enemy motorcycle. The rider spun from the onslaught, strafing wildly behind her, but her intent was not to win but to escape. Denied her prize, she raced away, slaloming wildly to present a harder target.

Anjing ran up and licked Seichan on the face, dancing in the sand around her.

She held the mutt off long enough to turn and see Ahmad come sliding down to her.

"How . . . ?" She glanced to the line of men rising along the ridge. "Who . . . ?"

Ahmad smiled, waving up. "From Rufaa. They come to kill you." From her shocked look, he patted her arm. "They think you kill two village elders. Find bodies this morning. Follow trail out here."

To exact revenge.

Seichan remembered the figure she had spotted lurking around their truck. She now knew that must have been the pale woman in disguise. Apparently her subterfuge that night also included murder.

"They find me in truck," Ahmad said. "I tell them *you* no kill. Then we see you." He wiggled his hand in the air to mimic her dust trail. "Come to meet you."

And save us.

Below, Jane had gained her feet and started climbing. Once she joined them, they hiked to the top of the dune. Hidden on its far side was a collection of sand bikes, along with a few camels, likely from nomads collected along the way by the hunting party.

But something was missing.

"Where's the Unimog?"

"Ah, not far. But too much noise, too much"—he wiggled his hand in the air again—"to sneak here."

Seichan craned the other way, looking off in the distance.

Near the horizon, she could make out the two hills that served as the giant's buttocks. A new cloud of dust hung in the air back there.

Gray...

Jane noted her attention. "Maybe they got out."

Seichan grabbed Ahmad's shoulder. "Only one way to find out."

20

Painter sat at his room's desk, reading through the translated book for a second time. He remained astounded by the story found here. It was split into two tales: One detailed Nikola Tesla's time spent in London, the other—set in the deserts of Nubia—featured Sir Henry Morton Stanley and of all people, Samuel Clemens.

Mark Twain . . .

Painter shook his head.

No wonder whoever stole this notebook after Tesla's death put no credence upon what was written in here. Painter wouldn't have believed it himself if not for the corroboration of recent events.

According to the inventor's story, he and Twain were summoned by Sir Stanley to stop a plague in London, the same one afflicting the world now. Painter knew enough of the story of David Livingstone's artifact and the disease it held to substantiate this claim.

The group took a steamship across the Atlantic, where they split up. Tesla went directly to the British Museum, which had been locked up and quarantined. There he experimented with a strange bloody sample found in the Egyptian artifact. He came to correctly recognize that the crimson-hued microbe seen under a microscope was the disease agent.

He named this germ *Pestis fulmen,* Latin for "a plague of lightning."

Even before Tesla had arrived, the Brits had noted the strange electrical properties of the bloody water, noting a glow from it during a lightning storm, as if it were reacting to the charge in the air. So they sought out an expert in electricity, sending Stanley to America. They had wanted Edison at first but apparently had to settle for Tesla, which from the Serbian's veiled comments in the text clearly rankled him.

Still, he did his best to see if electricity could cure the disease. While enough electricity could indeed overload and fry the microbe, it did the same to anyone afflicted. Tesla quoted Francis Bacon about his failed effort and tragic outcome: *I've cured the disease but killed the patient.*

Afterward, despondent yet determined, he set out to study the organism, to better understand it. He began to experiment with ways to harness its potential. Most of what followed had been redacted, clearly containing details Simon Hartnell did not want to share.

Painter glanced out the window at the spread of the antenna array.

Hartnell obviously learned something from Tesla's early efforts.

He returned his attention to the book.

In the end, Tesla abandoned his research, deeming it too dangerous, especially considering the nature of the microbe. This decision was further supported by the other half of the story.

After dropping Tesla in London, Twain and Stanley took the same steamer to Cairo, traveling incognito, following clues left by David Livingstone and hoping to find the source of the disease—and its possible cure.

Twain wrote Tesla about it.

> The manner in which our poor deceased friend hid his clues was clever, damnably clever, doubly so for a stuffy Brit. But we owe Livingstone a debt. He has led us straight forth to the deserts of Nubia. Unfortunately we also must lean upon Sir Stanley's memory, as some details were only imparted to the man via letters from Livingstone that no longer exist. Still, here I am again, back in these baked lands, while knee-deep in donkeys and neck-deep in dromedaries. We set off tomorrow with a baggage-wagon and a rabble of muscular Arabs and black-skinned Ethiopians. I hope we have paid them amply enough in bucksheesh, lest they abandon our pale selves in the middle of the desert.

Painter read further as Twain described the overland trek in general terms, clearly leaving out details on purpose. But at last, following those *damnably clever* clues, the group discovered a subterranean complex, dug out of a set of desert hills. From there the story defied plausibility. It was a tale of mummies and curses and of a great stone goddess buried in the sands.

The sight awed Twain to the point of poetic reverence.

> I imagine her face pressed into the sand, crushed by the burden she must carry, riven with sadness, eternally patient, waiting for redemption. Though I think it is of <u>our</u> salvation and deliverance that she dreams, not her own. She leaves her body behind as a beacon, a light shining through the darkness of the past to give hope to the future.

Within that sculpted tomb, Stanley and Twain must have discovered or recovered something important. A month later, they returned to England, where they were able to successfully cure the afflicted and halt the plague's spread.

Yet, again Twain was vague about the details of the cure. It sounded like they had discovered the *means* to a cure inside the tomb, but *not the actual medicinal tincture*, as Twain wrote. He was frustratingly enigmatic about it all, but he offered his reasons, warning not only of the dangers from within that tomb, but also of the dangers from without.

> I would not have the sledges and hammers of relic-hunters disturb her rest. Let her sleep, let her dream in peace, knowing she has saved us all.

So the story ended with Tesla and Twain returning home to continue their lives, keeping this secret. Tesla concluded by acknowledging the one man whose dedication to the people and lands of Africa had offered them a path to the cure.

We must thank David Livingstone, who risked all, even his
eternal soul, to deliver us from damnation. May we live up to his
sacrifice . . . and God forgive us if we don't.

Painter closed the bound pages and let his palm rest there.

He heard a soft whirring by the door. He glanced up as the camera on
the ceiling swung in his direction. He knew who was likely watching him,
waiting for him to finish.

He shoved the pages away.

Let's do this.

6:32 A.M.

Simon stared down at his prisoner, once again bound and shackled to a
chair in his library. He intended to make this man understand, to gain his
trust, if only enough to help him lure his companions out of the storm.

I need that data they stole.

Simon leaned back on his desk. "So now you know the story."

Painter shrugged, clinking his chains. "I think I'm even more in the
dark about what's going on here."

"In truth, so was I. When I first obtained Tesla's notebook back in
1985, I didn't have the financial resources I do now, so there was not
much I could do except review Tesla's experiments. I thought the man
was theorizing a hypothetical situation, positing the existence of such an
organism and extrapolating how its properties might be harnessed for the
betterment of mankind."

"But it wasn't hypothetical."

Simon shrugged. "Maybe, but no one knew that until a few years ago,
when some biologists in California discovered the first example of a bacterium that ate and excreted electrons, living directly off electricity." He
smiled. "But you can imagine my interest."

Painter lifted a brow, acknowledging this.

"By then, I was in a better financial position to explore this further."

"To the tune of a couple billion."

"Only *one,* if we're being precise." He waved this humble brag away. "Anyway, I funded researchers working on such microbes, both in the States and abroad. Investigating practical applications, like engineering *biocables*—living bacterial nanowires that could conduct electricity—or the creation of nanoscale engines powered by such microbes that could clean up pollution. The potential is thrilling."

"And quite profitable, I imagine." Painter shifted closer. "But that was not your ultimate goal. You were hoping to find an organism that could fuel Tesla's designs, those that you found in his old notebook."

Simon nodded, reminded again how sharp and intuitive this man could be.

Tread carefully.

"Nothing panned out, so I kept returning to the notebook. I grew more and more convinced that the story written there wasn't some rough draft for a future story by Twain, a wild tale featuring his personal friends instead of Huck Finn and Tom Sawyer."

"So you began following the bread crumbs found in that book."

"Not me personally. Like I had done with the biologists, I began funding *archaeologists,* anyone with an interest in that region."

"Like Professor McCabe."

"No, it was his son actually. The young man wanted desperately to show up his father, to escape his giant shadow. I gave him the clues to look into the relationship between Stanley and Livingstone, believing someone might be able to reconnect those old dots. When Rory failed, frustration drove him to seek his father's help—while still keeping his old man in the dark about who was pulling the strings."

"And Professor McCabe succeeded in connecting those dots."

"Somewhat, but to be honest, I think he succeeded mostly by pure dogged fieldwork. From his own past study of the region, along with the additional clues found in Livingstone's old papers, he simply went looking, taking his son with him." Simon lifted his hands. "So you can see, there wasn't anything particularly nefarious in this enterprise, mere scientific curiosity coupled with corporate backing."

"Granted, but what happened after that?"

Simon sighed. "Like I said, if it wasn't for Professor McCabe we wouldn't be in this mess. From his first steps *into* that tomb to his last steps *out,* he's cost lives. I'm just trying to mitigate the damage."

From Painter's sour expression, it did not look like he was swallowing this. Still, the man sat back and said, "For now I'll buy that, so go on with the rest of your story. I assume you found Tesla's *Pestis fulmen* microbe, but what are your plans for it?"

For capitulating this much, Simon rewarded him. "The microbe was the missing component of Tesla's dream for wireless energy. As I mentioned before, Tesla had already theorized using the ionosphere as the conductor, but for his plans to work, he would need a *battery* up there, something that could hold, distribute, and propagate that power."

Painter's eyes widened with understanding. "Tesla envisioned using the microbe as that battery—a *living* battery."

"His experiments at the museum supported this vision. He estimated— and I've proven it here—that this simple microbe could live for centuries up there, if not millennia, as long as it had a continual supply of food."

"In other words, electricity."

"Precisely. So not only is the microbe a *living* battery, it's a nearly *immortal* one."

6:40 A.M.

Painter sat in his chair, his mind reeling, following this path to where it must lead.

The man is insane . . . a genius, but insane.

He focused back on Hartnell. "You're planning to seed the ionosphere with this microbe."

He had recently heard that the air force was testing the feasibility of a similar plan, in their case to fuel the ionosphere with extra plasma to enhance radio signals. Plus he had read about the discovery of bacteria living in the upper troposphere, feeding on oxalic acid found at that level.

So it might be possible.

But this plan . . .

"I have a custom cargo jet equipped to dispatch high-altitude weather balloons. Each of them can ferry a quarter ton of the microbe up to the lower levels of ionosphere, where a small charge will disperse its load."

Painter found himself holding his breath in horror, picturing that scenario. Hartnell must have taken samples from the desert tomb and cultured vast loads of the plague-carrying microbe. Knowing now what the man intended to do with it, Painter understood the purpose for the station's ground installation.

"The Aurora Array," he sputtered out. "You're planning on using it to energize that load after it's sent up there."

"If my calculations and early prototypes hold true, the microbes should successfully store that energy." Hartnell looked up as if staring at the sky. "I envision the entire ionosphere seeded with Tesla's *Pestis fulmen,* a living, electron-breathing battery, one capable of storing not only energy passed *up* to it, but also collecting the natural electrical currents tracing through the ionosphere, driven by the solar winds."

"It would be a limitless power source."

Hartnell's gaze settled back to Painter. "Like Nikola, I see power plants around the world, even homes, with towers similar to the one outside, capable of tapping into the battery. Like a million Tesla coils hooked to the sky."

This scheme was beyond grand.

"Just think of it. No more burning fossil fuels, no more tearing apart the earth for resources, no more pouring carbon dioxide into the air. And there's an added bonus."

"What's that?"

"The crimson hue of the microbe would act as a natural sunscreen. A very mild one, but enough to push us back from the brink of turning this planet into a burnt cinder."

Painter appreciated his vision, but he could also think of a thousand variables that could turn this project into an unmitigated disaster—especially with regards to one glaringly obvious problem.

"But this organism is *deadly* . . . extinction-level-event deadly."

Simon sighed. "That's why we need the cure. I'm ready to perform a localized test in a couple of days. The conditions are perfect with the current geomagnetic storm, which is coursing the ionosphere with energy, the perfect soil in which to plant my seeds."

"But you don't have the cure."

"I could if you'd get your partner to cooperate. To return what they stole. I believe Dr. al-Maaz and Rory were close to a breakthrough, something that could help us discover the reins to control this unruly beast."

Painter now understood *why* Hartnell was being so forthcoming. "And if I don't help?"

Hartnell shrugged. "I'll still conduct the test."

Painter stiffened, the cuffs digging into his wrists. "What? Are you mad?"

"Not at all. I'm confident it would be harmless. Tesla has already supplied us with a failsafe. I could simply overcharge the ionosphere with the array, sterilizing what's up there, and achieve the same result."

Painter remembered the Francis Bacon quote he had read.

Cure the disease, kill the patient.

If not careful, this madman could do the same—only on a global level.

"But, of course, I'd prefer *not* to do that," Hartnell said, narrowing his eyes on Painter. "Especially if you help me find your friends."

6:50 A.M.

Exhausted, Kat let the Sno-Cat trundle down the next pass on its own, barely holding the wheel. Gusts pushed the vehicle from behind, as if encouraging them to get into the shelter of the next valley. Dark clouds roofed the world, brushing the ice-capped mountains on all sides.

Even in the eternal twilight of the storm, the view ahead was breathtaking.

The huge valley stretched in either direction, its ends lost in the mists. Directly below, a long, thin lake filled the basin. It was still frozen over, but some edges flashed a brilliant blue, indicative of the first signs of a summer thaw. Deeper into the lake, large black islands rose from the white ice.

"Lake Hazen," Kat mumbled.

Safia stirred, raising her head from where it had been leaning on the window.

Kat pointed below, hoping she had memorized the island map correctly on the flight here. "If that's Lake Hazen, we should be halfway to Alert."

"You don't look even a quarter *alert*," Safia teased. "Maybe we should take a rest. There's been no other sign of anyone on our tail for the past two hours."

After the ghostly passage of the caribou herd, Kat had sent their Sno-Cat into a region of barren rock to better hide their tracks, avoiding snow and ice. She didn't know if she had lost her pursuers or if they had even been there at all.

"Maybe you're right. If nothing else, I need to stretch my legs."

"Me, too," Rory said from the backseat.

Not likely, buddy.

Kat aimed for the nearest blue spot, where a thin river trickled into the lake. They could use more water. Safia had finished the last bottle from the emergency pack found in the back.

"Look at all the flowers," Safia said dreamily.

To either side of the Cat, the slopes were covered in purple saxifrage and arctic poppies. Even the rocks and boulders supported moss and yellow lichen.

Kat took heart at the signs of life. She guided the vehicle down and parked at the shale-encrusted bank of the lake. "I'll fill up our water bottles."

"What about Rory?" Safia asked.

"He stays put."

Upon hearing this, Rory slumped in his seat.

Kat gathered the empty bottles and cracked her door. The wind came close to tearing it out of her grip. The cold woke her up immediately, but she didn't mind. The air was crisp, smelling of ice. She hurried to the lake and topped off the bottles. In just a few seconds of touching that water, her fingers went numb from the cold.

She gathered the bottles and hunkered back against the wind. She had not had time to grab parkas during their hurried escape.

Okay, that's about all the fresh air I can take.

She climbed into the heated cab of the Cat and slammed the door.

Safia was turned in her seat, talking to Rory. "What happened after you and your father reached that tomb in the desert?"

Rory shook his head. "My father wanted to go in first. You know how he could be. He left me outside with two of the survey crew. The rest went in with him."

Rory glanced away, as if the memory was painful. "One of the crew hit a booby trap or mishandled something. I never got a good answer. All I heard was a bunch of yelling. I tried to go in, but my father warned me to stay away. Those inside were all contaminated in the enclosed space. From the records of what happened at the British Museum, my father knew the danger, knew the safest thing was for everyone afflicted to remain below."

"What did you do?"

He made a scoffing noise. "I panicked. I called Simon Hartnell."

Kat had already heard part of the story on the ride over, learning how Hartnell had been secretly funding and guiding Rory, who in turn manipulated his father.

"Simon sent over a medical team," Rory explained. "They buttoned everything up. There was some debate about trying to move the group to a hospital, but without knowing how communicable it was, it was decided to care for the men on-site."

"Was that Hartnell's decision?" Kat asked, figuring the man would do anything to keep his secret.

Rory turned to her. "No, it was my father's." He gave a tired shake of his head. "But I think his decision was based on a desire to remain at the site, to be the first to explore everything. I don't think he was concerned about the possible spread of the disease. I mean, look what he did in the end."

"So your father survived his initial exposure."

"Out of pure stubbornness more than anything. Two others also lived. But five men died."

"And after that?" Safia asked.

"Everything got locked down. I was flown here to work on the project."

Kat nodded to his missing finger. "And to ensure your father cooperated."

Rory stared at his hand and shrugged. "I accidentally shattered my finger after I got here. It had to be amputated anyway."

Kat could only imagine how horrified Professor McCabe must have been when they delivered his son's severed finger.

"My father worked the next twenty months searching for the cure. He discovered not only the tattooed mummy, but a whole batch of others. He tested all their tissues, everything in that damned place, trying to find the answer."

"But nothing worked?" Safia said.

"I think he must have gone a little mad in the end. Even tried to go through the ritual of self-mummification, to follow in the ancients' footsteps." Rory snorted. "Then he simply escaped. He waited until there was a rotation of researchers, when only two scientists and two guards were on the premises. He broke into a weapons locker and stole a rifle."

"He killed them all?"

"Only the guards. He tied up the researchers, then fled." Rory stared out at the frozen lake. "I don't understand . . . so many have died because of him."

Kat felt no need to console Rory, but she did anyway. "I don't think he meant to. We believe that act of mummification made him noncontagious. Unfortunately, it wasn't a cure. He still died from the pathogen, but I think he was trying to reach civilization, to warn about what was going on."

Rory turned back, his eyes welling with tears. "But he didn't have to do that. I didn't want him to die."

Safia leaned back to the boy, resting her fingers on his knee.

Kat did not share her sympathy.

You made this bed.

"What about afterward?" Kat asked. "Why would Hartnell want to destroy all of your father's work and go after your sister?"

"With all the renewed attention following my father's reappearance, Simon feared someone might discover the clues found in my dad's early papers and try to follow those bread crumbs to that location."

Kat frowned. "So he began cleaning house."

"Both in London and at the tomb. He removed everything of importance out in the desert, including the enthroned mummy. My father was sure she was vital to the cure."

And now she's gone, with only a ghostly digital record left.

Kat glanced at Safia's pocket.

"What about Jane?" Safia asked.

"Before my father fled, he left a strange sign, addressed to Jane. Simon believed my sister might find some meaning or significance in it. He hoped it might offer some new clue to the cure, something my father discerned near the end but never shared." Rory looked down. "Personally I think he was just saying good-bye."

Rory turned away, clearly done talking.

Safia shared a worried glance with Kat, then reached for a water bottle. Her arm visibly trembled.

"Safia . . . ?"

Kat noted how shiny the woman's face had become. She placed a hand on Safia's cheek, discovering the smoldering heat there.

"You're burning up."

6:58 A.M.

After Painter Crowe had been escorted out of the library, Simon sat quietly for several minutes at his desk. He had given Painter an hour to make up his mind about cooperating—then sterner measures would have to be taken if necessary.

Which might not be the case.

He had heard from Anton twenty minutes ago. Communication with his search team was spotty due to the geomagnetic storm. The only radio that worked was line-of-sight. Anton could only reach Aurora Station from the tops of the mountains, where he could send a direct microwave signal to the base.

The last report was that his team had picked up the Sno-Cat's trail again.

As Simon sat, he took this into account, his mind running various scenarios and projections through his head. He finally came to a decision and grabbed the phone. He tapped an extension and the project leader—Dr. Sunil Kapoor—promptly picked up. The physicist was likely troubleshooting all systems prior to the test firing of the array in two days.

"Sir?" Kapoor answered, knowing who was calling.

"Change of plans."

"Yes, sir."

Simon had weighed the variable concerning the two missing women and decided the risk was too significant to leave to chance—or even to Anton's skill. If the pair should reach help, everything could be shut down before it was even started.

I can't let that happen . . . not when I'm this close.

What was planned was an important proof-of-concept test. Even if those women succeeded, he wanted confirmation his system worked before facing any consequences.

The project here was too important, far larger than any one man.

Even myself.

"We're moving up the schedule," he told Kapoor.

"To when, sir?"

"To today."

21

Gray stood naked under a cold shower.

Sand swirled at his toes. Every muscle ached. He had already scrubbed his body with soap and hot water, and still more stubborn grains rinsed from cracks, crevices, and patches of hair. He was last to shower, so he took his time—to collect himself, to gather his thoughts. The white noise of the spray and the cold helped him focus.

Three hours ago, he had been hiking with Derek and Kowalski, following the trail left by Seichan's bike, when in the distance a great wall of dust climbed into the burning sky. Vehicles swept down on them, with the Unimog in the middle, flanked by a flock of motorcycles. Behind them came a clutch of camels driven hard by their riders to keep up.

Kowalski had noted their approach. "That's the most sorry-assed-looking cavalry I've ever seen."

After rejoining the others, they headed straight to Khartoum, using trails known to the nomads. Gray took the wheel of the Unimog, much to the disappointment of Ahmad, who needed to head back to Rufaa to return to his family. The boy was somewhat mollified after Seichan bought his bike—which had seen some rough last miles—for a price that was clearly exorbitant. Happy again, the boy and his dog headed back to his village in the sidecar of his cousin's cycle.

Seichan remained on the bike for the return trek, circling wide, watching the skies for any sign of a drone and the surrounding desert for any sign of pursuit.

They had safely reached Khartoum and settled into a cheap hotel at the edge of town.

After all that had befallen them, the team seemed to be back where they'd started, and no closer to discovering how to stop the pandemic. When Gray had headed to the shower, he had left Derek and Jane sitting at a table with their heads bent together, comparing notes. Their faces had not looked hopeful.

The door to the bathroom opened. Through the translucent shower curtain, a figure could be seen entering, shedding clothes with every step. Seichan pushed through and climbed in with him. Her only reaction to the cold was to push against him, sliding an arm around his waist. He pulled her closer, sheltering her body with his own.

He reached back to turn the valve to hot.

"Don't," she whispered into his chest.

He dropped his arm and held her. It was rare for her to be this tender, this vulnerable. He couldn't say he didn't like it. He stayed silent, knowing that's also what she wanted. Now was not the time for long conversations or heartfelt talks about their future. There was only now, this moment.

I'll take it.

He clung to her, their skins warming where they touched, cold where not. He felt himself stirring. A moment later they were kissing. But that was as far as matters progressed before there was a knock on the door. They broke apart. Cold water rushed between them, shattering the moment, pushing them farther apart.

"Gray!" It was Kowalski.

He closed his eyes. "I'm going to kill him."

"Get in line," Seichan growled.

"Monk's on the phone! Hurry it up in there."

Gray pulled back the curtain, stepping away, but turned back to her. He remembered an earlier offer of hers to run away and leave all of this behind them. "Tell me you found another fire escape here."

"A fire escape?" She reached to the top of the curtain, revealing the full breadth of her body. "You had your chance before. We're too in the thick of it now. But ask me again later, and who knows?"

She pulled the curtain, leaving the possibility hanging.

As he buffed his body dry, steam rose from the stall, fogging the curtain, but never fully enough to erase the shape luxuriating in the hot water.

He pulled on his dusty clothes.

Definitely murdering the guy.

As he stalked out to the bedroom, he saw Kowalski had left his satellite phone on the nightstand. He picked it up.

"Monk?"

"How're things in the desert?"

He looked at the closed bathroom door. "Hot. How about in Cairo?"

"Does this answer your question?" A faint spate of gunfire grew louder over the line. "NAMRU is under siege. Some nutcase decided the plague is all an American plot and that the base here is to blame."

"So just another day."

"Pretty much. So if you've made any headway toward a cure, I'd love to hear about it."

" 'Fraid not. We're still at the knocking-our-heads-together stage."

A loud blast echoed over the line. "Then knock a little harder."

"We'll do our best." Gray dropped his voice. "But, Monk, are you okay out there?"

"For now. We've got both American and Egyptian forces holding down the fort. But we can use some good news."

"Understood. Watch your back."

"Back atcha, my friend."

They signed off.

Gray headed to the others, more determined than ever now, but noted a text message waiting for him. He sighed at the number and pulled up the note:

> Dad took a turn for the worse. Stable again.
> Call when you can. Not an emergency, but you know.

Groaning, he called his brother's cell.

Where is that fire escape when you need it?

The phone rang and rang, then finally went to voicemail. He waited for the beep, then said, "Kenny, I got your message. Call back or text. Let me know what's going on and if there's anything I can do at my end."

He hung up the phone, frustrated at not being able to reach him—but also partly relieved. It allowed him to put off the inevitable a little longer. He closed his eyes, feeling guilty for the last part, then shook his head.

One problem at a time.

It was becoming his mantra.

He crossed to the next room. Derek and Jane looked up as he entered. "Any progress?" he asked.

Jane winced, her expression unsure. "Maybe . . . but it makes no sense."

2:24 P.M.

And it didn't . . .

Jane bit her lip, staring at the spread of paper, at Derek working on his iPad. Her father had left her a cryptic message, dying to deliver it, clearly believing she would readily understand it. To even struggle with the mystery made her feel inadequate, even undeserving of his love.

"Show me," Gray said. "Talk it out."

She nodded.

Who says I have to solve this on my own?

Hadn't her father taught her that true discoveries were a team effort? Not that he necessarily followed that dictate, at least when it came to taking credit. His name somehow always ended up being listed *first* on published papers.

Jane sighed. "When he circled that butterfly inside the stone heart, marking my name there, it could have been him merely acknowledging my love of butterflies, trying to share this last connection to me."

"But you don't think so."

"My father was often kind, sometimes generous, but never a sentimentalist."

"No, he was not," Derek concurred.

"So this last effort had to be more significant," Gray said.

"I racked my brain about why he would show me this. As I mentioned before, butterflies were a common image in Egyptian art representing transformation. The species typically depicted—as it was inside the heart—was the common tiger monarch, or *Danaus chrysippus,* a butterfly native to the Nile River basin."

"We were talking about it earlier," Derek said. "When she mentioned the scientific name, it struck me. I remembered seeing the butterfly in Livingstone's old letters. So I showed Jane."

Derek pulled up the page on his tablet and showed Gray.

Danaus chrysippus

"So it's a sketch of a caterpillar and a butterfly." Gray squinted at the name and read it off the screen. "*Danaus chrysippus,* just like you mentioned."

Jane reached and tapped the image. "Only that is *not* the common tiger monarch. The spotting on its wings is all wrong. My father would *know* I would never mistake this image for the true *Danaus chrysippus.*"

Gray leaned closer. "It must be another of Livingstone's maps. Like the Egyptian scarab that pointed to the buried goddess."

Jane nodded. "Yet another map hidden in another Egyptian image."

"But where's the map?" Gray asked. "I don't see it."

"Watch." Derek withdrew his tablet to manipulate the image. He tipped the butterfly up on the edge of a wing and showed them.

Then he set to work. "If you erase everything but the spotting in the lower wing, you can see the pattern that remains looks like a series of lakes and interconnecting waterways. And note the small X that Livingstone drew near one of the rivers."

"Let me guess," Gray said. "You figured out a place that corresponds to that configuration of rivers and lakes."

Derek nodded. "It's just down the road from where we are now . . . or more precisely, down the *river*."

He brought up a tiny map and placed it next to the drawing hidden in Livingstone's butterfly.

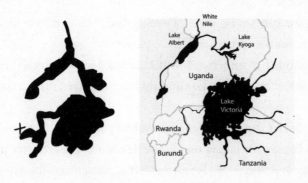

Derek explained, "Look how Lake Victoria matches up, as do the smaller lakes."

Gray took the pad to examine it closer. "And Livingstone's X sits along a small river that flows out of Rwanda and into Lake Victoria."

Jane's voice sharpened with excitement. "I believe what we're looking at might be the source of the Nile."

"Or at least *one* of the sources," Derek added. "You can see other rivers flowing into Victoria, which is why the true origin of the Nile is still disputed."

Gray frowned, looking suddenly concerned.

Jane turned to him. "What's wrong?"

Gray straightened and pulled out the test tube her father had buried in the sand. He removed the rubber stopper and unrolled the scrap of leather inside, revealing again the faint line of hieroglyphics.

"If I remember right," he said, "this translates roughly as *taking a boat to the mouth of the river*. And something about *elephants* or *elephant bones*."

Jane reached for the relic, then pulled her hand back. "The *mouth* of the river. Maybe that's referencing the *source* of the Nile. Just like we were talking about." She pointed to Derek's map. "Maybe it's saying go to that place marked with an X."

"But how can we be sure?" Derek asked. "How do we know what's written here is even important?"

Gray pointed to either end of the line of hieroglyphics. "There are a lion and a kneeling woman framing this section. Aren't those the symbols of Tutu?"

"And they're also found on Livingstone's *aryballos*," Jane added. "The two symbols are even facing the same direction as the artifact's profiles."

Gray looked at her. "Maybe your father recognized the same and cut this section off a mummy he found down there, seeking to hide it. Later he buried it to safeguard it, while leaving behind a clue for you to follow."

"And don't forget the elephants," Kowalski reminded them, his eyes flashing with a bit of excitement. "Remember that cute—I mean *small* elephant pot we saw before."

Jane nodded, sensing pieces were starting to come together—but not yet whole. "He's right."

Derek suddenly looked sick. "What if whatever was in those pots *was* the cure?"

Kowalski scowled. "I told you we should've taken one."

"No," Jane said. "My father would have tested anything found in those pots. That can't be it."

"Plus," Gray added, "whoever cleared the place out would have taken the pots if they thought they were important."

Jane pointed to Derek's map. "The answer must be there. My father knew it, but he couldn't get there himself, and he didn't want his captors to know about it."

"So he tried to escape and reach help." Derek turned to Jane. "And knowing he might fail, he left clues for his daughter to follow."

She knew Derek was right. With tears threatening, she turned away.

From the next room, Seichan entered, toweling her hair. She must have sensed the tension and excitement. "What's going on?"

Gray smiled. "Time to pack your bags."

Kowalski rubbed his palms together. "We're gonna find us some elephants."

3:03 P.M.

Valya refused to take any more chances.

She waited at a small airstrip outside Khartoum. The sun had baked the sand and dirt to a concrete hardness. The field was not on any map. It was used by drug smugglers and Sudanese rebels. The police and army were paid well to look the other way.

For all intents and purposes, this place didn't exist.

She took solace in this fact. *This* was her true home, the cracks of the world. After plunging her grandmother's dagger into the neck of the man who killed their mother, she took her brother and fled into those cracks, where, whether out of distaste or fear, no one truly looked. Back then, she and Anton had each other.

But no longer.

Anton had found a new home, a new heart.

So be it.

She would return to where she belonged, with or without him.

A grumble of an engine drew her attention to the right. An open-air truck crossed through a gate in a dilapidated chain link fence. A dark-skinned former Sudanese soldier with an assault rifle waved them through. Valya stepped around the parked Cessna to meet the truck.

Kruger hopped out, followed by four of his men. They were all that had survived the destruction under the desert hills. Four others had died. He had lost half his teammates down that hole. Kruger wore those deaths on his face as he stalked over. It had not been hard to convince him of the change in plans.

"Well?" she asked.

He nodded, rubbing a set of raw and bloody knuckles. "Took some convincing, but I confirmed what you overheard. Their flight manifest has them flying into Rwanda."

Valya had kept her distance from the enemy after being ambushed by the nomads in the desert. While Seichan and Jane McCabe had regrouped at the dunes, she had used the sharp eyes of the Raven in the sky to spot where the boy had abandoned the Unimog. She circled to that spot while the others were distracted, slowing to limit her dust trail. She finished her mission from last night and buried a GPS transmitter in the truck's wheel well—then sped off to rejoin Kruger.

She took a deep breath now, stretching her neck. She felt looser, less constrained, freer than in many years. Her mistake earlier had been to fix-ate on completing the task assigned her. While focused on capturing Jane

McCabe, she had let her attention on the fleeing truck lapse, even pulling the Raven assigned to it, allowing the boy to meet up with his people unseen.

That would not happen again.

After joining Kruger, she had easily tracked the truck's journey back to Khartoum and discovered where the group had holed up. Still, she kept her distance, having learned her lesson. From a quarter-mile away, she had eavesdropped upon their conversation, listening with a laser microphone, its invisible infrared beam fixed to the window, picking up minute vibrations in the glass and whispering their words in her ears. Unfortunately, such technology was not flawless. Words were missed. The conversation had annoying gaps. She got the gist of where they planned to go, but she had wanted confirmation and sent Kruger to get it.

It seemed her targets had hired a bush plane—a Cessna 208 Caravan—to ferry them south to Rwanda. She would follow them, even taking the same plane, only hers was a military variant arranged by friends of Kruger. It was a Combat Caravan, a plane used by rebels throughout the region, even in Iraq.

She glanced under the wings to the payload mounted there.

Two AGM-114 Hellfire missiles.

The edges of her lips tugged up in satisfaction.

She was done bowing to masters, of being reined in by their restraints and goaded into making mistakes to meet their expectations. She intended to be free again, free to return to cracks in this world. Knowing that, she saw no need to adhere to the prior restrictions placed on her.

"So are we sticking with the new plan?" Kruger asked as he stepped into the plane.

She followed him inside. "Yes, we kill them all."

FOURTH

THE PAINTED JUNGLE

22

By the time the guards came to collect him, Painter knew something was wrong.

Hartnell had given him an hour—until eight o'clock—to decide whether or not to cooperate in helping them capture Kat and Safia. That hour had come and gone, leaving him pacing his cell. Finally, after another two hours, a pair of guards barged into his room, guns raised, and forced him to don a parka and thick boots before cuffing his wrists in front of him and marching him out.

The delay was worrisome. Had something happened to Kat and Safia? Was his cooperation no longer a concern? If so, where were the guards taking him?

The outerwear and lack of ankle restraints suggested he'd be doing some walking, likely into the cold. Even the guards wore heavy coats. He tried to ask questions of them, only to be rebuffed.

They headed down three levels, rather than out.

It made no sense.

Where are we going?

At last, they reached a set of steel doors. One guard unlocked the way with a keycard and headed through first. The second man pushed Painter forward with the muzzle of his assault rifle.

The reason for the warmer clothes was immediately evident. The passage ahead had been cut out of the island rock. Though naturally insulated from the elements, the air was still Arctic-chilled. Each breath puffed white into the cold. The rough tunnel extended several hundred yards without a single door or side room. A wired string of caged bulbs lit the way.

Painter lifted his chained arms and ran his fingertips along one wall.

Must be an old mine tunnel.

He suddenly suspected where they were headed. At the far end, another identical set of steel doors sealed the passageway. His group followed the same dance to pass out of the tunnel and back into the modern age. Steel, glass, and concrete block opened around him, revealing another section of the station.

This extension of the base curved to either side, walled by blast windows across its front, all looking out into the tiered pit he had spotted from the air when he and Kat had first flown here. While this piece of the station failed to completely encircle that quarter-mile-wide hole, it did hug the half on this side, with its length subdivided into various workstations. People in lab coats and coveralls of various hues scurried about or sat hunched at monitors. Chatter was low, as if they were all inside a cathedral.

And maybe they were, but one built to worship science.

As Painter drew near the thick window, he could see storm clouds rolling darkly past the sky. He estimated this U-shaped perch was positioned halfway up the excavation's wall. Down below, lit by giant spotlights, the flat bottom of the old mining pit supported the massive square base of Hartnell's new incarnation of Wardenclyffe Tower. Steel beams rose past the window, forming a pyramidal skeletal skyscraper, ending at a massive bowl of concentric rings of copper and colossal electromagnets, all cradling a conducting sphere.

No, not a sphere.

From the air, the top of the tower had looked like a perfect globe, but from this lower vantage, Painter realized that what he had viewed was only the rounded *top* of a giant egg.

He pictured Clyffe Energy's logo—the Egg of Columbus.

Was this design purposeful or only a conceit?

"Ah, there you are!" Simon Hartnell came striding toward him from one of the stations. He wore a silver parka, unzipped at the moment. "I apologize for keeping you waiting."

"I'm on your schedule." Painter glanced at all the activity. "What's going on? This looks far busier than what I would imagine to be a typical workday."

"So it is, so it is."

The man set off again, clearly intending for Painter to follow, so he did. Not that he had much choice with the two guards at his back. Hartnell collected another figure in a parka along the way, a short Indian man with a pinched, concerned face.

Hartnell introduced him. "This is Dr. Sunil Kapoor."

Painter recognized the name of the physicist. He had won the Nobel Prize for his work with plasma, specifically involving a novel way of creating it using vaporized metal. Clearly Hartnell was standing on more than just Nikola Tesla's shoulders to complete his vision.

"We're about to head out and do a final systems check of the remote monitoring stations." Hartnell set off. "It's all very exciting."

Kapoor did not look as enthralled. The man kept glancing over his shoulder at the steel pyramid outside. Still, Hartnell would not be refused.

As they crossed along the curve of the tower's command station, a new window appeared, opposite the other. Painter slowed and peered through it to a neighboring cavern. It was nearly as deep as the pit outside, but not open to the sky. A black lake filled the bottom, but lights along an elevated catwalk revealed the water to be a deep crimson.

Painter went cold at the sight, knowing what he was seeing. Here was the fuel for Hartwell's vision. The bastard had cultured a whole sea of Tesla's *Pestis fulmen*. Men in hazmat suits worked along the catwalk, holding clipboards and shining lights along steel tubes that ran from the lake below to the roof above.

Oh my god . . .

"Everyone aboard," Hartwell said, welcoming them into the car of a funicular train whose tracks angled along the sloped wall of the pit, running the length from top to bottom.

Painter climbed inside with the others. A window of glass allowed him to peer at the tower as the car jerked and began to climb upward. "From all the commotion, I take it that you've moved up your schedule."

"Indeed. Upon further consideration, I thought it prudent."

Painter understood his logic. The man didn't want anyone interfering with his test run, especially if Kat and Safia reached outside help.

Painter turned to Hartnell. "So you're still planning to seed the ionosphere with the microbe as part of this test run."

"No reason to take half measures."

Painter looked at Dr. Kapoor. "And you have no qualms about this?"

The Indian physicist glanced to Hartnell, then back to Painter, and gave a small shake of his head.

Not exactly the most ringing endorsement.

"We've run countless scenarios," Hartnell assured him. "Considered every variable."

Painter looked to the sky. "When it comes to hacking the planet, you can't know all the variables. You could end up setting fire to the atmosphere."

Hartnell scoffed. "The very same concern was raised with the testing of the first atomic bomb, but it didn't stop the Manhattan Project from continuing." He cast a doleful eye at Painter. "Likewise, the same charges were made against HAARP."

That was certainly true.

"If we stopped progress for every Chicken Little's claim that the sky was falling, nothing would ever get done." Hartnell sighed loudly. "We'd still be huddling in cold caves, afraid of fire."

The train car reached the lip of the pit, and they all climbed out into the blowing wind and dry snow. Parkas were quickly zipped. The group set out across the steel forest of antennas. Thigh-thick cabling ran across the rock and through patches of stubborn snow.

Hartnell took them along a gravel path that led out of this forest.

No one spoke, hunched in their jackets, cheeks pulled into their hoods.

Far to Painter's right, a Boeing cargo jet was being hauled out of a hangar and into the storm. It looked sturdy enough to withstand the gale, especially as the storm had calmed slightly over the past hour.

Painter knew the payload the jet was set to carry, picturing that black lake.

The group reached the fringe of the array and found two vehicles waiting for them. One looked like a golf cart with a sealed cab and large knobbed tires. Painter imagined it would be used by Hartnell and Kapoor to make their survey run.

This was confirmed when Hartnell lifted an arm to the other vehicle, a Sno-Cat. "Here's your ride." He pointed to a neighboring tall hill. "We maintain a communication shack up top. It offers the tallest vantage for direct-sight-line communication during solar storms. It's to be your base of operation, to coordinate with Anton in convincing your companion and Dr. al-Maaz to deliver what they stole. For our sake and theirs. It can be very dangerous out there."

"And if I still refuse?"

Hartnell looked disappointed. "You can be part of the solution or part of the problem."

Painter imagined *problems* were promptly eliminated here.

He eyed the armed guards.

"I'll try my best," he said. "That's all I can do."

"And that's all I ask." Hartnell stared out at the storm. "It's what we should all do when faced with a challenge—at least *try* to do something about it, to make the world a better place."

Painter nodded.

I intend to do just that.

10:55 A.M.

Kat shivered as she poured the last of the diesel into their vehicle's thirsty tank. She estimated they had enough fuel to travel another eighty miles over such unforgiving terrain, maybe farther if she nursed the engine. Still, she had to accept that they might not reach the Canadian outpost at Alert.

And it's not like we can hoof it.

Without parkas, they would freeze.

And then there was Safia's deteriorating health. Her fever had been steadily climbing. She had been exposed six hours ago at the lab, so this was likely still the early stages of the disease.

For the moment, Kat and Rory both seemed fine, but trapped in the enclosed cab with the sick woman, how long would that last?

And what choice do we have?

She climbed back into the Cat and got them moving again. They were traveling along the northwest shore of Lake Hazen. It stretched forty miles long and only eight wide and pointed straight toward Alert. Unfortunately, beyond the lake's tip it was still another hundred miles over a treacherous terrain of mountains and glaciers.

At least the wind and snow had let up slightly, but she knew this was only a respite before the storm rallied again. The skies rolling toward them from the west were far darker.

As she stared in that direction, she caught tiny flashes of light along the mountains. She prayed it was lightning. It was not entirely unlikely, but she pressed the accelerator harder, speeding them up, forgoing any attempt to eke out better gas mileage.

She kept watching the west, but the lights never reappeared.

Safia stirred in the passenger seat, her lips dry, her eyes glazed with fatigue and fever. "It's hot . . ."

"You're burning up," Kat said. "Just try to rest."

She shared a glance in the rearview mirror with Rory.

"She needs medical help," he whispered. "Maybe if we go back . . ."

Kat knew that would be certain death for Safia. The station would not risk exposing everyone. Plus Kat refused to turn over their hard-won data.

Safia had risked her life—and now might be paying with it—to keep that information out of Hartnell's hands.

"No," she said. "We're not turning back."

Rory's gaze shifted to the windshield. "Kat, look! Out on the lake."

She focused forward. Off to her right, a trio of hide tents, frosted white by the snow on their windward sides, sat on the ice. In front of each tent, small circular holes glowed blue, with poles planted next to them, trailing lines. The grumbling noise of their approach stirred the ice fishermen from their warm tents.

From this distance, they looked like small bears in fur coats and thick pants.

"I think they're Inuit," Rory said, leaning forward as much as his restraints would allow.

Safia showed no interest, even shading her eyes from the sight. "It's bright," she mumbled.

Kat's worry for her friend flared. One of the signs of encephalitis was photophobia, an aversion to light.

Safia's head lolled back, her eyes rolling even farther. "So bright . . ."

11:04 A.M.

Safia struggles to turn her face from the sun. It stings her eyes, hanging in an achingly blue sky. She gasps at the heat, each breath fiery. Her bare feet sink in the burning sands as she struggles toward the cool promise of the river.

"Safia, Safia . . . you have to drink . . ."

She searches for the voice.

The world shimmers before her, shaking the palm trees. Through the ripples of the mirage, she sees a strange white land, frozen over and dark. Her ears hear distant thunder.

"C'mon, just a few sips . . ."

Then it's gone, and she sees only sand and death again. Fly-encrusted beasts lay bloated all around. Scavengers tear into their flesh, screaming at her passage. She continues stumbling forward, cresting a dune to look upon the river.

As thirst closes her throat, she sees her salvation is a lie.

The river runs red with blood, draining the life from the lands.

She searches the heavens, begging.

"Drink, Safia . . ."

Beyond the river, the sky is black, coursing with lightning, angry and punishing. It falls toward her, toward the world, intending to crush it.

She backs one step, then another. "It's coming . . ."

Then a coolness flows down her throat, spills along her neck.

She is drowning under the sun.

"Stop fighting, Safia, please . . ."

Again the world shimmers like a veil. The sun dims to darkness, and sand becomes snow, and a shadow becomes a face.

One she knows.

"Kat?"

"I've got you, honey. I've got you. You've had a small seizure."

She can't help it and begins to sob.

"What's wrong?"

"Something bad . . . something horrible is coming."

11:32 A.M.

At least they're consistent.

Painter waited for the first guard to key open the communication shack. It sat at the summit of a tall hill, a squat concrete bunker festooned with antennas on the roof.

As he waited at the threshold, he took a moment to appreciate the view from here. To one side stretched the Arctic tundra; on the other, the breadth of Aurora Station. The spiral of the array was clear from this height, as was the tower poking from the old mining pit.

The cargo jet he had spotted earlier was parked near the runway, its rear-loading ramp lowered. A fleet of laden forklifts headed its way.

Beyond that island of activity, nothing else moved out there. It was as if everything was holding its breath for what's to come.

"Quit gawking," the guard behind him said, urging him at gunpoint into the shack. He clearly wanted out of the cold.

Can't blame him.

Painter sighed, slumping into the one-room bunker. He paused at the threshold, noting a rumpled bed to one side. The back of the space was packed with communication gear, including multiple radios, even a VLF transmitter used to contact submarines.

In the center of that nest hunched a heavyset young man wearing headphones. With his back to his new guests, his only greeting was a raised arm.

"How's it going, Ray?" the first guard asked.

The other man poked Painter again.

About time.

Painter twisted sideways and stepped back. With the barrel of the rifle now across his belly, he swung his arms up and hooked the links of his cuffs around the startled guard's neck, then lunged at the waist and tossed the man over his shoulder and into the room.

The first guard spun, firing in his direction.

Painter had already dropped to his butt, shielded by his choking prisoner. As the first panicked rounds pelted into the man, Painter drew his bound wrists in front of the prisoner, as if hugging him from behind. Painter's hands found the wounded man's weapon, and he snagged a finger on the trigger.

He strafed wildly.

A lucky couple of shots hit the exposed guard: in the knee, in the chest. The man crashed to the side. Painter firmed his aim and only needed one more shot, which he took. The guard slumped. Still cradling his prisoner, who gasped and choked in his arms, Painter swung the rifle toward the radio operator, who sat stunned, a deer in headlights.

"Hey, Ray, how about you pat down your friend, find the keys to these cuffs, and let me free?"

Ray hesitated, glancing back at his equipment, then to Painter.

"Now, Ray, either I shoot you and find the keys myself, or you help me and you end up wearing these cuffs and live to see another sunrise. And up here, that might be a good long while."

In the end, Ray proved to be a reasonable guy.

Painter rubbed his wrists after cuffing the operator to the bed and tying his ankles with his own headphones. For good measure, he had also stuffed a sock in the man's mouth and duct-taped it in place.

"Okay, Ray, unless you have an objection, I'm going to take that Sno-Cat out there and go find my friends. And you're not going to say a word, right?"

The man nodded vigorously.

So very reasonable.

Painter grabbed one of the rifles and pocketed the two extra magazines found on the dead guards. Armed, he headed out into the cold, climbed into the Cat, and put his back to Aurora Station. The open tundra spread before him.

Now down to business.

12:45 P.M.

Simon stood at the helm of the command station for the Aurora array. His heart pounded as he stared through the window at the massive tower, a testament to Tesla's genius.

And my own.

Men and women continued to prepare for the test firing, triple- and quadruple-checking every system. He had green lights across his board from all stations.

On a monitor to his left, he watched the Boeing cargo jet steam across the heated runway, gaining speed. Its flaps dropped and it lifted skyward, carrying its package toward the heavens.

Simon grinned, following its trajectory toward the clouds.

Then he heard the patter of feet behind him and turned to see a man in black coveralls rush to his side, one of Anton's crew.

"Sir?"

Simon hoped it was good news from the search crew, but from the man's pale face, it was not. "What is it?"

"We just got word that the prisoner who was being escorted to the communication shack has escaped, killing the guards. According to the radio operator, the man took off with a Sno-Cat, going after his friends. He was well armed."

Simon clenched a fist in frustration, his cheeks flushing, close to exploding. Clearly Painter Crowe was far more than a DARPA investigator. Still, Simon forced his fingers to relax and to take a deep breath.

Look at the bigger picture.

Nothing had fundamentally changed. With the two women still free, the situation here was already compromised—but fixable. This new development did not significantly worsen matters.

At least not for me.

He took a deep steadying breath. "Let Anton know what has happened. Tell him to watch his back out there."

"Yes, sir." The security guard turned on a heel and dashed away.

Simon shook his head at Painter Crowe's futile actions.

Where does he think he can go?

1:04 P.M.

Painter crouched in the cavernous hold of the cargo jet.

Under his boots, he felt the vibrations of the jet's four engines as they fought the storm winds. The plane jostled and rocked. Cargo creaked and shifted around him ominously, threatening to crush him.

He was aboard a wide-bellied Boeing C-17 Globemaster, normally used by the military for long-haul transport, moving troops, equipment, even battle tanks. It was uniquely built for dropping air loads in midflight from its rear hatch. While the behemoth had recently gone out of production, Hartnell must have acquired one that he had redesigned and configured for his needs.

After leaving the communication shack, Painter had set out into the storm in the Sno-Cat. He drove it deep into the blowing snow until he reached a relatively open stretch of tundra, then jammed a crowbar found in a tool chest against the gas pedal and sent the vehicle trundling away on its own, leaving a false trail.

He didn't expect his ruse to last for long. He just needed enough time to backtrack to the station and over to the idling Globemaster waiting on the tarmac.

Using the cover of the storm, he had run behind hillocks of plowed snow and through netted piles of crates until he could get under the plane. He had flown aboard these big birds in the past, back when he was still with the Navy SEALs, which seemed a lifetime ago.

Still, some things never changed.

He knew when you packed a big bus like this there were plenty of places to hide.

So he scurried to the aft of the plane, to where its rear-loading ramp still touched the tarmac. He slid under it and waited for a forklift to back out, turn, and zip away. A couple of peeks and he saw his opportunity to roll onto the ramp and dash into the hold.

As expected, the entire space was crowded. Two rows of pallets, nine to a side, held aluminum crates as tall as Painter, each crowned by parachute-like pouches. They sat atop a hydraulic air delivery system designed to push the two rows of cargo out the rear hatch in midflight.

Painter wasted no time cramming himself between two of the pallets, dropping low, ready to shift to keep hidden if necessary. Though he doubted anyone would dally too long with a search of this hold. Red biohazard labels were plastered on each side of the aluminum crates.

He knew what these containers held.

Cultured vats of *Pestis fulmen*.

The parachutes on top must be Hartnell's weather balloon system. Painter imagined they must self-inflate once the crates were ejected, carrying aloft their deadly cargo. Once high enough, the crates would burst open like toxic seedpods.

Picturing that, Painter stared at the label near his cheek.

Maybe this wasn't such a bright idea.

23

We need to keep moving . . .

With the sun hovering low on the horizon, Gray wanted to take advantage of what little day they had left. He remembered the blasts and gunfire heard over the phone with Monk. Matters were worsening by the hour in Cairo, and likely to boil over throughout the volatile region and beyond.

If there was something to be found here, they dared not delay.

To that end, Gray had gathered with his team on an open wooden deck overlooking Lake Ihema, the second-largest lake in Rwanda. They had flown by bush plane from Khartoum and landed as close as they could to the X marked on Livingstone's map, setting down at a dirt airstrip in Akagera National Park. They were awaiting the arrival of a local guide who had worked here for twenty-five years.

From the park map spread on the table, they certainly needed someone with boots-on-the-ground knowledge of this place. Akagera National Park spread across five hundred square miles, encompassing rolling savannas, papyrus swamps, and mountainous jungles. It held a labyrinth of lakes and interconnecting waterways, all branching off the Kagera River, which formed the park's eastern border.

Jane ran her finger along the same river on the map. "This must be the correct tributary, right?"

Back in Khartoum, the group had charted the rivers flowing into Lake Victoria—which served as the headwaters for the White Nile—trying to determine which of its many feeders best corresponded to the one drawn on Livingstone's secret map. The Kagera River was a perfect match, flowing west out of Victoria and coursing between Uganda and Tanzania before turning south along the Rwandan border.

Still, they couldn't be a hundred percent sure.

"Look at this," Derek said.

While they waited for their guide, he had been seeking further corroboration, using his tablet to study more maps, both new and old. He showed them a chart of the region with the Kagera River highlighted and some measurements drawn on it.

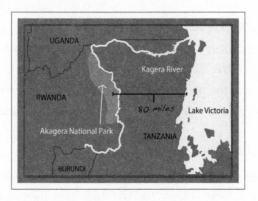

"As you can see," Derek said, "the park lies about eighty miles due west of Lake Victoria."

"And that's significant, why?" Gray asked.

Derek pulled up the sketch that Livingstone had drawn of the butterfly and caterpillar. He zoomed in on the latter.

"Look how the caterpillar is drawn with *eight* segments. I think Livingstone was using the worm as a legend for his hidden map. As a yardstick, if you will."

Gray nodded. "Eight segments, eighty miles."

While not definitive proof that they were on the right course, it did support the case. Even Jane smiled, patting Derek's hand appreciatively. Plainly they all needed this little measure of reassurance.

Seichan turned from the deck rail, where she had been watching the lake and skies. "I think this is our guy coming."

A rumble of a motor grew louder and drew them all to her side. An odd-looking watercraft charged toward the dock below. The boat had clearly seen some rough miles over the years. The scarred green metal hull bore dents along its sides, and the windshield had a crack in it that looked ominously like a bullet hole.

"Lake's low," Seichan noted. "Not sure he has enough draft to dock here."

This fact did not seem to concern the man behind the wheel.

"He's not even slowing," Derek said, backing a step.

The craft reached the dock—and continued past it. The bow lifted as the boat hit the bank, riding up to reveal a pair of treads, like the undercarriage of a tank. The amphibious craft continued out of the water and rode up alongside their deck and finally stopped with its port-side gunwale even with their rail.

The driver smiled, clearly enjoying their surprise. "*Muraho!*" he greeted them in his native Kinyarwanda. He wore a khaki safari jacket with matching pants. Despite being sixty, he looked fit, with only some specking of gray in his dark hair.

"Welcome to Akagera," he said. "My name is Noah Mutabazi, and while I don't bring an ark with me"—he patted the flank of his boat—"I assure you this vessel will not disappoint."

But the *method* of arrival wasn't his only surprise.

He hadn't come alone.

Kowalski retreated two steps. "Okay, what's with the lion?"

From behind his seat, a creature rose into view, spine arching in a typical feline stretch. A yawn revealed long fangs and a pink tongue.

"Ah," the guide said, "that is my navigator. His name is Roho, which means *ghost* in Swahili."

The name certainly fit the beast. The lion's coat was a tawny white, his eyes a rich amber. The mutation that produced white lions was not albinism but a rarer genetic trait called leucism, which resulted in only a partial loss of pigmentation.

Noah scratched his partner's neck, earning a rumble that served as the equivalent of a feline purr. "He's just a cub."

"*That's* a cub?" Kowalski asked.

Gray understood the man's shock. The cat had to weigh over a hundred pounds.

"He is indeed," Noah said. When the man spoke English, his words took on a slight British accent. "His first birthday is next month. So hopefully he'll soon grow into this."

Noah tussled a mohawk of brighter white fur that ran from the crown of the cub's head and down his neck. "As you see, his mane is still immature. In fact, he's not even learned to roar yet. He won't do that for a few more months."

Roho growled, pretending to bite at his hand, as if insulted.

Jane looked like she wanted to go pet him. "How did you acquire him?"

Noah's face grew more serious, glancing across the lake to the breadth of the park. "Two years ago, seven Transvaal lions were reintroduced to our park, in an attempt to restore a population that's been gone from these lands for decades. With the addition of the lions—and perhaps one day, black rhinos—Akagera may soon return to its full glory."

He turned to them, his face wistful with hope.

"And Roho?" Jane pressed.

"Oh, yes, one of our new lionesses was pregnant when she arrived. She gave birth to three cubs, one of them Roho. Since survival rates are poor for cubs in the wild, we culled him from her litter to give the other two cubs a better chance of surviving, but also because we feared poachers might hunt him for the color of his pelt. And as indiscriminate as such men are, Roho's presence risked the lives of the entire new pride."

"So you kept him."

"To train him. The hope is still to release him, when he's older and better able to fend for himself. He's now of the age when his mother usually begins teaching him to hunt, so I take him whenever I can."

Gray glanced to the sun as it sat lower over the lake. "We should be going. I want to be at the site we mapped before sunset."

Noah climbed from the boat to the deck. "Show me. I was told basically where you wanted to go, but perhaps I could offer further guidance."

Roho followed him with a single leap, plainly ready to do the same.

"He's friendly," Noah assured everyone while crossing to the maps strewn on the table.

Gray joined the guide, while the others took the opportunity to meet Roho.

"This is where we were thinking of going." Gray pointed to a region to the north that most closely corresponded to the X marked on Livingstone's map.

Noah studied the chart while inhaling deeply. "May I ask, why there?"

"Is it a problem?"

"Compared to other places in Africa, Akagera sees few visitors. When I lead a safari, I am often the only one out there. And that's in the *southern* end of the park. Up north, no one goes there. Not really."

"Why doesn't anyone go there?"

"Difficult terrain. Mountainous, thick jungles. It's as untouched as you'll find in Africa. Many believe those dense forests are haunted. Even rebels and poachers don't go there."

Gray looked at his amphibious boat. "But can that get us there?"

"To the edge, certainly. Beyond that . . ." The man shrugged. "But again, why *there*? What are you seeking?"

Gray frowned. "Elephants."

Noah's eyes widened, looking relieved. "Oh, that is easy then. No need to go all the way up there. I can show you many elephants. Much closer. Here in the south."

"And what about in the north?" Gray stared at the map. "Are there any elephants up there?"

Noah considered his question. "Not yet. While the park has had good success at reestablishing an elephant herd here—we have over ninety now—they mostly stay in the south. Even they don't like to venture into the northern jungles, preferring the savannas and marshlands."

Gray took stock of what he had just said. "What do you mean by *reestablishing* the park's herd?"

"Like with the reintroduction of the lions, elephants were added back to the park in 1975."

"What happened to the original herds?"

He shrugged again. "Poachers, big-game hunters. All I know is that the indigenous elephants vanished some sixty years ago."

Vanished?

Gray's stomach sank with despair. If there was some cure to be found here, was it already gone?

Are we decades too late?

Noah shook his head. "When I first came here as a young man, some of the older guides would talk of the park's former glory. There had been many herds back then, even shy forest elephants who roamed those northern mountain jungles. No longer, but hopefully, those times will return."

"But can you be sure?" Gray asked.

"Of those times returning?"

"No, of those forest elephants being gone." Gray looked at the spot on the map. "You said those mountains are rarely traveled, even avoided. If the elephants were truly that shy, maybe a few of them are still up there."

Noah looked skeptical.

Gray straightened, eyeing the sun. "What's the harm in looking?"

5:31 P.M.

Jane sat with Derek in the middle of Noah's amphibious ark.

Ahead of them, Gray murmured with the ship's captain, while Seichan crouched at the point of the bow, her gaze alert for any threat ahead. Kowalski did the same in the back, sprawled in the stern, his shotgun across his knees.

Jane did her best to ignore the peril.

Instead, she stared at the beauty around her, enjoying the tropical weather after the searing heat of the Sudan.

All around, the flat waters of Lake Ihema mirrored the blue sky, marred only by the boat's wake, which dappled the last rays of the sun across the water. It looked like they had the vast lake all to themselves.

But she knew that wasn't true. Though they might be the only boat, the lake teemed with life. Hippos bobbed along the shoreline as their craft plied past their roosting spots, sometimes opening their massive jaws in territorial displays of threat. Elsewhere, hidden in the papyrus, the long black logs of crocodiles were reminders that swimming these waters was a sport only for the most foolhardy. A few brave creatures took that risk, but those lumbering adult Cape water buffaloes had little to fear.

She gazed out at the flocks of crowned cranes and open-billed storks working the shallows. They weren't the only hunters of the lake. An African fish eagle dove down, snagged something wiggling and silver, and shot back skyward. Thousands of other birds flitted and darted, too quick to identify, too numerous to even try.

Out in the surrounding marshes and grasses, life spread far and wide. Herds of klipspringer antelope grazed alongside impalas and zebra. In the distance, the stately bob of giraffe necks moved through a savanna, like the masts of tall ships.

With the sun sunk to the horizon, shadows stretched everywhere, adding dark brushstrokes across the meadows and hills.

Jane sighed, knowing how easy it would be to be lulled into the pace of this land, but they still had much to do.

A sharp slap reminded her of this.

Derek rubbed his arm, leaving a tiny smear of blood from whatever had bit him. Throughout this region, it was those same bloodsuckers that spread disease and death: West Nile, dengue and yellow fever, even Zika, which originated in a Ugandan monkey. She had also learned that those same pathogens were *all* flaviviruses. Same as the virus harboring inside the microbe they hunted, a genetic Trojan horse capable of killing male offspring.

So maybe it's no surprise we ended up here.

As she dwelled on this fact, the wonder of the park faded.

She sank back into her seat. Derek followed her. She took his arm and pulled it over her shoulders, wanting to feel his solidness. She nestled into him.

Derek must have sensed her dismay and tried to combat it. "I keep imagining the likes of David Livingstone and his fellow explorers, trudging through these swamps, battling the elements, wild animals, not to mention"—he lifted his bitten arm—"the smallest of predators."

He craned around. "Livingstone likely searched this very region. We know Stanley famously found the good doctor languishing in a village along the shores of Lake Tanganyika, which lies only a hundred miles away. And while Stanley returned home, Livingstone remained to continue his quest for the source of the Nile. His explorations might have very well led him here."

"As I recall, it was along those same shores where a tribesman gave him his talisman."

He nodded. "The same tribe honored him later, burying his heart under a local plum tree."

"Then mummified him," she added sourly, thinking of her father's fate.

"Out of respect. They packed his remains in salt and shipped him home in a coffin made of bark. He's now buried in Westminster Abbey."

"But was it worth it? He gave his life to add a few lines to a map."

"Perhaps, but he also helped many of the natives here, fighting against slavers, teaching them. And besides, even if he never did any of that, the pursuit of knowledge is never for naught. Each line drawn on a map gets us closer to understanding the world and our place in it."

She rewarded him with a small smile. "You, Dr. Rankin, are a better person than I."

He drew her closer. "I'm not about to dispute that."

By now they had reached the end of the lake and entered the labyrinth of lakes, rolling hills, and swamps that separated them from the low mountains darkening the horizon. The terrain here proved the utility of their unique mode of transportation. No matter the challenge—deep water, slippery mud, sinking sand, or tall grass—Noah's amphibious ark forged on.

Still, not everyone was content.

A growled complaint rose behind Jane. "Why does he keep licking me?"

She turned to find Roho nosing the big guy, smearing a long wet tongue across his cheek. Kowalski pushed him away.

Seichan commented from the bow. "He's tasting you, Kowalski. Seeing if you're worth eating."

Noah gave her a scolding look. "It's just the salt from your sweat."

This information failed to calm the man. "So he *is* tasting me."

Jane turned back around and nestled deeper next to Derek. "What was that about knowledge always being a good thing?"

5:55 P.M.

Valya wanted as much intel as possible before acting.

Seated in the copilot seat, she ordered the Cessna to bank wide again, to keep its reflection off the wide lake below. In the back cabin, Kruger had the side cargo door slid open. One hand clutched a grip against the wind, the other held a pair of binoculars. He watched their targets progress across a landscape of lakes, marshes, and grasslands, likely recalling his teammates killed by those below.

She was tempted to order the Cessna to dive down, to fire one or both of their Hellfire missiles at the amphibious craft. But while that would certainly annihilate them, it would fail to be fully satisfying. She absently rubbed the hilt of her grandmother's *athamé*.

No, not nearly satisfying enough.

Plus there was a practical reason. She and Kruger had decided to follow the others, see where they might lead. And if the situation presented itself, they would grab whatever prize might be hidden down there for themselves.

To sell to the highest bidder.

Best of all, she knew someone who had a personal stake in all of this and who had very deep pockets. It was time to turn that to her advantage.

To hell with Simon Hartnell—and my brother.

With the decision made, she intended not to fail, which meant heeding the instructions of her former masters in the Guild: to be patient and wait for her moment. All the failure up until now was due to her moving too hastily, acting upon her baser emotions of revenge. She needed to be cold and calculating.

Like her quarry.

She pictured Seichan's face.

"Sun's about to set!" Kruger called up to her.

She twisted in her seat, eyeing the Raven UAV sharing the cabin with Kruger and his three men. "Wait until it's fully dark before launching."

The plan was to hold off until nightfall and send the drone to continue the hunt by air, using its thermal and low-light optics to continue tracking their prey. She could not risk the bird being spotted during the day. Once it was aloft, they would refuel and maintain a high-altitude vigil, waiting for their moment. When that came, they would sweep low. Kruger and his men would bail out in base-jumping gear to secure the area. She would follow in a more conventional chute. The pilot would circle and wait for their command to unleash his missiles, which guided by a fire-and-forget radar system would clean up behind them.

Alternatively, if it looked like their targets had failed in their search, then her team would go with the missiles first. Though such a scheme was far from satisfying or profitable, it would get the job done.

Still, she preferred the first plan.

So she stared below and wished the others the best of luck.

6:35 P.M.

Now I understand what Noah meant.

The dark forest ahead looked impenetrable. Their vehicle had climbed out of the swamps and savannas forty minutes ago, just as the sun was beginning to set. The northern mountains rose like broken fangs, cutting across the world. The very tops were exposed granite, but the rest was dense jungle. It looked trackless and forbidding.

Still, Jane and Derek had plotted their best approach into the mountains, using hydrological and topographical maps of the park. They believed a river flowing out of the mountains and winding across the plains might be the small extension off the Kagera seen on Livingstone's sketch ending at an X.

Or so they all hoped.

With no other good choice, they set off into the mountains, following along the river. Though more times than not, Noah simply rode up the stream, fighting the current, sometimes afloat, sometimes climbing over boulders.

By now they were all drenched from water splashing over the gunwales. It was hard to say who was grouchier about this development, Kowalski or Roho. Both complained just as miserably. It also didn't help that the temperature had dropped rapidly as night fell.

Two beams of light led the way deeper, but eventually Noah's ark reached a sheer waterfall. It blocked the way forward as the river tumbled down over a series of small cliffs ahead of them.

Gray stood and looked at the top of the cascade. The forest appeared even thicker up there.

Noah joined him. "End of the road. From here, the only way forward is on foot."

Gray glanced to the others, judging their fortitude to continue.

Jane must have realized what he was doing and climbed up. "We've come this far, what's a little hike through the woods?"

Derek looked less convinced, but nodded, heaving to his feet.

Noah accepted their decision, slinging a rifle over one shoulder and pack over the other. He whistled and Roho bounded from where he had been lounging with Kowalski, shaking his wet fur. Noah fixed a red collar with a black weight hanging from it around the cat's neck.

Roho accepted the attention begrudgingly, swishing his tail.

"Shock collar," Noah explained.

Jane looked concern. "Isn't that cruel?"

"Necessary. Despite appearances, he's still a baby. Which means he can easily get distracted and just as easily hurt. I need to be able to get his attention. But don't worry." He pulled what looked like a small beeper from his pocket. "I can control the level of shock. From one to ten. I seldom have to go to three, and one and two are really no more than a tap on his shoulder, telling him *listen up, buddy.*"

Once outfitted, Roho rubbed his head against Noah's thigh.

"Yes, that's right. You're a good boy."

Seichan sidled past Gray on her way off the boat. "Can we get one of those for Kowalski?"

"I heard that," the big man said, following her.

"You were supposed to." She hopped over the gunwale, landed on the riverbank, and headed for the jumble of cliffs.

Everyone offloaded and followed.

Gray had bought a new set of caving helmets after their earlier adventure and passed them around. He didn't know what they might encounter out here, but considering how dark it was under the forest canopy, they might as well be underground.

Lamps clicked on in the dark, and the group set off to tackle the cliffs.

The climb alongside the cataract was not as arduous as it first appeared, especially working as a team. Using vines, roots, crevices, they worked step by step up the series of cliffs, helping one another when necessary. Only Roho managed the ascent without any assistance.

Three-quarters of the way up, Gray hauled himself onto a ledge after a rather precarious section. Jane puffed heavily, and Derek's face was flushed. Recognizing this, he called for a short break. Their perch was five or six stories above their abandoned vehicle.

"Good job," he told Jane.

She nodded, too winded to speak.

Noah looked like he could go for hours. He pointed to the far side of the waterfall. "Apparently we're tonight's entertainment."

Gray turned and spotted a troop of small apes squatted on a tumble of rocks over there. Some carried tiny babies on their backs.

"*Papio anubis,*" Noah said. "The olive baboon."

"Should we be worried?"

"No. If you leave them alone, they'll leave you alone. They're just curious. It's the vervets you have to watch out for." He looked to the branches overhanging their perch. "Those little monkeys will pelt you with nuts . . . and sometimes worse."

Jane finally regained the power of speech. "The baboons don't seem bothered by us being here at all."

"True, and you'll find it quite common here. The park truly sees few visitors, so many of the animals have not developed a natural fear of humans. Last month, a woman woke in the tent with a blue monkey cuddled up next to her, which is quite amazing considering the species was once considered extinct here in the park. But give nature a chance, and it will surprise you."

Kowalski scowled at the troop across the river. "If one of those wakes up next to me, *surprise* won't be the word. More like shi—"

Gray cut him off and pointed up. "Let's keep going."

They scaled the last quarter without any mishaps. Up top, the river snaked into a dark forest that looked even more impenetrable. Birdcalls and screeches echoed from its depths.

Derek eyed the path ahead. "The jungle looks primeval, like we're traveling back in time."

"In some ways, we are." Noah pulled out a machete, ready to hack a path if necessary, and set off along the river's edge.

Roho kept close, his tail swishing nervously.

"This region of Rwanda is part of the East African Rift Valley, a great crevice that hugs around the western side of Lake Victoria, like a big crescent moon curving from Lake Tanganyika to the south and ending at the edge of the Nile basin."

Derek mumbled to Jane, "If Livingstone ever followed that path, he would have come straight through here."

Noah continued, pointing his machete. "These are some of the oldest mountains in Africa, made of Precambrian basement rock." He glanced back at them. "Basically the very crust of the continent. And these forests have been around for nearly as long."

Gray searched the jungle, appreciating the living history surrounding him.

Almost in reverence, the group continued in silence for the next mile, walking in single file, their line of helmet lamps an illuminated caterpillar worming its way deeper into the mysteries here.

Roho became a tad braver. He began to venture from Noah's side, sniffing here, squatting there, but he always circled back to get a reassuring pat or a kind word.

Noah smiled like a proud papa, maybe a bit sadly knowing he would eventually have to say good-bye. On one pass, Noah bent down and nuzzled his friend.

"*Ndagukunda, Roho. Ndagukunda,*" he whispered in the lion's ear, which earned the man an appreciative rumble back.

Gray didn't know a lick of Kinyarwanda, but he suspected *Ndagukunda* meant *I love you.*

And clearly that sentiment flowed both ways.

After a time, the trail opened enough for Gray to walk next to Noah. "So how did you end up working here at the park?"

Gray meant it to be a casual inquiry, but from Noah's pained expression it was a touchy subject. He didn't shy from answering, though. "When I was a young man, I lived in Kigali."

"Your capital."

"Yes, I joined our national army when I was sixteen. I was very proud, even earning the rank of corporal by 1994."

Gray began to understand the pain he heard in his voice. In July of that year, one of the worst acts of genocide occurred in Rwanda, as a tribal war broke out. The Hutu-run government sought to purge the Tutsi. By some estimates, a million people were slaughtered over the course of a hundred days.

Noah sighed, looking out at the jungle. "I was Hutu."

He didn't say anything else.

Roho came back around, as if sensing his master's distress, circling and rubbing. Noah ignored him, lost in memories he must continually fight to keep buried.

After several quiet minutes, he finally spoke. "It is better here. Animals teach you much. Teach you how to live . . ."

His voice trailed off, but Gray could finish it on his own.

. . . when you don't deserve to.

Gray fell back, allowing the man to continue ahead. Clearly Noah had sought to rediscover himself here by caring for the defenseless to make up for what he had failed to do in the past.

Again they marched in silence, putting one foot in front of the other. They slowly crossed into a section of forest where the river had overrun its banks and flooded the forests to either side. It reminded Gray of regions of the Amazon that would seasonally inundate, changing woods into swamps. But this region looked stable, an eternally drowned forest in the middle of the mountains.

Noah used his machete to cut branches to make walking sticks for them all. "Careful of snakes." He demonstrated poking ahead of them. "And for patches of quicksand."

"You take us to the best places, Gray," Kowalski groused.

They set off again, moving more slowly. Their lights reflected off the dark water, making it harder to see what lurked below. But it was rarely deeper than midcalf, the depth rising and falling with the landscape. Islands dotted the swamp around them, and occasional bright pairs of round eyes stared at them from high branches.

"Bush babies," Noah said. "Small nocturnal primates."

They continued onward. After another twenty minutes of hiking, Jane reached forward and lightly touched Gray's shoulder. "Look over to your right. Are those lights or are my eyes playing tricks?"

He turned to where she pointed. Far in the drowned forest, he could make out faint glimmers, softly glowing patches. They shimmered in a kaleidoscope of hues.

Curious, he waved to the others. "Turn off your lamps."

As the lights were doused, the effect grew more dramatic. It spread deeper and wider than it had first appeared. Some patches were iridescent, others a soft glimmer. It was phosphorescent and incandescent. There were streaks and whorls and splatters. It was like Jackson Pollock had come out here with a paintbrush and a palette of luminescent paint.

"What's causing it?" Derek whispered.

Jane frowned. "Maybe a glowing moss or fungus."

But in so many colors?

It made no sense.

Gray turned to Noah. "Have you seen anything like that?"

He shook his head. "Never."

Apparently neither had another member of their party. Roho, ever curious, bounded toward the phenomenon. His paws splashed loudly through the shallow water.

"Roho, no!" Noah headed after him, fumbling in his pocket for the control to the shock collar.

Gray clicked on his lamp and followed, drawing the others with him. He had heard tales of fiery will-o'-the-wisps luring the unwary into swamps and bog. He prayed they weren't falling for the same trap.

Ahead, Noah tried to get Roho to obey, holding out his controller, pressing the button. But the cub continued his playful pursuit.

As they neared the patch of painted forest, Noah must have raised the collar's charge. Roho let out a small yelp, bouncing off his paws and finally coming to a stop.

Noah hurried to the lion's side, quickly reassuring the cub, who did figure eights around the man's legs. "*Babarira, Roho*," he apologized. "*Babarira.*"

Gray and the others gathered around the pair. Now that he was closer, standing at its edge, he saw the effect was stunning. It was an ethereal starscape trapped under the canopy, glowing softly, reflected in the water.

"It's beautiful," Jane whispered.

And the forest responded to her admiration.

From its farthest depths rose a low murmur, a chatter of many voices, the words too faint to make clear.

The eerie noise shivered all the hairs over Gray's body. He remembered Noah saying how these forests were said to be haunted.

Seichan grabbed his arm. "We need to get out of here."

He stepped back—but the painted forest had already begun to move.

24

If I wasn't so scared, I'd be dizzy.

Still hidden in the cargo hold, Painter felt the Boeing C-17 Globemaster bank for another slow turn above the storm.

After the turbulent, teeth-rattling ride through the cloud layer, the aircraft had reached the calmer air above the storm and had been circling for more than an hour. The crew was likely coordinating and preparing for the release of the eighteen quarter-ton canisters of *Pestis fulmen*, but with the tempest *below* and the geomagnetic storm *above*, communication between Aurora Station and the Globemaster had to be challenging.

Or maybe everyone was being extra careful.

With his cheek near the biohazard label on the crate next to him, he appreciated such caution.

He had used the passing time to figure out how many others were aboard the airship. He had to be careful, sneaking between the containers.

He spotted two men in black coveralls—Anton's crew—both carrying the same assault rifle Painter had slung over his own shoulder. While waiting, he had made sure the two extra magazines he had stolen from the guards at the communication shack were fully loaded. He also timed the security men's movements. Unfortunately they rotated regularly and refused to gather in one spot together.

Too bad.

A few moments ago, Painter had almost been caught by one of the aircraft's flight crew. The man had needed to relieve himself, but the plane's single restroom was in use, so he came back to the rear hold to avail himself of a relief tube, basically a funnel that piped outside. The man had stood near enough to Painter that he could have tapped the guy on the shoulder. Still, the close call had allowed Painter to note the holstered sidearm. He estimated there had to be at least two people in the flight crew, plus a loadmaster for helping with the cargo.

The final members aboard the aircraft were six scientists, a worrisome mix of men and women. From their excessive chatter, they were clearly civilians, which was problematic, as they could very well be innocent of any malicious intent, just enthusiastic researchers.

If Painter burst out with his gun blazing, he might be able to take out the two armed guards, but he could end up with the scientists caught in the crossfire. And what would it get him in the end? At the first sign of a problem, the flight crew would simply button up the cockpit and leave Painter pounding on the bulletproof door in frustration. Plus the loadmaster inside could activate the automatic air-delivery system from the flight deck.

His plan was far simpler.

At the front of the row of pallets were two red emergency shutdown buttons, one on each side of the hold. They would cut power to the hydraulic plows up there, each designed to push their row of nine pallets across rollers and dump the load out the rear hatch. The plan had only two hiccups. First, the cutoff switches only worked once everything was powered and in motion, which meant he could not act until the very last moment. Second, even if he hit the switch, the loadmaster could still override and get things moving again.

So Painter needed the time between the first hiccup and the second to convince everybody on board to stop what they were doing.

To accomplish that, he needed one other thing.

Hostages.

A commotion stirred the scientists around a makeshift station. A monitor showed a scintillation map of the storm surging through the ionosphere. They made appreciative comments about its turbulence, speaking in cryptic scientific code.

"Look at the plasma spike. Definitely an HSS."

"It could be a co-rotating interaction region."

"A CIR? No, the G-scale is through the roof."

With no windows in the hold, Painter could only imagine the view of the aurora borealis at this height. Above the cloud layer, the midday sun still shone, but from its low arc this time of year, an aurora of this magnitude was likely still visible. He wished he could see it.

Regrettably, a genie heard him.

A low moan of hydraulics rose all around him. He glanced over a shoulder as the back of the plane began to open. Daylight blazed into the dim hold through a ship-wide crack.

Giddy shouts rose from the front, along with some clapping.

Painter tucked himself more tightly between two pallets. Winds roared outside but failed to enter the hold due to the giant ship's draft as it flew onward. The aircraft bobbled a bit due to the sudden drag from the opening doors, but the pilot proved his skill at keeping the wings even and steadying their flight.

At the moment, the plane headed toward the low sun, which allowed Painter a view to the dark blue sky behind their tail. Scintillating waves of green and red washed across the heavens, dancing and weaving. Momentarily mesmerized, Painter failed to immediately recognize a change in timbre of the hydraulics, but a grind of a motor drew him immediately around.

One of the plows had been engaged.

Painter had suspected they would eject one row at a time, lessening the chance that the cascade of blooming weather balloons would tangle.

Unfortunately, the row of nine crates he was hiding among was going overboard first.

With everything starting, Painter took one last look, fixing the position of everyone in the hold—then ducked out of hiding and ran low between the towering crates and the curve of the plane's hull.

He reached the red shutdown button and slapped it with his palm.

The plow, which had been closing down on his row along the port side, halted with a disappointed sigh of its hydraulics.

All eyes turned to him, shocked, as if he had appeared out of thin air.

It was time to threaten his hostages.

He lunged behind the first portside crate and sheltered behind it. Staying out of view, he pointed his assault rifle at the row of crates along the starboard hull and centered his sights on one of the biohazard labels.

He hollered to those gathered at the front. "No one moves, or I start shooting my hostages!"

Let's see how much they value their lives—and any future male children.

Apparently his threat failed to reach the loadmaster on the flight deck. The second steel plow groaned and began pushing toward the opposite row, about to roll his hostages away. The loadmaster must have noted the red light on his board for the first row and decided to eject the second instead to keep to the schedule, which would also give him time to investigate the reason for the interruption.

Regrettably, that didn't work for Painter's schedule.

Pinned down, he had no way to reach the cutoff on the starboard side of the hold, so the plow continued unimpeded. The sledge reached the first pallet and shoved it into the next and the whole deadly parade began to roll toward the open aft doors.

Painter waited until the plow drew abreast of his position. He aimed his rifle at the hydraulic lines, hoping to sever one or two and force the plow to a halt. He squeezed his trigger for a cautious spurt, fearful of ricochets in the enclosed space.

Two rounds ruptured a line, but it didn't seem to have any effect.

At least, not for the plow.

One of the guards, mistaking his shots for an attack, panicked and opened fire toward Painter's position. As he was still safely sheltered, none of the rounds hit him, but it might have been better if they had.

At such short range, the shots pierced the aluminum case of the *Pestis* vessel, passing fully through and over Painter's head. The rounds lost enough momentum to only ping off the next container.

Still, the damage was done.

Fountains of crimson poured out, showering Painter. From the screams of alarm and terror, he imagined the same was spilling from the holes out front. But the disaster wasn't done.

Painter heard a sharp hissing overhead.

Oh no . . .

As he glanced up, the weather balloon exploded out of its sealed package on top, bursting like an air bag during a car crash. A bullet must have struck its inflation tank. It blasted to the roof of the hold, shaking and whipping, trying to escape. The balloon then did what it had been designed to do and flew toward the open hatch. The damaged, leaking container got yanked off its pallet and dragged with it.

Painter dove out of its way, crashing headlong into the hull.

The quarter-ton crate came within inches of cracking his head open.

Other crates in line were knocked over, but their combined drag finally captured their wayward companion. The balloon ripped and deflated, falling over the rest of the row, tangling everything up.

On the starboard side of the hold, the plow continued its duty, oblivious to the chaos on the portside.

Painter watched as one crate after the other was dumped overboard. They fell leadenly away, but then moments later, white mushrooms bloomed against the blue skies, backlit by the shimmering aurora borealis.

Nine balloons rose heavenward, swinging their deadly cargo beneath.

Helpless, Painter remained slumped against the side hull.

A loud voice rose from up front. "What the hell happened?"

Painter turned, guessing the shocked man was the plane's loadmaster, come to check on his handiwork. Rifles pointed accusingly at Painter.

Soaked to the skin like Carrie on prom night, he shrugged. "You think you're having a bad day."

3:39 P.M.

Hang in there . . .

Kat crouched over Safia, holding a cold compress to her forehead. After the first seizure, Kat had moved the half-conscious woman out of the Sno-Cat and over to one of the Inuit's hide tents. Despite outward appearances, the nomadic dwelling on Lake Hazen had a camp cot and piles of fur blankets and was heated by a camp stove vented to the outside.

The three Inuit ice fishermen—Tagak, Joseph, and Natan—had offered their help, but Kat feared exposing them, so had them stay back. Still, she had accepted the use of their tent and a first-aid kit, which contained a welcome bottle of aspirin, both for her and Safia.

She had downed three, hoping not to get sick.

She made Rory do the same. He hovered behind her, pacing the small space. She had realized keeping him bound was a waste of a useful resource, especially when it came to hauling Safia here.

Besides, where could he go? She still had the Sno-Cat's keys, and the Inuits' only means of transportation were snowshoes and a dogsled. And an hour ago, Natan had taken off with his tethered team toward Alert, intending to get help.

Lake Hazen had a small makeshift airstrip. It was one of the park's three spots where you could land a plane. This early in the season, it was snowed over and so far unused, but hopefully Camp Alert could dispatch help here.

At least, that was the plan.

She also had Tagak and Joseph standing guard, watching the mountaintops for any sign of hunters from the station. Like everyone traveling in the Arctic, they carried rifles.

Safia moaned, thrashing her limbs under the blankets. Kat had found a digital thermometer in the first-aid kit and checked her fever: 103.4. High but not deadly. Still, to protect her brain, Kat kept swapping out compresses soaked in ice water, which she sent Rory out to freshen periodically. She kept one under Safia's neck and another on her forehead.

The cold did seem to calm her, and she had not had another seizure after the first one. Since then, Safia had been fading into and out of consciousness, sometimes recognizing them, other times not.

She mumbled in a fever dream.

Rory shifted closer, cocking his head. "I think she's speaking early Egyptian Coptic."

"Are you sure?"

"Not one hundred percent. And it might make no difference. Dr. al-Maaz is an expert on Egyptian history and knows the Coptic language well. She may be just drudging up words out of her feverish consciousness."

Kat looked at him. "But you don't think that's the explanation."

"When my father got sick—and the others—they reported vivid hallucinations."

"Which is common with high fevers and encephalitis."

"Yes, but it was how *similar* their deliriums were. All about Egypt, burning sands, diseases."

"Your father and his men could have been responding to the heat and their fear of this disease. The similarities could have been nothing more than the power of suggestion, triggering a mass delusion."

"You could be right. In the end, some of the hallucinations never even fit this pattern."

"Then there you go."

Rory sighed. "My father's gotten into my head."

"What do you mean?"

"We had long talks via the Internet. He had his own theory. He thought it was possible the organism could record the memory pattern of a person it infected and carry it forward to the next victim, replaying it by stimulating the second brain in the same manner."

"Why would it do that? What's the evolutionary advantage?"

"He believed only *strong* memories would be captured and recorded, especially something frightening, which would excite the brain more fully, feeding the microbe. Then by carrying it forward and repeating the pattern in the next victim—"

"—it would quickly energize that new feeding ground." Kat nodded her head. "Intriguing, but where does that get us?"

"According to my father, it takes us all the way back to the biblical plagues."

"How's that?"

"He believed the strain of microbe that infected him, that infected Safia, the same strain he spread to Cairo and beyond, all came from the time the organism first bloomed in the Nile, turning it red. He thought it might have captured that period of panic and horror, and now repeats it over and over again, an echo out of the distant past."

"After so long?"

"It may not be *long* for this organism. Simon Hartnell tested the microbe and found it's nearly immortal, capable of going into dormancy until it gets its next electrical fix." Rory finally shrugged. "Like I said, it was just something my father dwelled upon. And with Safia speaking ancient Egyptian, it reminded me of that conversation."

Kat considered this theory. Human memories were organized in the hippocampus region, but recent research suggested the information was only stored there on a *short-term* basis. Later, the hippocampus recoded these memories as electrical patterns across billions of synapses and distributed them for *long-term* storage over the entire cerebral cortex.

She also remembered Dr. Kano mentioning the unique shapeshifting biology of the Archaea domain, how these species were capable of chaining together into wires or cables. Could a web of interconnected microbes capture the brain's pattern, especially if it was cast by a strong enough memory, and mimic it later?

Safia stirred, her lips moving silently in some dream.

Kat felt a chill, picturing what she had just imagined happening in her brain.

Rory shifted closer and whispered in Safia's ear, "*Khére, nim pe pu-ran?*"

Kat frowned. "What did you say?"

He glanced over. "I asked what her name was, using ancient Coptic."

"But why—?"

Safia answered faintly, as if speaking from a deep well. *"Sabah pe pa-ran . . . Sabah."*

Rory jolted at this response, pushing away, his face scared.

"What?"

He looked to the laptop sitting atop a folded fur, then back to Safia. "She said her name is Sabah."

"Why is that significant?"

"Before all hell broke loose, Safia learned the name of the woman mummified on the throne, the one who infected her. Her name was Sabah."

Kat wanted to dismiss this again as the power of suggestion. If Safia had been working on his puzzle, her feverish mind could have latched on to this.

Still . . .

She stared at Rory. "How did you know her name?"

"From the tattoos found on her body."

She thought for a moment, then pulled out the data disk she had removed from Safia's pocket. She shoved it at Rory and pointed it to the laptop. "See what else you can figure out."

She refused to leave any stone unturned.

He eagerly took the disk and sat cross-legged before the computer.

She returned her attention to Safia, willing the woman to fight. She checked her temperature again, freshened the compresses, and managed to get her to swallow another aspirin along with a few sips of water.

Rory tapped away behind her, mumbling, sounding sometimes frustrated, sometimes astounded. She let him concentrate on his work.

A voice rose from outside the tent flap. "Hello." It was Joseph, the oldest of the Inuit trio. "Someone comes. Many lights sweeping down into the valley from the mountains."

Kat stood, grabbing her gun.

Seems it's time for me to go to work, too.

3:58 P.M.

Sabah pe pa-ran . . .

She walks for the thousandth time through the burning sands, past the carcasses of water buffaloes, through the crushed bodies of birds of every feather, where even the vultures have fallen where they fed.

Screams rise from the village to her left, weeping, mourning.

Still, she continues to the blood-red river. Crocodiles float leadenly past, bellies to the sun. The reeds are choked with the dried husks of frogs. And everywhere clouds of flies rise and fall, like the waves of the sea beyond the delta.

Other images swim, overlaying this one.

—a woman holds a dying baby boy to her chest.

It is my child.

—a young girl gasps for air as her body burns.

I am that girl.

—a bent-backed hag is stoned for blaspheming the gods.

I feel those rocks break my skull.

On and on.

She is a hundred women, tracing back to that time of misery. She is Sabah and all others who carried that memory. It is what they were all trained for, to be the *hemet netjer* . . . the maid of God. They learned to take the water and let it wash through them, to hold down their own fears so they did not taint the memory of the time of misery, to preserve it for the next woman in line, to never forget.

To carry the memory is a curse.

To know what we know, a blessing.

And now I am another.

She reaches the muddy bank and stares yet again at where the world ends in a wall of darkness far beyond the river. The storm eats the sun and is not satisfied. Lightning crackles, and hail pounds the sands like the hooves of a thousand angry stallions. She knows it is both the past and what might yet come.

She speaks to the new woman.

You must warn them.

4:05 P.M.

"Conditions remain within the baseline for an optimal test firing," Dr. Kapoor informed Simon.

The pair stood at the helm of the control station with a panoramic view through the curved window to his tower. Over the past half hour, his emotions alternated between fury and elation.

He could not fathom how Painter Crowe suddenly appeared aboard the cargo plane. It was like the bastard was the living embodiment of his name and flew up there on his own. Now the aircraft was contaminated and in the process of being locked down. Unfortunately half the crates of *Pestis fulmen* still remained aboard the plane, but despite the sabotage, *nine* had made it safely out.

He stared down at the map of the ionosphere. Small blips marked where the balloons had discharged their loads at the lower edges of that charged layer of the atmosphere. Digital estimates of the energized streams from the geomagnetic storm swirled and eddied in waves across his screen.

Kapoor nodded to where he was looking. "Projections remain good, even without the additional load. Still, we should give our seeds time to settle into this pool." He pointed to a spot on the screen where energy whirled tightly. "I've already calibrated the beam to this site. But we don't want to wait too long and allow the ionosphere's currents to spread the seed too thin."

"What's your estimate for firing?"

"Ten minutes."

"Very good."

Simon rose up and down on his toes with excitement.

Ten more minutes and Tesla's dream will finally be realized—along with my own.

A phone chimed at his station. He picked it up and heard rasps of static. He knew who had been patched to his private line.

"Anton?"

"We've found them, sir."

"And the data?"

"It will be secure in the next ten minutes."

He smiled at the serendipity of the timing.

Perfect.

"You have your orders," he said.

"And the women?"

He stared at another screen that showed the circling aircraft. Painter Crowe was no longer a problem, only a loose end. He saw no need to retain a bargaining chip.

"Clean your mess up."

"Understood."

Simon clutched his hands behind his back in an attempt to reel in his excitement. He paced back and forth. He looked at his board.

All green lights.

After what seemed like forever, Kapoor returned.

"Well?" Simon asked, as the man seemed to hesitate.

The physicist grinned and pointed to the key inserted into his console. "We're go for ignition."

Simon felt this moment needed some momentous words, a grand speech about changing the world, but he let his actions do his speaking. He stepped to the console, gripped the key, and turned it.

He felt the vibration of power in his fingers as systems engaged—or maybe it was his own exhilaration.

At last . . .

Faces across the station swung toward the view.

"Look at the top of the tower," Kapoor said.

He drew his gaze upward. Copper rings began to revolve, dragging with them the massive electromagnets. Within that metal nest, an egg of superconductors shelled in titanium slowly turned, its tip pointed down.

"Amazing," Kapoor whispered.

Over the course of a minute, the rings whipped faster, the magnets becoming a blur. The egg spun like a perfectly balanced top, rising weightless within its cocoon of energy—then slowly it began to tip, rolling its narrow end toward the dark sky.

Simon took a breathless step forward, drawing Kapoor with him.

Once the egg's axis pointed to the heavens, Simon let out his breath.

With a blast that sounded like the world cracking, a shaft of pure plasma shot from the tower. Cheers and whistles rose throughout the control station, everyone knowing this was the first step to saving the planet. Blue crackles of energy burst from the tip of the tower and coursed out to the spiral array, dancing among the limbs of that steel forest. It reminded Simon of Saint Elmo's fire, a natural fiery display that had once shot along the masts of sailing ships plying uncharted seas.

Only this journey explored an ocean far more mysterious.

The column of plasma struck the clouds, driving them apart. Lightning shattered outward along the belly of the clouds, trying to dispel the energy. The beam continued toward the heavens—where it finally struck its intended target.

It smashed into the ionosphere, slamming into the shield he had cast overhead, a barrier made of the smallest bits of life. The energy spread outward, visible as an aurora of such brilliance that Simon had to shy from it.

Kapoor passed him a set of tinted goggles.

He held them to his eyes, too excited to strap them on. More and more energy rocketed from the tower to the sky, charging the aurora even further. Waves of energy cascaded outward in all directions.

"You've done it," Kapoor said, turning his gaze to the board. "It's holding stable."

Simon smiled.

At long last . . .

4:21 P.M.

Something was dreadfully wrong.

Painter stood near the open rear hatch of the Globemaster, one fist wrapped in a scrap of weather balloon. Outside, a column of fire blazed through the storm and shattered across the roof of the world. Fed by this energy, the aurora spread outward in all directions, outshining even the arctic sun.

He felt the charge across his skin as the microbes soaking his clothes responded to the energy in the air. A glance back to the dark hold showed the crimson pools from the bullet-riddled container shimmered with a soft glow.

As he watched, one of those pools spilled into a river flowing toward him, toward the open door. He yelled to those gathered behind a translucent tarp hastily erected between the cargo hold and the front quarter of the aircraft.

"Keep the plane's nose down!"

He didn't want this poisonous soup pouring from the plane. He suspected some might have already dribbled out the back, before order was restored. He pictured the plane painting a red circle over the top of the clouds, seeding the storm below as readily as it had the skies above.

After the catastrophe aboard the plane, he had been quarantined away from the rest of the crew. He was the only one drenched by the damaged container, which still lay on its side, slowly leaking with each rock of the aircraft. Painter had no doubt he would have been shot outright, except the others needed a maintenance crew and no one was willing to venture into this toxic swamp.

So it was up to him to do something about the rear hatch, which was stuck open, its works gummed up from the weather balloon it tried to chew up. Aurora Station refused to let them land until the issue was rectified. The station did not want a rough landing to send the remaining load of crates scattering across the tundra or over the base.

Which meant for now, the crew needed him.

While down deep the others must know they were breathing an airborne pathogen, he let them clutch to whatever false hope they wanted.

It's keeping me alive.

A loud boom shook the ship, accompanied by a blinding flash. He had been aboard enough airplanes to recognize what had happened.

Lightning strike.

He turned back to the open skies. As he feared, matters were beginning to change outside. The aurora borealis filled the bowl of the sky. It was no longer shimmering waves, gently lapping at the arch of the world. It had become a raging tempest, roiling and surging.

Sharper crackles popped earthward.

He knew the effect he was witnessing. It was called upper-atmospheric lightning, but in reality, it was streams of luminous plasma being cast off the ionosphere. It presented in various ways, each with a cute name— *sprites, blue jets,* and *elves.* But in fact, the displays were large-scale electrical discharges.

But Painter knew nothing this *large* had ever been recorded.

A dozen glowing sprite halos bloomed in the air, then burst into crimson balls of flame, trailing tendrils of energy toward the clouds, while brilliant blue cones of gas spun across the skies.

The storm below wasn't happy about any of this and spat up forks of lightning, strafing the skies, which only added to the dance of fire between the heavens and the clouds.

Painter knew even a medium-sized storm contained the potential energy of a hundred Hiroshimas, and the sprawling arctic beast below could easily hold ten times that.

As he watched the interplay, he realized he was witnessing a feedback loop between the ionosphere and the storm, each exciting the other, escalating faster and stronger.

The station below must have realized the same. The column of plasma blasting from the tower to the sky suddenly extinguished.

But it was too late.

Simon Hartwell had managed the impossible.

He lit the skies on fire.

25

"No one move," Gray warned.

Only his helmet lamp was still on. Its beam shone past where Noah crouched over the lion cub after shocking the cat to a splashing stop. The others were spread out behind him.

Their commotion in getting here had sent ripples through the drowned forest, shimmering the reflection of the starscape ahead, enhancing its prismatic effect. The spread of tiny glows and glimmers failed to truly illuminate the shadowy bower under the dense canopy. In fact, the opposite was true. The phosphorescent dabs and luminous whorls made the dark spaces darker. And the longer one looked, the more those brighter bits burned into the retina, creating false glows as one's eyes searched the forest, doubling and tripling the trickery.

Still, Gray swore entire sections of paint shifted across the forest, as if tiny snatches of a larger canvas suddenly came to life. The faint murmurs he had heard when they'd arrived had gone silent. The entire flooded jungle had gone dead quiet.

"What's out there?" Noah whispered.

Roho rumbled, slipping from his master's side. The cub stalked forward, moving with great care, his legs barely stirring the water. He slunk his belly low, tail swishing just over the surface.

"*Roho, oya,*" Noah scolded, waving him back.

Gray touched the man's shoulder. "Let him go."

At the farthest reach of his lamp's beam, a tiny section of the painted forest broke free, moving closer.

Jane gasped behind him.

Moving with the same care as Roho, a tiny shape appeared, as curious as the cub and maybe not much older. A tiny trunk, daubed in motes of blushing crimson, lifted higher, sniffing at the stranger's scent.

A larger section of the canvas followed, drawing others.

A low trumpet of warning flowed out of the dark shadows.

"Elephants," Noah said, straightening in wonder.

The small curious calf, no taller than Gray's waist, hesitated, clearly balancing between obeying and not. It tossed its wide ears.

As the calf hovered at the edge of his light, Gray recognized what else might have drawn out the young animal. Its skin—painted in glowing phosphorescence to match the forest—was otherwise a pinkish-white, revealing the calf to be an albino. The inquisitive fellow must have been lured out of hiding by the novelty of the white cat, perhaps also recognizing their genetic commonality.

The calf's tiny dark eyes watched Roho, as the cat continued his cautious approach, slinking forward in a submissive posture.

As if encouraging him, the calf lifted his trunk and made a tiny piping whistle.

That was all it took.

Roho bounded forward, splashing excitedly, which involved much bouncing and slapping of water. His antics emboldened the shy calf. With an airy trumpet, it tilted up on it hind legs in faux aggression—revealing itself to be a bull calf—then dropped back down. It loped forward, its little body half-turned, making tiny hops, then swinging its body the other way.

The earlier rumbling trumpet of warning grew louder, echoed by others hidden in the forest.

Still, the calf would have none of it. The two youngsters met and danced in the water. They circled, bumped, and splashed together.

"What do we do?" Noah whispered.

Gray shrugged. "For now, let Roho be our ambassador."

Their play expanded outward, circling wider through the trees. Each took turns chasing the other. As Gray's eyes adjusted, he discerned darker shadows under the canopy, their flanks as decorated as the calf's.

"Who painted them?" Jane asked, keeping her voice hushed.

It was a good question.

Gray remembered the whispered voices in the darkness.

Who else was out there?

Noah spoke, his words awed. "I think . . . I think they did it themselves."

Gray frowned. "How could—?"

A loud splash and a trumpet of distress cut him off. They all turned to where the cub and calf had rounded a small island. Roho danced back into view, tail swishing in distress, then darted behind the island again.

They all moved, driven faster by an upset cry from Roho.

Gray and the others rounded one side of the island. Across the way, a lumbering shadow with painted flanks thundered through the water toward the same spot.

There was no sign of the calf.

Then Noah pointed. "There!"

A few inches of pale trunk waved frantically above the water.

"Stay back," Gray warned.

He took two steps and dove. With his helmet strapped under his chin, his waterproof lamp cast a weak glow through the murk. The bottom fell steeply away from the island, forming a depression. His hands discovered a floor of sucking muck.

A shape appeared out of the gloom ahead.

He kicked over to the calf. Its legs were sunk to its ankles in the mud. It writhed in panic, fighting the grip but only managing to sink deeper. Gray placed a palm on the calf's side, trying to reassure the young animal.

He then popped back up, floating to keep his own limbs free.

"Blanket and a rope!" he called out and pointed to the island. "We'll use the tree for leverage."

"Got it." Kowalski was already in motion, hauling toward the island.

Noah pulled a coil of climbing rope from his pack, while Jane and Derek fished a camp blanket from theirs.

Everything was tossed toward Gray.

Seichan nodded past the island. "Be quick, Gray."

A large shape hovered at the edge of their light. It was an elephant cow, likely the calf's mother. She hung back for now, perhaps sensing they were trying to help.

Gray knew that hesitancy might not last.

By now, the calf's nostrils flared and puffed at the surface.

Gray dove back down. He reached the trapped animal and shoved the waterlogged blanket behind its front leg and under its barrel chest. He looped the rope over it, catching it on the other side—though it took two tries.

He burst back up, tied a quick double half-hitch knot, and tossed the other end to Kowalski. The big man caught it, dashed around the trunk of a tree, and hauled on the rope, digging in his heels.

Gray stayed with the calf. He cupped the end of its trunk and tried to keep the nostrils clear of the water. He also wanted to reassure the panicked youngster that it hadn't been abandoned.

On the island, Kowalski groaned and swore, fighting the grip of the mud that held the calf, but it looked like he might not succeed. Derek and Noah joined him, adding their strength to the tug-of-war.

Finally, inch by stubborn inch, the calf's trunk rose out of the water.

"Keep going!" Gray urged.

With a final grunt and heave from Kowalski, the mud finally let go. As they dragged the calf out of the water, Gray stayed beside it, rubbing and patting the pink flank. Once on the island, he removed the rope and blanket.

The calf shivered, plainly shaken up.

A concerned trumpet sounded from his mother.

Having had enough of this adventure, the calf turned to her, but he looked frightened of the dark water.

Noah leaned down, rubbing a tender spot behind the youngster's ear.

"*Wakize, umsore,*" he reassured the fellow. He guided the calf to the other side of the island, where the water was shallower and the footing more solid. "Come, little boy, you're safe."

Gray followed but stayed a few yards back, so their group didn't overwhelm the nervous mother waiting for her calf's return.

Roho kept to his new friend's side, nudging now and then, his head hung apologetically.

Once near his mother, the calf broke away and trotted to her side. She bent her head and wrapped her trunk around her boy. Nostrils sniffed him all over, snuffling with relief.

The pair then turned and headed into the forest.

"Should we follow them?" Jane asked.

Gray nodded. "That's why we came here."

The group set off, but another did not agree with this plan.

A huge bull blocked their path. His glowing decorations looked like war paint. He raised his trunk, chuffing and brandishing a pair of yellowed ivory tusks. Other large shadows stirred behind him.

Noah lifted an arm for them all to stop. "We don't want him to charge."

"No kidding," Kowalski said, then under his breath, "Some gratitude. I got rope burns that'll last weeks."

As if hearing this, a firmer trumpet came from the retreating mother.

The bull rolled his head toward her, then lowered his tusks and lumbered his muscular bulk around.

"Seems he got overruled," Seichan said.

"Elephants are matriarchal," Noah explained. "It's the females that rule a herd."

Seichan shrugged. "Works for me."

As the team waded after the elephants, the herd closed around them but still kept to the painted shadows. The females might rule here, but the group remained wary. Gray didn't know how long their presence would be tolerated, but he hoped the herd's graciousness lasted long enough to discover what else might be hidden in this forest.

Gray studied the surrounding bower, trying to find a pattern in the brilliant display through which they walked. He was both awed and strangely calmed. Like traipsing through a candlelit cathedral. Their journey through here was hushed, just the whisper of rubbing skin, the gentle huffs of elephantine breaths, and the quiet burble of water.

After a time, they passed out of the painted jungle. He could now appreciate the number of elephants, who carried bits of that glowing artwork with them, great lumbering canvases moving through the dark drowned forest.

Gray counted at least thirty, maybe more, mostly adults, but also a handful of calves.

But even this revelation of the herd faded as their glowing body paint grew dimmer. He glanced back and saw the same happening to the forest. Apparently this magic was fleeting, which made it all the more lovely for some reason.

Noah had tried to capture and hold that wonder, collecting glowing samples from the trunks and low branches. He had sniffed, rubbed, even dabbed a finger on his tongue.

"Hmm . . ." he mumbled as the magic disappeared from his palms.

"What?" Gray asked.

"Definitely bioluminescent mushrooms and fungus. I could identify mycelia and fruiting bodies, crushed and macerated to create this paint." He stared around the darkening forest. "They must have gathered specimens from far and wide throughout this ancient forest."

"Who?"

"I told you before." Noah frowned at him. "The elephants."

8:25 P.M.

Derek shifted forward, as incredulous as Gray. Jane came with him, but her face looked more amazed than disbelieving.

"How can that be?" Derek asked. "We heard voices. There must be a tribe hiding here, too."

Noah stared at the group. "No. That was also the elephants."

Kowalski blew an exasperated breath. "I know elephants are smart, but ones that can talk?"

"No, not talk . . . *mimic*." Noah waved back the way they had come. "Elephants have been shown to mimic sounds, ranging from other forest animals to the grumble of a truck. And yes, even humanlike voices. They do this by using their trunks like complex whistles. Here in Akagera, one bull elephant does a perfect imitation of a water buffalo's mating grunt." He smiled. "It's caused some confusion during the rutting season."

Jane stared toward one of the hulking shadows moving through the forest. "But why would they do that just now?"

"I can't be sure. But I think they were trying to scare us off. I'm sure they were aware of our approach as soon as we entered the mountains."

Derek had to admit the effect was unnerving.

"And the painted forest?" Gray asked.

"I think we were lucky to come when we did. I expect we stumbled upon a special ritual, one rarely performed due to its elaborate nature and the preparation necessary. But elephants are known to develop complex social ceremonies within a herd. They're the only mammals, besides us, who ritually bury their dead amid touching displays of grief."

Derek glanced over his shoulder. "Then what's the meaning behind decorating the jungle like that?"

"I have no idea. You'll have to ask them." He smiled. "But we know from countless examples that these big giants are innate painters, seeming to have an affinity for color and patterns."

Jane nodded. "I remember the London Zoo even sells paintings in their gift shops done by elephants."

"Indeed. At another zoo, a canvas by a pachyderm Picasso named Ruby fetched tens of thousands of dollars."

"But would they do this in the wild?" Derek asked.

"It's been seen before." Noah nodded ahead. "Elephants who would grind natural pigments and paint one another. Like I said, I think this was a ritual we stumbled upon. You could almost feel the reverence in the air."

Derek had felt something akin to that.

"So when we arrived at that opportune time," Noah said, "they tried to scare us off." He waved forward. "But it may also be one of the reasons they're letting us come now. Beyond rescuing the calf, the herd may have placed extra significance in our arrival during this time." He patted his feline companion. "Of course, Roho also helped."

Derek pictured the two young animals playing, building a bridge, but that's not what Noah meant, at least not entirely.

"Did you get a look at the bull and the mother cow?" Noah asked. "They're albino, same as the calf."

"But they weren't white," Jane said. "More a reddish brown."

"Ah, that's typical for the species. Albino elephants are born pink and darken a bit as they age. A truly white elephant is very rare." He gave Roho a rub. "But perhaps us coming with someone sharing their genetic heritage gave us a foot up."

"Whatever the reason," Gray said, "at least they're allowing us to follow them."

By now, the trees had begun to grow taller. The water receded to mere puddles and wide, shallow ponds. Slowly the normal sounds of the jungle returned with hooting calls of monkeys and sharper cries of nesting birds.

Noah gazed appreciatively around. "If the entire herd shares this genetic quirk, it might be why they've chosen the shadowy forest to make their home. Albino elephants often go blind or get skin diseases because of the harsh African sun. Here they could thrive."

"And hide," Gray added.

Noah sobered. "Yes. That is true. Poachers would certainly target them. Perhaps it is why the herd has receded so far and been so shy. I wager they may even be nocturnal for both the same reasons. To avoid the sun and keep themselves secret."

Derek glanced around, wondering what other *secrets* the herd might be hiding here.

They continued in silence for another mile.

The curious calf eventually wandered back to their group, seeming to have shaken off his fright. He drew his mother with him, who lingered farther away, but kept a close watch.

The calf sniffed and snortled and poked at their group. He seemed especially enamored with Gray, wrapping his tiny trunk around his wrist, as if holding his hand.

"I think he's thanking you," Noah said.

Kowalski grumbled. "What, no love for the guy who did all the heavy lifting? Gray just tied a knot."

Eventually, the forest ran up against a massive jungle-strewn cliff, a towering black wave cresting far above them. He remembered Noah's description of the area's geology, how the region was the oldest in Africa, where the very crust of the earth cracked and was thrust up here.

Derek didn't doubt it as he stared at the giant edifice blocking their way. The wall before them looked as if a chunk of that crust had been dropped, shattering along its forward edge. Fissures and narrow crevices cut deep into that rock face.

The herd closed in on their group, drawing down to a line in front and behind. The procession aimed for one fissure that looked no different from the next.

"Check behind us," Noah whispered. "Near the end."

All their faces turned.

A trio of bull elephants trailed the group, walking backward, sweeping the path with giant fronds.

"They're erasing their tracks," Gray said.

"I've seen our park elephants using the same fronds to swat flies. And once I saw an elephant during an exceptionally dry season dig a watering hole, then plug it up with a wad of chewed bark and sand to keep it from evaporating. He preserved his little well like that throughout the summer." Noah looked like he wanted to cry. "I know the great beasts are tremendously clever, using their big brains to survive, to problem solve, to work together, to use tools. But just look at what wonderful beasts they are. Who would dare shoot them for sport or ivory?"

Jane touched his arm in sympathy.

Kowalski looked concerned, but for a very different reason. "If these big guys are covering their tracks, they're covering ours, too. What if that's on purpose?"

He clearly worried about some sinister intention.

Gray pointed ahead. "Only one way to find out."

9:02 P.M.

Nearly breathless with anticipation, Jane stayed close to Derek. She was drawn by the mysteries ahead, yet worried about what they might find. Still, a larger fear clutched her throat.

What if there's nothing?

Despite the wonders demonstrated by these giants, they were still just elephants. What could they hope to learn from them? How did any of this connect to the burning sands of Egypt, to a mystery going back millennia, to the time of Moses and the plagues?

Ahead of them, the lead elephants entered a narrow fissure, vanishing away. One by one, the others followed, until it was their turn. As she entered the slot canyon, she gaped at the top of the cliffs to either side. Far above her, more jungle grew at the summit, casting a thick canopy over their path.

Trapped between these walls, the musk of the elephants grew stronger, smelling of sweet dung and old hides. She swallowed her fear and followed with the others. The path grew ever narrower, until she was sure some of the bigger bulls could not pass, but they somehow did. She imagined them sucking in their broad chests to squeeze their bulks forward.

They continued for what seemed like miles, though the distance was probably less than one. At last the walls began to fall away, promising an end to their long journey—but there remained one last obstacle.

She watched the column of elephants shift to the left. The herd scaled a steep stone ramp on that side, little calves clinging to their mothers' tails with their trunks. The procession had a timeless quality to it, as if this same path had been walked for thousands of years. The ramp confirmed this, its center worn down by the passage of countless elephants tramping over it.

The need for this route was evident.

It bridged over a high wall that spanned the breadth of the fissure.

The odd formation piqued her curiosity. It did not look natural.

Derek came to the same conclusion. He bent down and ran his fingertips over the coarse surface of the bridge. "White limestone," he said as he straightened. "This didn't come from these granite mountains. It had to have been quarried somewhere else."

She shifted to the ramp's edge and studied the wall. It was made up of giant bricks, each the size of a small car. She had seen blocks of this shape and magnitude before, also made of limestone.

At the Great Pyramid of Giza.

"Elephants didn't build this," Derek said. "I don't care how good they are at tool use."

The elephants behind them did not let their group tarry there for long, grunting their displeasure at being kept from their home.

Jane reluctantly allowed herself to be herded over the ramp and down the far side.

Beyond the wall, the cliffs circled wide and around to enclose a small valley. On the far side, the fissure continued yet again, but it was the sight at hand that captured Jane's full attention.

The valley held a piece of the forest along with a spread of green meadow, though all of it had a manicured look, as if maintained by its caretakers. Other elephants greeted those that returned, trumpeting softly, entwining trunks, rubbing flanks. The ones left here looked far older, with sagging skin and bony chests, likely elders who were too enfeebled for the journey.

The arriving herd spread out toward various little trampled homesteads within the larger valley, mostly located near the cliffs where the overhanging jungle canopy offered shade. Jane knew elephants were normally nomadic and didn't truly have homes or nests, but this group was unique in their isolation, driven by their biology and genetics to hide from the sun, developing a new way of living.

Still, none of this fully captured her attention.

Instead, she stared off to her far right. A small grotto lake filled one corner of the valley, half in the open, half buried into the cliffside. She imagined the pool was fed by an ancient spring rising from the unique hydrology of these rift mountains. The scalloped granite roof that overhung the grotto glowed with what looked like incandescent lights, blinking and shimmering, but flurries of those lights fell away, fluttering low across the water, then swirling across the valley like a gust of burning embers.

"Fireflies," Noah said.

Their illumination was enough to reveal the dark crimson surface of the lake.

They all knew what that portended.

"My god . . ." Derek murmured.

Still, as they all watched, a juvenile bull sauntered over to the pond's rocky bank, dipped his trunk, and drank deeply from that toxic font. Jane cringed, but the elephant flapped his ears as a few fireflies pestered him, then wandered away.

Their party gave that side of the valley a wide berth.

Gray gathered them at the edge of a copse of broad-leaved trees. The elephants mostly ignored them, going about their usual routine. Still, a few larger bulls stood nearby, plainly on guard, tails swishing.

"What do you make of this place?" Gray asked.

Jane cast her gaze from the lake to the limestone barrier wall. "I know exactly where we are."

Gray turned to her.

"We're standing in the *mouth* of the river. Like it was written on that tattooed scrap left by my father. It's all so clear now."

Kowalski frowned. "To you, maybe."

Derek understood. "Thousands of years ago, there must have been a dramatic shift in the weather pattern, a rainy season like no other. It flooded this region, enough to swell the Kagera River and all of its feeders."

Jane pictured a storm surge flowing through these mountains. "That drowned forest we passed through would have been neck-deep, maybe more. It would have swamped these highlands, filling in all the cracks of this cliff, flowing all the way here."

"Where it merged with that toxic pool," Derek said. "Allowing the microbe to escape this valley and flow out of the mountains, spreading to the Kagera River, then Lake Victoria."

Gray stared off to the north. "Where it eventually flowed down the rest of the Nile Valley."

Jane nodded. "Spreading death in its wake, cascading into the other plagues like we talked about before. Even the eruption of Thera—as it swept a dark column of ash over this area—may have been the atmospheric change that triggered the flooding to begin with."

Gray stared toward the tall wall, understanding dawning on his face. "During or shortly after that, someone from Egypt came looking for the source. Following that bloody trail."

"To here," Jane said. "And to prevent that tragedy from ever happening again, they built a tall wall, a stone dike to make sure any future flooding didn't reach this inner valley."

"But that's not all they found," Gray said, turning his attention to the elephants. "Like us, they must have wondered how these elephants survived. We know the beasts were living here at the time since they were mentioned on that same tattooed scrap."

Jane put a palm on her forehead. "But how *do* they survive here? Is it some natural immunity? Something unique to their genetics?"

"I don't think so," Gray said.

"Why?"

"Whoever came here long ago discovered their secret. I don't think the Egyptian explorer who found this place came with the equipment necessary to perform immunological or genetic assays. No, something else is going on here." He stared toward the lake. "But what would make these elephants risk drinking from that pool to begin with?"

Noah offered a possible explanation. "Because it might have given them an evolutionary advantage."

Gray turned to him. On the boat ride here, Jane had overheard Gray giving their guide the gist of what they were looking for. "How is it an advantage?"

"Life in this region revolves around water. Each animal develops unique strategies to survive the dry seasons, which many times in the past, have turned into decade-long droughts. I told you about that elephant plugging up his watering hole to protect it." Noah waved to encompass this valley. "This is a biological version of that. If you're the only ones who can safely drink this water, then no one could compete with you for it."

Derek conceded this point with a nod. "But how did they learn to drink the water?"

Noah smiled. "Elephants are smart and patient. They love a puzzle to solve. So the adaptation strategy could have taken them decades to figure out through trial and error. So the better question is, why reinvent the wheel? Why don't we simply try to learn what they already know?"

Jane wondered if whoever had come here thousands of years ago had done exactly that.

Noah offered a modern example to support his position. "In Kenya, elephants chew on leaves of a certain tree to induce labor. Local tribesmen learned to follow that example for the same medical benefit. So you see, you *can* learn much from our large friends."

"But if you're right, where do we even begin?" Jane asked.

Gray stepped away from the shadow of the trees and searched the dark valley, his gaze lingering on the flickering glow of the grotto. He finally faced the group. "The strip of tattooed skin that your father hid. It didn't just mention *elephants*. It mentioned something about *elephant bones*."

Jane stood straighter. "That's right."

Gray turned to Noah. "You mentioned that elephants are the only mammals to have a ritual surrounding their dead. What do they do exactly?"

"It's about respecting the deceased. It involves a period of mourning over the body, then a ritual burial of tossing dirt and twigs over the remains, sometimes covering them with branches. Afterward the bones are revered, even if they're not from your own family. Sometimes herds will even take bones and move them with them."

"So where are the *bones* of this tribe?" Gray asked. "As secretive as they are, I wager they wouldn't want their dead to be found out in the open valley."

"And they'd still want them close by." Derek nodded toward the fissure at the back of the valley. "How about through there?"

Gray nodded. "We should go look."

Before they set off, Seichan pointed back to the wall. "As far as we know, that's the only way in or out of this place. So while you go look for bones, I'm going to go man those ramparts."

Gray nodded. "Stay on radio. Holler if there's trouble."

She patted a large gun at her hip. "Oh, you'll hear me."

He gave her a fast hug, and she trotted away.

Gray got them all moving the other way.

Noah kept Roho close by, especially as they passed the toxic grotto. They circled far from its shores, crossing through a meadow of knee-high grass. Elephants stirred as they passed, snuffling and piping at them. A young bull came charging, ears splayed wide. Everyone froze, but when it was about ten yards off, it stopped, shook its earflaps, then sauntered off with its tail held high.

"Juvenile posturing," Noah explained.

Kowalski frowned after it. "Typical teenager."

They crossed the rest of the way unmolested.

Noah nodded as they neared the cleft in the cliff. "The idea of an elephant's graveyard is only a legend," he said, as if warning against disappointment. "Old elephants don't go to a place to die. There's a good chance this herd is no different than others and simply lets their bones lie where they've fallen."

Jane wasn't so sure. She suspected there was nothing ordinary about this tribe. As they neared the opening, a bull elephant—the biggest seen so far—suddenly pushed out of the dark fissure, confronting them, blocking their way. His ears flared, trunk curling high.

"Something tells me that's not *juvenile* posturing," Kowalski grumbled.

"What now?" Derek whispered.

The answer came from beyond the bull, a wheezing trumpet, almost sounding exasperated. The bull eyed them a moment longer, staring daggers at the group, and shifted reluctantly out of the fissure, stepping aside.

"Looks like someone wants to see us," Derek said.

With the way open, the group set off into the fissure. The bull closed up behind them, blocking the exit with his bulk. He followed from a distance, moving quietly, barely making a sound, as if he placed much reverence upon the ground he tread.

Or maybe it was more about *who* waited for them.

Jane stared ahead. This fissure was darker, heavily canopied above, but Gray's helmet lamp offered enough illumination for them to see. The path was jagged, cutting back and forth. But eventually it ended at a bowl with no outlet.

End of the road.

And Jane meant that in more ways than one.

The floor of the next canyon was covered in mounded piles of branches and twigs, some intact, others scattered. Curled yellow tusks poked from a few, along with bleached white bones. At the back of the bowl rose a small grove of tall trees, but otherwise there was little sign of life. The barren ground was salted with white sand, pebbled with round stones, mixed what looked like broken shells cast up by an ancient sea long gone.

Jane stepped out with the others and realized she was wrong.

Underfoot was not sand and shells—but crushed bones.

She stared down, overwhelmed with horror, wondering at the depth of this grim bed. She pictured millennia of elephants coming here to die, crushed by others, ground down by time and the elements into this gritty sand.

Kowalski was no less pleased. "So much for an elephant graveyard being a myth."

But they were not alone here.

A handful of elephants stirred throughout the canyon, walking slowly, or standing vigil over a pile of sticks, or gently touching a trunk to a protruding bone. No sound was made, except for the gravelly tread of those visiting the dead.

Some of the horror faded from Jane, as she recognized the respect shown here, the genuine grief. One young bull hung his head over a mound, a glistening tear track running from the eye on this side.

No wonder the bull tried to block them from entering.

We don't belong here.

But as Derek had mentioned, they had been summoned.

An ancient elephant strode feebly toward where they stood, a grand matriarch. Her skin was gray-white, a near match to the bone crushed around her. She seemed to beckon them forward with her trunk.

They went to greet her, sensing she deserved this respect.

"I think she's nearly blind," Noah whispered.

It seemed he was right. The beam of Gray's light swept over her face, and she didn't blink or shy from its glare.

As they gathered, she came forward, her trunk arched before her. Drawing on senses keener than sight, she came first to Jane. Her nostrils sniffed, then her trunk found her wrist and wrapped softly there. Jane was tugged closer, drawn away from the others.

She glanced back, but Noah nodded to her reassuringly. So she let herself be guided forward, placing her trust in his years of experience working with the great beasts.

After a few steps, her wrist was released.

Then the great lady returned to the group, weaving her trunk, and chose one more.

Noah also encouraged this reluctant recipient of the matriarch's attention.

"*Komeza, Roho*," he whispered to his friend. "Go on now."

The cub followed the tip of the trunk as it fluttered through his tiny
mane, huffing and rubbing his neck. The cat was drawn to join Jane.

The two stood before the majestic beast. Jane noted the curled white
lashes of her old eyes as the elephant bowed her head, bringing her crown
to touch Jane's chest. At the same time, the side of her trunk rubbed
Roho's side, earning a contented rumble from him.

When the queen lifted her head again, tears glistened from those tired
eyes.

9:32 P.M.

Gray studied the old matriarch as she communed with the pair. The pink
tip of her white trunk explored tenderly, almost sadly.

"What is she doing?" Derek whispered.

Noah shook his head. "The old girl's grieving, but I don't know why."

Gray did. "She's remembering."

Derek turned to him.

He nodded forward, surprised it wasn't obvious to Derek. "A woman
and a lion."

Derek's eyes got huge, returning his attention to the tableau playing
out here. "You can't think . . ."

"She picked those two. That seems beyond coincidence." He pictured
the symbols carved in the tomb and sculpted on Livingstone's oil vessel. "Perhaps whoever came here looking for the source of the Nile was a
woman, someone who brought along a unique hunting partner for such a
long journey. Didn't Egyptians worship cats, occasionally raising lions as
pets or as hunters?"

Derek slowly nodded. "According to records, some pharaohs and others did. But while an elephant may never forget, I don't think they have
memories that go back thousands of years."

"Normally, no. But *that* old elephant certainly seems to remember this ancient pairing. I can't explain how yet, but maybe that evolutionary advantage we talked about before was not so one-sided." He turned to Noah. "You mentioned before about the big brains of elephants."

"Indeed. Bigger than any other land animal. Around eleven pounds. With a cortex holding as many neurons as our brains."

Gray nodded. "So for a microbe that has a predilection for electrically charged nervous systems, such a host would be perfect, a veritable feast. So maybe over time the two worked together, achieving other benefits. Maybe the microbe is able to electrically stimulate the elephant's brain, enhancing its already considerable memory . . . and maybe it serves somehow as a vehicle for passing knowledge from generation to generation."

Kowalski interrupted his train of thought. "Look. She's moving. Taking those guys somewhere."

The ancient elephant had turned and worked her way slowly across the canyon, urging Jane and Roho to follow with quiet huffs from her trunk.

"C'mon." Gray set off after them, keeping his distance so as not to spook the beast.

She took the pair over to the edge of the only stand of trees here, to where a mother and calf were rooting near a pile of dry branches. She drew Jane and Roho to a stop, blocking them from interfering with her trunk.

Gray hung back, too.

Derek gazed toward the wide bower of the neighboring trees and pointed toward its fruit-laden branches. "Plums," he said. "Those are Mobola plums."

Gray didn't understand the significance.

Derek must have realized this and explained. "When Livingstone died, his heart was buried under a Mobola plum tree. And when his body was shipped back to England, it was in a coffin made of this tree's bark."

"Why?"

"That particular bark has resins used for tanning purposes. It was part of the natives' method in mummifying Livingstone's remains for the long journey home."

Gray frowned and looked over at the pile of branches covering these mounds. He wagered they all came from these trees. Were the elephants using the branches to serve the same purpose? He sensed something important about this detail, but it still escaped him.

"What are they doing?" Kowalski asked.

The disgust in his partner's voice drew Gray's attention back to the mother and her calf. The elephant cow drew a chunk of bone from the burial mound. From its concave shape, it looked to be a piece of a skull. She placed it gently down and cracked it into smaller pieces with the hard nails and pads of her foot. She picked up a sliver, drew it to her mouth, and set about chewing it. She encouraged her calf to do the same.

The cow moved her jaw, likely grinding the sliver between her molars. She did this for half a minute, then a small rounded pebble fell out of her lips. It was a polished piece of the bone she had been gnashing.

Gray looked down at his boots, at the crushed bed of bone. All around, the ground was littered with these pebbles.

What the hell?

Again he felt that itch at the back of his brain, telling him this was important, but he couldn't put it all together.

I've got the pieces, but I can't see the puzzle.

As he stared across the canyon, the brilliant white of the boneyard had begun to shimmer with waves of color. It took Gray a moment to realize the source. The crystalline bed was reflecting the sky.

He craned his neck as waves of energy swept across the stars.

It made no sense.

It was some sort of aurora.

As if responding to the same strange sign, the elephants began to trumpet across the canyon. Even the old beast here raised her trunk and whistled out a mournful note, full of melancholy and grief.

Gray stared over at the others.

What is going on?

9:55 P.M.

From the open side door of the Cessna, Valya watched the dance of energies across the skies, great undulating ripples of emerald and blue. She knew what she was witnessing, having viewed the aurora countless nights up in the Arctic.

A flicker of superstitious unease accompanied the sight now. She imagined it was some warning from Anton, a message meant for her.

She gave her head a shake, dismissing such thoughts.

To her side, Kruger and his men were suited up in helmets with basejump parachutes strapped to their backs. Their faces were staring up, too, but she needed their focus below.

"Are you ready?" she yelled to Kruger.

He gave her a thumbs-up.

They had been tracking their targets all night, easily watching their progress up into the mountains through the infrared eyes of the Raven. The enemy had bottled themselves up into a set of box canyons, where it appeared a herd of elephants made their home. The oddity of it and the fact that they lingered there was enough to warrant dropping down and discovering what the others might have learned or acquired before dispatching them.

The pilot would swoop low but to the north of those canyons, dropping Kruger and his three men. Each had an AK74M assault rifle mounted with under-barrel grenade launchers strapped across their bellies. They would drop in dark, wearing night-vision gear, landing in the larger canyon. She would follow, sweeping down to cover the cliffside entrance into the canyon system, guarding any escape back into the outer woods. Her weapon was a Heckler & Koch MP7A1 submachine gun with night sight and silencer. She had four extended magazines, each holding forty rounds.

But her best weapon was strapped to her wrist.

Its blade would be bloodied this night. She would carve her mark deep, down to the bone, hopefully while her victim still lived.

The plane dipped, readying to unload its passengers. Under its wings, the two Hellfire missiles waited to be called down from above, to burn everything behind Valya and her team.

Up in the sky, the blaze of the equatorial aurora flared brighter, whipping energies across the heavens. She no longer took the sign as warning, but as a flaming banner.

The plane raced lower; Kruger glanced back to her.

She nodded.

Let it begin.

One by one, the five men fell down from the fiery sky.

26

Painter's skin crawled with the charge in the air. As he grabbed a strut to lean farther out of the rear cargo hatch of the Globemaster, a snap of static fired through the muscles of his hand, constricting the fibers, clenching his fingers to his grip. He ignored the pain and held tight.

Beyond the cargo hold, the skies were on fire.

The air smelled of ozone, sharp, like chlorine mixed with the smell of an amusement park bumper car ride. The hairs on his arms stood on end.

The sky overhead raged with an aurora that surged and billowed, a storm-swept sea of electrical whitecaps and fiery breakers. It cast out sprites and blue jets of plasma. Thunder boomed in continuous cannon fire. Lightning forked up from the dark clouds below.

The plane jolted from strikes, its wings shook as if trying to cast off the discharge, and one of the Pratt & Whitney engines trailed black smoke.

"What can we do?" the loadmaster shouted, hanging from a grip on the other side.

Painter glanced back into the hold. Past the tumbled blocks of the aluminum crates, the temporary barrier had been ripped down. Scientists worked at their station, braced as best they could, trying to answer the loadmaster's question. Anton's two men struggled to anchor the nest of containers within an orange cargo net, clipping its edges to braces along the hull. The two guys splashed through the glowing pools of crimson on the floor, oblivious to the toxic threat.

What did it matter now?

As the fireworks worsened outside, everyone had realized one truth.

We're all in this together now.

Painter yelled across the open hatch. "Things are about to get worse!"

The loadmaster—a young, red-faced man named Willet—looked at him, his horrified expression easy to read. *How could this get worse?*

Painter pointed down to their starboard. One section of the dark storm churned ominously, a monstrous whirlpool of energy and fire. Across its maw, lightning danced. But worst of all, the blaze of the borealis above dipped toward it, as if being sucked toward the tempest.

Painter had been watching this build for the past minute. He pictured the ionosphere dimpling, about to be torn by those tidal forces. He could even guess the cause. The heart of the fiery cauldron shone a rich crimson.

Painter recognized that particular glow.

It soaked his clothes, smoldered his skin, and ran in shimmering pools across the cargo deck. He had suspected all along that some of the toxin had spilled from the back of the plane, seeding the clouds below.

Here was the proof.

He pictured each particle acting like a superconducting speck, unbinding the potential energy trapped in those storm clouds, triggering a chain reaction, the effect cascading outward. It would soon liberate all that power, a thousand nuclear bombs' worth of energy.

Painter turned to the loadmaster. "Tell the pilot to keep us away from that!"

They had to get clear of that fiery whirlpool.

Now.

Willet nodded and ran toward the flight deck at the front.

Painter held his breath—then slowly the plane banked away, heeding his warning.

He sighed out a breath.

We're gonna—

From out of the clouds to the port side, a new column of fire burst forth, booming as it ripped the air, spiraling to the sky.

The plane had been turning in that direction. To avoid a collision, the pilot heaved the aircraft around, rolling the massive aircraft onto the tip of a wing. The cargo net ripped from the hull. Crates tumbled across the hold. One of the guards was crushed.

As the Globemaster fought to avoid the blaze, Painter gaped at this new threat, knowing from where it must have risen.

Aurora Station.

He stared down in disbelief.

What was that bastard thinking?

5:12 P.M.

"It's our only hope," Simon Hartnell whispered.

He stood at the helm of the control station, still captain of this ship, refusing to abandon his post. The evacuation Klaxon rang throughout the station. On a monitor, he saw Sno-Cats and snow machines dashing away. Other figures ran on foot, parkas flapping from their panicked forms.

Only a skeleton crew was here, helping him try to stop what he had started.

Dr. Kapoor ran up, out of breath, his face shiny with sweat. "It's too much." He shook his head. "We have to shut it down. It won't hold."

"It must."

Simon felt the floor tremble under his feet. With goggles strapped to his face, he stared up at the giant tower, willing it all to hold. Blue coruscations of fire ran from the spinning superconductor on top down to the bottom of the old mining pit. Its entire floor raged with a sea of burning plasma, surging and lapping around the base of his tower. Through the thick glass, the heat of a blast furnace reached him.

Still, he knew the fierce energy churning below was only the dregs of the full force he was channeling deep into the earth. After his test firing of the array had such a disastrous outcome, he had sought a way to reverse what he had started, to snuff the fire from the sky. He and Kapoor's team had run panicked scenarios and hasty calculations and come to one possible solution.

Following Tesla's design, Simon had built his Wardenclyffe not only to *transmit* power but also to *receive* it. Tesla's dream was to build a network of hundreds of towers, each casting energy wirelessly into a huge pool of power that circled the globe—either through the skies above or the earth below. But he also envisioned that each of those same towers could *tap* into that source, making its energy readily available to all.

Looking to the future, Simon had done the same.

And it was what he was attempting to do now.

He and Kapoor had reversed the polarity of his tower, something untested and untried but they had had no choice but to attempt it. While the fiery beam of plasma looked the same, it was no longer shooting power *up*, but sapping that energy *down* from the ionosphere.

His tower was now a lightning rod, trying to pull the fire from the sky.

Still, they had needed somewhere to *send* that energy, and again it was Tesla who offered an answer. When Simon had built his tower, he had to drive footings deep into the bedrock to support its massive structure. It was simply a matter of engineering necessity, but it had amused him how similar it was to the three-hundred-foot pilings that Tesla had designed for his tower, mighty iron rods meant to "grip the earth."

Tesla had intended to use that grip and those rods to send energy deep into the earth, to reach the resonance frequency of the planet, a potential bottomless well that could be filled and shared around the world.

Tesla had failed, but his reasoning was sound.

So Simon sought to fill that same well now with the fires from the sky. His hope was to balance the two visions of his mentor, two possible sources of global wireless energy: the ionosphere enclosing the planet and the dark well at its core.

He intended for his tower to act as a massive Tesla coil, connecting sky to the earth, a conduit for the fires above to flow deep underground. With luck, a point of equilibrium might be reached, allowing order to be restored.

Unfortunately, luck wasn't with them.

The ground jolted under his feet, tossing him across his console. He heard a boom of shattering glass. He cringed, believing it was the curve of window overlooking the tower. Instead, giant jagged panes crashed off to his right, near the back of the station. He knew what the window had once sealed. He pictured that dark lake.

"Sir!" Kapoor yelled, drawing him back to the more immediate threat. "We need to shut this down. We're getting massive voltage spikes. Plasma currents are surging wildly both ways."

As the floor continued to rattle and bump, he pictured waves crashing back and forth, traveling between the earth and sky.

"But isn't that what we want?" Simon said. "Didn't we anticipate that as equilibrium neared we'd get this effect? A sloshing back and forth as the two forces tried to stabilize?"

Kapoor shook his head. "You don't understand."

"Then tell me."

"The two sloshing waves . . ." he sputtered, struggling to explain, using his hands. "One traveling up, the other down. Their amplitudes and wavelengths are the same. They're beginning to superimpose as they cross each other."

Simon sucked in air, understanding the danger. "They could build to a standing wave."

He imagined a taut vibrating string of energy connecting sky to earth, stable and permanent.

Kapoor stared out at the tower in horror. "It would form a massive circuit."

Simon lunged forward, knowing such a circuit would not hold for long, not with the herculean forces at play. It would all short-circuit. If that happened, it could shred the sky and shatter the globe.

He twisted the key to cut the power, to shut everything down.

Nothing happened.

He tried a few more times.

"It's already powering itself." Kapoor backed a step. "The circuit's complete."

Simon straightened.

We're too late.

5:18 P.M.

"Hold on!"

At breakneck speeds, Kat drove the Sno-Cat down the far side of Johns Island. The long sliver of black rock jutted from the ice of Lake Hazen, looking like a submarine cracking through an arctic sea—only this sub was four miles long and half a mile wide. A scatter of smaller islands clustered close by, offering places to hide.

Tagak braced himself in the passenger seat, while his father, John, was sprawled in back. Both men had rifles in hand.

For the past forty-five minutes, Kat had engaged in a game of cat-and-mouse across the islands of Lake Hazen, hunted by Anton's men. When John had first alerted her of their approach, she had intended to take the Sno-Cat by herself and lure the enemy away from Safia and the others. Instead, the two Inuit had insisted on coming. She had tried to discourage them, warning them off with the threat of contagion, but John had eyed the number of snow machines sweeping down out of the mountains and climbed into the Sno-Cat with his son.

Kat was lucky they had.

While the storm had worsened, offering some shelter, it was their local knowledge of the lake and islands that had kept her alive. Using the lights of her Sno-Cat as a beacon in the storm, she had successfully drawn the enemy to the south. The trio of hide tents, covered in snow, had never even been spotted.

Once she reached the islands, she had turned her headlights off and became both the hunted and the hunter. The ensuing guerrilla war kept both sides at an impasse. The Sno-Cat had two new bullet holes in its windshield, but Kat knew she had taken out three snow machines.

Then everything changed.

"Go, go, go!" Tagak urged as the vehicle's treads hit the lake ice.

To either side, tiny glowing motes sped through the blowing snow, marking the enemy's swifter vehicles. But they weren't the danger any longer.

Lightning shattered across the low sky. Bolts crashed down all around, striking the ice with explosive force. Huge cracks skittered outward. Overhead, the entire cloud bank above the lake had begun to churn, forming a maelstrom of impossible magnitude.

Worse yet, it glowed a dark crimson, as if a fire were stoked inside.

Which Kat suspected was true.

She raced that storm, as did Anton's men, who scattered in all directions, heedless now of their prior targets, fleeing the hellfire above.

Kat had to reach Safia and Rory, grab them, and get out of this valley.

The back window suddenly shattered. John gasped, his palm flying to his ear, blood flowing immediately through his fingers.

"Down!" Kat yelled as she hunched lower.

Tagak rolled over the seat to join his father in back. He pointed his rifle out the fist-sized hole in the rear window and blindly shot into the storm pall behind them.

Kat raced faster as thunder boomed and lightning bolts seared her retinas. The Sno-Cat suddenly tilted as a section of ice proved to be a broken floe. It shifted under the vehicle's weight. She didn't slow, using the momentum to escape and get back to solid ice.

Tagak continued to take potshots at the storm, but Anton had to be running dark. Kat knew it was the Russian back there. Who else would still be doggedly continuing this chase?

To her right, something ripped through the swirling snow and struck the ice. It exploded with such force that it shook the Sno-Cat. Her first thought was a mortar attack. Then the skies opened up and unleashed its full fury.

Giant chunks of ice crashed to the lake, shattering into splinters or bouncing across the surface. Pumpkin-sized hail pelted all around. The roof of the Cat rang with their impacts, denting toward them. The bombardment worsened, pounding the landscape, the view lit by flashes of lightning.

Kat dared not slow down.

Finally, she outraced the worst of the hailstorm, clearing its deadly salvo, but the cannonade of ice and lightning continued to pursue them. She ran from its onslaught, struggling to keep ahead of it.

In her rearview mirror, she noted a change in the storm. As if partially spent by the barrage, the churning clouds had shredded, revealing streaks of the skies above. Flaming plasma raged across the blue vault, while chains of lightning ripped apart the heavens. It was as if the barriers between worlds had parted, and she was peering into the burning heart of hell itself.

And maybe I am.

She remembered descriptions of the biblical seventh plague: *Moses stretched out his staff toward heaven, and the Lord sent thunder and hail, and fire ran down to the earth.*

She stared at the shattering forks of lightning, the explosive barrage of ice, the fires burning across the skies. Thunderclaps boomed all around, shaking the ice and rattling the windows.

Is that what I'm witnessing?

Slowly, the maelstrom closed again, hiding what it had briefly revealed. It looked even stronger and darker now, yet still retaining that dread glow.

"Watch out!" Tagak hollered from the back.

She twitched her gaze from the mirror to the lake.

Across the ice ran a familiar sight, more ethereal than ever. Small shapes flew silently before her, their panicked hoofbeats covered by the storm, their bodies fading into and out of the swirls of snow. It was the ghostly herd of caribou.

But these were no apparitions.

A big buck suddenly burst directly across the bumper of the Sno-Cat. She swerved to miss it, sending the vehicle into a skid on the slick ice. The animal bounded safely past, as the Sno-Cat spun full circle.

Kat fought them back around, her heart pounding.

Then in the distance, she spotted humps on the ice.

The hide tents.

Thank god . . .

With their goal in sight, she got them moving again. But with her focus fixed ahead, she missed the cracks in the ice. The shelf under the Cat canted to the side. With her momentum bled away by the near collision, she didn't have the speed to get clear. As the center of gravity inexorably shifted, the floe tipped faster and faster.

Kat pointed to the high-side doors. "Out!"

They all scrambled up the slanting cabin. Doors were shoved and flung open. Bodies jettisoned. By the time Kat was out, the Sno-Cat was nearly upended to one side. Its bulk slid down the slanted shelf, hastening its demise. She planted her feet on the door sill and leaped away, abandoning ship. As Kat flew over open blue water, the Cat slowly toppled into the lake behind her. She hit the solid ice headlong and rolled across its frozen surface. She caught glimpses of Tagak doing the same, cradling his wounded father.

She gained her feet in time to see the shelf of ice falling back into place, its edges cracking further, bobbing in place. The Sno-Cat was gone, swallowed by this frozen trapdoor, as if it had never been there.

John and Tagak joined her.

John sighed. "A dogsled is much better."

She didn't disagree.

They set off for the tents, but after they had trekked fifty yards, a low rumble rose out of the storm to the left. A shadow passed through the storm pall, a shark in dark water.

It was a snow machine, traveling without lights.

"Run," Kat said.

She pointed ahead and motioned to stay low, hoping her group hadn't been spotted. In their haste to escape the Cat, they'd lost their weapons. The only hope was to reach the snow-covered tents and pray the enemy passed them by.

They moved as a tight group, sticking close.

The camp grew clearer.

Kat's ears strained for the sound of a motor, but the storm closed down upon them from behind, booming with thunder and cracking ice. Still, the group reached the site safely.

Kat hurried toward the tent where she had left Rory and Safia.

Before she could reach the flap, a gunshot blasted. Ice exploded at her toes.

She stopped and turned.

Anton appeared from behind the neighboring tent, accompanied by another figure bundled in a parka. Both had assault rifles leveled. They must have parked their machine out of sight and set up this ambush.

Anton addressed the two Inuit. "On your knees. Hands on your heads."

They hesitated, but Kat waved them down.

Anton's partner circled behind them, keeping aim on their backs.

"Rory, come out!" Anton called.

The tent flap was thrown open, and the young man climbed through, looking apologetically toward Kat. He was wearing a new parka.

"I'm sorry," he said, looking down. "They caught us by surprise. I didn't want this all to happen."

You and me both . . .

But from the looks of that parka, he would be getting out of here.

"How is Safia?" she asked.

He shook his head. "Bad. It's like she's worsening with the storm."

So at least they hadn't killed—

The tent flap flew open, and Safia stumbled out between Rory and Anton. Her eyes were on the maelstrom filling the world to the south. For a moment, Kat swore her eyes were aglow, but it was likely just a reflection of lightning.

She swung an arm up.

Then everything happened in slow motion.

The guard behind Kat must have thought Safia was brandishing a weapon. He fired, but Rory was facing that same direction and noted the threat.

He flung himself in front of Safia. "No!"

In turn, Anton reacted with a skill born of his Guild training and rolled in front of Rory, his back to the shooter. The bullet struck him in the spine. He fell forward into Rory's arms.

As the two went down, Kat lunged low, grabbed Anton's weapon, and spun onto her rear, squeezing off a three-round burst.

One bullet found the guard's neck, blowing most of it away, and sending him crashing backward.

In that breathless moment, only one of them still stood.

Safia's eyes never left the skies.

She spoke, as if to the storm. "It must not be . . ."

5:32 P.M.

As flames burn brighter through her skull, she stares out of two sets of eyes.

One old, one fresh.

She sees a cold storm roll across a burning desert toward a blood-red river. She sees a frozen lake that defies the fiery tempest rolling over it. The two sights waver and shimmer over each other, as if trying to snuff each other out.

It is a war of ice and fire, a battle as old as the world.

She ignores this, knowing it is but a distraction.

Her gaze shifts farther away, to a beacon that blazes out there.

It must not be.

5:33 P.M.

"You want us to do what?" Painter asked.

He sat up on the flight deck with the pilot and loadmaster, who apparently also doubled as copilot. Behind him, the others on board crowded the stairs that led up here, all listening to their former boss over the plane's microwave radio.

"You must crash the jet into the Aurora array," Hartnell said, his voice breathless with fear. "Straight into the tower."

Painter looked past the nose of the jet toward the blazing column of plasma. Hartnell had already told them roughly what was happening, how in an attempt to reverse the damage he had wrought, he had made matters worse. He pictured the circuit that Hartnell had described, knowing it was only a crude analogy for the colossal energies at play here, but he understood the gist.

Hartnell needed someone to break that circuit before it collapsed on its own.

On the ground, Hartnell and Kapoor fought to keep it stable but that could not last. Painter only had to look out the window to recognize this truth. The fiery whirlpool had been growing steadily larger, a swirling hurricane of potential energy.

The kiloton equivalent of a thousand nuclear bombs.

Once that reached the fragile circuit blazing brightly in the sky, it was game over.

Painter estimated they had another twenty minutes at best.

So there was no time for long debates.

"We'll do it," he said.

The pilot glanced over to him, his face terrified. He clearly recognized that someone had to take this bird down manually. With all the interference and storm conditions, it would not be an instrument landing.

And they would only have one shot at this.

Painter had also noted the photograph next to the pilot's seat: a smiling wife and two small children. He reached and squeezed the man's shoulder. "I got this."

The pilot frowned. "You've flown a C-17 Globemaster before?"

"Nothing this big. Mostly private jets." He patted the man's shoulder. "But it's not like I have to land this—just crash it."

The pilot looked dubious and clearly fought between arguing with Painter and letting him take over this kamikaze mission. His face firmed. "I'll talk you through the basics. If you don't feel confident—or I don't feel you know your flight stick from your dick—then I'll take her down."

"Fair enough." Painter pointed to the throttle. "That's the stick, right?"

The pilot looked aghast.

Painter grinned. "It's the throttle, I know. And that's your stick.

There's the HUD, the IAS, and of course, the PFD." He ended by pointing to his crotch. "And that's my dick, the last time I looked. We good?"

The pilot grumbled and sank deeper into his seat. "Let's do this."

Everyone on board quickly made evacuation plans, while the pilot banked for the best approach to the array. The plan was to do a fast dive through the storm layer, which Painter was happy to leave to the pilot. Once low enough, the aircraft would level off, allowing everyone to offload out the back with parachutes, leaving Painter to take the Globemaster the rest of the way down.

Simple enough, if you weren't the one left in the hot seat.

"Hold tight!" the pilot radioed throughout the aircraft. "Starting descent!"

Painter sat in the jump seat behind Willet, which offered him a bird's-eye view as the nose of the aircraft tipped toward the cloud bank. The pilot had aligned the course to be a straight, long shot.

As they dove steeply, Painter stared at the column of fire to the right and the dark, churning pool to the left. The space between them had narrowed considerably, even faster than Painter had initially estimated. He could guess why. The plasma storm raging through the ionosphere had worsened. The aurora boiled across the heavens, casting great fiery loops earthward and blasting out a flurry of sprites and jets.

Such a display could mean only one thing.

Hartnell was losing control, the situation already destabilizing.

The pilot must have sensed this and drove the aircraft into a steeper approach. "Hold tight!" he hollered.

The Globemaster swept down to the black clouds. Painter cringed and gripped his seat harness, leaning back. As they dropped through the storm, the ship was immediately battered and tossed, rattled and rolled. The pilot hunched over his controls, a hand on the stick, the other on the throttle. Through the windshield, the world was nothing but blackness. Even the green lines of the heads-up display were awash with static. It seemed to go on forever, then suddenly they dropped out of the clouds, and the world returned in a grayscale of whipping snow, black crags, and white glaciers.

The pilot raised the nose, flaring the craft, to level and slow their descent. Once back to an even slope, he adjusted a few switches, scratched his chin, then turned to Painter. "You're up."

Painter unsnapped his seat harness.

Into the hot seat.

He changed places with the pilot, who took a few moments to make sure Painter was ready, like a doting hen.

Painter finally waved him off. "Go. Get everyone offloaded."

He nodded, turned away, then back. "Thank you."

"Don't thank me yet."

The pilot patted him on the shoulder, then dropped out of the flight deck.

Willet stayed another moment. "You're only going to have seconds."

"I know."

The man sighed, staring ahead. Directly in front of the nose of the aircraft, the storm glowed with blue fire. The beast was waiting for him.

"I can stay," Willet offered. Though from the strain in his voice, it took every ounce of willpower to utter those three words.

Painter pointed a thumb behind him. "Mr. Willet, get off my ship. That's an order."

The man smiled, tossing him a salute. "Aye, aye, Captain."

He unstrapped and climbed out of the neighboring seat, clapping him on the shoulder. "You better pull this off."

Painter knew Willet was talking about more than just taking out the array.

That's the plan.

As Willet headed below, Painter slipped on a radio earpiece. He used a minute to further acquaint himself with the controls. There were hundreds of switches above his head and over his instrument panel, but the most important control was the flight stick at his knee.

I can do this.

He finally heard Willet again on his earpiece. "Birds have safely flown the coop. Heading overboard. Ship is yours."

Though he didn't know for sure when the loadmaster abandoned ship, Painter sensed it. He was alone on this great big bird.

To distract himself, he checked his attitude indicators, eyed his primary flight display for his airspeed, and made subtle adjustments to his pitch. Two minutes out, he eased on the throttle, slowing the craft for the final approach.

Here we go.

He hit a switch for the microwave radio. "Hartnell, are you there? Pick up."

The man came on the line, his voice surprised, almost amused. "Painter? You're bringing the plane down?"

"Someone's got to clean up your mess. Just letting you know I'm a hundred seconds out. So you and Kapoor should get to the bomb shelter."

"I already sent Dr. Kapoor. But somebody's got to keep watch at the helm. Even if it's only to buy you another second or two."

Painter heard the strain and remembered the raging storm in the ionosphere, indicative of the situation destabilizing. "How much time do I have?"

"You may need those extra seconds or two."

Painter silently cursed and pushed the throttle forward, regaining the speed he had just bled off.

Ahead, he was close enough to make out the sprawling antenna array. It ran with blue sparks of energy, illuminating its spiral, turning it into a shimmery galaxy sprawled across the tundra. In the center, the column of plasma rose from the blazing tip of the steel tower. Even from this distance, he could note spasms vibrating along the fiery column's length, shaking it with destabilizing pulses of plasma energy.

Painter increased the airspeed. He dared not slow down like he had planned. His window of opportunity had narrowed considerably—leaving him no second to spare.

Hartnell suddenly yelled in his ear. "Painter!"

He saw it at the same time. A thick ball of plasma swept up from the mining pit, heading toward the ionosphere. Energy was no longer flowing *down.* The tower's polarity was shifting, about to collapse. As Painter followed that lightning ball toward the clouds, he saw the likely reason.

The fiery cauldron in the sky had arrived. Its outer edges brushed close to the column of plasma rising from Aurora Station.

Painter was out of time.

He throttled up and used the flight stick to drop the nose. His airspeed spun up, turning the Globemaster into a missile.

He was about to make his move when a crosswind crashed into the flank of the aircraft. Cursing, Painter crabbed the plane's nose into the wind, fighting to return the ship to the correct angle of approach. He lost precious seconds during this maneuver but finally reset the course.

He hovered his hands for a breath over the controls.

Looks good.

Once satisfied, he flew out of the hot seat, rolled to the stairs, and dropped to the cargo deck. He sprang immediately away, racing toward the back, while the aircraft flew ahead, a missile about to crash.

His feet pounded across the deck. There was no way he could survive bailing out the back. He was too low to use a parachute, too high to jump without one.

So he improvised.

Near the open cargo door, he snatched what he had prepared and strapped it to his back, then grabbed the assault rifle next to it.

He flung himself toward the hatch—just as the outer edge of the scintillating spiral galaxy appeared to either side. The wings clipped the antenna tops as the bow of the bird slammed through the steel trunks in front.

Oh crap . . .

Painter reached back and slapped his palm on the ignition for the inflation tank.

The weather balloon burst out the pack on his back, whipped into the wind drafting behind the plane, and yanked him out of the rear of the craft.

He sailed away and up, watching the wide-bellied Globemaster plow through the glowing spiral, aiming for the flaming beast at the center.

5:52 P.M.

Simon Hartnell stood at the helm.

He heard the roaring approach of the huge cargo jet, and now its splintering crash through the array. He stared up at the tower before him, aflame with energy. He remembered thinking earlier how the display had reminded him of the blazes of Saint Elmo's fire, which would dance through the masts and riggings of sailing ships.

He pictured the tower here as the mast to his own personal HMS *Erebus* or *Terror*. He also recalled Painter's admonition to his ancestor who had been a crew member aboard one of those original ships.

It seems some men reach too far.

Yet even now he didn't accept that.

He stared up at his masterpiece, doomed though it may be.

What's far worse is never trying.

The world exploded before him, taking away his life and all his dreams.

5:53 P.M.

Sailing high, Painter watched the Globemaster finish its last flight.

The cargo plane dragged its belly through the shining array and slammed nose-first into the top of the tower. As it canted into the wide mining pit, it crushed the tower beneath its bulk, snuffing the flame of that incandescent candle.

For just a moment, seared across his retina, he saw the remaining column of plasma whip into the sky like the angry tail of a cat—then it was gone.

A moment later, the airplane exploded, wiping that image away. A great ball of fire rolled into the sky and quickly became a column of smoke, a dark shadow of the brilliance from a moment ago.

Out of harm's way—but far from safe—Painter raised his assault rifle and shot at the balloon overhead. He took great care, shooting one round at a time, letting the air out slowly. His ascent finally topped off, and he began to fall back to earth. He had prepared himself for a hard landing, but in the end, he touched down rather softly.

The weather balloon collapsed behind him, settling like a shroud over rock and snow. He shrugged off the pack but kept the weapon. He guessed he was a couple of miles from Aurora Station and didn't want any polar bears marring his hike back.

Still, he stood for a breath, staring at the sky. With the array shut down—no longer feeding fire into the sky and having sucked a fair amount of energy back into the ground—the raging vortex in the clouds appeared to be calming down. The dull crimson glow was all but gone, its inner fire no longer stoked by the plasma storm as the ionosphere cleared.

Still, while the weather might be cooperating, Painter knew there was much cleanup yet to be done. There was no telling *how* contaminated this whole island might be. They could not count on the play of electricity to have eradicated all the microbes cast into the air.

He sighed, returned his attention earthward, and set off for Aurora Station.

Even with his parka, he had thought it would be cooler here in the Arctic.

He touched a palm to his forehead.

I'm burning up.

6:25 P.M.

"How are you feeling?" Kat asked.

Safia sat on the camp cot in the Inuit's hide tent. She cradled a cup of hot fish soup in her hands, courtesy of John and Tagak. "Better."

They had the place to themselves for the moment. Rory had retreated to another tent, where John had done his best to make Anton comfortable, but the bullet he had taken for Rory—and in turn, Safia—had severed his spine, paralyzing him from the waist down. The round had also shredded through his chest, leaving him coughing blood.

He would not make it.

Rory seemed to know this and stayed with him.

"Can you tell me what happened?" Kat asked. "You were hallucinating quite dramatically?"

"It's foggy. I remember bits and pieces mostly. My feet burning in sand. The stench of dead animals." She shook her head. "But there at the end, just before I collapsed, I saw stronger images. It was like I was seeing through two sets of eyes. I could see the storm here, but also another, looming above a blood-red Nile. It felt so real—as real as the ice and snow here."

Kat glanced toward the tent flap. The weather had abruptly calmed. The lightning and hailstorm about to sweep over the camp had died away. It coincided with Safia collapsing to the snow, as if she were a puppet whose strings had been cut.

"Rory—and his father, too, for that matter—believed that your infection by that microbe could have been the source of those dreams, that the organism was replaying past patterns it had been imprinted with. Carrying forward memories, thoughts, maybe even personalities. And possibly tracing all the way back to ancient Egypt."

Kat wondered if the storm's energy had enhanced that effect, possibly explaining why Safia remembered the last hallucinations more vividly.

Safia shrugged. "I don't know. Like I said, I don't remember much."

"When you were hallucinating, Rory asked your name in ancient Egyptian Coptic. You answered in the same language, saying your name was Sabah."

This clearly surprised her. "That's the name of the mummy on the throne." She touched her face, clearly also remembering how she had become infected in the first place.

"And you're feeling better now?"

"I am."

After her sudden collapse, they had gotten her inside. She woke shortly thereafter, seeming much better. Her fever had definitely broken, her temperature returning to normal. Kat wondered if she had simply recovered or if her sudden recuperation had something to do with all the electricity in the air. She wanted to run tests on Safia as soon as possible.

Which raised another question.

With as much time as has passed, how come Rory and I are still fine?

They were missing something important.

The tent flap stirred and Rory pushed inside. His eyes were puffy.

"Anton?" Kat asked.

He shook his head and sank to the floor, sitting cross-legged, plainly not wanting to be alone. He looked shell-shocked and dazed. She imagined his loss had not fully hit him yet.

"I'm sorry," Safia said.

Kat could not find her way to sympathy yet, but the man had tried to save Safia, throwing himself between her and the shooter. So she tolerated his presence.

Rory took a deep breath. "I need you to know . . . I never got a chance to tell you."

"What?" Kat asked.

"You left me to study the topographic map of the mummy's tattoos." He glanced over to Safia. "The scan was impressive, and I used your method for converting the Egyptian hieroglyphs into early Hebrew. I made some progress before . . ."

He waved toward where Anton had died.

"Go on," Kat pressed. "What did you learn?"

"The mummy was the cure."

Kat stood up. "What?"

"Or the body at least was carrying it, along with a load of the pathogenic microbe in her skull. But I still don't understand. My father had her tissues tested. Over and over again. He found nothing except what would make you *sick*, certainly nothing that would *cure* you." Rory scowled. "He missed something."

He waved to Safia. "But that's why she's better. Whatever she was exposed to acted like a live-virus vaccine. Made her a little feverish in the process, but in the end harmless."

"You got that all from the mummy's tattoos?"

"I had to infer much. And there's still more to translate. But I'm also pretty sure that's why we never got sick. The cure must have also made

Safia harmless, attenuating the load of the pathogen she was exposed to in the lab."

Kat stared at Safia. "Then maybe we can use her blood or spinal fluid and develop a cure . . . ?"

Rory sighed and shook his head. "For some reason, it doesn't work that way. That much was clear. There is only *one* cure and *one* way to obtain it. Directly from the source." He stared over at Kat. "And we burned it to ash."

Kat pictured the failsafe at the lab, remembered the roaring rush of fire.

The cure is gone.

27

The trumpeting of the elephants continued throughout the canyons, echoing off the walls, trebling and quadrupling in volume.

Concerned by the strange behavior and afraid to aggravate the herd further, Gray kept his group gathered and quiet in the elephant graveyard. He could readily enough guess what had triggered this dramatic display. In the middle of the small canyon, the ancient white-skinned matriarch stared blindly up, as if she could sense the dazzle of the equatorial aurora dancing across the night sky.

Finally, the commotion began to subside. While ribbons and waves of shimmering energy still washed over the stars, it seemed to be fading, too.

Noah let out a breath, as if the guide had been holding it all this time. "I've never seen anything like that." He waved to the skies but also stared toward the grand dame sharing the canyon. "And I doubt this group has ever been this vocal. Especially for such a shy and secretive herd. Their chorus must have been heard for a hundred miles."

Roho had stuck close to Noah during all of this. The cub clearly did not appreciate this musical display.

Neither did another. Kowalski rubbed his ears and popped his jaw. "I may never hear right again."

To the side, Derek held Jane's hand. "But did you notice their song? It didn't sound angry or distressed . . ."

"Almost sorrowful," Jane murmured. "Like the entire herd had suddenly remembered something that tore at their hearts."

Noah nodded. "She's right. I've listened to elephants mourning the passing of members of their herd. This reminded me of that."

"But what could they be remembering?" Derek looked to the skies. "I doubt any of them would have witnessed an aurora at the equator, not in their lifetimes."

"Maybe it wasn't their lifetimes." Gray eyed Jane and Roho. He pictured the old elephant drawing the two out, as if she had recognized them, possibly confusing the pair with another from long ago. "Maybe it's a much older memory, one tied to a great tragedy that has echoed over millennia."

Derek still seemed dubious, clearly guessing Gray was referencing their prior talk. "You're suggesting from the time another woman and lion arrived on their doorstep."

"After a great flood washed the microbe out of this valley and poisoned the Nile." Gray stared up. "If that ancient flood was triggered by atmospheric changes following the volcanic explosion of Thera, as you imagined before, it could have been accompanied by a localized aurora."

Jane followed his gaze to the shimmering sky. "We know Thera exploded with a force never seen before, but how could it change the sky?"

"Because ash plumes are full of energy, crackling with lightning. If all that cataclysmic energy was exploded upward by Thera, it could have created an aurora in the ionosphere over this region." He listened as the last mournful trumpet ended. "And these great beasts remembered . . . along with all the death that followed."

Noah stared across the canyon. "If you're right, maybe that also explains the purpose behind the painted forest. The multitudes of glowing colors, the shimmering reflection in the water, even the movement as their decorated bodies shifted among the trees. Could they have been trying to evoke some memory of an aurora? Was that the origin of their ritual?"

Gray recalled how the very air under that painted bower had seemed sacred, full of reverence. "And then we arrived at that ceremony with a woman and a lion in tow. Perhaps that's why they so readily accepted us."

Noah nodded. "Merging our arrival with an ancient memory, one full of heartache and grief."

Jane stared over to the old queen. "It makes you wonder if they knew, even back then, what was unleashed from their valley. Maybe they allowed the Egyptians to build that wall—a wall the elephants could have easily taken down if they had wanted to—then taught the newcomers the cure in order to make amends."

Gray remembered the elder taking Jane by the hand and possibly trying to do the same, an echo of another time.

"But what have we learned?" Jane asked. "I don't understand."

Gray had begun to get an inkling, but it seemed that would have to wait. As if responding to some unseen signal from the matriarchal queen or just agitated by the fading sky, the big bull had returned. He stared at their group and tossed his head, grunting and baring his tusks in a clearly aggressive posture.

"Looks like we've overstayed our welcome," Kowalski said, "and are being shown the door."

Respecting their wishes, Gray waved them forward. They skirted past the matriarch's guardian and headed back down the fissure. No one spoke, each lost in the mysteries and wonders of the last hours. As they reached the greater canyon and headed through it, Gray stared around the enclosed valley, lit by the fading aurora, trying to imagine Egyptians arriving here, discovering this place.

"Look," Derek said, pointing toward the grotto and the small pond it sheltered.

The water's surface glowed a blushing crimson, but it wasn't a reflection of the colony of fireflies roosting across the scalloped overhang. Instead, it came from the depths of the pond itself.

"It must be responding to the energy in the air," Gray said.

Derek turned to him, his eyes wide. "Maybe you were right before." He gazed out at the elephants. "Maybe it was this same energy that gave rise to that melancholy chorus from before, stirring up those ancient memories, stoked by the fire of what they carry in their skulls."

And now it was ending.

Gray watched the glow receding in the water, fading with the aurora, too. He felt a deep sense of peace—which was a mistake.

A single gunshot made them all turn.

Seichan's voice crackled in his radio earpiece. "Look up! We're under attack!"

Gray studied the skies, not seeing anything at first. Then he noted dark shadows falling swiftly against the stars. As they reached the level of the cliffs, parachutes snapped wide.

Gunfire crackled from above.

Rounds shredded through the trees and ripped into the ground all around them.

Gray realized his helmet lamp was still lit, a beacon for the gunfire. He flicked it off, got the others moving, and waved them toward the shelter of the cliffs.

"Get into cover! Hide!" He pointed to Kowalski. "Keep them safe!"

"How—?"

"Figure it out!"

Gray grabbed what he needed from them and headed away. He glanced toward the canyon entrance, toward the shield wall built by ancient Egyptians. He wanted to radio Seichan, but he feared the enemy would overhear.

He willed her silently instead.

Watch your back.

11:09 P.M.

From atop the wall, Seichan noted Gray's lamp go dark.

She prayed he was all right, while cursing herself for not recognizing the threat sooner. For the past two hours, she had stayed posted here, using the vantage of the dike's height to watch the valley on one side and the path leading here on the other. She had focused most of her attention on that dark fissure through the cliffs, guarding their team's only exit.

So she had failed to spot the figures falling through the sky until it was too late. The only reason she was alerted was the faintest rumble of a plane engine, heard as the deafening chorus of the elephants ended. With her paranoia running high, she had searched the skies and spotted the specks plummeting toward the canyon.

She had fired a warning shot for Gray, while radioing him.

It was all she could do to help him and the others.

With the alarm now raised, she ran atop the wall to the ramp. She was tempted to take the path to the right that led into the valley, to add her firepower to the battle about to begin, but she pictured a pale face marred by a black sun.

That's what you want me to do, don't you?

She suspected that was the purpose behind this aerial attack, to keep everyone's attention in the canyon. She had counted five parachutes, but she knew there was still another threat. Back in the Sudan, the pale assassin had sent a team underground, while setting up an ambush outside, guarding all exits.

And it had almost worked.

Seichan pictured the blazing desert sun, being trapped on the side of a dune, watching the rider aim her rifle, imagining that savage smile hidden under the scarf.

Reaching the ramp, Seichan turned left and headed into the fissure.

Not this time, bitch.

11:11 P.M.

Valya chose a spot well back in the woods, close to where the forest was flooded.

This will do.

Ten minutes ago, she had landed outside the cliffs as the crackle of gunfire echoed from the distant canyons. Still, she didn't rush and calmly folded her parachute.

While drifting down out of the skies, she hadn't come alone. The Raven UAV had circled wide around her. She used its infrared optics to scan the last of the fissure and the surrounding forest, spying for any hidden dangers.

She wanted no more surprises.

Once safely on the ground, she moved to this vantage, which gave her an unobstructed view to the mouth of the fissure. She discovered a nest of boulders, the perfect sniper's roost. So she set up her camp, rolling out a dark blanket behind the cover of the rocks. She dropped to her belly, balancing her Heckler & Koch MP7A1 submachine gun atop its small tripod. Equipped with a night sight and a silencer, it would be nearly impossible for an enemy to spot her position.

She lined up three of her extra magazines on the blanket next to her, but kept a reserve tucked into her belt, in case she needed to move fast.

Last, she positioned the portable receiver near her elbow, masked from direct view of the canyon by one of the boulders. A glance allowed her to continue to spy from above.

Satisfied, she lowered her eye to her sights and waited. A fresh spate of gunfire echoed to her. She didn't know what was happening, as she had demanded radio silence from Kruger's team until the canyon was secured.

Still, she did know one thing for certain.

She'll come for me.

11:13 P.M.

With rounds sparking from the rocks around him, Gray ducked into the tight fissure that led to the graveyard. He took a hard turn at the first jag. Once out of direct view of the canyon, he shifted one of the helmets to the crook of his elbow and thumbed off its lamp. He did the same to the one on his head and the one held in his other arm.

He had borrowed the additional two helmets from Jane and Derek.

A bullet ricocheted around the turn in the fissure, setting him to running again.

My trick seemed to have worked . . . but how well?

After Kowalski had headed away with the others for the canyon wall, Gray had sprinted the opposite direction, hoping to lure the enemy to chase him—at least long enough for the others to reach cover. To bait his lure, Gray had taken the helmets and clicked on the lamps. He was sure the five-man assault team had come with night-vision gear, so the three lights should be flaming torches in the shadowy canyon. He hoped their glare would hide the fact that only one man hid within that blaze. He wanted the enemy to believe Gray's team was still with him and come after the fleeing targets with a majority of their strength.

He sprinted the rest of the way to the graveyard, nearly bouncing off the walls to keep ahead of whoever was taking potshots at him. At last, he burst back into the smaller canyon, his boots crunching through the crushed bones.

He clicked the three helmet lamps back on and flung them in all directions as he worked across the space. Only the queen was still here, plainly on edge from the spatter of gunfire, but not so panicked as to squint her old eyes at Gray's strange antics.

Wanting her out of harm's way—*this isn't your fight*—he shooed her toward the back of the canyon, waving his arms. "Heeyah! Get over there now! C'mon."

She took this as an affront, raising her trunk as if in disgust at his rudeness, but she did lumber around and slowly work farther back.

Good enough.

Gray glanced to the three scattered lamps, wanting them to confuse whoever came, to divide their attention. Satisfied, he hurried to one of the stacks of branches over moldering bones and burrowed his way undercover, facing the cavern entrance, SIG Sauer in hand.

It didn't take long.

A shadow shifted within the fissure, cautious. The assailant popped his head out and did a fast sweep, then ducked back. He had exposed himself only for a second. Hidden again, he was likely strategizing how to proceed, analyzing the information from his mental snapshot of the canyon.

Guy's good.

Gray listened, ears straining, and realized one other detail about his adversary.

The man had come alone.

The fact that he hadn't been fooled into dragging his teammates along with him told Gray this was likely the team's leader, probably the same one who had hunted them in the Sudanese tomb. If so, the bastard would want revenge.

Gray tightened his jaw, worried about his friends.

11:18 P.M.

Derek crouched at the back of the grotto.

After separating from Gray, their group had fled to the canyon wall. The best hiding place was also the most dangerous. The toxic pond had gone dark again, but the small cave that sheltered half of it remained lit by the firefly colony nesting in the vegetation that covered its roof. Derek had hoped the flickering bioluminescence would negate the enemy's night-vision advantage. He knew even this much light would blind the sensitive gear.

So they carefully circled the bank of the pond to the back of the grotto. There they found a low cave, one big enough to hide everyone in their group, except for the hulking form of Kowalski. He hadn't minded, telling them to lie low while he dealt with the enemy. He left them with a disconcerting grin and some final words.

I have a plan.

Behind Derek, Jane hid with Noah, both of them sheltering Roho.

They all held their breaths as a dark shadow circled the far side of the pond, hunkered low, weapon raised. Derek pushed deeper into the cave, trying to stay hidden, praying for the hunter to continue past. But the man paused, seeming to stare straight at them, his eyes beetled by his night-vision goggles.

Derek cringed, suddenly having no confidence in his choice of hiding places.

Keep going . . .

As the hunter continued to hold, Derek searched past him, hoping Kowalski was close by, rushing already to help them. Instead, a loud shotgun blasted, followed by a gurgling scream. The noise rose from the middle of the canyon, likely Kowalski taking out one of the men—unfortunately, that also meant he wasn't nearby to help them.

Still, the attack seemed to have achieved the same result.

The hunter had dropped low, spinning his weapon in that direction. He now lifted to a crouch and started toward the commotion.

Phew . . .

But one other reacted to the blast.

Roho let out a low nervous whine of complaint.

Noah scolded him softly, quieting the cat down mostly by touch—but the damage was done.

The hunter turned back around, his head cocking, still unsure. The jungle above the canyon beckoned with the hooting calls of monkeys and the occasional yowl of night predators, all further confounded by the acoustics of the high walls.

Unfortunately, the gunman shifted to the side and headed toward the apron of rock that served as the pond's bank, plainly intending to investigate.

Derek glanced over his shoulder. The only weapon they had was Noah's machete. Heading into the thick of the fight, Kowalski had needed his shotgun, and their guide had forgotten his rifle on the island where they had engineered the rescue of the elephant calf. In all the excitement and wonder of the painted forest, Noah had left it leaning against a tree.

Derek eyed Roho, but Noah had already told them that the cub was too young and inexperienced, that he was only beginning to learn to hunt. Derek also suspected the guide didn't want his friend to become a man-killer. And from the way the cub was shaking, Noah was right about Roho being a lover and not a fighter.

Derek shifted forward, accepting the inevitable.

It's up to me.

Noah still held the machete, but only as backup, a second level of defense to protect Jane.

By now the gunman had reached the pond and edged around its

bank. He swatted one-handed at a couple of disturbed fireflies. From his exaggerated reaction, the bugs' bioluminescence must have flared explosively in his goggles. Still, he kept them in place, displaying his deference for the military tech.

As he circled around, he stared both out at the canyon and into the grotto.

Derek waited until he was only a few steps away—then lunged out as the man swung his gaze out to the canyon. Sadly, the scrape of a boot heel drew the hunter's attention straight back.

But Derek was already committed.

He reached both hands for the man's throat, while hitting him broadside. He grappled with the man, and they both crashed into the deep pond. That wasn't Derek's plan, but he knew it was a risk.

And for Jane he was willing to take it.

He sputtered up, flung himself back onto the bank, and yelled "Now!"

Jane lifted the controller in her hand as the hunter raised his rifle. Beating him to the draw, she pressed the button. The shock collar Derek had snapped around the gunman's neck sparked brilliantly, with its charge set to 10. Still, the effect was more dramatic than anyone had anticipated. Rather than merely incapacitating their target, the electric shock ignited his drenched form—along with the entire pond—as if the microbes unleashed their trapped energy in one fell swoop.

The man screamed, writhing, his back arching.

As his body finally slumped into the pond, electricity still danced over the surface, Derek backed away warily. "Um, Jane, I think you can stop pressing the button."

"Oh, right." She let her hand drop and stepped toward him.

He retreated, knowing full well what soaked his clothes. "No . . ."

She ignored him and hugged him anyway. "It's too late. We're in this together."

He stood with his arms wide, fearful of returning her hug—then realized she was right and folded her up against him, knowing this was worth dying for.

Not that I want that to happen, especially not now.

11:24 P.M.

As Jane held tight to Derek, a volley of blasts rose from the canyon, drawing all their attention. They stared silently, as a belligerent complaint rose from the elephants.

What is going on?

Derek got them moving out of the grotto. "We can't stay here."

Jane recognized he was right. With all the pyrotechnics, not to mention the screaming, their hiding place was compromised.

As they cleared the pond, Derek guided them along the wall, sticking to the deeper shadows of the canopy far above. The rest of the canyon was dark, but the moon and stars were bright enough to reveal a strange sight.

A large clutch of elephants—maybe twenty—stirred out there, milling, but generally heading toward the walled-off opening to the fissure.

Jane squinted. "What are they—?"

Then suddenly another volley of shotgun blasts rang out. Brilliant blue scintillations of piezoelectric crystals burst like fireworks with each concussion. Kowalski was firing, but not at the enemy. He stood behind the herd, blasting at the rear ends of the largest beasts, driving them ahead of him. He accompanied this with loud curses that would normally have made Jane blush, but instead she was impressed by the sheer range and imagination.

Jane remembered his last words to them.

I have a plan.

Finally, it came to fruition. The herd moved faster across the canyon floor, trying to escape their tormentor, confused by the bright lights, the stinging swats on their backside. Their bumping bodies amplified the perplexity—until a tipping point was reached. Legs churned, the trumpeting grew louder, and in a moment, it became a stampede.

And the target was clear.

Gunfire flashed from both the top and bottom of the ramp, revealing the presence of two combatants. A grenade exploded, casting up a geyser of dirt. Luckily the aim was poor as the enemy manning the ramparts panicked at the wall of tusks, stamping feet, and bellowing trunks heading straight at them.

The man at the bottom swung around and sprinted up the ramp, but the sandy surface betrayed him. He went down and vanished under the herd as it surged up and over the wall. A moment later, a muffled cry rose on the far side, the scream echoing out into the canyon as the second gunman was trampled in the narrow chute.

The last of the stampede crested the ramp and fled down the fissure, likely seeking the refuge of flooded forest.

Fresh gunfire drew all their faces to the opposite side of the canyon.

Clearly the battle was not yet over.

11:32 P.M.

I'm not falling for that.

Gray kept hidden in his burrow of branches and bones. His assailant reached around again and fired blindly into the graveyard. Rounds chattered toward one of the glowing helmets, pelting into the crush of bones. The hunter was trying to goad Gray into responding, to reveal his location.

The strategy behind this was likely born from the sounds of battle reaching the two of them: screams, gunfire, shotgun blasts, all amid cries and bellows from the canyon's elephants.

Gray sensed the brooding presence of the old matriarch at the back of the small canyon. She haunted the copse of tall plum trees back there. Guilt ate at him, knowing the carnage his arrival had wrought to the peaceful, shy creatures who had opened their home to them.

And look how we repaid their generosity.

As if sensing the subject of his concern, the gunman shoved low and blasted toward the trees. A sharp, pained bleat rose from back there.

You bastard . . .

Gray shifted to see if she was okay.

As he did so, a branch fell from atop his pile and rattled down the mound's side.

Gray did not wait and burst out of his burrow, knowing the keen hunter would act on that movement and noise. He flung himself to the side and rolled away. A grenade struck the gravesite and exploded, casting broken bones and flaming tinder high into the air. The concussive force threw him farther, showering him with debris, peppering his skin with slivered shards.

He kept his arms long, extended in front of him, still gripping his SIG Sauer with both hands. He fired back at the shadow, earning a sharp curse from his opponent as he ducked back into cover.

Gray stayed flat on his belly, his aim fixed, but he was exposed, stretched across the white crystalline bed. If he tried to run, even move, the crunch would give him away. The impasse felt like it lasted minutes but was only seconds.

The hunter finally strafed blindly at his location, likely hoping for a lucky hit.

And he came close, as a bullet seared past Gray's ear.

Gray fired back at the exposed weapon, but he had no better success.

I won't last another round.

Behind Gray, a heavy shift and sigh was accompanied by gravelly footfalls. Branches cracked. He risked a glance to see the matriarch pushing through the copse. Blood stained her white skin, flowing down the side of her chest. Her near-blind eyes stared toward him, looking mournful but determined. She came forward, shifting in front of him, dropping to her knees, then chest.

A trunk curled back to him, huffing at his cheek. She leaned her own cheek down to stare back at him. Soft nostrils touched him.

Gray understood.

She's trying to shield me, even as she's dying.

Gray heard a brush of boot. He stood up, accepting this gift from the great beast. He aimed over her back as the hunter showed himself, plainly aggravated by the intrusion. Gray fired first, driving the man back a step, but no blood was shed.

Still, that wasn't Gray's intention.

Just focus on me.

The hunter obliged, centering his grenade launcher.

Past the man's shoulders, a giant shadow pushed from the fissure. The bull elephant loomed, as silent as ever, always the guardian. With a slowness that seemed unreal, he pushed a tusk through the man's back, lifting him to his toes, then off his feet.

Blood poured, and his weapon dropped.

Finally, with a toss of his head, the broken body was flung back into the fissure, so the man's bones would never defile this sacred ground.

Gray sank to his knees, placing a palm on the dry cheek of the matriarch. "I'm so sorry."

Her trunk rose and rubbed his forearm, as if to acknowledge his grief—then circled his wrist and gently urged him up and away. The bull came forward to take his place, his tusk bloody, his eyes not as forgiving.

Gray accepted that judgment and headed away.

When he reached the exit, he glanced back. The bull had his head bowed, his trunk entwined with the dying matriarch's. Gray turned away, knowing he did not deserve to witness this.

He ran down the fissure, both relieved and ashamed.

But others needed him now.

11:39 P.M.

Seichan crouched forty yards from the end of the mile-long cleft through the cliffs. On the cautious trek here, she had heard echoes of the firefight behind her, rising from the distant canyon. She cast off her fears, knowing it did her no good. Instead, she placed her trust in Gray—even Kowalski—to survive and keep the others safe.

She had her own responsibility this night.

With the exit in sight, she remained in place. Her ears strained for any noises that didn't belong to the forest, her eyes sharp for any suspicious shifts of shadows.

While all seemed quiet and safe, she knew better.

You're out there.

Every nerve screamed this.

Seichan had two options from here, diverging paths defined by two words drilled into her by those who trained her in the Guild as an assassin.

Shadow or *fire.*

She could proceed by stealth, sticking to *shadows,* scaling the cliffs and dropping outside unseen. Or she could *fire* up her blood, spiking her adrenaline for a run and bursting free under a hail of gunfire.

Instead, she waited because there was a third path not taught by the rigid structure of the Guild. Something she learned from Gray, a mix of improvisation and intuition—though this night, perhaps Kowalski was her true mentor.

She heard them well before they arrived, a low thunder. She refused to move lest she alert the lurker in the woods of her plans. Once she felt the ground shake under her toes, she scaled the cliff.

A moment later, the first of a stampede of elephants rushed under her, near enough she could reach down and brush her fingertips along their rolling backs. She looked for her chance and found it in a large female. As the beast passed her position, she leaped out, grabbed its tail in both hands, and braced her boots on the back of her thick thighs.

Shocked at the sudden stowaway, the beast sped faster, trying to escape what clung to her. Seichan held tight, only needing to hitch this ride for a handful of seconds. Still, an elephant in back batted at this stranger in their midst, almost knocking Seichan off her perch. She ducked low and clung with all her strength, her boots bucking from her ride's hindquarters. The world blurred around her.

Then the cliff walls suddenly fell away.

Seichan waited until the herd burst into the apron of the forest, then leaped free, rolling across the leafy mulch. She immediately regained her feet and ran low to the side and ducked behind the bole of a towering tree.

She dropped to a knee and studied the booming, crashing passage of the herd as it spread out into the forest, so she could see if something would be flushed into the open.

Far to her right, a massive bull hip-checked into a pile of boulders.

As the rocks tumbled from the impact, something dark and low fled from behind that shelter.

There you are.

Still, Seichan noted the flash of dark metal as the figure ran.

Definitely armed.

I wouldn't expect any less.

She set off after her quarry.

With a change of plan from here.

Fire.

11:43 P.M.

Valya took a low, careening path through the forest.

Elephants crashed all around her, driving her farther away from the cliffs. Water soon splashed under her boots, first in puddles, then in a wide lake that stretched endlessly before her. Finally, the dark bulks of the rampaging beasts spread out, their panic seeming to dissipate.

Still, she didn't stop—needing time to regroup.

She checked her weapon. The night sight had snapped off but the gun was otherwise serviceable. Regrettably she had not had time to grab the controller to her Raven.

Before the chaos, with her trap set, she had noted movement deep in the fissure, a flicker of body heat picked up by the UAV's sensors.

Definitely a person, but identification had been impossible.

Still, from the furtive actions, Valya knew who glowed on her small screen.

Valya waited for Seichan to make her decision.

Shadow or fire.

Then from down the tunnel, seen via the optics of the Raven, a surging river of body heat flowed through the narrow fissure, sweeping the tiny glow away. As she tried to fathom what she was seeing, she reacted too slowly. The elephants burst out, stampeding straight for her. She had barely gotten away in time.

But what had become of Seichan?

Had she been trampled?

Valya knew the answer.

No.

The bullet that splintered into the trunk near her head confirmed this.

Valya ducked and rolled, putting the trunk between her and her adversary. She fired back along the trajectory of the attack, but she surmised the woman was already moving.

Valya began to do the same.

She turned and ran low, weaving a path into the denser thicket of forest. From the sound of the one shot, Seichan came with a pistol. Valya hefted her submachine gun, feeling the additional forty-round extended magazine still tucked in her belt.

In this game of *fire,* she intended to win.

She just needed cover.

And reached it.

She dove into the thicket, where she had plenty of thick trunks to pick from, allowing her to shift from position to position unseen. She hunkered down, fully out of sight.

A pistol blasted, and she felt a punch to her shoulder, spinning her around.

She closed her mind against the pain and sidled to a new position, deeper into the thicket.

Another shot.

And her ear became fire.

She spun in a panicked circle.

How?

Then she heard a low whining drone and realized she'd been playing the wrong game. This wasn't *fire*. It was *shadow*—stealth and trickery. Seichan must have searched where she had hidden, found the UAV control, and commandeered it.

A voice called out to her. "Only seemed fair I got my turn to play with the toys."

Valya cursed.

Then *shadow* it is—and *fire*.

She pulled out her radio, reached the pilot. "Fire both Hellfire missiles. Target both canyons. Now."

11:48 P.M.

Hellfire....

Seichan knew the pale woman had wanted her to hear that radio call.

But was it true about the missiles?

She remembered back in the Sudan, when she didn't know if they were being tracked, that the best course was to assume they were.

This was no different.

"Hunt me or help your friends," the woman called out, taunting.

Seichan ignored her, having already made her decision. She turned and sprinted for the cliffs, knowing she had to do everything she could to help the others.

She cast one silent promise to the pale woman.

We'll meet again.

11:50 P.M.

"Go, go, go!" Gray hollered, doing his best to empty the canyon, moving everyone over the wall and into the shelter of the dark fissure.

Seichan had radioed two minutes ago, panicked and breathless.

"Get out of there now!"

The call had come as he regrouped with the others in the main canyon. With helmet lamps blazing, everyone now worked to get the remaining herd moving in the same direction. Seichan sought to help by sending a drone she had commandeered over the valley, both to confirm the threat and to hassle the bigger bird with her smaller one.

Seichan radioed again, her voice in his ear. *"Cessna closing on your position. Hellfires are hot."*

"You gotta buy us more time," he urged.

"Working on that."

Kowalski fired his shotgun into the air to urge the last few stragglers in the right direction. "Move your wrinkly asses!"

Noah took a gentler approach with a pair of elderly elephants, touching and encouraging them to follow, leaving Roho to do his best imitation of a sheepdog.

Ahead, Derek and Jane manned the wall, waving fronds, compelling the herd over the ramp.

Luckily the earlier stampede had already cleared a number of head, but there remained one stubborn holdout.

Gray stared across the dark canyon. The shadowy figure of the large bull stood vigil by the back wall, having appeared from the crack ten minutes ago, indicating the great matriarch had passed. A handful of the adults still in the canyon had wandered over, entwining trunks, sharing their grief.

The bull now refused to budge.

Jane suddenly called from the rampart, pointing, "A calf! Over in the grass!"

They all turned, but from their low vantage, they couldn't spot the youngster.

Kowalski headed over, running hard. "Where?" he hollered back.

Jane yelled directions, guiding him.

Then Seichan was in his ear again, her voice rife with panic. "Gray! Drone's damaged. Cessna's almost on top of you."

Gray looked up, hearing a faint rumble of an engine.

Not good.

He cupped a hand around his mouth. "Kowalski, get back here!" He waved to everyone else. "Over the wall. Get as far back as you can!"

"I see the tyke!" Kowalski ran faster.

He ducked into the grass, vanishing for a breath, then hauled back up, carrying the baby elephant in his arms. It had to weigh two hundred pounds. He ran with it in his arms. The baby wailed plaintively.

He'll never make it.

Confirmation appeared in the sky, sweeping past the stars. A small plane banked on a wing, preparing for a bombing run over the canyons.

Then came the sound of thunder.

From the back of the canyon, the bull came charging forward—whether stirred by the calf's trumpet of fear or out of some altruistic recognition that Kowalski was struggling. The bull reached the big man, plucked the child from his arms, and continued toward the wall.

Unburdened, Kowalski put his head down and ran.

Past him, the Cessna dropped over the smaller canyon. Fire shot from under one wing. The missile screamed, then a deafening blast shook the ground. Flame and smoke shot up, spiraling for a breath, before collapsing into a dark pall.

The bull reached the ramp and charged over the ancient dike.

Kowalski followed, and Gray ran with him. They cleared the wall as the world exploded again behind them. The concussive force channeled up the chute and sent both men flying and rolling across the ground, nearly under the bull's trampling legs.

Once they came to a stop, Kowalski stayed on his back. "Remind me to listen to you next time."

Gray stood up with a groan. The others joined them, and together the group hobbled back over to the wall and climbed to its top.

Off to the left, a loud, splintering crash sounded, coming from the jungle on top of the canyon wall on that side. A moment later, an oily black cloud of smoke rose against the stars.

Seichan whispered in his ear. "Gray?"

"I'm fine."

"Good. Just wanted to let you know I got the drone working again."

He stared toward the column of smoke, knowing it must be the Cessna, brought down by Seichan. "Better late than never, I suppose."

Jane and Derek joined him, both looking forlornly across the ruins of the valley. The back half was rubble and smoke. As they watched, more of the canyon wall to the right collapsed, further burying the former grotto.

"It's all gone," Jane said. "Now we'll never find the cure."

"It doesn't matter," Gray murmured.

Derek gave him a hard look. "It bloody well matters to me. I took a header into that pond."

"I just meant that the cure was never here . . . at least not for us."

Neither of them looked any happier with this news.

Gray sought to reassure them. "I know where the cure is."

"What?" Jane gasped. "Where?"

Gray turned and headed away. "Right back where we started."

28

Two weeks later, Gray stood at the window overlooking a small surgical suite at the Francis Crick Institute, outside London. He stared down at the draped figure on the table of the sealed room.

We all owe you a great debt.

Finally cleared medically after a battery of testing, Gray was scheduled to return to the States tomorrow. And while Seichan and Kowalski also passed their tests and would be on the same flight, neither of them had any interest in joining him here. As Kowalski had said, *I've had my fill of mummies.*

Gray smiled, doubting the man realized how apt his words were in regards to this situation. He pictured the macabre dead faces found inscribed inside the stone stomach of the buried goddess.

That had been one of the more obvious clues. He even remembered thinking at the time: *Everything here is a lesson.*

And it had been, but not the only one on this journey.

He pictured the old matriarch taking Jane by the hand and sharing her knowledge, teaching her like a child. There truly was no cure to be found in those canyons.

Only another lesson to be learned.

What Jane had been shown—what they'd all been taught—was a *recipe* for making the cure, not the cure itself.

The door opened behind him, and two familiar faces who were fighting the pandemic came to join him, to honor the man while they had this last moment.

Monk smiled and gave him a bear hug, while Dr. Ileara Kano simply shook his hand.

Monk looked into the next room, his face lined by exhaustion. "Seems we've come full circle, you and I. From one mummy to another."

That was certainly true.

In another wing of this very same medical complex, Professor Mc-Cabe's mummified body had been destroyed in an arson attack. Gray remembered standing on the street outside, learning for the first time about this strange microbial disease.

Full circle indeed.

Only it wasn't Professor McCabe on the table this time.

Ileara gazed sadly at the figure draped out there. "His work is done," she said. "He's scheduled to be reinterred at Westminster Abbey tomorrow morning."

Monk attempted a British accent—and failed. "Dr. Livingstone, I presume."

Gray cocked an eyebrow. "*Exhume,* you mean."

"Good one." He jabbed his elbow into Gray. "I'm going to use that at the next meeting."

"Feel free."

Shortly after Gray's team had arrived from Rwanda, David Livingstone's body had been disinterred from his crypt at Westminster Abbey, where he had lain undisturbed for more than a century. The poor man's remains had had so many tissue samples collected that Gray was surprised there was still anything left under the drape.

Still, all that was truly important was hidden in his skull.

The cure.

Monk frowned at the mystery before him. "I've heard it in bits and pieces," he said, "but never the whole story."

Knowing his friend wanted him to fill in those blanks, Gray turned to him. "Where do you want me to start?"

"How about with Moses."

Gray smiled and sighed. "If you really want to understand, we may have to start even earlier. Back to when a thirsty group of elephants discovered a challenging water source, one toxic to most life."

He remembered Noah's admiration for the great beasts. "Being such profound problem solvers, they learned a method to drink it safely. *How* this accommodation came about we may never know, but I suspect it had something to do with the respect they had for their ancestor's bones."

Ileara nodded. "Nature is full of examples of these odd biological relationships. Sometimes we never know how they truly formed and lump the explanation into the category: *Life finds a way.*"

Gray rubbed his chin. "Regardless, the elephants eventually *found* a method. They learned to store their remains under piles of branches from the Mobola plum tree, in order for the bark's tannins to effect a chemical transformation in the dead body, turning what was toxic to curative."

"We've confirmed this in the lab," Ileara added. "After someone dies, the microbe goes into a dormant stage, as it's no longer being fed electricity from a living brain. It is only *then* that the microbe becomes sensitive to the bark's tannin. A chemical in the tannin basically turns off a handful of genes, making the microbe nontoxic, but better yet, if this nontoxic microbe runs into its toxic cousin in living tissue, it neutralizes it there, too."

"The cure," Gray said.

Monk scratched his head. "So the recipe for making the cure is to let an infected body mummify under the effects of that bark's tannin, then wait a year or two and harvest the transformed good version."

Gray pictured the mother elephant cracking the skull of the tannin-soaked remains of an ancestor and showing her child how to chew it, to extract the curative version of the microbe.

"But this method is species specific," Gray stressed. "It's why the elephant bones are useless to *us* as a cure. We have to do it to ourselves. Elephant bones for elephant bones."

Monk grimaced. "And human for human."

"And skulls work best," Ileara added. "As that's where you'll find most of the microbes. Of course, now with modern methods we can simply culture the cure, but back then that was the only way of getting it done."

Gray knew the labs at Francis Crick had been doing just that, using samples of the curative microbe found in Livingstone's skull.

"So when do we get to Moses?" Monk asked.

Gray checked his watch, happy to skip ahead. "The plagues. Yes. That part of the story starts when a spectacularly wet season—possibly due to atmospheric changes from a volcanic eruption—flooded the elephant's source and spread the organism up the Nile Valley, triggering the chain reaction of biblical plagues. After that, a group of Egyptian explorers went looking for the source and discovered the elephants. Shocked that the beasts could safely drink the water, they studied their behavior and learned how to make the cure."

Gray recalled Noah's story of the Kenyan tribesmen who had learned from elephants how to induce labor by chewing on leaves. He gave a small shake of his head at both man's ingenuity and nature's resilience.

Life finds a way.

He continued, sensing the press of time. "The explorers returned north with this cure, where this knowledge was preserved by a sect that worshipped a feminine version of Tutu, the god of sleep and dreams."

"Why feminine?" Monk asked.

"I think because the original explorer who discovered the cure was possibly a woman, maybe a Hebrew scholar who came with a lion. At least that's who I think led the Egyptian explorers, from the way the old matriarch reacted to Jane and Roho. Or it could be a female goddess because this microbe causes genetic damage to *male* offspring of those afflicted." Gray shrugged. "Either way, I'm guessing they picked a god of *dreams* because of the strange hallucinations this microbe triggers in the brain."

Gray decided to skip over his theories about how this microbe might be able to record strong memories and repeat them. Instead, he continued with its historical trail.

"During a tumultuous time of war in Egypt around 1300 BC, over a century after the plagues, the sect feared this knowledge could be lost, so they built the tomb to their goddess to serve two purposes. They first carved lessons into the tomb to record the recipe, then left a sample of it, a mummified and preserved body holding the cure."

"Where it was buried for millennia," Monk said.

"But nothing stays buried forever, and no secret is perfectly kept. Some locals knew about the tomb—possibly the descendants of the original Nubian servants who helped the sect, passing their secret from generation to generation. Until eventually a British explorer came through looking for the source of the Nile, a man whom the natives came to revere."

Gray stared over at the draped body, knowing how much good David Livingstone had done during his time in Africa, both helping tribes and fighting the slave trade across the continent.

"To honor him, they revealed all of this to Livingstone, even gifting him with artifacts. Afterward, perhaps wanting to preserve this knowledge himself, yet keep it secret, he locked the mystery away in coded messages to his friend Stanley. And upon his death—either with his consent or as part of a tribal ritual—his body was transformed into the same vessel as the enthroned woman. When his body arrived in London, it was found to be mummified, wrapped in a coffin made of Mobola plum."

Ileara gave a sad shake of her head. "Then late in the nineteenth century, somebody had to go and *open* one of Livingstone's artifacts, unleashing the plague into the British Museum."

Gray checked his watch again.

I'm late.

He faced Monk. "That's right, but Painter and Kat know more about that part of the story than I do, involving Tesla, Twain, and Stanley. So you might want to ask your wife about those details. Or Painter. I heard he's out of quarantine." He rubbed his hands. "I have to get going. I have a lunch date with a certain woman who gets very impatient if I'm not punctual. And I'd hate to tell her *you* were the cause."

Monk lifted his hands. "Hey, go, I don't want to get on Seichan's bad side."

Gray headed away, content to have acknowledged the great explorer and happy to leave him to his well-deserved rest. He wound his way through the sprawling medical complex, bustling with the ongoing battle against the plague, and out to the sunshine of a bright new morning.

He hailed a taxi and gave the driver the directions Seichan had left him. She had been very mysterious about this lunch, which, considering the woman, was a tad worrisome.

When the cab pulled up to the curb, there was a large crowd queued up outside. He climbed out, shading his eyes. Where was—

A hand grabbed his elbow, fingers digging deep. "You're late."

"Monk can be a bit gabby."

Seichan drew him through the crowd and around the corner. He gaped at what loomed ahead. It was the London Eye, a giant Ferris wheel towering over the Thames, each car a large clear spherical compartment able to hold a couple dozen riders.

She dragged him to the front of the line. "Do you know how much it cost to hold this up? Why do you think I said *be on time*?"

"What're we—?"

"Shut up."

She dragged him up the ramp to a waiting car of the great wheel. Inside, a private table had been set up with fine linens and crystal stemware. On a neighboring serving cart, domed silver cloches hid culinary mysteries, while a bottle of champagne chilled in an ice bucket.

She pushed him inside and waved to the waiting operator.

Her face flushed, she turned to Gray. "You are a hard man to surprise."

He smiled. "A trait that's kept me alive."

As the car began to move, she stepped forward and slipped her arms around him. "Then I'll have to try harder tonight."

"I'm certainly up for the challenge."

"You'd better be."

She drew him to the table, where a small bench on one side faced the Thames. They settled together before considering the food. The car slowly arced up, offering an ever-widening view of the sprawling city of London.

"Why all this fuss? I'd be happy with a burger and a beer." He scooted her closer. "It's the company that matters."

"I thought we deserved this."

"Where did you get the idea to—?" He looked harder at her. "You stole this from when Derek and Jane rode that Ferris wheel in Khartoum."

She smiled. "You truly don't let anything get past you." She pulled *him* closer this time. "Who says those two should get all the fun?"

He sighed, realizing how few moments the two of them got like this. He suspected that might be part of the intent here, one not purposefully contrived by Seichan, but still there, hanging in the air between them like an unspoken question. Did they dare recognize the forces that kept them from more moments like this—and did they dare shed them?

With no answer, they both remained silent, having to find contentment in this moment.

Seichan stirred, turning slightly toward him. "I heard from Kat earlier. She thought I should know."

"What?"

Seichan gazed out over the river. "Yesterday, up in Canada, at the gravesite of Anton Mikhailov, somebody left a single white rose."

He knew her worry. After events in Africa, the pale assassin had vanished, escaping through the forest, a woman whose name they now knew.

Valya Mikhailov.

Gray touched Seichan's hand. "You can't know for sure it was—"

She turned her palm and wrapped her fingers around his. "The white rose had a single black petal."

11:38 A.M.

"You've got a couple of visitors," Kat said as she entered the room.

Painter sat up in his hospital bed.

Finally.

He had been cooped up in the infectious ward at Francis Crick for too long, undergoing treatment, testing, and observation. He was ready for any distraction.

Behind Kat, Safia ducked her head through the door. "Just coming to check on the patient." She stepped in, dragging a bouquet of balloons. "Thought you could use a little cheering up."

Painter groaned. "I think I've had enough of *balloons* for a while."

She smiled. "Then how about an old friend."

The door shifted wider, and a tall, broad-shouldered figure with shaggy blond hair and darkly tanned skin stepped into the room.

Painter smiled. "Omaha Dunn . . ."

The man grinned, his eyes crinkling. He pulled Safia to his hip as he entered with her. "I leave you with my wife, and you go about almost getting her killed . . . *again*."

Painter shrugged. "What can I say? Someone's got to put a little excitement in her life."

Safia shook her head with a sigh and crossed over to the gathering of cards and gifts, adding her balloons. The group spent the next several minutes filling in the blanks in one another's lives.

"So someone actually married you?" Omaha chuckled. "Where's the unlucky woman?"

Painter grimaced a little. "Lisa's holding down the fort back in D.C. She wasn't too pleased to hear I was joining everyone here at Francis Crick. At this point, the place has practically become Sigma U.K. But she understood. The center here is far ahead of the rest of the world in understanding this pathogen, and after what happened in the Arctic, we need all hands on deck."

Safia sat on the edge of his hospital bed. "So how are things up at Ellesmere and Aurora?"

"Still a mess. At this point there are more microbiologists and infectious disease experts on that island than polar bears. It'll be a while before we know the full environmental impact of the release of that microbe into the wild by Hartnell. But right now we're cautiously optimistic. As cold as the Arctic gets, that tropical microbe will not likely find a foothold outside of a warm host."

"Then let's hope the Arctic *stays* cold."

He nodded, reminded that Simon Hartnell's method for saving the planet might have been misguided, but the goal remained a noble one.

Omaha nudged Kat. "Now show him his real present."

Painter crinkled his brow. "What present?"

Kat smiled. "We were saving this until you were out of quarantine, so you could hold it in person." She crossed to her briefcase and snapped it open. She slipped out a clear sleeve protecting a yellowed sheet of paper with faint writing on it. "We found this inside David Livingstone's crypt, left by a gentleman who apparently was very good at keeping secrets, unlike a certain friend of his."

Painter took the fragile-looking letter, holding it gently, especially when he saw the signature at the bottom.

$$S.L.\ Clemens$$

$$Mark\ Twain$$

"This is from Mark Twain," he murmured.

Painter remembered the account found in Tesla's journal, describing events back in 1895, including Twain and Stanley's trip to the Sudan, following the clues left by Livingstone.

Curious at this last addition to that story, he read the letter, dated August 20, 1895.

> To the gentlemen and most gentle ladies who read this,
> First of all, shame on you for trespassing upon David Living-
> stone's grave and into those sandy tombs where you did not belong,
> but likewise my heartiest congratulations for your good fortune or
> good judgment (or both!) that led you to disturb poor Livingstone's
> sleep. How fitting that the good doctor is once again available to cure
> the ills of those who come knocking upon his gravestone here in the

abbey. I assure you we've left you ample remedy of his most gruesome tincture.

Be forewarned, however, the treatment comes with some rather enlightening and alarming effects. I myself as a precaution partook of said treatment and during the feverish recuperation of it found myself dreaming sights and sounds that were not my own, but memories of another, the very man whose bones lie before you. I saw blue lakes that my own eyes never set upon, dark jungles my feet never traipsed, and other views both gentle and horrific, including the cruelty of man upon those of darker skin in even darker Africa. Likewise, I felt the passion, as if it were my own, of the same bearer of these memories, his deep devotion to those less fortunate, his pious belief in a God that could love all, his boundless curiosity for what lies beyond the next horizon.

Now I am certainly a man of words more than a man of science, so do not purport to know more than your average street sweeper when it comes to how the world works. Still, I wish all of mankind could walk in another's shoes like I did, to truly know another's soul—if only in a fever dream—what a kinder world it would be.

So drink deep of the draught before you and appreciate the days that await you, because one day we will all end up here. While there is no escaping death, may we all have done as much with our days as our good Dr. Livingstone.

Painter smiled at the last sentiment.

How true.

From this note, it was clear Twain and Stanley had learned that Livingstone's mummified body held the cure. He remembered reading of Twain's account of his time in the Sudan, how he and Stanley had discovered the *means* if not the actual *medicinal tincture* inside the tomb. The pair had likely never understood the pathogenesis of this disease or its treatment—any more than the Egyptians or elephants had—but they had learned that the process of mummification was the *means* and that Livingstone's body was the actual *tincture*.

Painter also suspected the pair must have been aided in this realization by additional clues or knowledge given to Stanley by Livingstone, information that had either been lost or never written down, making later efforts all the more difficult.

Still, Painter was drawn by one other intriguing part of Twain's note.

"Did you notice how he references what he calls *fever dreams,* hallucinations that he seems convinced were David Livingstone's memories? Gray and I discussed the possibility of that microbe actually recording details from a person's life and passing them on." He turned to Safia. "It sounded like you might have had a similar experience, but unlike Twain—who was dosed with Livingstone's microbes—you were exposed to the desert mummy's."

Safia shook her head, plainly uncomfortable with this line of inquiry. "I can barely remember now. It's like trying to remember a dream."

Painter nodded. "And I didn't experience anything of the sort from my treatment."

Kat offered an explanation. "It may be because you were dosed with the lab-grown cure, not a natural elixir."

"Lab-grown?" Omaha grinned. "In that case, Painter, I'm surprised you didn't dream of cheese and a spinning wheel in a rat's cage."

Painter ignored him and stared down at the letter in his hand. "Still, it makes you wonder if there's not more . . ."

"More what?" Kat asked.

He shook his head. "Certain details still don't make sense."

Kat frowned. "Like what?"

"Like why did Professor McCabe circle the seventh plague in his journal?" Painter looked out his window toward the north. "I mean, look what happened up in the Arctic. It was like something right out of the Bible."

"I think you're still feverish," Kat said. "We know from further interviews with Rory that his father circled it after translating hieroglyphics from an Egyptian stela found near the Sudan dam project, one that described the seventh plague. It was early during his investigation, before the professor vanished into the desert."

"Still, what if it was a prophecy of what we experienced in the Arctic?"

"More likely it was simply an account of a bad storm by an ancient Egyptian meteorologist." Kat pointed at his chest. "I'm having a doctor recheck your vitals."

He scowled at her. "I was just wondering, that's all."

Omaha clapped his palms atop his thighs and stood up. "Life is indeed a wonder, but we should get going."

"He's right." Safia scooted over, gave Painter a hug, and whispered in his ear. "Thank you."

Omaha was having none of it. "Painter, if you all start kissing, I'm calling your wife."

Safia smiled and held Painter's cheeks between her palms so he could see the sincerity shining in her eyes. "Thank you."

"Anytime, Safia, anytime."

1:07 P.M.

As the taxicab crept its way through the congestion of a midday London traffic jam, Safia stared out the window. Omaha sat next to her, holding her hand. She squeezed his fingers, needing his physicality as an anchor.

Out the window, she watched the bustle of a city she loved—from the local pubs crowded with patrons laughing and finishing their lunches to a lumbering red double-decker bus that grumbled at the traffic ruining its schedule.

Yet, over it all, another image shimmered.

Rolling sands burning under a desert sun . . . the golden points of pyramids reflecting those rays into a blinding dazzle . . . the slow line of camels moving along the edge of a dune in a dark silhouette against that blaze . . .

She gripped Omaha's hand more tightly. These flashes were growing less and less frequent, so she refrained from talking about them. Still, she knew that wasn't the only reason for her reticence. Back when the skies had been burning with fire up in the Arctic, she had experienced so much more than she had shared with Kat. She had felt the hundreds of women who had led to that moment, a solemn chain of life, one linking to the next. She experienced, as if it were her own, snatches of their lives, mostly the harsher elements as if that's what the microbe captured best.

It grew to be a force, like a wind at her back—pushing her *forward*.

Though not as clear as the past, other images had begun to shimmer, glimpses of what might come. She had witnessed the fiery storm above the ice, well before it broke, knew it was coming. And even more dangers lay beyond that one, stacking one upon the other into the future. They were vague, just shadows, storm clouds beyond the horizon. If she had known more, she would have shared them, but she had no details, only fears.

Knowing what was to come, she was glad there were men like Painter—and all those he led in Sigma—who were willing to face those storm clouds. It was what she had tried to convey to the man back at the hospital.

Thank you.

Omaha must have sensed something and drew her closer. "Saf, what's wrong?"

She nestled against his warm side. Slowly the shimmering image of burning sands faded, replaced with life's usual commotion and flurry.

"Nothing," she murmured. "Nothing you need worry about."

4:24 P.M.

There's nothing left.

Back in Ashwell for the day, Jane stood before the ruins of her family home. The fires had consumed all, leaving nothing but a few charred beams.

"You can always rebuild," Derek offered.

She considered it, but the memories would be too painful. It was time to move on. Her fingers reached back and found Derek's. After being under quarantine at Francis Crick for the past two weeks, it was good to be out, back in fresh air. Though she truly did not expect to find anything here, she needed to take this pilgrimage, to truly say good-bye to her father.

"He thought he was bringing out the cure," Derek reminded her, as if reading her thoughts.

"But he brought us the plague."

Over the past many days, with time on their hands, they had been putting together pieces of her father's past. What had stung her the most—and still did—was learning of Rory's part in all this. She still could not bring herself to make contact with her brother, who was incarcerated at a Canadian military prison, pending the fallout from his involvement in events above the Arctic Circle.

She had also learned of Simon Hartnell, of his manipulation and imprisonment of her father, of his obsession and discovery of a lost Nikola Tesla text that had started this whole chain of events. Her father eventually found the organism described in Tesla's text and searched for the cure, but it was a herculean task considering the strange recipe.

She pictured the little elephant pots, which they now knew were sculpted of wood and bark from Mobola plum trees, whose tannins were part of the mummification process in the production of the cure.

But how could my father have known that?

The tannins worked only on dormant microbes found in dead bodies; they were not curative on their own, so the bark pots were ignored as useless decoration.

Likewise, she knew from Rory's accounting of events that her father had tested the mummy on the throne—the actual cure—but only found microbes that looked identical to the pathogenic variety, as it would have taken a molecular assay to differentiate the two.

Still, after nearly two years, he had his breakthrough, realizing that the tattoos on the enthroned mummy were ancient Hebrew written with Egyptian glyphs. The story found on her body had offered enough clues for her father to connect mummification to the cure. Not wanting Hartnell to learn the truth, he had left clues for Jane to follow and begun the self-mummification process himself, consuming the bark and following the ritual written on the tattooed woman. He did this for two or three months, prepping his body, then dosed himself with the active microbe stored in the goddess's stone skull, hoping the bark's tannin would turn what was toxic into a cure.

"You came so close," Jane whispered to the blackened ruins.

"Still, his failure was as much *ours*," Derek said. "He was bringing us the cure. He knew the disease had to kill him in order for the microbes to go dormant and become susceptible to the tannin. Only we opened his skull prematurely, before the transformation was complete, releasing the plague instead of the cure." He drew her closer. "But he also reached out to *you*. Near the end, I think he must have realized that Hartnell had co-opted Rory, that your brother was complicit in—"

"Rory *betrayed* us all," she said bitterly. "He stole my father from me, left me thinking they were both dead all this time."

"I know." He turned her to face him. "But Jane, your father knew you'd be able to follow those clues. It was his fallback plan. And he was right. You figured it out."

"*We* did."

He lifted a brow. "An archaeologist willing to share credit. Are you sure you're Harold's daughter?"

She smacked him in the shoulder and tugged him down the road. "Let's get a pint."

They headed toward the Bushel and Strike.

He took her hand. "And, Jane, in the end, your father achieved what he set out to do from the very beginning. He found proof that the Biblical plagues did occur, that the events chronicled in the Book of Exodus were *historical*, not mere legend or story. His discovery has turned archaeology on its ear."

She nodded, taking a small amount of comfort in this fact. She squeezed Derek's hand in thanks, and they continued in silence for a couple of minutes.

"Oh, I heard from Noah earlier today," Derek finally said.

She glanced to him. "Did he ever find the elephants?"

"He *says* no, but I'm not sure I believe him. And he's certainly not talking about them to anyone."

"Good." She pulled closer to Derek. "They're better off—"

A pealing of bells interrupted her, drawing her attention past the pub to the old stone church. Apparently they'd repaired the bell tower, which made her happy. It was a small sign of resilience in the face of all the horrors.

Faintly she also heard a chorus of voices echoing out the church's open door.

She drew Derek across the street, drawn by the music, a haunting hymn full of sorrow and grace. Once they were through the doors, the smell of incense warmed through her. To her right, the choir practiced in the nave. She took Derek in that direction but drew him into a little chapel opposite the century-old pipe organ.

"What're we—?"

"Hush."

She stopped at a pillar. She ran her fingers along an inscription scrawled across the stone. She remembered coming here as a child with her father, using charcoal and paper to rub a copy of this bit of ancient graffiti. It was in Latin, written when the plague struck this village, another reminder of its resilience.

Praetereo fini tempori in cello pace.

She whispered the translation to herself, "I pass at death into the peace of Heaven . . ."

She let her palm rest there, feeling so close to her father at this moment, reminded that not all memories here were bad. A tear rolled down her cheek.

"Jane?"

She looked up at Derek, his eyes shining with concern. She pulled him close and kissed him deeply as the chorus sang, as it had for ages.

But noting the young lovers, the choir stopped and started clapping.

Blushing and smiling, she pulled back and stared around a church that had stood for centuries, resolute and steadfast against every storm—then finally back to Derek.

"I want to rebuild my home."

EPILOGUE

Promise me.

Gray sat at his father's bedside in the nursing home. Those words had haunted him for weeks after his father first uttered them in this room, but now he understood. He studied his father's face, noting the broken blood vessels on his nose, remembering the drunken rages he could get into, especially after he lost his leg.

He was a proud man, brought low by disability and a disability check. Gray's mother had to continue to work, while his father languished looking after two belligerent sons, who grew only more so with age. *It's your Welsh blood,* her mother would excoriate the men in her house after some fight.

She was wrong about the *Welsh* part but right about the *blood.*

Gray had come to recognize the true source of the friction between father and son. They were too alike, too much of the same blood.

He continued to study that lined face, the sunken eyes, trying to find that fire. He wished the man would rail again—against him, against the disease that had stripped his mind, against chance, which had taken his leg.

Promise me.

Now his father fussed with the edges of his blanket as if trying to find meaning. He barely spoke any longer. He battled demons when he slept, pawing at the air, kicking feebly with his one leg, enough to get a bedsore on his heel.

Gray had spoken to the nurse practitioner yesterday. While Gray had been away, his father had a small stroke, and according to her, he was stable, on blood thinners, but he might never improve from his current baselines. The prognosis was that he could stay this way for months, if not years.

As Gray sat now, he held his father's hand, feeling the bones. He rubbed a thumb over the thin skin, trying to remember the last time he had held his father's hand, or really even touched him. So he took advantage of that now.

His father mumbled in his sleep, but when Gray shifted his gaze from those frail fingers to his father's face, his eyes were open, staring back at him.

"Hey, Dad, didn't mean to wake you."

Lips moved, cracked and dry. He swallowed, then tried again.

"Gray . . ."

It had been ten days since his father had recognized him.

"Gray, your mother . . . your mother's coming."

He patted his father's hand, long past trying to find significance in the needle-skips of the man's memory. Better to just go along. "Is she? When's she coming?"

His brow knit, as if posed a challenging question. "Huh?"

"When's Mom coming?"

"Harriet?"

"That's right."

His father searched, even lifting his head from the pillow. He stared toward an empty chair in the corner. "What're you talking about? She's right there."

Gray stared at the empty chair, then back to his father. His head had settled back to the pillow, but his gaze remained on the chair, his lips moving as if speaking to the apparition sitting there.

Then his eyes closed, and he was gone again, fingers twitching at the edge of his blanket.

Promise me . . .

He now knew what his father had been asking him, and filled in the words that disease had silenced.

. . . when the time is right . . .

Gray kept holding his father's hand, but with his other, he pushed the plunger on the morphine syringe stabbed into the IV line.

Now's the time, Pop.

He leaned over and kissed his forehead.

Fingers squeezed his, then relaxed.

He moved his lips to his father's ear. "Go see Mom."

Gray clutched that hand one last time, stood up, and left.

He strode through the nursing home, out the front door, and to the woman waiting in the bright morning sunlight. He took her hand, never breaking stride, and together they headed away.

"Are you ready to find that fire escape?" he asked.

She smiled and gripped his hand so very tight. "I thought you'd never ask."

ETERNAL AND UNKNOWABLE

The large bull leads the others up the narrow canyon. His shoulders brush the vines and leaves to either side. His chest rumbles his solemnity as he leads the herd.

Behind him lies their new home, a deep bowl warmed by steaming vents. There, the forest grows far taller, its canopy more sheltered than their old home. Water flows from its high edges, splashes into many pools.

It is a good place.

The man who brought them here follows now. The bull allows it. He senses no threat from the man, only wellness and concern. So for now, the man is herd, too. He must come.

The bull follows the cleft to a grotto at its end. Small, flat stones cover the ground, shaded in half by an overhanging shelf of rock. A small pool shines to one side. When they first came here, the bull carried old water in his trunk and blew it deep into the pool. The surface is already starting to blush with promise.

But that is not why the herd is here.

He takes them to the other side.

Upon the smooth stones rests a broken body. It is not whole, but it is enough. The man has brought these pieces, too, dug from their old home and brought here.

The bull comes first. He smells the burns upon the flesh, but he brings his trunk to the curve of her head, lets his nostrils brush her white skin.

He then gently places the branch he carries over her and backs away.

He stands beside her as the others come, each placing another bough. One by one, stick by stick, she is covered. The man comes last and places his branch, then steps aside, revealing there still is one more.

It is he who will protect them.

The bull knows this because she had shown him, before she died.

The large white cat draws forward, splayed paws crunching the stone. He carries a long bough in his teeth and drops it on the pile. He nudges it with his flat nose to rest it better.

The cat shifts to the man, who pats him.

It is good. It is done.

She will be remembered.

The bull lifts his trunk high and trumpets to the skies, mournful yet hopeful, challenging yet respectful. The others follow, adding their lungs, their voices. Their song is eternal.

One other joins in.

The cat steps forward, stretching his neck high—and roars for the very first time.

AUTHOR'S NOTE TO READERS: TRUTH OR FICTION

I am a collector of bread crumbs, all those bits of science and history that I mash and knead together to build my stories. And now that the bread is baked and served, my goal here is to try to separate those slices of the story that are based on substantial fact from those that are pure fabrication.

So here we go.

Historical Characters

I thought I'd pair these guys up, as I found it fascinating that so many bigger-than-life historical figures not only knew each other, but were involved in each other's lives and pursuits. I knew I wanted to write a story sometime that highlighted such a coming together of giants. And, of course, for that to happen, it would require an adventure of biblical proportions.

Stanley and Livingstone

While doing research on these two characters, I was struck by how different the pair of them were. When taken at face value, the much-publicized and ballyhooed story of Henry Morton Stanley's rescue of Dr. David

Livingstone seems to cast Livingstone as an inept, bumbling adventurer who nearly got himself killed. But upon deeper reading, it's discovered that David Livingstone was the true hero of the story of Africa. He was a missionary and explorer who sought to better the lives of the tribes in Africa. Even after being rescued, near death, he stayed on the continent to continue his fight against the slave trade. Whereas the "heroic" Stanley, a notable racist, had to be pressured into going to Africa in the first place, and he treated his porters and any tribesmen he encountered with brutality and cruelty. To make matters worse, he was eventually employed by King Leopold II of Belgium to open the Congo, which involved forced labor and the slaughter of tribes, and ended with a large swath of the Congo privately owned by the Belgian king.

It is this difference in character and outcome that ended with Livingstone being interred in Westminster Abbey and Stanley being denied this honor. So for my story, I wanted to highlight Livingstone's life and death. And, yes, it is true that his body was indeed mummified by the natives and sent back to England in a cylinder of bark. But his heart remains in Africa, buried under a Mobola plum tree.

Stanley and Twain

Yes, Henry Morton Stanley and Samuel Clemens (aka Mark Twain) were indeed friends. To get a better flavor of their close and intimate relationship, I suggest you read the novelization of that friendship:

Twain and Stanley Enter Paradise, by Oscar Hijuelos

And, no, I don't think the pair had their own adventures in Egypt, but how much fun is it to think they did?

Twain and Tesla

I find this relationship the most delightful. Mark Twain and Nikola Tesla were great buddies. Twain even spent time in Tesla's lab, helping with experiments, and I'm sure being a general nuisance. The anecdote of Twain testing Tesla's "earthquake machine" to help with his constipation is true. Twain stepped on the inventor's large oscillating device and promptly excused himself to the restroom.

So again, I had to write a story where Twain and Tesla get into some Sigma-style adventure of their own. But let's talk more about Tesla.

Nikola Tesla truly was a visionary genius—if not the most business savvy or practical. I could spend pages writing about his life, his work, and his legacy. Luckily I don't have to, as there are multiple books that could expand on this for the intellectually curious. Here are two I found most enlightening while writing this book:

Nikola Tesla: Imagination and the Man That Invented the 20th Century, by Sean Patrick

Tesla: Inventor of the Electrical Age, by W. Bernard Carlson

But I do want to talk more about the specific aspects of his life and inventions that played a role in this novel. He truly believed in wireless energy, to the point that everything I talked about in regard to Wardenclyffe Tower is factual; so too were his later claims to have stumbled upon a new, never-before-seen energy source. His inventions and claims so worried the U.S. government that upon the man's death his rooms at the New Yorker were raided and most of his papers taken. It took years of pressure from Tesla's nephew before the government finally returned them, but not *all* of them. The one notebook that Tesla's nephew was specifically told by his uncle to secure upon his death remains missing. And, yes, the National Defense Research Committee, who were called in to review all of Tesla's papers after his death, was run at the time by John G. Trump, the uncle of a certain New York real estate magnate (or president of the United States, as I'm writing this before the election of 2016).

So let's continue with the historical aspects of the novel, but for that, we're going a little further back in time.

The Book of Exodus and the Biblical Plagues

This novel proposes an alternate historical timeline to the events in Exodus. For a more thorough exploration of this New Chronology, I recommend the following books both written by the same author.

Exodus: Myth or History, by David Rohl

The Lords of Avaris, by David Rohl

There have been numerous attempts to scientifically explain the ten plagues inflicted on the Egyptians by Moses, so I figured I'd add my voice to that chorus. Most of what is written here is, of course, conjecture and speculation, but it's based on real science. For example, the eruption of the Mediterranean volcano, Thera, some 3,500 years ago is believed to have been the strongest eruption ever witnessed by humans. The atmospheric and climatic changes associated with an ash plume of that magnitude would have been significant. Could it have created an equatorial aurora? The 2006 eruption of Augustine Volcano in Alaska was studied because of the dramatic lightning associated with its ash plume. It is said to have been so powerful that it even affected the aurora borealis.

So let's move on to some of the novel's science.

Electric Bacteria and the Archaea Domain

This novel features a rather nasty little microorganism, but most everything about it is actually real. Scientists have discovered a whole slew of these electron-eating bacteria by shocking mud and seeing what comes to feed. Various labs around the world are exploring practical applications for these newly revealed and strange microbes, from looking into growing living biocables that could transmit electricity to using them to power nanomachines capable of all sorts of industrial uses, including cleaning up the environment.

As to the strange Archaea microbes featured in this novel, those aspects of the story are all true. Archaea are distinctly different from bacteria and are indeed shapeshifters able to form long filaments (perfect for rewiring a brain). And this third branch of life did evolve alongside viruses, often incorporating their genetic material. So in this novel, I devised a very unique disease, using a pathogenic Archaea that is itself deadly, yet also holds a virus in its back pocket, similar to Zika, that could cause birth defects. And when I learned that many Archaea species turn waters red (from a lake in Iran to the salt lakes of Utah), I thought it was the perfect organism to trigger a biblical plague (maybe even ten of them).

One other part of the story that is true: The outer layers of the planet's atmosphere do indeed harbor bacterial colonies, who are up there feeding and multiplying all on their own.

Climate Change and the State of the Arctic

As Twain writes in the novel, I'm a man of words more than a man of science, so I'm not about to get on a soapbox and debate the merits of climate science or how man might play a role in it. But it's hard to deny that the Arctic is getting warmer, the ice caps are getting smaller, and it's opening up the entire north to exploration. Cruise ships are indeed plying the Northwest Passage, a trek once considered too hazardous to even contemplate and which led to the deaths of countless explorers, including the crews of the HMS *Erebus* and *Terror*.

By the way, if you want to get a flavor of that fateful journey, I highly recommend the novel by one of my favorite writers:

The Terror, by Dan Simmons

Most climate scientists believe we are near, at, or past the tipping point to do something about the imperiled state of the world. Some researchers are looking to geo-engineering as a possible solution. These are massive projects, such as enclosing the earth in a solar shield, or flooding Death Valley, or even wrapping Greenland in a blanket. The only problem— beyond the feasibility of funding or accomplishing them—is the danger of unintended consequences, disasters that no one could predict because the number of variables is so huge when talking about a globe-wide engineering project. So, of course, I wanted to explore what might happen.

This book also talks about the HAARP installation in Alaska, along with the rumors and conspiracy theories that surround it. Since the Aurora Station featured in this novel is basically a giant version of HAARP, I decided to make all those rumors true and set the sky on fire (which is indeed one of the charges claimed about HAARP).

Mummification and Tattooed Mummies

This book opens with a body from a person who underwent a ritual of self-mummification. As gruesome and painful as that may sound, it is real. *Sokushinbutsu*—or Buddhas in the flesh—are found in Japan, where the practitioners undergo great lengths to preserve their tissues after death. This involves fasting, consuming special bark and teas, and swallowing stones—then entombing oneself alive. You'll also find similar practices in China and India.

As to tattoos found on mummies, there have been twelve Egyptian mummies who have been discovered covered in skin art. Using modern imaging software and infrared scanners that can see through layers of skin, archaeologists are able to bring these tattoos to life.

Elephants

Everything that the elephants do in this novel may seem amazing but is easily within behavior noted about elephants at zoos or in the wild. That includes painting, vocalizing in human voices, observing death ceremonies, mimicry, even self-medicating. The story of people in Kenya being "taught" by elephants how to induce labor by chewing on leaves is true. Mankind has a long history of observing nature and its survival methods to keep ourselves alive.

All of this elephant behavior is attributable to their big brains—all eleven pounds' worth. And they do have the same number of neurons and synapses in their cerebral cortexes as us humans. Likewise, they put all that brainpower to good use. They use tools and solve problems and even show altruistic behavior. They are also self-aware and have a concept of art.

So quit shooting them, please.

A Few Miscellaneous Bread Crumbs

I had a chance to visit SAINT MARY'S CHURCH in Ashwell. Most of the details are accurate but my visit was a decade ago, so memory and time may have altered a few aspects. But the church does indeed have medieval graffiti scribbled all over inside, some meaningful and some quite comical. There is also a spring behind the church, set in a park and crossed via stepping-stones. I shifted the cemetery over a touch for the action sequence, but mostly everything else is as written.

I based **NOAH'S ARK** on an amphibious vehicle called a Swamp Spryte. It looked so much fun, I had to put it in a book.

The same is true of Kowalski's **PIEZER** weapon. It is based on the Department of Homeland Security's concept for a shotgun that can fire showers of piezoelectric crystals to shock their target from 150 feet away, all without those pesky Taser wires. So, of course, Sigma Force would be perfect to field test such a weapon.

Lastly, the book talks a bit about the electrical nature of **MEMORY**— from the storage of short-term reflections in the hippocampus to the fact that long-term memories are recoded and spread in a network across our brain. It's also been demonstrated that our memories can be made stronger and more vivid via electric stimulation. So what might happen if one of those electric-loving microbes were pathogenic? How might it affect our memories? I think I'd rather write about it than experience it.

So that covers the basics of the novel. There are, of course, a thousand more bread crumbs that are true, but I'd need tweezers to get them all out, and it would take many more pages to cover them. So I suggest you simply believe everything in the book.

I've peppered this novel with a few Nikola Tesla quotes, so I thought I'd end with one more, a testament to the connectivity that joins all humanity:

Though free to think and act, we are all held together, like the stars in the firmament, with ties inseparable.

Except that I must separate from you all for now—at least until Sigma gets into more trouble, which of course won't take them too long.

RESOURCES

Wear your Dharma. Remind yourself to stay on your path by wearing your Dharma symbol close to your heart with beautiful shirts created especially for us. Designs for Bhakti, Karma, Jnana and Raja.

"These meaningful Dharma designs will help you to keep your commitment to the your personal path in your awareness every time you wear them!"
~Lissa Coffey

www.WearLuck.com

~

Energy Muse Jewelry

Jewelry with Gemstones for your Dharma.

www.EnergyMuse.com

~

yogaworks

Yoga classes, and yoga teacher training. Yoga products. Yoga workshops and retreats.

www.yogaworks.com

~

GAIAM

Products for your personal yoga and meditation practice. Yoga and meditation gear.

www.gaiam.com